Island of Fog, Book 9

Castle
of Spells

Castle of Spells

by Keith Robinson

Printed in the United States of America
Published by Unearthly Tales on August 20th, 2014
ISBN-13 9780984390687

Visit www.unearthlytales.com

Island of Fog, Book 9

Castle of Spells

a novel by
KEITH ROBINSON

Meet the Shapeshifters

In this story there are nine twelve-year-old children, each able to transform into a creature of myth and legend . . .

Hal Franklin *(dragon)* – Thanks to a werewolf bite, Hal had to be cleansed of his shapeshifter blood, rendering him ordinary. But the new and improved Shapeshifter Program allowed him to become a much bigger, adult dragon.

Robbie Strickland *(ogre)* – At three times his normal height, and with long, powerful arms, Robbie is a mass of shaggy hair and muscle.

Abigail Porter *(faerie)* – She can sprout insect-like wings and shrink to six inches tall. She once owned a magical glass ball, a gift from her faerie kinfolk, but she left it in a cave by the sea after a run-in with the miengu.

Dewey Morgan *(centaur)* – Although impressive in his half-equine form, this small, shy boy is ashamed of his roots after discovering what some of the centaurs had done to humankind many years ago.

Lauren Hunter *(harpy)* – With enormous owl-like wings, yellow eyes, and powerful talons for feet, this beautiful white-feathered human-creature soars and swoops like a bird of prey.

Fenton Bridges *(rare lizard monster)* – Able to spit a stream of water that turns to glue, Fenton is black and reptilian with an impossibly long tail. Though tentatively dubbed an 'ouroboros,' he's still compared to a gargoyle.

Darcy O'Tanner *(dryad)* – As a wood nymph, she has the ability to blend into the background like a chameleon, allowing her to sneak around unseen.

Emily Stanton *(naga)* – Part human, part serpent, the naga come in three different forms, only two of which Emily has explored.

Thomas Patten *(manticore)* – The redheaded boy spent six years in the form of a vicious, red-furred, blue-eyed lion creature with a scorpion's tail. Now he's struggling to adjust to human life.

Other shapeshifters include Miss Simone, the resident mermaid and esteemed leader of the village; Molly the gorgon; Blair the phoenix;

Bo and Astrid the sphinxes (although Bo refuses to utilize his shapeshifting talent); Orson the pegasus; and Jolie the jengu, who is literally half her former self.

Now that the hostage situation is under control, Hal and his friends have other problems to deal with: first rescuing Molly and Blair, and then trying to prevent Queen Bee and her scrags from becoming shapeshifters . . .

Chapter One
The Cavern Under the Cliff

Hal flew low over the sea, heading toward Old Earth's familiar coastline. Crashing waves sprayed the sheer cliffs. Up on top, long grass blew in the wind. In the distance to the south, a city gleamed under the morning sun.

The last time Hal and Abigail had been here, they'd had no magic. With Robbie's help, they'd half-dragged a very sick Emily along the sandy clifftop trail, eventually veering inland toward a military building nestled in the trees. Rather than seek help from the soldiers there, who at the time had been 'the enemy,' Hal and his friends had instead hopped into the back of a truck for a ride into the city. And that was where their trouble with scrags had begun.

A few things had changed since then. Soldiers were allies now, the young shapeshifters had regained their magic, and portals between the two worlds had been reopened. But the scrags were still a deadly threat, and right now the scarred gang had Molly and Blair hostage in a castle overlooking the town of Brodon.

When Hal reached the cliff, he turned to follow the long, overgrown trail that ran for miles along its edge.

"Slow down," Abigail called. She was perched on his back, her legs slung over his powerful reptilian shoulders and around his neck, clinging to him as he flapped his leathery wings. "I think it was just up ahead."

Hal squinted down at the trail, seeing nothing in particular that stood out, just grass and a few trees. Then he spotted a cluster of boulders, and his heart leapt with excitement—and a touch of dread. This was the place.

He thumped down on the backside of the boulders, away from the cliff's edge. The long grass had been brown last time he'd been here, the weeds dead and cold. Now everything was turning green and thickening up, which made their search a little more difficult. But the tunnel was here somewhere. They just had to nose around.

Abigail slid down off his back and began picking her way through the grass as Hal reverted to his human form. He'd barely noticed the wind on his hard, green scales, but it felt cool on his pale, sensitive skin, and he shivered and pulled his thin shirt tight around his shoulders. His enchanted 'smart' clothes gave out a bit of heat, but not much.

"Here!" Abigail exclaimed, dropping to her knees. She pulled the grass back, exposing a narrow but very deep pit.

"Down you go, then," Hal said, kneeling beside her. "I'll wait here."

"No, that's okay, you go. Honestly, I don't mind."

"I don't mind, either. You found it, so you should be the one."

"Seriously, I'm okay with you taking my place. Be my guest."

They grinned at each other. Hal leaned forward and peered into the shaft. There was nothing to see, and all was quiet, but that didn't mean those weird *miengu* creatures weren't down there. "Think they're still alive?" he whispered, afraid his voice would echo around the cave.

"Not if they're still trapped," Abigail said. "It's been almost exactly four months since we were here last. If any of those executed people were still trapped down there, they'd be dead by now."

Executed, Hal thought idly. Over many years, Molly's calcifying death-gaze had been the harsh punishment for a substantial number of *miengu* misdemeanors, all at the request of their leader. In return, the lake people offered neighborly consideration and respect, not to mention enchanted material that smart clothes were made from. As it had turned out, the victims had only been suspended.

But when a thousand-year-old phoenix had gone up in flames and drained the land of magic, the calcification spell had broken, and dozens of executed *miengu* had been given a second chance at life. This particular group had ended up stuck in a cave, their way back to the lake cut off with the closure of the smoky portal between worlds.

"Maybe they crawled out through this hole," Abigail suggested, looking down into the darkness.

"Without legs?" Hal said doubtfully. "Just fishtails?"

She looked sideways at him. "If you were desperate enough, you'd crawl out even if you had the back end of a rhinoceros to drag up the tunnel."

Hal pursed his lips. "Yeah, but they have gills. I know they can switch to lungs and breathe air, but that's quite a climb for fishtailed people."

Abigail rolled her eyes. "Quit stalling and get in there."

Sighing, Hal sat on the grassy rim of the shaft and dangled his legs inside. Once he'd gotten a slight grip on the rocky sides, he let himself down carefully.

The hole was tight, but it opened up after about four feet of solid rock. Then he was in a cavern lit by thin, slanted shafts of light from numerous holes in the ceiling—holes he and Abigail had been lucky not to put their feet through. The smooth rock walls gradually leveled off below, and he started shuffling down while his eyes adjusted to the gloom.

The pool of water at the bottom was as still as a mirror until he slipped and almost stumbled into it. He crawled back from the edge of the rocky ledge, flinging droplets from his sleeve.

"You okay?" a voice echoed from above.

"Fine," Hal said, looking around. He was relieved to find no miengu waiting for him, although it occurred to him they could be swimming around underwater. He scanned the surface in alarm, but all he saw were a few ripples where he'd disturbed the pool. If they were in there, he was sure the water would be lapping at the rocks quite a bit more. They must have escaped after all.

He padded along the ledge. It skirted the edge of the pool and widened out. "Where is it?" he murmured.

It was missing. The bronze box he'd come for was not here. Maybe the miengu had stolen it. If so, it was long gone. Either that or . . .

He knelt and peered over the ledge into the water. The ripples had calmed now, and he saw his wobbly reflection staring back. The pool was clear but dark, and he saw nothing. If the box had fallen off the ledge, or been thrown in by angry miengu, or even just knocked in by accident, it would be lying on the bottom of the pool, lurking in the depths along with the tiny glass faerie ball and magnifying glass that had been fixed inside.

Sighing, he slid into the water, transforming as he did so. He realized then that his adult dragon form was quite a bit bigger now than it had been last time, and he found the space alarmingly small as his huge body sank below the surface and hit bottom. He scrabbled for a foothold on the smooth, slippery rock, then ducked his head under.

Although his keen dragon sight permeated the darkness, he blew underwater fireballs to light his way. This resulted in a lot of bubbles that hindered more than helped as he scoured the pool.

To his astonishment, he found the box within thirty seconds. It lay on its side, the lid open. The magnifying glass lay about three feet away, skittering along the rock because Hal was causing a disturbance. The faerie ball was missing.

Groaning, he knew the tiny artifact was going to be much more difficult to find. It might have slipped down into any number of cracks . . . although, as he looked around, he conceded there weren't actually that many. He became still, knowing his movements might cause eddies and currents liable to send that precious glass ball out of reach.

As a dragon, he could hold his breath a long time. He turned slowly, piercing the darkness, looking for the slightest glimmer of light, the tiniest reflection.

What he found instead shocked him.

It took a while to register what he was seeing. For a moment he thought it was one of the miengu—a jengu, as a single creature was called—lurking at the bottom of the pool, trying to wriggle through an impossibly narrow passage. Why else would he be looking at the fishtail end of a jengu with no sign of the upper human half? But this creature didn't move. It was *only* the fishtail end, neatly severed below the waist.

Jolie, he thought.

Just above where the severed end of the tail nudged against the wall had once been a smoky portal leading to New Earth. It was through there Jolie had tried to escape before the thousand-year-old phoenix had burst into flame and wiped out all the magic. All the portals had closed, and she hadn't made it through in time. It had cut her in half. Luckily for her, it was like being cauterized by magic. Instead of bleeding out and suffering pain, it was as though she'd been born that way.

Hal moved closer. Should he return the fishtail to Jolie? He immediately abandoned that idea when he saw how decayed the skin and flesh were, swollen and blotchy. When he disturbed the water, the tail moved and seemed to dissolve, a cloud of nastiness seeping out . . .

Gagging, Hal backed away, bubbles erupting from his throat. This was an image he'd never shake, far worse than the skeletal remains of six or seven miengu creatures, an idea he'd conjured in his mind before arriving.

He turned his back on the rotting fishtail and frantically hunted for the glass ball, doubtful he would find it now. Still, he ducked low, grateful he could hold his breath and not breathe in the murky rot that was now clouding up the pool. How was the tail *still here*? He guessed the water had been frigid over winter, perhaps even frozen, and there didn't seem to be much in the way of other fish to peck and chew at the half-corpse. And no wonder—it was cut off from the lake, the only fresh source of water trickling down through holes in the roof every time it rained.

A sparkle caught his eye, and he froze.

There!

It was lodged in the smallest of crevices, and it rolled slightly as he moved, following the path of the crack.

The faerie ball was tiny, delicate even in the hands of a normal twelve-year-old boy, let alone a dragon. Hal knew even as he approached that he'd need to revert back to his human form in order to pick it up. Repulsed, he steeled himself and steadied his clumsy paw over the ball.

When he transformed, he shut his eyes and mouth tight, slapped his hand down on the rock, felt the glass ball in his palm, gently worked it out of its crevice, and shot up to the surface. He emerged gagging, not because the water tasted or smelled foul but because his mind kept replaying the image of Jolie's tail dissolving before his eyes.

He scrambled out of the water, extra careful to keep hold of the glass ball. Shivering and wet, he took a moment to place the object in his pocket. Then he scurried up the smooth rock as fast as he could go, slipping and stumbling all the way. When he struggled out of the narrow aperture in the cavern's ceiling, Abigail jerked back in surprise.

"Whoa! What's the hurry?"

"N-nasty," he stammered, breathing hard as he rolled in the grass and climbed to his feet. He checked for the glass ball again, then took it out and handed it to Abigail. "You take it. I need a bath."

"A bath? It looks like you just *had* a bath—"

Hal held up his index finger, halting her midsentence. "Be right back."

He practically threw himself into the air, transforming as he did so. Rather than beat his huge leathery wings and struggle into the sky, he hopped over the huge boulders and took a dive off the cliff. Dangerous rocks poked out of the churning water below, but he angled his wings and glided away from the cliff, then plunged into the clean ocean.

He imagined rather than saw a cloud of rot floating away from him. He was probably being a little overdramatic, he decided as he swam around . . . but still it was a relief to rinse the filth off.

It was as he was swimming back toward the cliff that he spotted figures in the water with him—three man-sized fishlike creatures that darted this way and that. Hal paused to watch them. *Were* they fish? Or . . .

Miengu! They had a distinctive glow about them. He remained still, not wanting to spook them. Ordinarily, *they* would be the ones doing the spooking. Seen from a distance like this, nothing but eerie silhouettes within their glowing auras, they might be radioactive sharks circling for the kill. Seen up close, they were altogether more sinister, at least to those who knew them.

One swam close enough that Hal made out his features—a heavily muscled male, probably handsome to women. He had no doubt Abigail would find this jengu "hot," though he suspected her opinion would be skewed by the enchantment. The miengu were masked in illusion, an enviably attractive people despite their pointed ears and completely black eyes. In reality, though, they were hideous. Without their magic, they were gaunt and oily-haired with creepy, translucent skin.

Hal shuddered. If there were females nearby, he needed to steer clear. Miengu magic was powerful. No matter how much he tried to reason that the beauty he saw was illusory, another part of his brain would start arguing, suggesting he was mistaken about this particular jengu, that she was special, as attractive and wonderful as she appeared . . .

He blinked. Their magic was already working, and there wasn't even a female in sight! Putting on a burst of furious speed, he shot upward and exploded out of the sea so fast that he only had to beat his wings once to reach the clifftop where Abigail waited.

She looked puzzled when he landed next to her. "Happy now?"

* * *

Hal didn't bother reverting back just to explain what he'd seen. They flew home to find Miss Simone, and it was only when he'd thumped

6

down outside her small house on the outskirts of Carter that he explained everything.

Abigail was appalled. "You saw her rotting *tail*?"

Miss Simone stepped outside at that moment. Her blond-haired, blue-eyed beauty was almost as false as the miengu's. Being a mermaid shapeshifter, her alter-kind were somewhat nicer cousins to the manipulative lake people. "Whose tail?" she asked, joining them on the doorstep.

Hal quickly recapped his experience in the cavern and his quick bath in the sea. "Three of them, probably more, swimming about like they lived there," he finished. "And in the sea! I thought they preferred lakes."

Miss Simone shrugged. "It's not unusual for lake-dwelling miengu to convert to seawater and vice versa. They have that ability, as do mermaids. Even the sea serpent that guarded your island originally came from a lake. Besides, that little group of miengu you saw couldn't get back to their lake even if they wanted to, not without that underwater portal." She paused a moment, thinking. "And Jolie's tail was preserved? I guess the water froze over winter."

"Her tail *dissolved*," Hal said with distaste. "Fell apart as soon as I disturbed the water. It was gross."

Miss Simone abruptly changed the subject. "So you found it, then? The faerie ball, I mean?"

Abigail carefully extracted it from her pocket and held it up. "What a lot of fuss over such a tiny thing."

"And it probably won't work anyway," Hal added. "Not for Queen Bee and her gang."

It had worked well for *him*, though. He'd been unable to fly when he'd first transformed. Flapping wings and actually flying were two entirely different things. It took an instinctive knowledge to angle wings correctly and apply the right amount of power, and he hadn't possessed that knowledge. Or so he'd thought.

Somehow, he and his friends had inherited crucial memories from the creatures they'd been cloned from. This included dialects and skills they couldn't possibly have learned in a classroom. When it came time to transform, they instinctively knew how to control their new bodies and converse with others of their kind. Dewey could speak centaur, Emily found herself fluent in naga, and Hal could talk to dragons in rudimentary grunts and growls. Science alone could not explain this phenomenon. By accident, the old Shapeshifter Program happened to include a subtle but important dose of magic.

However, some of those inherited skills were buried a little too deep, just out of reach. Peering into the faerie's glass ball had clarified things. With a flood of resurfaced memories, Hal had suddenly known how to fly.

But the new Shapeshifter Program was different. Miss Simone had said it was mostly about the blood. The procedure was fast, able to be applied to full-grown adults. Literally anybody could be turned into a shapeshifter if they desired. The downside to this speedier, more portable science was the lack of inherited memories and instincts. New shifters were in for a brutal shock.

"I doubt it even has any power left," Abigail said, staring into it. "The magic was drained. It *might* have recharged itself, but I don't know . . ."

"As long as it buys us back our friends," Miss Simone said, "then I don't care if it works or not. Let Queen Bee believe what she wants." She slipped it carefully into a pocket and brushed her hands. "All right, let's go."

Hal said goodbye to his parents before heading out. They usually did well at letting him embark on dangerous missions even though he was only twelve, but they at least liked to see him off and give him a hug. His mom's tears and dad's grim expression always made him think they didn't expect to see him again, that he might be killed in action . . . but that was always left unsaid.

Hal made sure to tell them he would be thirteen soon. They laughed and rolled their eyes, saying, "Oh, well, that makes us feel *so* much better."

Abigail popped in to say goodbye to her mom, too. Since she lived close to Hal on the outskirts of the village, it wasn't a huge surprise when, as the two of them prepared to leave with Miss Simone, all their shapeshifting classmates came running up: Robbie, Lauren, Emily, Fenton, Thomas, Darcy, and Dewey.

"Did you find it?" Robbie demanded.

Abigail answered first. "If you mean my glass ball, then yes, we found it. We're just off to Brodon now."

"How come *we're* not needed?" Fenton complained, turning to Miss Simone. "You could use us. She wouldn't dare mess with you if we were by your side."

Miss Simone sighed. "First of all, Hal can't carry you all—"

"Astrid and Orson could," Darcy immediately pointed out.

"—and second, too many of us might spook Queen Bee and set her off. Don't forget poor Molly looked in a mirror and calcified herself. She's probably still teetering on the edge of those steps. So we want to keep this quiet and calm. Hopefully the exchange will be simple."

"And then Queen Bee creates a gang of evil shapeshifters?" Robbie said.

Miss Simone shook her head. "Not a chance. But that's another mission." She pursed her lips, looking around the disgruntled faces. "And for that I'd like your help to put an end to Queen Bee's experiments. Why don't you plan to leave for Brodon tomorrow morning? Check with your parents first, though."

The crestfallen faces brightened into smiles. "We'll be there," Darcy said. "But why not *today*? Maybe this afternoon, after lunch?"

"Tomorrow," Miss Simone said. "We'll negotiate for the release of Molly and Blair, then do some secret investigating to find another way into the castle. By the time you get there, we'll be ready for action."

Hal knew she was placating them all, and he suspected they knew it, too. Even so, permission to join the mission tomorrow was good enough, and they relented and bid their farewells.

"Good luck!" Lauren shouted as Hal took to the sky with Miss Simone and Abigail astride his back. "Bring Molly and Blair home safely!"

On his way east, Hal looked down on Carter and thought, not for the first time, how vulnerable it would be if determined enemy shapeshifters decided to attack. A few nasty dragons, a flock of harpies, a horde of ogres, maybe other creatures Hal wasn't so familiar with . . . The village would be flattened in no time, thatched roofs easily set alight and homes burned down. Hundreds of people could be homeless or dead in a matter of hours.

Nine giant helicopters rested on the treeless hills between the woodlands, a platoon of soldiers at the ready. They'd returned the previous night along with all the rescued hostages. Of course there had been tears of joy and relief throughout the village, but the celebration had been tainted by an abject fear that Queen Bee would strike again soon—hence the strong military presence.

"So when are the soldiers planning to attack the Swarm?" Abigail asked as they flew east.

Miss Simone sounded tired. "The council met late last night. They ordered Lieutenant Briskle to stand down for now. Councilman Frobisher doesn't want to order an attack of any sort until he's figured out if the mayor's involved."

"But we *know* the mayor's involved!" Abigail practically squawked with indignation. "He gave Queen Bee permission to take over the castle! What more proof do we need?"

Hal listened without uttering a grunt as he soared higher toward the morning sun. Brodon was just a couple of hours away.

"We don't know for sure the mayor really knows what he's gotten into," Miss Simone said carefully. Hal knew she was being diplomatic, not wanting to speak ill of the council despite her misgivings. "Frobisher wants to organize a civil face-to-face with the man and get to the bottom of it all. He'll be heading out to Brodon this afternoon. By that time we should have Molly and Blair back. If not, the face-to-face will be rather tense."

"A civil face-to-face," Abigail repeated.

Hal imagined she was shaking her head in disgust right about now. He had to agree. The mayor had apparently agreed to the kidnapping of fifty-two people from their homes in Carter! One had been *killed*, his poor family destroyed by the loss of a husband and father. The rest had been safely released—but then the scrags had snatched Blair back and tricked Molly into calcifying herself in a mirror. How could the council not order an immediate attack?

Because the people of Brodon are innocent, a more logical voice in his mind told him. *Queen Bee and her Swarm are behind this. The mayor might be, too, but maybe he's just an idiot who can't see what's going on in front of his nose.*

Hal scoffed at the idea of the mayor not being aware of the goings-on at the castle. Rocs delivering cages full of prisoners in the early hours of the morning? Dozens of people must have seen that.

Had the prisoners screamed for help, though? Had anyone actually heard?

After a while, Abigail said thoughtfully, "Maybe a team of shapeshifters would be best. We can sneak in a back way, disarm the scrags, and take away the Shapeshifter Program before it's too late."

"That's what I'm hoping for," Miss Simone agreed.

Hal knew from personal experience that a shapeshifter could be created within hours. The procedure itself was a secret; he'd been sedated when Miss Simone and Dr. Kessler had worked on him. All he knew was that it involved an injection of blood from a magical creature. The finer details were probably fairly complicated, but Queen Bee would figure it out. She had a lot of willing subjects to experiment on.

It was doubtful she'd work on them all at once, Hal decided. She'd want to try one and wait, then try another, with a few hours of rest for each plus a bit of testing to make sure the procedure had actually worked. Still, if she'd worked at it all the previous night, it was highly possible she already had five or ten shapeshifting scrags at her command.

Hal shuddered with apprehension.

Chapter Two
The Exchange

Brodon sprawled on the coast north of Bad Rock Gulch, the collapsed mines where the fabled Chamber of Ghosts now lay buried under tons of rock. Timber-framed homes crowded the narrow, cobbled streets and leaked columns of smoke into the clear sky. A river zigzagged from one end to the other, cutting past the market square. Forestland surrounded the town to the south and west, a calm bay and narrow beach bordered the north, and a wall of craggy rocks and high cliffs stood to the east. It was on these cliffs that Castle Brodon perched.

This was the first and only castle Hal had ever seen, and it was smaller than he'd imagined, though still pretty spectacular. Much of it was blocky and square, including the grand entrance hall with windows along its sides and a huge archway in the courtyard. A short, fat tower stood at its rear, so close to the cliff edge that Hal couldn't help seeing it as a frightened stone gargoyle standing on a narrow ledge with his toes sticking out over the side.

"Land in the courtyard," Miss Simone told him.

A road cut into the inland side of the craggy mountain. This allowed Brodon residents steep but easy access to the castle. Hal descended toward the courtyard at the top. At least a dozen statues stood around, all calcified scrags thanks to Molly's gorgon death-gaze the day before. The iron gates were busted open where Robbie had forced his way in.

Five large wooden cages also littered the place. Carried here by enormous roc birds, these cages had been used to transport the fifty-two hostages to the castle. Hal envisioned the cages being used again soon, only this time for scrags. He kept that happy thought in mind as he thumped down.

Scrags appeared at once, four of them brandishing spears as they rushed out of the castle's main entrance. As with the courtyard's iron gates, Robbie had busted open the huge oak doors the day before while Hal had been busy smashing his way in through a side window. The debris had since been cleared up, but the doors still hung in pieces off their hinges.

The scrags took up a defensive posture with spears pointing his way. More scrags appeared, mostly men but a few women, and they joined the ranks so that now ten of them stood between Hal and the castle entrance.

He let out a bellowing roar and playfully seared the air with a burst of flame. The scrags ducked, two of them yelling and scuttling backward. Hal stomped forward, and all ten retreated toward the doorway, clearly uncertain about what they were supposed to do next.

Then Queen Bee appeared. She weaved through her jumpy gang and, looking annoyed, gave one of the most frightened guards a smack on the back of his head. "Stand your ground like the man you're supposed to be. That goes for the rest of you, women included."

The scrags immediately halted and stood up straight and stiff, their posture suggesting fearless bravery but their wide, darting eyes saying otherwise. Queen Bee sauntered up to Hal and stood mere feet from his snout. She stared up at him with interest, her head tilted and a faint smile on her lips.

Her straight black hair hung loose across her shoulders, framing her scarred face. Many scrags were much worse off, their skin dry and crusty with blackened lesions. In comparison, her skin was merely blotchy as though peeling after a heavy suntan. She wore black leather pants and a sleeveless vest complete with a belt that held a collection of wicked-looking implements: a corkscrew, serrated knife, claw hammer, a loop of wire with a wooden handle at each end, and more. Hal suspected she chose her weapons each morning the way some people dithered over clothing. She probably had a drawer full of gadgets.

"You see?" she called back over her shoulder to her anxious gang. "Hal is just a sweet, twelve-year-old boy. He won't bite. Not right now, anyway. Because if he does, his friends Molly and Blair might suffer." She turned her back on Hal, spread her hands, and added, "You just have to understand the situation instead of letting fear get the better of you."

Hal desperately wanted to roast her alive right now.

Queen Bee turned to face him again and looked over his head to where Miss Simone and Abigail perched on his back. "Are you coming down or what?"

Hal lowered himself to make dismounting a little easier.

"Stay here," Miss Simone murmured to Abigail as she slid down. She came around to stand before Queen Bee and looked down on the smaller woman. "Where are my friends? Bring them out."

"Do you have what I need?" Queen Bee asked.

Miss Simone patted her pocket. "You'll get it after you bring my friends out."

The queen pursed her lips. "Now, see, that's a little difficult. Molly is still on the steps where she was turned to stone. We *could* carry her up here, but we don't want to drop her, do we? Why do you think I left my faithful friends out here all alone?" She swept her hand around at the scrag statues littering the courtyard, silent and staring.

Hal had to admit she was probably right about that. Molly's magic worked in mysterious ways, not only turning flesh and bone to stone, but clothes as well, and the resulting statue was appropriately heavy and breakable.

"Bring her up," Miss Simone said anyway. "And if you drop her, I promise it'll be the last thing you ever do."

Queen Bee frowned. "You're being unreasonable. Why don't we just let Blair do what he needs to do, and then—"

"I want Molly and Blair outside in this courtyard, in full view."

"So Hal can snatch her up and—"

"No argument," Miss Simone snapped. Her face was reddening. "I'm done playing games, lady. Bring them up here and make this exchange in a civil, businesslike manner, otherwise I'll ask Hal to tear this place apart and burn everyone—starting with you."

Queen Bee spent a moment considering. Clearly she had an agenda of her own, forever scheming and angling toward an even better deal. But this time she sighed and nodded. "All right. But I want that glass ball now."

Miss Simone shook her head and climbed onto Hal's back, leaving a puzzled Queen Bee standing there. Only when she was settled next to Abigail did she speak again. "When Blair regenerates, anything in range will be drained of magic—shapeshifters, geo-rocks, the statues, even this glass ball."

If it's not drained already, Hal thought. It might have recharged the same way faerie hotspots did, though.

"We'll be watching from high above while Blair regenerates," Miss Simone went on. "After that, we'll be back to collect Molly. You'll release Blair so he can fly away. Then—and *only* then—will I give you this tiny glass ball in my pocket."

"I don't trust you," Queen Bee said shortly.

"I don't care."

Hal felt the tiniest of kicks, which he recognized as a signal to leave. He reared up and began thumping his wings, causing a draft that sent a number of watchful scrags back a step or two. He was pleased to see Queen Bee duck and move away, too, as he lifted off and picked up speed.

"Now we wait," Miss Simone said as they rose high above the castle. "While they're struggling to bring Molly upstairs, fly around the cliff and see if there's some kind of second entrance we missed."

"Wait," Abigail said. She sounded excited. "Will Blair's regeneration drain the magic from the blood samples? Because if so—"

"Then there won't be a Shapeshifter Program," Miss Simone agreed. "Let's hope Queen Bee doesn't think to move those samples out of range."

The scrags were scrambling in the courtyard as Queen Bee issued commands Hal couldn't hear. He swooped down low, circling around the jutting mountain of rocks. Though craggy along much of the coast, these cliff faces were smooth, dropping straight down into the ocean with no narrow trails or passes or even a manmade jetty. There was nothing but smooth cliff all around—except for one shallow, square-shaped cave that clearly didn't go anywhere. It was jammed with boulders.

"Well, that's not very good," Abigail said.

Miss Simone sounded like she wasn't ready to abandon the idea of a second entrance. "Before the castle was built, an old mansion stood atop that same cliff. It stood there for six hundred years before burning down one night, a fiery beacon that was seen up and down the coast. The castle is fairly new in comparison, built on the foundation of the old mansion."

She paused, and Abigail had to prompt her. "So?"

"So there are plenty of old tales of people being washed away in the tunnels below the mansion, trapped and drowned. I *know* there are tunnels in those cliffs, and it stands to reason they would be used as another way into the castle, probably by boat. If that square cave was the way in, then it's obviously blocked now. But maybe there's another way in. We need to speak to a few of the locals."

Hal flew around again, his keen sight scouring the low mountain. He saw nothing besides the square cave. If there was another entrance, it had to be underwater.

A shiver of excitement prickled his spine as he thought about that possibility. An underwater tunnel? He wanted to voice his idea, but to do so would mean reverting to his human form—which would be a disaster in midflight.

He circled over the courtyard again. There was no sign of anybody now, and it would take time for Queen Bee and her gang to carefully manhandle Molly's statue up the stairs and out to the courtyard. *And they'd better be careful*, Hal thought with fire deep in his chest.

To pass the time, he turned to glide over the town of Brodon, peering down into the narrow streets as his impressive shadow flitted across the rooftops. He smelled something enticing in the market square and wished he could take a minute to eat. Maybe after Molly and Blair were safe, they could pop into town and gobble a few meat pies or fresh-baked bread.

With a little sightseeing out of the way and five or ten minutes killed, he turned back to the castle and focused on the distant courtyard. He saw movement there and picked up speed. By the time he got close enough to make out the details, Queen Bee and two dozen scrags—her faithful Swarm—were milling about, arranging statues in a row.

Hal's heart missed a beat. There was Molly, balanced awkwardly in a frozen, calcified state, her left foot pulled backward and propped on a makeshift step of tough wood from the broken castle doors. She'd been descending a flight of stairs when she'd met herself in a poorly lit, hastily erected mirror. She'd turned herself to stone before realizing who she was looking at. Her hand was raised to hold her veil up, though her death-gaze was harmless in her current state.

And it'll be harmless when she wakes, Hal thought. *She'll have no magic after Blair's regeneration stunt.*

Queen Bee clearly wasn't taking that risk, though. She pulled a sack over Molly's head, arm and all, so there would be no accidental calcifications the moment the gorgon blinked awake.

"We're ready!" Queen Bee yelled as Hal came around again. "Statues are lined up, geo-rocks taken down below, Blair is fully charged and ready to set light to himself—oh, and the blood samples are safely stashed."

She looked smug at that last comment, and Miss Simone sighed.

Hal let out a bellow to indicate he'd heard, and Queen Bee waved for her Swarm to bring forth her final prisoner, Blair.

He was shackled, but the scrags quickly removed his wrist irons and stepped back. Blair was now free to fly away, and he looked sorely tempted as he looked up at the sky and squinted. Of course he wouldn't leave Molly behind, though. Hal knew he would go through with his phoenix rebirth. But once he'd done so, and Molly was free . . .

Hal grinned to himself. He could snatch up Molly as soon as she was awake, and then Blair could fly to safety. Miss Simone still had the glass ball, and there would be no need to give it to Queen Bee.

His jubilation faltered as Queen Bee gave a simple gesture with her hand and a long line of Brodon residents emerged from the castle. Led by grinning scrags, they seemed happy enough, walking freely as though part of a guided tour. Hal counted fifteen in the group, mostly in their late teens but some as young as eight or nine, an even mix of boys and girls. Queen Bee waved her arms around as she talked to them, and they nodded and grinned, clearly excited about something. Finally, she put her arms around a couple of the young children and hugged them tight as she nodded to Blair.

An expectant hush fell in the crowded courtyard as Hal glided around and around. With a scattered group of statues and three times as many scrags, plus the blissfully ignorant Brodon residents, there was barely room for Hal to land if he needed to. And surely he *would* need to if Queen Bee used these poor, innocent people as leverage to make sure she got her glass ball after all.

He sighed. The woman had endless tricks up her sleeves—and she didn't even have sleeves!

Blair, looking pretty fed up, abruptly transformed. His smart clothes reformed just as fast, though Hal was too high above to see what they had become. It hardly mattered. Even smart clothes couldn't survive the intense burning they were about to be subjected to.

A phoenix stood there, six feet tall, deep red in color with yellow, blue and green across its chest, a smattering of gold around its throat, and an impressive fanned tail that was also gold. Blair shuffled and planted his huge talons wide on the flagstones. He was already beginning to smoke as he began his regeneration.

Everyone in the courtyard gasped, scrags and Brodon residents alike. It was one thing to see giant roc birds but quite another to witness the spectacular colors of the phoenix slowly blackening as tiny flames curled off the ends of his wings and smoke poured up over his body. A wave of heat hit Hal as he came by for another flyby, and he saw the crowds below recoil and edge backward.

"Not so close, Hal," Miss Simone warned.

He shot away with a jolt of fear, remembering that the fiery rebirth would deplete his own magic if he wasn't careful. He retreated to a safe distance and contented himself to a faraway view of the event.

Fire engulfed Blair with a *whump!* sound, bright yellow flames that licked high and ate hungrily. He barely flinched and instead held out his wings as if basking in the heat. He turned slowly and deliberately. Hal thought for moment he was simply showing off, as Blair tended to do with his pyrotechnic displays. But when he stopped turning, it became clear that he was targeting Molly, who stood absolutely still twenty feet away.

Unlike an ancient, thousand-year-old phoenix, Blair's range was limited. If any of the statues woke from his rebirth, it would be Molly.

His yellow flames turned blue. The courtyard spectators cringed again, and a second later Hal felt a wave of heat rising past him. Then the heat faded as the blue aura brightened. Within the dazzling inferno, black feathers turned to dust and floated free on a breeze . . . and underneath those feathers, bright red and gold shone through.

A *bang!* like a clap of thunder caused glass to crack in the castle, and people yelled out and clutched at each other. Hal gasped at the sight of the shockwave spreading outward, an oval-shaped dome, much of it projecting in front of Blair and upward maybe a hundred feet. Hal was well clear, but he knew his skin would be tingling right now if he had been within range.

Queen Bee stood perfectly still, mesmerized, as her hair lifted and stuck outward like a giant fuzzball, charged with energy. The Brodon residents experienced the same phenomenon, and they exclaimed and laughed at the same time. Most of the Swarm seemed unaffected by this, perhaps because they were unwashed, their hair too greasy and matted to react to the static in the air.

A second later, the rebirth was over. Blair stood there amid a pile of ashes looking even more colorful and vibrant than before. Hal knew he'd kept a little residual magic back for himself.

All around him, what had once been statues slowly began to move. Molly stumbled off her wooden block and squirmed to free herself from the sack covering her head. She paused a moment, then pulled the sack off more slowly. Her hair hung limply, and though she'd tugged her veil safely into place, Hal knew she had no magic now.

Scrags greeted their reawakened friends. The residents of Brodon stood in wide-eyed awe, huge grins on their faces. Queen Bee nodded with satisfaction and gave a thumbs-up to Blair, who remained in his phoenix form, looking on impassively through cold, unblinking eyes.

"Go get Molly," Miss Simone said, giving Hal a hard prod.

Hal snapped to it. He'd been so wrapped up in what was happening below that he'd almost forgotten he was still flying around in the sky two hundred feet above. He dive-bombed the courtyard, pulling up at the last moment and thumping down in the largest clear space he could find.

Queen Bee had resumed her position behind a couple of the Brodon children, her hands clamped on their shoulders, smiling broadly while shooting Miss Simone a warning glare. "My gift?" she said above all the noise.

Miss Simone slid off Hal's back and strode over to Queen Bee, delving into her pocket and fishing out the glass ball as she approached. It was almost too small to see, and a look of suspicion crossed Queen Bee's face.

"Take it," Miss Simone said. "You'll need a magnifying glass."

Queen Bee took it silently, her expression now one of bemusement. "That's it? I expected something bigger. This is the size of a pea."

It was actually a little bigger, more like a fingernail. "We're going now," Miss Simone told her. She stepped closer, putting her face close to her opponent's. "If you do *anything* to these people—"

The scrag laughed and smoothed down her frizzy hair. "Like impress them to death?" She pushed the glass ball into a small pocket in her pants and patted the young boy and girl on their shoulders. They couldn't be more than eight or nine. "What do you think, kids? Can you stand any more excitement?"

"I don't know, Queen Bee," the girl said, grinning broadly. "That phoenix is *amazing*." She pointed directly at Hal. "And the dragon over there! I've never seen one up close before. This is the best day of my life." She turned back to the scrag. "Are you going to show us more monsters today? Please say you will!"

Queen Bee laughed. "Maybe tomorrow, Chrissy." She stood up straight, facing Miss Simone with a less-than-pleasant smile. "These young people are so excited. Their parents are caretakers, living in various rooms below the castle. They can't wait for the official announcement tomorrow evening."

She let her words hang for a moment. Miss Simone narrowed her eyes and finally took the bait. "What announcement?"

The queen feigned surprise. "The mayor's. He's going to stand up here and talk to Brodon's residents—you know, introduce his new shapeshifter protectors. We're to be formally recognized as citizens."

"And they're going to show us how they can change!" the girl named Chrissy blurted. "They're going to put on a demonstration and prove they can protect us from bad people."

Hal had nudged closer to eavesdrop on this entire conversation. Now he was just a few yards away in case Queen Bee tried anything. But he doubted she would. She was keeping up a pretense, and she wouldn't want to spoil the happiness and end up with frightened hostages again. Blissfully ignorant and willing helpers were far more preferable. The problem was, this group of young people weren't alone. As live-in caretakers, their parents and perhaps siblings were around somewhere, maybe downstairs on the subfloor level where Hal couldn't reach them in his dragon form.

Miss Simone looked like she was biting her tongue, itching to scream a warning and send these children running for the open gates and down the hill to safety. Hal was ready to help if that happened. So, too, was Molly judging by her wary stance as she edged closer, though she may have forgotten she had no magic now and couldn't rely on her death-gaze.

But Queen Bee had already moved on, mingling with her young and happy helpers, smiling and talking with them, though she kept shooting glances at Hal and his friends as her Swarm stood silently with their hands resting on the hilts of their knives. Her message was clear: *You should go now.*

And they did. Feeling like he was in a dream, Hal waited while Molly climbed aboard, then Miss Simone. He heard Molly greet Abigail, but their voices were drowned out when Blair spread his wings and launched into the sky at an incredible speed, his wings flapping noisily. Some of the younger children rushed forward to claim brightly colored feathers that had come loose.

Hal launched after him, though nowhere near as fluidly. He left the castle far below and turned to head home, leaving the scrags to cheer and celebrate their victory, even if that victory was a temporary status quo where none of the shapeshifters dared interfere with the Swarm's dastardly plans.

Miss Simone wasn't done yet, though. "Go on home, Blair!" she yelled when they caught up to the phoenix.

The bird's scarlet-and-gold wings stopped flapping. Gliding gracefully, Blair peered back at them.

"Bring the other shapeshifters out here tomorrow morning," Miss Simone continued. "Wait on the beach. And if we don't show up, storm the castle."

After a long pause, Blair gave a nod.

Miss Simone then patted Hal's back. "As for us, we need to circle around and head back to Brodon. Let's keep this quiet. If we're going to put an end to Queen Bee's nonsense, we need to find a secret way into that castle."

Chapter Three
Undercover Shifters

Molly appeared at the end of the dark, narrow alley where Hal was waiting impatiently with Miss Simone and Abigail. "Here you go," she said, heaving an armful of clothes at them.

Some items dropped into the dirt. This particular alley wasn't important enough to warrant a cobblestone surface like the main streets. It was a little smelly and cold in the shadows of the cantilevered buildings, but at least the group was away from prying eyes.

"Nice," Abigail said, holding up a shabby red frock with long sleeves.

"It's your color," Hal mused.

Miss Simone peered dubiously at an adult-sized dark-grey robe, then handed the rest of the pile to Hal. He grimaced at the brown pants and cream shirt, both well worn.

"Stop moaning and put 'em on," Molly said. She grinned from under her wide-brimmed hat, and Hal did a double take for the tenth time that morning. Seeing her face was unnerving. Seeing her *eyes*. It didn't sit well with him. What if she suddenly regained her magic and accidentally calcified everyone?

They each donned their disguises over their clothes. Miss Simone, with her blond hair, startling blue eyes, and flashy silk cloak was the most noticeable of the four, so the dull robe she climbed into helped some. Molly took off her hat and stuck it on Miss Simone's head, then stepped back and pursed her lips.

"Better," she commented. "But put your hair up."

Molly was the only one of them not wearing a disguise. Her long robe was drab enough, and she wore grubby leather boots to match. Her normally veiled face was unusually white, her cheeks sunken, and she had dark rings under her hazel-colored eyes. With her black, curly hair hanging down rather untidily, nobody would ever guess she was a gorgon.

"Quit staring," Molly said, giving Hal a wink. "I know I'm gorgeous, but you're too young for me."

Hal's face heated up. "I, uh . . . I was just wondering where your veil is. In case you need it in a hurry?"

Molly patted her side where, apparently, a pocket was hidden in the folds.

"All right," Miss Simone said briskly. "To business. It's about lunchtime, so I suggest we mingle with the crowds and grab a bite to eat."

"Do you have money?" Molly asked. "I used up all mine paying for these expensive togs."

Miss Simone nodded. "I smell meat pies. Let's follow the scent."

Hal didn't need to be told twice. He grabbed Abigail's hand and followed the older women out of the alley and around the corner.

They were on the outskirts of the town. Hal had landed in the forest on the riverbank, and they'd walked in. The cobbled streets grew busier as the disguised shapeshifters moved toward the town center. People bustled about, completely ignoring them except to say "excuse me" when jostling occurred.

When they finally reached the market square, Hal and Abigail ate hungrily, forgetting everything else while they stood in the middle of a crowded street munching on steaming pies filled with beef, onions, potatoes, carrots, and a healthy dose of pepper.

"Robbie would *love* this," Hal said between mouthfuls.

Abigail nodded slowly. "He can have one tomorrow for lunch. Maybe we'll buy a bunch and take them down to the beach when they arrive."

They were large pies and took a full five minutes to chomp through. Miss Simone only ate half. She said she was too distracted to be hungry, but Molly rolled her eyes and said, "Watching your figure, more like. As if you need to."

Her compliment was completely wasted on Miss Simone, who stared off into the distance with her half-pie forgotten. A small, skinny boy slipped out of the crowd and stared at it longingly, and it was only when Molly nudged Miss Simone that she jerked back into the here and now and offered the remainder to him. He grinned and took off running.

"Let's go down to the docks and find a fisherman," Miss Simone said, brushing her hands off. "If anyone knows about secret tunnels into the cliff, it'll be a fisherman."

With a mission in mind, they navigated their way through the market. A girl appeared ahead of them, probably no older than Hal. She was grasping a stack of paper in one hand and a single sheet in the other, holding it aloft so people could see it as they bustled past.

Miss Simone sucked in a breath and spun around so her back was to the girl. She pulled Molly, Hal, and Abigail together. "She's one of the castle caretakers. Or her parents are, anyway. See the fliers she's handing out? They're for the mayor's official announcement tomorrow night."

"Well then, let's talk to the poor girl," Molly said. "She doesn't know it, but she's safely away from danger now. We'll tell her what's going on so she—"

"No," Miss Simone said, shaking her head. "She might have family in the castle, or friends. What if we try to convince her to abandon Queen Bee but she rejects us? She'll go straight back and warn her."

"But she might have valuable information—"

"Stay away. Come on."

Miss Simone headed off in a different direction, leaving Molly to sigh and click her tongue. But she followed Miss Simone anyway, gesturing for Hal and Abigail to keep up.

They hung back to watch the girl, though. She was smiling and talking to a group of women, her cheeks red with excitement as she explained about "the new shapeshifters in town." She handed each woman a flier, and they read it with interest as the girl moved on.

"Shapeshifters," Hal muttered.

"I guess we should go," Abigail said, giving his hand a tug.

They weaved through the crowd following the wide-brimmed hat Miss Simone was borrowing. Several minutes later, they left the packed streets behind and made their way through a more relaxed, sleepy part of town. Two jovial old men sat in rickety wooden chairs right outside their open front doors, taking up half the narrow lane. Past them, five small children hopped and skipped across a grid of chalk lines on the cobblestone. A large woman with a basket over her arm stepped out of a doorway at that moment, pulling her door shut with a bang before giving a cheery smile and setting off for the market.

"They seem happy here," Molly remarked. Right around the corner ahead, a stubborn donkey brayed as the owner tried unsuccessfully to yank it along on the end of a rope while swearing and panting. "Well, apart from him," she added as they hurried past. "Brodon is a busy, noisy place, but it has a nice sense of community spirit about it. Like Carter, only . . . more cheerful?"

"Carter's not cheerful at all these days," Miss Simone said. "Frobisher's right. I've brought a lot of strife to the village. Look at the place now—soldiers everywhere, portals clogging up bathrooms, hostages being taken in the night . . ."

Molly snorted. "Hush, woman. Old coots like Frobisher shouldn't be on the council. We need young blood, people with a brighter outlook on the future. Brodon has a castle, and in that castle they host events. When was the last time we did that? They bring people together for celebrations. There's music and dancing, food and drink, fun and games. It's just a brighter, happier place."

"Not for long," Abigail said. "Not if Queen Bee takes over the place."

"She almost has," Miss Simone muttered as she stopped at an intersection and looked both ways. She chose left. "Somehow that woman has Mayor Seymour Priggle in her pocket."

They reached the end of a street, turned a corner, and emerged quite suddenly into bright daylight. The town had ended, and they stood upon an old but sturdy wooden walkway built practically on the doorsteps of a few dozen homes that faced the ocean.

"What a view!" Abigail exclaimed as they headed along the boardwalk. It had no railings, so they could jump down onto the beach at any time or make use of occasional steps. "Imagine living here and opening the front door to this every morning. The sea's right outside."

Hal snorted. "Back home, the sea's right there in my bathroom!" *Though not for much longer*, he admitted privately. *Dad's promised to wall up that smoky hole soon. It only took a bunch of scrag intruders to convince him.*

"I'd like to be here during a storm," Molly said, her robe whipping about in the breeze. The wind had picked up now that they'd left the network of narrow alleys. "Look how short the beach is. Maybe fifty, sixty feet? I'll bet the waves crash all over the houses."

"I see fishing boats," Miss Simone said, pointing around the bay where half a dozen rowing boats were clustered together on the sand. Three of them had simple masts sticking up at angles.

Molly shielded her eyes. "I see bigger ones in the distance. Looks like there's a small harbor a bit farther along the coast."

"I don't really care about the boats," Miss Simone told her, walking at a brisk pace now. "We just need a fisherman to talk to."

Hal glanced around as they stamped along the boardwalk. He couldn't see much beyond the tall, timber-framed houses he walked alongside, but at the far end of the bay behind him, the cliff and its castle rose high under a blue sky with patches of wispy clouds.

They found a fisherman painting some thick, sticky liquid onto the front end of a boat. He was so engrossed in his task that he didn't notice the visitors until Molly cleared her throat. He whirled around, his paintbrush held high, and stared at them with eyes as blue as Miss Simone's. His cheeks were full and ruddy, his curly grey hair and beard as thick and wiry as his brush. "Who are you?"

"Just a bunch of tourists," Molly said. "I bet you get a lot of us nosing around, asking questions about the castle and its dark, forgotten secrets."

Hal had to admire the way she launched straight into the interrogation.

The man, probably in his sixties, frowned. "What secrets?"

"People drowning in the tunnels under the cliff?" Miss Simone ventured.

"Oh, *that*." The fisherman sighed and looked at his brush as if he'd forgotten he held it. "Nothing exciting. Not exactly a secret, either. There are tunnels, and plenty of people have died in them, but if you're thinking about visiting, then forget it. It's impossible except during low tide, and even then it's dangerous. That's why they're out of bounds."

"And these tunnels are the only way into the castle other than the front door?" Molly said, sounding doubtful.

"Well, there was once a passage high above sea level, easily accessible, big and wide with a rickety elevator leading straight up to Brodon Heights. But that passage collapsed long ago. You can see it if you look carefully."

They all shielded their eyes and studied the distant cliff face. There was the square cave they'd seen earlier, perhaps about fifteen feet wide.

"Like I said, it collapsed," the man went on. "Rocks came tumbling out one night, crashing into the sea below. The passage was jammed tight the next morning. Now there are just the natural tunnels below. Very, very dangerous."

"Can you show us?" Hal blurted.

The man squinted down at Hal. "Think you can survive the old catacombs, sonny?" he said with a crooked smile. "The old house that used to be on top of that rock saw a lot of tragedy in its day. The fire was the final straw. You should speak to my granddaughter about it. All us locals know the stories, but she really loves that old history." He tapped the side of his nose. "She's been there a time or two, as well."

Abigail gripped Hal's arm with excitement. "She's been into the tunnels?"

"Go ask her," the old man suggested as he turned back to his boat and resumed plastering the bow with the sticky tarlike substance. "She just got home from school. Name's Kinsey. Excuse her manners, though. She's a good girl at heart, just rough around the edges. She'll be walking her dog on the beach."

With that, the conversation was over. The group turned and peered up and down the beach, seeing quite a few tiny figures, most of them alone. It was a moment before Molly let out an exclamation. "There! Is that her?"

The distant figure she pointed to, back the way they'd come and closer to the overlooking castle, was lying down on the sand, letting the waves lap up over her bare feet. What gave her away as the old man's granddaughter was the huge dog that sat next to her. There was something strange about it. It looked like there were three dogs merged into one . . .

"Is that . . . is that a *cerberus*?" Miss Simone gasped.

Behind them, the old man chuckled. "Aye, Kinsey's a strange one, good with animals. No respect for people but will die for her pets."

As was usual with beach walks, it seemed to take forever to get anywhere. They passed the alleyway they'd emerged from earlier and continued another ten minutes. "This is where the helicopters landed," Miss Simone commented. "I remember it was near this pier."

The pier stuck out across the sand and into the water. At least a dozen small boats were moored there, some with masts and others without. They bounced and bobbed with the waves.

"Our young friends should be here tomorrow morning," Miss Simone added. "Though I hope to have taken care of the problem by then. I fear a large group of us will only complicate things."

"That's why you put them off?" Abigail said. "To keep them out of the way?"

Molly gave Abigail a gentle nudge. "She means no disrespect. Sometimes a job is best done quietly. If we can take care of Queen Bee ourselves today, then we won't need your friends. But they'll be here tomorrow if we run into trouble."

Run into trouble, Hal thought. He didn't like the sound of that. He was amazed and a little nervous that Miss Simone thought the four of them alone could take care of Queen Bee's plan—and all before morning!

Eventually, Miss Simone jumped down off the boardwalk onto the beach and made a beeline for the girl lying twenty yards away. Hal and Abigail followed close behind, holding hands, while Molly hung back a little. "Be careful," she whispered over the crashing waves. "I've never seen a tame cerberus before."

As they approached, the three-headed dog suddenly whipped around and began snarling. It was much bigger than a normal dog, and its shoulders widened considerably to accommodate three necks and heads. Because of that extra weight, its front legs were thick and muscular. The heads themselves looked ordinary enough, just in triplicate. Two looked wary, the third downright angry, but all three had teeth bared and ears flattened.

The girl reached out to pat her companion's side as she sat up and twisted around, shielding her eyes against the sun to squint at Miss Simone. Wearing a raggedy sleeveless shirt and equally threadbare pants that she'd ripped off at the knees, one might think she was homeless. Her hair was short and curly, sticking up on top and shaved at the sides and back as though she couldn't be bothered to mess with it every day.

"Who are you?" she demanded almost exactly like her grandfather had done a short time before.

"Are you Kinsey? Your grandfather sent us to you," Miss Simone said. She'd stopped fifteen feet from the girl and her savage pet, and the others huddled behind. "We're from out of town. We want to talk to you about the castle."

Although Miss Simone gestured up at it, the girl flatly refused to glance that way. Instead, she glared around the group while her pet continued to snarl, a fearsome sound that came from deep within.

"What's in it for me?" Kinsey said sullenly.

Miss Simone patted her hidden pockets. Something clinked in there. "I have money. Just name your price."

It occurred to Hal that she could carry coins without fear of losing them because her knee-length silky dress hardly altered. If Hal carried money, it would scatter to the winds when his clothes became a strap around his neck.

"I don't care about money," Kinsey retorted. Her cerberus inched forward, its ears flattening even more. "And I'm not in the mood to talk to tourists. Leave me alone or I'll set Dog on you."

Abigail stifled a giggle, then sidled around Hal and Miss Simone to the front of the group. "Sorry, but is that his name? You call him Dog?"

"Her," Kinsey growled, her teeth bared almost as dangerously as her pet's. "Don't come any closer."

To Hal's astonishment, Abigail ignored the girl's warning, took a few more steps toward her, and collapsed on the sand a few feet away. She stretched out her legs and spread her toes as much as the waxy smart shoes would allow. "How old are you?" she asked. "I'm twelve. Thirteen in a few weeks. My name's Abi."

Kinsey looked incredulous, her mouth opening and closing like she was a stranded fish. "I don't care!" she finally exploded. "Go away!"

She let go of her cerberus, and the creature came around and snapped its jaws while slobbering on the sand. The creature was enormous, standing as high as Hal's chest and towering over his girlfriend as she sat staring out to sea.

"I don't think so," Abigail said quietly. "Because if we go away, this whole town will be taken over by monsters and you won't get *any* peace and quiet to walk Dog." She grinned at Kinsey. "Plus, we're just about the coolest people you'll ever meet."

Although Kinsey had removed her hand from Dog, the cerberus seemed to understand she hadn't given an order to attack. Hal wondered if she ever had. She came across sullen and bad-tempered, and no doubt most people steered clear of her and her three-headed beast, but Abigail already had her figured out. *Kinsey's all bluff,* Hal thought. *Of course she wouldn't let her monster-dog attack anyone. If she did, nobody would allow her to keep it.*

Steeling himself, he went to sit by Abigail, ignoring the thunderous expression on Kinsey's face and the three-headed dog's snarl.

After that, Miss Simone and Molly tentatively sat down as well. Having invited themselves to join Kinsey, the girl apparently decided she didn't want to be here anymore and started to get up, her face red with anger. "Come on, Dog," she muttered.

"Have you ever seen a shapeshifter?" Hal called after her. "Do you want a ride in the sky or something?"

Kinsey paused, her back to them.

Abigail winked at Hal and squeezed his hand. She said loudly, "I don't think she does, Hal. Too bad. Not many people get to ride on the back of a dragon. Oh well, maybe someone else will instead. We could walk down to the harbor and see if there's somebody there who knows about the tunnels under the castle."

"Yeah," Hal agreed. "I'm not sure how much Kinsey would know anyway. She can't be more than eleven."

"I know more than *anyone!*" Kinsey snapped, spinning around. The cerberus spun with her, instantly starting up with the snarling again. "Oh, be quiet, Dog." She stepped closer and glared down at them all. "One of you had *better* be a dragon shapeshifter, or I'll set Dog on you, and he'll tear your throats out. I'm not just saying that, either. I really will!"

Abigail put on a wide-eyed expression. "I believe you. And we're telling the truth. I promise you'll get a ride on a dragon's back—but *after* you've helped us. Now, will you please sit down and let us ask you some questions?"

Kinsey, looking flustered and muttering incoherently, threw herself down in the sand and ordered Dog to lie down next to her. She glared at Abigail and pouted for a moment, then folded her arms and said, "So get on with it, then. *Ask* me already!"

Abigail ignored her rotten attitude. "There's a way into the castle from the sea, yes?"

Kinsey gave a curt nod.

"Is it dangerous?"

Again, a nod.

Miss Simone broke in. "Will you show us?"

This time, Kinsey looked skyward as if considering the request.

"If you're allowed, that is," Hal added quietly.

Kinsey threw him such an intense glare that he wondered if she had been a gorgon in another life. "Of *course* I'm allowed. I can do what I want. And I'll prove it!"

Yes! Hal thought, mentally punching the air.

Molly seemed a little doubtful, though. "Surely you need to check with your parents first?"

"My parents are dead. I live with Grandpa."

"Oh. I'm sorry."

An extra powerful wave swept up around them, and it was too late to jump clear. As the seawater soaked through their clothing and made them all gasp, a faint smile flitted across Kinsey's face.

"I can show you the tunnels," she said, her mood having lifted a fraction. "If you promise me a ride in the sky. Which of you is a dragon?"

"Guess," Abigail challenged her.

Kinsey looked from one to the other. She eventually shrugged and pointed at Abigail's feet. "Three of you are wearing weird shoes. I reckon you three are shapeshifters and *she's* not." She pointed at Molly with an accusing finger as she said this.

"*She* is a shapeshifter like the others," Molly corrected her. "I'm just wearing boots, is all. I don't change much. At the moment I can't change at all."

Frowning, Kinsey looked around again. "Well, who is it, then? Tell me! Who's the dragon?"

Hal was ready. He obliged her with a quick puff of fire and smoke, and she leapt back in fright. Dog jumped up and backed off, one of the heads whining and the others looking at him in shock.

What followed was a conversation about how they had become shapeshifters and why they were there. Miss Simone took the lead, obviously deciding to trust the moody girl with the truth and laying it on thick so there was no doubt who the enemy was. By the time she was finished, Kinsey's hostility was hidden behind a barrage of questions that all four shifters patiently answered.

"So Queen Bee must be stopped, do you understand?" Miss Simone finished up. "We have to get into the castle."

"If it were me," Kinsey said with half-closed eyes and raised eyebrows, some kind of superior, all-knowing expression, "I'd just smash my way in through the window like you did before and burn them all. Why's that so difficult?"

Molly sighed. "Because, like Simone said, there are lots of children your age in the castle. They think they're helping Queen Bee, but she's using them as willing hostages. She'll slit all their throats in a heartbeat if she needs to. We need to sneak in and deal with the situation quietly."

"From below," Abigail added.

Kinsey nodded. "Well, you can't go right now. It'll have to wait until low tide, and that's either later tonight or early in the morning."

"So tonight, then," Molly said firmly.

Kinsey shook her head. "I wouldn't. It's dark enough in the daytime. You need light, and it's hard to take lanterns underwater. I've tried wrapping one to keep it dry, but then you have to light it, and—"

"Fire isn't a problem," Hal interrupted. "I can make light easily."

She stared at him with a scowl and stuck her bottom lip out. Apparently she didn't like her authority on the matter being usurped. "The tunnels are really narrow, a tight squeeze. You can't breathe fire in a space like that."

"I can."

"For two hours?" she demanded, raising her voice.

This gave Hal pause for thought. "Why two hours?"

"That's how long it takes to climb through and up. I'm telling you, it's tight. In the daytime there are little rays of light here and there. It's not much, but it's *something*. It makes all the difference."

"We'll manage," Hal said, suddenly not so sure. Two hours to climb tunnels to the castle?

"Don't you have school in the morning?" Molly added.

Kinsey shrugged. "I could skip class . . ."

"We'll go tonight," Miss Simone said sternly. "The sooner the better. Where shall we meet you, Kinsey? And at what time?"

The girl looked troubled now. She chewed her lip, and Hal was sure she was about to back out. Maybe she was all talk. The reality was suddenly upon her and doubts had crept in. 'Later tonight' was most likely past her bedtime. Maybe she wasn't cut out for adventure—

"I'm not going all the way to the top," Kinsey said. "I don't want to get stuck inside all night. I'll take you halfway, and that's all."

"Good enough," Molly said. "We don't want to drag you in anyway."

Kinsey nodded. "Meet by my boat, then. See where Grandpa is?" She pointed back along the beach. The old man had finished his sticky painting job and was sitting on a wooden beach chair, puffing on a pipe as he stared out to sea. "My boat is there. Meet me after sunset. The tide goes out then."

With that settled, Miss Simone got up and brushed clumps of wet sand from her ugly robe. The back of it clung to her. "Let's go. I'm expecting a visit from Councilman Frobisher this afternoon. I want to make sure we hear what he and the mayor discuss."

"What about my ride on a dragon's back?" Kinsey demanded.

Abigail reached out to touch her arm. "Be patient. If we do that now, we'll give ourselves away. It'll have to be after we've dealt with Queen Bee, when everything is back to normal. We won't forget."

The girl reluctantly agreed, her pout and glare making her look like she'd sat on a wasp.

Chapter Four
Secrets and Lies

Molly, Hal, and Abigail grew impatient waiting for Miss Simone to return from her 'quick nose-around.' There was only so long a tiny square park in the middle of a bustling town could hold interest.

Thankfully, Miss Simone returned after an hour with her dull robe flapping open, revealing flashes of silky green underneath. She kept her face low and the wide-brimmed hat pulled down as she rejoined the others on the park bench. "Apparently the mayor is a bigger imbecile than I previously imagined. He's arranged to meet Councilman Frobisher in his favorite haunt, an old tavern inn called The Crooked Chimney."

They stared at her in amazement. "He's meeting at the local *pub?*" Molly exclaimed. "An important meeting between town officials to discuss a potentially dangerous political situation—in a dirty, smelly *drinking house?*"

"I never said it was dirty or smelly," Miss Simone said, "but it does have a crooked chimney. It's quite a nice place, family oriented, several rooms to rent. They serve food as well."

Molly leaned toward her. "Don't tell me we're staying the night?"

"What? Good grief, no! We'll be far too busy to sleep. But we should get along there and wait for Frobisher to show. Maybe things can be resolved amicably and we won't need to go creeping around in tunnels tonight."

Abigail squeezed Hal's hand. He could tell from the look on her face that she doubted things would be sorted out with a simple conversation.

The Crooked Chimney surprised them all. The two-story building was so old and twisted that it looked like it had been picked up by a giant and wrung out like a wet cloth. Every window had warped out of shape over the years, slate roof tiles replaced one at a time. Of its three chimneys, the tallest one in the middle had earned the inn its name, being so twisted and acutely angled that builders must have been fretting over it for decades.

Despite the obvious age of the building—a small plaque on the door suggested it had stood for three hundred years—the place looked fresh and clean, the leaded window panes sparkled, and the fabulous smells wafting out the door indicated good food.

Just beyond the foyer, tables and booths filled the space. The inn was like a maze with various hallways running off to other lounges and dining rooms. Some of these hallways had steps to accommodate the street's gentle incline. The ceiling was impossibly low in places; one thick beam forced customers to duck, a sign dutifully warning to 'WATCH YOUR HEAD.'

Miss Simone led the way to a booth in the corner and gestured for Molly, Hal, and Abigail to sit. Then she went off again, her hat tipped low in front.

"Where's she going?" Abigail asked. She twisted around on the bench seat, trying to peer over the partial wall that separated their booth from the next.

Molly smiled. "When you come to a place like this, you're expected to buy something from the bar—food, drink, or both. I expect she's getting drinks."

"What, like . . . like *ale*?" Hal said, thrilled. Ever since arriving in Carter and visiting places like Louis and now Brodon, he'd wondered what the foul-smelling adult beverage tasted like. He'd never been allowed to try it, but if beer was on offer right now, well, he was willing to give it a go. He was nearly thirteen, after all. He was pretty sure he could down half an ale in one sip like he'd glimpsed men doing. How impressed would Abigail be if—

"Not a chance, young man," Molly said with a wink. "Juice or water for you. You're only twelve, you know."

"Thirteen soon," he grumbled.

"Still too young." Molly grinned. "You know, by a staggering coincidence, I too was thirteen when I was your age."

"Never heard *that* one before," Hal said, rolling his eyes. But he returned her grin. It was nice to see her like this, without her veil, her expressions unmasked. "Molly? When was the last time you walked around without covering up?"

She leaned on the table and touched her fingers to her cheeks. "When I was little, my death-gaze would switch itself on even when I was in human form. Then I learned to control it and spent many years without a problem. I was young and strong. But my inner gorgon has been trying to push through for the past fifteen years, and it's winning. You've seen me in my full gorgon form—all slithery and dark green with a tail like a mermaid and snakes for hair? I can control the transformation except for the snakes and the death-gaze. I have to wear a veil."

"Except when Blair drains you of magic," Abigail said.

Molly smiled. "I admit I do enjoy these brief respites from being a monster. It's almost a shame the magic always comes back."

Miss Simone returned with a tray. She handed tankards out, and Hal peered hopefully into his, sniffing it cautiously. "Apple cider," she said. "It was either that or lemonade."

After a moment's thought, she threw her hat down on the seat next to her and made an attempt to shield her face in case anyone looked over. She seemed a little less conspicuous now, though. Nobody wore large hats indoors.

"And what do *you* have?" Abigail asked, looking at Miss Simone's tankard.

"Molly and I have barley tea. Would you like a taste?"

It was as they were sipping in silence that a distant throbbing sound came to their attention. Hal recognized it as an army helicopter, one of the smaller ones. It had to be Councilman Frobisher arriving for his meeting. It made sense that he'd enlist the military for a fast journey rather than trundle across land by horse-drawn cart. If the helicopter was landing on the beach, Frobisher would be here soon.

They passed the next thirty minutes enjoying a rare, unhurried chat about anything and everything. Molly mentioned Hal's forthcoming birthday.

Miss Simone smiled. "Thirteen. It's hard to believe. These last six months have been interesting." She looked from Hal to Abigail and back again. "You two and your friends have fared so much better than my own classmates ever did. We were a mess, weren't we, Molly? I think dealing with serious threats has brought you together and—"

A sudden hush fell across the inn, and Miss Simone broke off. The noise level had been a constant drone ever since they'd arrived, and suddenly it was gone as everyone stared at the main entrance door. Twisting around in his seat, with Abigail hanging over him, Hal spotted a familiar face—an old man in a fine long coat, bending over his cane as he shuffled in and looked around.

"Councilman Frobisher," Molly whispered.

Dipping her head, Miss Simone said, "Look away, everyone. He mustn't know we're here. If he sees us and reacts, then everyone else will see us, and word will get back to Queen Bee."

Hal and Abigail faced front again and studied Miss Simone and Molly as they, in turn, watched the councilman approach the bar. While Miss Simone made some attempt to hide herself, Molly did not, and after a while Hal realized it was because nobody, not even Frobisher, knew what she looked like. Ironically, her missing veil masked her identity.

Miss Simone reached for the wide-brimmed hat. Molly stopped her. "That thing is more recognizable than your hair. Leave it. He's not looking this way."

Now that the councilman had reached the bar and was talking to the man behind the counter, a murmur had started up again. It was obvious everyone was whispering about the visitor. "Do people know who he is?" Abigail said.

"They probably guessed," Molly murmured. "A finely dressed gentleman with a couple of goblin escorts? Who else could it be?"

Hal blinked and twisted around again. "Goblins? Where?"

"By the door."

Miss Simone nodded. "My good friend Gristletooth is one of them. The other is Knottynose, I believe. Have you noticed there are no goblins in this town? The village of Carter has a very strong relationship with goblins thanks to our own resident goblin shapeshifter—"

"Blacknail," Hal said.

"Riley," Miss Simone said at the same time. "Most other towns think it's strange mixing with goblins, so when a man walks into a bar with a couple of them, it's obvious he's from Carter. And everyone here knows of the meeting."

In fact, with Frobisher's arrival, the place was filling up quickly. Pretty soon, all empty tables and booths were filled, and then newcomers started lining the walls, standing there and leaning with their arms folded.

Word evidently got back to the mayor, too, for he showed up fifteen minutes later. By this time, Frobisher had been offered a table of his own, and it was around this table that people started to congregate, drifting in from all sides until a crowd had formed. When a wall of customers blocked Hal's booth in the corner, Molly cleared her throat loudly and asked them to move aside. They ignored her. "Can't see a thing," she grumbled into her barley tea.

"Yes, but Frobisher can't see us, either," Miss Simone said, looking much happier about it than her friend. She was still trying to hide her hair, fearful that she'd be recognized.

When Mayor Seymour Priggle entered, the audience shifted around again. He was a large man to part way for, especially with his entourage: the scrag named Duke, who had declared himself Queen Bee's liaison—and Queen Bee herself, half the size and weight of the town's overweight leader but carrying just as much presence. Both scrags hung back while the mayor approached Frobisher at his small round table.

"Glad we're hidden back here," Miss Simone whispered, barely audible over the hushed murmur that filled the inn's lounge.

"I still want to *see*," Molly complained, looking like she was ready to climb up onto the table.

Miss Simone touched her arm. "We'll hear just fine. We don't need to see."

Abigail clearly wanted to, though. She leaned heavily on Hal, trying to peer past the wall of expectant townsfolk. In the end, he slipped out of his seat and edged between a couple of people with Abigail clinging to his hand.

"Hal! Sit down!" Miss Simone hissed.

He pretended not to hear. He and Abigail jammed themselves between a smelly man on one side and a rotund woman on the other. Another line of people stood in front, but a gap presented itself. Through that gap they could see Frobisher struggling to rise as the mayor pulled a chair out.

"Please, don't get up," Priggle said, waving his hand dismissively as he eased his great bulk into the chair. Someone let out a sharp intake of breath as the flimsy wooden legs creaked under his weight. Queen Bee casually slid into a third chair and rested her elbow on the table. Duke chose to stand, looking down his nose at Frobisher.

"This venue is highly unsuitable," the councilman said stiffly. "A bar in the middle of town? At happy hour, no less! Don't you think we should migrate to somewhere a little more private?"

The mayor shook his head. "I want everyone to know where I stand on this matter. I want it heard loud and clear." He pointed a pudgy finger at Frobisher. "You, sir, are wasting your time. You're here to demand an explanation and an apology for the unfortunate death of a man from Carter, yes?"

The old man blinked. "Why, yes, and to—"

"The truth is, that man was killed by one of your own."

A heavy silence fell. Frobisher's mouth hung open, a frown plastered across his forehead. "Now, wait a minute," he said finally. "Your scrag friends took hostages, and they murdered one and sent him back to us as a warning."

"As I said, he was actually killed by one of your own."

Frobisher stared in amazement. "A fellow hostage killed him?"

"A fellow *prisoner*," the mayor corrected him. "Yes, a man found it difficult to control his frustration at being locked up. He lashed out at the woman next to him. A brawl started, and that woman's husband punched him. Apparently it was a hefty punch."

The councilman gripped the edge of the table and rose out of his seat a few inches. "What kind of nonsense is this? That poor man had a look of absolute terror and pain on his—"

"Of course he did," the mayor barked. "Who wouldn't be scared facing a strapping big man like that?"

Hal shared the councilman's indignation. When the giant roc bird had flown into Carter and delivered a casket containing a dead man, it was perfectly clear at first sight that he'd been the victim of a stinging courtesy of the Swarm. A post-mortem examination had confirmed it. The mayor was a liar.

The huge man reached across to pat Queen Bee on the shoulder. "My colleague here treated those criminals with great respect, but a petty squabble broke out and resulted in a tragic death."

"Criminals? They were *hostages!*" Frobisher exploded. "They were taken from their homes against their will and—"

"Treated very well, all things considered." While the councilman blinked in amazement, the mayor addressed the silent onlookers. "Yes, my friends, the rumors are true. I arranged for that group of people to be extracted from their homes in Carter."

"Why?" a woman asked.

Hal couldn't see who'd spoken, but Mayor Priggle focused on her. "Because all those people and more have been plotting to overthrow the leadership of various towns and villages in this region."

"Preposterous!" Frobisher exploded. "We've been plotting no such thing!"

The mayor shook his head. "*You* haven't, my old friend. You and your council colleagues appear to be blissfully ignorant of what's going on around you. In fact, your people plan to turn on you also. They want to sweep you aside, take control, establish a new governing body that extends to the far reaches of these lands—and all with the help of military men from the other world."

"And errant shapeshifters," Queen Bee added softly.

The mayor nodded. "Indeed. Let's not forget about Carter's infamous Shapeshifter Program—an army of shapeshifters to aid in the takeover."

Frobisher had been sitting there shaking with indignation. He finally found his tongue. "This is—I've never heard—You can't be serious! The Shapeshifter Program is nothing more than a way to bridge the communication gap between our species and—"

The mayor thumped the table so hard that even Queen Bee looked surprised. "A public relations cover story! What you really want is an army."

A silence fell, the audience frozen. Standing by his side, Duke nodded soberly.

Mayor Priggle sat back and folded his arms as he glared at Frobisher. "I have close allies, people with their ears to the ground. I know what's going on even if you don't. I'm afraid the situation is already out of your control, Councilman. When half your town is plotting against you, and the military men and shapeshifters are preparing for battle behind your back, there's hardly any point talking to an elderly councilman such as yourself. But here we are. Out of respect, I felt you deserved to know, and that's why I allowed this meeting."

Frobisher looked flabbergasted. "This is *ridiculous!*" He pointed accusingly at Queen Bee. "These people are deranged killers, and this woman is the worst of them all. You've been brainwashed, sir."

The mayor shook his head. "You're blind, old man. You want to hear about deranged killers?" He struggled to turn in his chair as he again glanced around the audience. "Look at this poor young woman at my side. Can you believe the shapeshifters of Carter fed her to a sea serpent? She was lucky to survive."

Everyone in the crowd gasped.

Hal was so dumbfounded by the stream of absolute garbage coming from the mayor's lips that heat began to rise in his chest. He wanted to rush forward and shout the truth, but he knew that would be a huge mistake. Instead he gripped Abigail's hand, squeezing tighter and tighter.

"Citizens of Brodon," the mayor said softly, "the only way we can protect ourselves against a rising army is to gather intelligence and form an army of our own. That's why I took prisoners, and that's why I've gathered shapeshifters from afar. But I believe in restraint. Our new protectors are primarily for show, a display of strength. Last night, shapeshifters from Carter—a dragon and an ogre—attacked us in an effort to rescue their kin. We have a much larger force of shapeshifters in residence at the castle, but rather than provoke a war, I decided to stand down and release the prisoners. In doing so, the people of Carter glimpsed our strength lurking in the wings but also recognized our restraint and mercy. Perhaps that will make them think twice about returning here again."

"You kidnapped innocent people!" Frobisher roared, trembling with rage as he rose to his feet. "Your so-called protectors are hoodlums and thugs!"

He looked around the packed room, looking desperate.

"People of Brodon, taking hostages is the work of a madman! These people your mayor has sided with are incredibly dangerous. This woman right here, who calls herself Queen Bee, has a large gang of scrags called the Swarm, and they sting people to death with poison-tipped spears! Do you really want to call these people your protectors?"

Queen Bee jumped up and stood very close to the councilman, looking at him in the eye about two inches from his face. She raised her voice. "The councilman should leave now before his insanely inaccurate and hurtful accusations land him in jail. My extended family may look a little rough and ready, but that's because we spent over a decade surviving in a virus-stricken world. Now we're shapeshifters, and all we want is honest work and somewhere to call home."

"Shapeshifters? You're *scrags*!" the councilman shouted.

The mayor spoke loudly, addressing to the crowd. "Notice how Councilman Frobisher uses the derogatory word *scrags*? That's what he calls these poor, afflicted people. He doesn't understand what they've been through, doesn't care that they had to scavenge for food the past decade using nothing but spears. When they crossed into our world, they stumbled upon the ancient and dangerous art of shapeshifting. They embraced the secret and were successful where many in the past have failed. Now they need a mission." The mayor shook his head, putting on a sad expression. "But the councilman here still sees Queen Bee and her people as animals, fit only for scavenging."

"Th-that's not true!" Frobisher cried in a strangled voice.

Hal couldn't stand anymore. He turned and dragged Abigail back to the corner booth where Miss Simone and Molly listened intently. They were staring at each other, their fingers gripping the edge of the table.

"Can't I do something?" Hal whispered. "I could—"

"You'll do *nothing*," Miss Simone snapped, her voice low. Her eyes blazed with fury. "Sit down and be quiet."

He and Abigail slid into their long bench seat and waited it out. Lies continued to spew from the mouths of the mayor, Queen Bee, and Duke while the councilman sputtered with indignation.

Eventually the mayor ended the meeting. "Go home, Councilman Frobisher, and take a good hard look at the people you call your neighbors."

"This isn't finished," Frobisher warned. "My village demands justice for the death of a loved one and the trauma of being kidnapped. If you don't willingly hand over these scrags as prisoners and offer a sincere and public apology, then we'll have to hold you personally accountable."

"Is that some kind of threat, Councilman?"

"It's—it's a *promise*. We have the military on our side, Mayor Priggle. We have the manpower to come here and—and—"

"Enough said!" the mayor barked. Although Hal couldn't see it from his booth, he clearly heard the large man's chair scrape and topple over. "Escort this man and his goblins to the beach and make sure he leaves at once."

The meeting was over. The packed audience immediately burst into noisy chatter as people milled about, jostling one another in their efforts to stream outside after the mayor, the scrags, and the humiliated councilman. Hal heard thuds and clanks along with the annoyed shouts of the innkeeper.

Within a minute, the place was almost completely empty. Several tables and chairs lay on their sides, and a maid dashed out with a mop to clean up spilled drinks. Hal could see through one of the small windows that a mob was herding the frightened councilman and his two goblin escorts along the street, presumably to the beach where his helicopter waited.

"Well, I believe the councilman's trip was a waste of time," Molly said with a sigh, her voice now strangely loud in the empty lounge.

Miss Simone shook her head. "Not a waste of time. Now our path is clearer than ever, and I'm glad we're already here and ready to take action."

"I wish we didn't have to wait until this evening," Abigail said. "I wish Kinsey would just show us the way into the cliff. Maybe we can get in without her. We're not like normal people, you know." She smiled at that.

"Perhaps so," Miss Simone agreed. "If flooding and drowning is the only concern, I certainly don't have anything to worry about. Let's go."

Chapter Five
Low Tide

They couldn't find Kinsey anywhere. She wasn't on the beach, and her grandfather mentioned she had probably gone off with some friends. "But if she agreed to meet you at low tide, she'll be there," he said with a smile.

"Do you happen to know where the tunnel entrance is?" Miss Simone asked.

The old man rubbed his chin. "Sure, it's no big secret. It's around the cliff on the far side. Look for some mooring rings stuck in the rock. But don't go in while the water's high. You'll never make it."

"Thank you," Miss Simone told him, and Hal could see from her expression that she had every intention of ignoring his advice.

The four of them walked to the far end of the beach where the boardwalk ended and the rocky cliff towered above. The beach sloped away rather steeply until it was lost to the frothy waves, but the small mountain continued out across the water. The blocked entrance to the original passage was much more obvious up close, high above the water with iron pegs sticking out, signs of where an old platform and perhaps a staircase had once hung.

"I'm going for a swim," Miss Simone said, handing her hat back to Molly and peeling off her dull robe. Underneath, her silky green smart dress gleamed in the sun, and suddenly she stood out a mile as a shapeshifter. Without waiting for a response, she headed off down the sand to the water.

"Can't we come with you?" Hal called after her.

"No, wait here."

She threw herself into the water and began splashing away. Seconds later, she dipped under. A fishtail rose briefly before disappearing.

Molly glanced around, peering up the beach toward the boardwalk and houses, and the road that ran alongside the cliff. "Good thing nobody saw that. We need to be careful about transforming in public."

Hal knew a mermaid wouldn't take long to swim out around the gentle bend of the cliff to the far side, but still he hopped up and down with impatience. Abigail grinned at him. "She'll be back soon. Just relax."

Miss Simone returned after an agonizing wait. She splashed out of the water to her waist, then paused. After a moment she adjusted her dress and continued out, her tail now reformed into legs.

"It's not going to be fun," she said as she padded up the beach.

She pushed her wet hair back over her head. Almost immediately it began to dry, puffing up and becoming springy as seawater streamed off in torrents—one of the stranger aspects of her mermaid magic.

"There's a tunnel entrance just below the water," she went on, "but it starts narrow and gets tighter. Completely filled with water, impossible for most people to navigate without diving equipment. Lots of branch-offs, too. I explored a few and gave up. We could easily get lost without a guide. I do hope Kinsey knows her way."

"So we have to wait for her after all?" Hal said.

"We do. Every route I took led to a dead end. We'll just have to be patient."

* * *

Kinsey showed up as promised after dark, rowing her small boat across the bay close to the beach. She veered inland until she hit sand, then waited while Miss Simone, Molly, Hal, and Abigail rushed to join her.

It was a small boat, and it didn't help that Dog took up half of it. She glared balefully with three pairs of eyes that gleamed in the moonlight as Miss Simone climbed in. Hal and Abigail followed next, their seat thankfully out of nipping distance. If Dog decided to bite, it would be hard to shake her loose; she could easily chow down with three pairs of jaws.

Molly stayed on the beach. Abigail squeezed closer to Hal and patted the remaining portion of wooden seat next to her. "There's room here, Molly."

"I'm not going," the woman said, folding her arms. Her robe flapped in the breeze, and her hat, which Miss Simone had returned earlier, threatened to blow away. "If I can't turn anyone to stone, then I'm more a hindrance than a help, just a gangly, clumsy woman."

Miss Simone nodded as if they'd had this discussion already. "Keep an eye out for the other shapeshifters when they arrive tomorrow morning and tell them where we are." She peered up at the castle. Except for a few feebly lit windows, it was nothing more than a black outline against the almost-black cloudy sky. "Maybe by then we'll have made our way up and dealt with Queen Bee."

"Be safe," Molly said, struggling to push the boat out.

Only when Kinsey got turned around and started rowing out around the cliff did she say her first words of the evening. "Hope you're ready for this. It's going to be very dark and very tight."

"Well," Abigail said, "*two* of us won't have a problem. Miss Simone is a mermaid, so being underwater is easy. I'm a faerie and can shrink down small, so tight spaces won't feel tight at all. Hal, though . . ." She nudged him. "He's a great big dragon, so he's utterly useless."

Kinsey's eyes widened. She forgot to row for a moment, and the boat drifted. "There won't be room to turn into a dragon."

"I know. That's what I said. He'll have to stay as he is—utterly useless."

"Thanks," Hal muttered.

When they made it around to the other side of the cliff, the choppier waves caused them to bounce up and down. Kinsey squinted in the darkness and rowed straight for a couple of iron rings embedded in the wall a few feet above the water. Directly below was a funnel-like opening in the rock, partially submerged.

"Low tide has started," Kinsey said, reaching for one of the rings. She held onto it while deftly threading a rope through and tying it off. She made sure to leave some slack. "This entrance is normally below water. The water will drop a bit more before the current changes direction. Then it'll rise again."

"How long do we have?" Hal said.

She paused. "Enough time to get up to the castle, but not enough time to get out again. That's why I can't go all the way with you. I'll have to turn back so I can get out while you're still on your way in."

"Fair enough," Miss Simone said. "Do you have a lantern or something?"

"There's no point. Come on, we haven't got all night. Stay here, Dog."

Leaving the cerberus to whine in triplicate, the curly-headed girl clambered fully clothed over the side of the boat and swam into the tunnel entrance. Miss Simone followed. When it was Hal's turn, he gasped at the water's icy chill and clung to the boat, watching Kinsey as she bobbed around in the shadows.

With a popping sound, Abigail shrank down small and began buzzing around Hal's head like an annoying gnat. He playfully swatted at her, and he heard a high-pitched giggle. Miss Simone gave them both a glare.

Kinsey stared open-mouthed at them, almost letting in a flood of water as she floated up to her chin. After a while she composed herself. "This way," she said rather unnecessarily as she twisted around and headed deeper into the darkness.

Hal squinted and tried to make out where the walls were. Abigail zipped this way and that, glowing faintly, the only source of light now.

Several yards in, Miss Simone said, "Floor," and a second later Hal's feet touched bottom. It had come up to meet them, the coarse rock sloping gently upward. As the three of them climbed, the sound of splashing water increased until they were wading thigh-deep.

"That wasn't so bad," Hal muttered, surprised.

In front of him, Miss Simone let out a soft grunt. "Ouch. Watch your head."

Hal groped and found that the ceiling was easily within reach. Miss Simone must be bent double already.

"Why couldn't we bring a lamp?" Hal asked, focusing on the small faerie glow as Abigail flitted about. "If we're going to walk through tunnels—"

Kinsey's voice echoed back out of the darkness. "We won't for long. The water's not deep here, but it will be in a minute."

A shiver went down Hal's spine, and not just from the cold water. "The tide's coming in already?"

"No. It's just that the tunnel's not level. It slopes up and down, so the water will be at our ankles then up to our chins and back to our waists and so on."

Still could have brought a lamp, Hal thought.

He was glad Abigail was with them. She zipped deeper into the tunnel and back, all the time giving off a faint light that Hal steadfastly focused on. Before long, the water had dropped to ankle-deep just as Kinsey had promised—and then the tunnel sloped down again, and the level rose until it was at Hal's waist. Not only that, but the walls closed in so that he had to turn sideways and squeeze through. Gasps and grunts filled the blackness.

"The first tricky part is ahead," Kinsey said, her voice seemingly far off.

It isn't already tricky? Hal thought. He would have lit up with a blast of fire to see what to expect, but Miss Simone was directly in front of him.

"Mind your footing," Kinsey said, closer now.

Hal bumped into Miss Simone, who had now stopped. "The floor's gone," she warned over her shoulder. "Just drop into the water."

The flooded tunnel was waist-deep at the moment. Hal didn't mind that. But the idea of having no floor, having to paddle around in darkness trusting the word of this girl they hardly knew, filled him with doubt.

Miss Simone made a splash in front of him. Hal waded forward, groping for the walls on both sides until they abruptly ended. He felt with his foot. Sure enough, his firm footing had also terminated.

Abigail buzzed past him, and she said something in a high-pitched voice that sounded like "Last one in's a chicken!"

"It's all right for you," he muttered.

As carefully as he could, Hal stepped forward and dropped into the pool. Once he was busy treading water, Kinsey spoke loudly as though she were right by his side. "All right, now swim to the wall on the other side. There are a few crevices to grab hold of once you get there."

Blindly following her directions, Hal surged forward just a few strokes and came up against a smooth rock face. He felt for handholds and became aware of Miss Simone bobbing around on his left.

"Okay?" she asked.

"Yeah."

A splash indicated that Kinsey had just swum behind him. She nudged up against his right side so he was sandwiched between her and Miss Simone. "Now we need to swim under," she said. "This is why it's pointless bringing a lantern. There's nowhere to hang it, either. There are quite a few lanterns lying twenty feet below us, lost underwater."

"How far do we swim?" Hal said, unable to keep his teeth from chattering.

Miss Simone touched his arm. "I did this bit earlier. These tunnels were completely underwater then, but I had a quick look. It's not far.

Maybe about twenty seconds if you keep moving. You can't get lost. Just follow the walls."

"Abi?" he said, looking around.

She appeared at once, her light brighter than before. Or maybe it just seemed that way. She landed on his shoulder and wormed her way into his collar. Clinging tight, she patted his neck and made it clear she planned to hold tight while he swam.

"It's easy," Kinsey said, sounding a little like she was bragging. "I've done this a million times."

"Does your grandfather know how dangerous it is down here?" Miss Simone asked her.

Kinsey laughed. "No. Are you ready?"

Without waiting for an answer, she splashed and disappeared below.

Miss Simone said, "You go next, Hal. It's very narrow, so if you get in trouble, stop kicking and let me push your feet."

Hal nodded—something she couldn't possibly see—and counted to three, more for Abigail's benefit than his own. He could feel her nestled inside his collar. He bobbed up and down with each count, getting higher and higher before diving.

Turning upside down and feeling for some sort of opening, he wished desperately he could switch to his dragon form. Swimming underwater was no problem for his reptilian counterpart. Squeezing through tight tunnels was, though. He fought to calm his nerves, knowing that to panic about drowning might lead to an instinctive transformation—which would be a disaster.

He found the opening. It felt triangle-shaped. He squeezed in, thinking this was the craziest thing he had ever done. Panic surged as he pulled himself through. Everything he did was painfully slow, and there were barely any handholds to help him. The only thing that kept him from backing out was the realization that reversing his direction would be even slower—and the fact that Miss Simone was right behind him, giving his feet gentle shoves.

How many seconds had passed? He was sure it had to be twenty or thirty by now. His chest felt like it would burst. The journey wasn't made easier by the fact that he kept jamming into the wedge-shaped ceiling. But when he exhaled slightly and let out a few large bubbles, his buoyancy decreased a little, which helped. He focused on that, grasping at the thought like a lifeline. The less air in his chest, the more of a deadweight he was . . .

Miss Simone pushed at his feet, and suddenly he sped along. He concentrated only on using his hands to keep from bumping against the slanted walls above.

Then those walls were gone, and he shot upward, burst out of the water, and sucked in huge breaths of sweet, cold air.

"Man, you're *slow*," Kinsey said from afar. "Swim forward and follow my voice." She kept talking, chatting incessantly about how this pool branched off into seven different tunnels, two of them drilling directly downward, the rest relatively level. "Five of them dead-end," she explained, "and one runs all the way through the cliff to a gorgeous cavern. But only one tunnel leads up to the castle."

As she talked, Hal drifted toward her, seeing nothing but suffocating blackness and wondering how on earth she managed to find her way.

"Okay, Hal?" Miss Simone whispered.

"Yeah, fine," he gasped. "I thought that was much longer than twenty seconds, though."

"It was. Nearly a minute. You *were* pretty slow."

Abigail emerged from his collar. She vigorously shook her soggy wings, then rose into the air with a high-pitched whine accompanied by a welcoming glow. Her tiny faerie figure, no more than six inches tall, was plain to see at this close distance, but it faded to a blurred smudge of light as she zipped over to where Kinsey was waiting.

In Abigail's feeble light, Kinsey knelt on a protruding ledge. Hal hoisted himself onto it, feeling extremely heavy in his saturated state. Glancing back, he watched Miss Simone drag herself out, her fishtail already a pair of legs again.

"This was where I got confused," she said. "I tried all these tunnels earlier and found no way through."

Kinsey's self-satisfied smile was obvious in the glow of the faerie light. "That's why you need *me*. Get ready, because the easy part's over."

She turned and crawled through a two-foot wide gap that Abigail's feeble glow was unable to penetrate. "Seriously?" Hal murmured. "Are we going to be on hands and knees the rest of the way?"

"I spotted this tiny opening when I came here earlier," Miss Simone muttered. "I didn't bother with it."

She said nothing more as she wriggled through the gap. After her feet were out of the way, Hal pulled himself through and felt around. To his dismay, the passage remained two or three feet in diameter, and he could hear both Kinsey and Miss Simone panting as they struggled ahead.

Abigail stayed with Hal, shedding a tiny amount of light on his oppressive surroundings. He forged on, wishing he could pad his elbows against the rock.

It went on like that for a while. Then the passage abruptly sloped downward. Ahead of him, Miss Simone muttered something under her breath.

"What?" Hal grunted.

"I said, I thought we'd be heading upward by now."

Kinsey's voice floated out of the darkness. "We'll go upward soon. I'll let you know when."

After another few minutes of wriggling down a slope, Hal heard splashing ahead. Then Miss Simone exclaimed, "We're back down to sea level!"

"Only for a bit," Kinsey said. "This is where most people give up even when they know the way. The tide is about as low as it's going to get right now, but it's not quite low enough. We need to crawl down into the water and up through a hole in the ceiling. It's just a few yards. Swim through and feel for my hand."

More splashing, and then silence. Miss Simone sighed. "All right, Hal. Are you up for this?"

"What choice is there?" he said. Nerves and chilled water were causing his bones to rattle. "It's not like I can turn around."

Miss Simone slid a little farther down the slope and splashed into water. Abigail buzzed ahead of Hal so he could see what to expect. The water was there, filling the tunnel, black and cold.

Abigail huddled against his neck, slipping inside his collar and clinging tight. Hal crawled toward the water, trembling. He'd spent way too much time in tunnels since he'd crossed into New Earth. After this, he was officially done with them. And no matter what happened in the castle above, he was certain of one thing: He was *not* coming back this way!

He counted aloud and thrust himself headfirst into the water. As fast as he could, he pulled himself onward down the slope, his eyes shut tight against the stinging salt. It wasn't like he'd be able to see anything anyway. He put every ounce of trust in Kinsey and Miss Simone as he crawled deeper and deeper.

Something slapped him in the face. He grasped for it, felt a hand, gripped it hard, and allowed himself to be tugged upward. An opening above his head meant he could rise up onto his knees, then stagger to his feet. And as soon as he kicked upward, he broke the surface and sucked in a gulp of precious air.

Abigail immediately lit up and buzzed free, but she plopped back into the water and floated there. Hal scooped her up, holding her in his hand. Her glow was strangely warm, and as he peered closer, he saw that she was shaking her tiny wings dry. Then she buzzed into the air again.

"That wasn't so bad, was it?" Kinsey said.

With great care, Hal breathed a few puffs of fire, just enough to get a good glimpse of his surroundings. The three of them were treading water in a craggy shaft about twelve feet wide and five across, no obvious exits anywhere.

"The only way out of here is back the way we came," Kinsey said, "or straight up to the castle. About twenty feet above our heads is the old passage that collapsed a long time ago. The way into that passage from outside is blocked, but the rest is still clear. You just need to reach it."

"How?" Miss Simone asked.

"Well, you *could* float up with the rising tide for the next hour, then climb some more to the top. Or you can use that rope ladder over there. See it?"

They all agreed to climb.

Kinsey did so first. Miss Simone went next while Hal lit up the shaft with regular blasts of fire to light the way. Kinsey commented that dragon shapeshifters were pretty useful despite what Abigail had said earlier.

Then it was Hal's turn. It was easy enough, and he was glad to drag himself out of the water. The ladder swung around, sometimes slamming against the rough rock wall. Abigail buzzed to the top, glowing faintly.

They emerged in a sizeable passage, again utterly black. Hal lit up several more times and discovered an immovable roof fall not ten feet to his right. "That way used to lead outside," Kinsey explained. "There was a platform fixed to the cliff, and ladders and everything, and boats used to moor there for loading. It was really simple. But the roof fell in."

"And nobody tried to clear it?" Miss Simone asked.

"It's a good hundred feet of rubble. And not just loose rock, either. The whole mountain is resting on it. If anyone tried to clear it, more might come down."

"Oh."

"And so people have been using this awkward back door ever since," Kinsey said. "Not very convenient but doable if you know the way."

Awkward, Hal thought, her words echoing in his mind. *Not very convenient. The understatements of the year.*

"Most of this passage is naturally formed, but the floor has been leveled off," Kinsey said cheerfully. Her sour mood when they'd first met her had completely lifted now that she was where she loved to be— acting as a tour guide in this awful, cold, waterlogged blackness. "This shaft was always here, too, just a big old crack in the ground."

Hal turned and breathed fire in the other direction. A long passage opened up before him. "So we go this way," he said. "Looks easy enough."

"Just lots of steps," Kinsey said. "This is where we part ways. I could go on a bit farther, but there's no point. I'm going back down and out. You carry on up to the castle."

"On our own?" Miss Simone said. "Is it easy to get lost?"

"No, you won't get lost. There's an old elevator, but it's broken, which means you'll have to take the stairs. Just go to the end of the passage and start climbing. There should be lanterns if the last explorers were kind enough to put them back."

In the darkness, Hal heard her grunts as she felt around for the rope ladder and began descending. He belched a sheet of fire and saw her already halfway down. "Uh, see you later, then," he said.

"You'd better keep your promise about letting me ride in the sky," Kinsey warned, a hint of her grumpiness returning, "or I'll come find you and poke your eyes out."

And with that, she was gone.

Miss Simone sighed. "Well, I guess the worst is over."

Hal began walking immediately. "Let's find these steps. I'm sick of this place. I'd rather be up in the castle fighting scrags than tripping around down here. I nearly drowned ten times tonight!"

Abigail abruptly grew to full size beside him. He felt rather than saw her presence as she jostled him and clung to his arm. "You sound like Robbie now, exaggerating like that. Light the way, fire-breath."

The three of them traipsed along the passage, their footfalls echoing off the cold, damp, rock walls.

Chapter Six
Under the Castle

They found the circular stairwell at the end of the passage. It reminded Hal of the old lighthouse on the island, only much narrower and steeper. These steps were made of stone rather than metal, and the walls let in no light whatsoever. It was a long climb.

"One hundred and three," Abigail said, panting in the darkness as she placed one foot after another right behind Hal. "One hundred and four . . ."

"Save your breath," Miss Simone complained, a few steps above. "Anyway, we should be getting close by now. Let's keep our noise down."

Hal had stopped belching fire a while back. Despite what Kinsey had said, none of them had spotted any lanterns—they were missing from their hooks—and so they ascended in absolute blackness, feeling their way, stumbling through cobwebs and treading on all manner of things that squelched or crunched.

Another twenty steps later, Miss Simone whispered, "I just bumped into something hanging off the wall. Hal, take a look."

So Hal breathed fire, and the orange light from his flames flickered all around. There on the wall, smothered in more cobwebs, was one of Kinsey's elusive lanterns. Miss Simone brushed it off and took it down, and Hal carefully lit it with the tiniest flame he could muster.

Finally illuminating the stairwell did nothing to lift Hal's spirits. Now he could see the cobwebs they stumbled through and the hand-sized spiders that scuttled away. He also became aware that all the squelchy, crunchy things they'd been treading on were large snails. He shuddered, wishing he wore something more substantial on his feet than open-toed smart shoes.

"Looks like we're close," Miss Simone said in a low voice.

Instantly, Hal forgot about his aching legs and the sticky cobwebs. He focused instead on a soft light permeating the gloom just around the next bend in the stairwell. A doorway!

After climbing in darkness and at last finding a lantern, now it seemed they didn't need it. Miss Simone carefully placed it at her feet, still flickering, and crept up the remaining seven or eight steps. Hal and Abigail followed close behind. They squatted in the doorway and peered around the frame.

Flickering torches lit the corridor beyond: stone floor, walls and ceiling, with archways at both sides all along its length. With the telltale squeak of a door's hinges, a scrag emerged from one of these archways, crossed the hall, and disappeared into another.

"This is it," Abigail whispered. "Darcy and I came down here before. This is the floor below the castle where the hostages were locked up. In fact . . ." She paused, then pointed. "See this room closest to us? That's where Lauren was held. And at the far end of the corridor is a narrow staircase leading up to the castle. That's where Molly was turned to stone."

Hal saw only archways from where he squatted, but he guessed a recessed doorway stood in each. And he remembered the narrow staircase Abigail was talking about. Aside from Molly calcifying herself, it was where he'd run into scrags and gotten a taste of a Swarm stinging.

"So now what?" he asked, his mind going blank.

From a room on the left, a tall scrag with a hump appeared. He seemed preoccupied with a notebook, which he wrote in as he ambled along the corridor before vanishing into another room at the far end. Voices sounded as a nearby door opened and three people wandered into view. Even from behind, Hal could tell they weren't scrags. They were dressed too nicely and had no scars on their hands or the sides of their faces.

"It's busy here," Abigail said.

"Too busy," Miss Simone agreed. "It's late, but perhaps not late enough. We should wait awhile. Maybe they'll all go to bed soon."

So they waited, crouching in the darkness of the stairwell. People came and went, scrags and Brodon caretakers alike. The residents seemed perfectly comfortable wandering around below the castle even though the dimly lit corridor struck Hal as a little creepy. Why didn't the caretakers live upstairs in the castle itself? He supposed the grand upper floors were meant for the droves of tourists who came to visit, perhaps even when paying out-of-towners wanted to stay overnight.

The place had to be kept clean and tidy, so the large team of caretakers lived downstairs out of the way.

Hal was tired. He wished he could sneak into an empty room and sleep in a comfortable bed instead of sitting upright on a cold, hard step with snails leaving a sticky mess around him. Abigail snuggled close, and they tried to relax but grew bored very quickly. Miss Simone seemed to have endless patience, just sitting there peering along the corridor as the night dragged on.

"Wake up," she said at last.

He jolted awake. "What?"

"Things are a little quieter, now. The caretakers seem to have retired for the night, and a lot of the scrags have gathered in a room to the left about halfway along. I don't think they've gone to bed, though. We'll need to be careful."

"How long were we asleep?" Abigail asked, rubbing her eyes.

Ignoring her, Miss Simone touched Hal's shoulder. "Would you have room to transform if you needed to?"

Hal looked doubtfully at the corridor. "Maybe. It's kind of tight."

"Well, let's try not to bump into any scrags, then. Our primary objective is to find the blood samples. We can put an immediate stop to any shapeshifting experiments simply by destroying them."

The small glass vials stolen from Miss Simone's laboratory had been divvied up between the scrags rather than transported together. But they were probably back in one place again. Maybe.

"What if everyone held on to them?" Hal wondered aloud. "If every scrag is carrying around his own bottle of blood, it's going to be difficult to—"

"I suspect Queen Bee would have gathered them up once she got here," Miss Simone interrupted softly. "Let's stop wondering and start looking."

"And you don't care if they're smashed on the floor?" Hal asked. "It must have taken ages to get all those samples!"

Miss Simone sighed. "It did. Months and months. Some will be easy to fetch again, but others will be very difficult and dangerous. The chimera, for instance, was a nightmare to pin down and extract a sample from . . ."

"So why don't we try and steal the blood instead?" Abigail suggested.

"That's fine if we can. But we'll destroy it if we have to. I'd rather have no blood at all than let the scrags use it for themselves. Now, are you ready? All of us together, as quietly as possible. No talking."

With that, she stepped out from the shadows of the stairwell into the corridor. She padded lightly across the stone floor, and Hal followed next, trying to keep his footfalls as silent as possible. He heard a faint popping sound behind him, then the whine of tiny wings as Abigail buzzed past his ear and rushed ahead.

A continuous run of archways formed the corridor's walls. Behind each was a doorway, set back a few feet so each had its own private porch. Though many doors were shut, Hal still saw into plenty of rooms of varying sizes, all with windowless stone walls, some crammed with furniture and others sparse—staff quarters, meeting rooms, stores, pantries, and more. Fifty-two hostages had been brought down here, split into groups, and locked up with whatever happened to be in the room.

What had the caretakers thought about that? Having frightened, yelling people locked up in storerooms up and down the corridor? Queen Bee had really sold her story. Of course, the mayor was on her side. She'd somehow persuaded him to go along with all this, offered him a reward he couldn't possibly refuse, and he in turn had convinced his staff that the hostages were a short-term, necessary step in securing Brodon's long-term safety.

The corridor stretched quite a way, what Hal guessed was the length of the castle above plus its expansive courtyard. As they tiptoed along, Hal picked up the sound of voices from one or more rooms ahead.

Miss Simone slowed and sidestepped into one of the archways. Hal joined her in the shadowed recess. The door to this particular room stood ajar, and he glimpsed surprisingly plush furnishings within—a four-poster bed, chest of drawers, wardrobe, table and chairs . . . and a woman tilting back and forth in a wicker rocking chair with a sleepy baby in her arms. She was fanning her face with what looked like peacock feathers tied to a short stick. She must have opened her door to let a breeze into the warm, stuffy room.

Judging by her unblemished face, she obviously wasn't a scrag. This, Hal thought, was why Miss Simone had insisted on entering the castle secretly from below—to avoid an ugly confrontation that might get innocent people like these caught in the crossfire.

Miss Simone silently urged Hal out of the archway and into the next. Once there, they peeked into the room and found it full of old books. It looked like a library and was, thankfully, empty.

"It's still a little busier than I'd like," Miss Simone whispered. "It would take only a shout to bring the scrags running."

Hal nodded. "This is where Darcy would come in handy. She could easily sneak about unseen. Maybe we should wait for Abi to come back?"

"She shouldn't have rushed off in the first place," Miss Simone said through gritted teeth.

The faerie had disappeared ahead. If anyone saw or heard her, hopefully they would think she was just an annoying bug.

Hal and Miss Simone waited in the shadows, peering around the archway along the corridor. The way back gave Hal a chill. He could see the narrow opening leading to the steep, dark, cobwebbed stairwell, and the thought of going back down there now filled him with horror. But ahead looked promising.

From time to time, a scrag emerged from an archway and disappeared into another. Then a couple of Brodon girls about Hal's age, wearing pajamas, tore out of a room, giggling softly as they headed up the main stairwell at the far end. What were *they* doing up? The place was a dangerous mix of scrags and residents. If the alarm were raised, Queen Bee had plenty of innocent people to pick on.

Hal loitered there while muffled voices sounded from various places, most distant but a few very close, perhaps in the room next door or opposite. He eased back behind the archway's column, grateful for so many hiding places.

Abigail returned after five minutes. She landed on Hal's shoulder and shouted in his ear, her voice high-pitched. "Looks like Queen Bee's set up a lab in a room near the stairs. No sign of her, but there are a lot of scrags about. You can't just wander down this corridor and expect nobody to see you."

Miss Simone cupped a hand to her ear, frowning as she tried to pick up what Abigail was saying in her tiny, high-pitched voice. Hal repeated her message.

At that moment, the door directly opposite flew open and two scrags stormed out, arguing loudly. "—Just because you *want* something doesn't mean you *get* something," the first said, a burly man with a face ravaged by lesions. "I'm telling you, there isn't enough to go around. If everyone wants to be a dragon, we're gonna need more dragon blood, and that means catching a dragon."

"Why should Duke get it, though, just because he's Queen Bee's go-between?" the second scrag muttered. He was much older, his hair grey. "Should be a system where seniority gets to choose first."

"You *would* say that, old-timer . . ."

The argument continued all the way along the corridor. Through the open door of the room they'd vacated, more scrags sat around tables and lounged in chairs. There had to be ten of them in there. Maybe this was a gathering place for off-duty scrags. For a second, Hal found the idea of scrags taking breaks from their evil duties mildly amusing . . . but then he shook the thought from his head and eased back behind the archway. They weren't off-duty. They had to be the nightshift, on standby in case of intruders.

He waited with Miss Simone and Abigail for someone to shut the door to the scrags' break room. Nobody did. After a while, he sighed with frustration. To step out into the corridor now would be too risky. "We can't stand around here all day!" he hissed.

"And we'd be in trouble if a scrag came along to check a book out of this library," Miss Simone replied, jerking a thumb over her shoulder.

Hal glanced at her in surprise. Had she just made a *joke*?

She leaned closer to him, and he wondered for a moment why she was staring at his neck. Then he realized she was looking at Abigail, who still perched there. "Do you think you can close that door?"

A doubtful expression crossed her tiny face. "I can try."

She zipped into the corridor and dropped lightly to the stone floor. Her wings now still, she scurried through the wide-open doorway into the break room. Nobody looked toward her. Scrags continued talking and snoozing, some laughing from time to time. One got up and strolled across to join two more at a table, and he thumped one hard on the shoulder before sitting to interrupt whatever conversation was going on.

Inch by inch and in absolute silence, the door started to move. As tiny as she was, Abigail had to be using all her strength to push it shut. And she would be in full view if anyone glanced her way.

The gap in the doorway gradually narrowed. When the door was maybe a foot away from being completely shut, it stopped moving and Abigail appeared, staggering back out into the corridor. She looked exhausted, her face red. She fell, picked herself up, and fell again. Hal rushed to help, mindful that at least a couple of scrags were still visible through the gap in the door.

He scooped her up and darted past the doorway. Miss Simone was right behind him. On the move at last, Hal threw caution to the wind and hurried past three, four, then five doorways, some of them open. Adrenaline fueled him as the soft chatter of scrags in the break room faded and a new sound rose ahead—a strange, mournful, groaning sound.

The end of the corridor lay just a few doors away. Just beyond the final archways, the walls widened into a foyer of some kind, a dead end except for a single opening in the wall to one side—the staircase leading up to the castle.

Miss Simone grabbed Hal by the collar and yanked hard, causing him to stumble and halt. She pulled him behind an archway and pushed him roughly into the corner. "Slow down!" she whispered furiously. "Are you *trying* to be seen?"

"Sorry," he said meekly. He checked for Abigail. She was on his shoulder where he'd put her, clinging to his collar despite Miss Simone's rough handling of him. "You okay there?"

She nodded.

The mournful groan rose again. A woman's voice sounded, then a man's.

"What's that noise?" Hal asked quietly.

Miss Simone risked a peek. "If I didn't know better, I'd say it was a shapeshifting experiment." She looked at Abigail. "You said there's a makeshift lab in one of these rooms at the end?"

"On the left," Abigail squeaked.

Hal snatched a glance. They were literally three doors from the end. The blood samples were in that very last room opposite the staircase. They were so close.

He withdrew his head and squeezed back into his sheltered corner. "Maybe we can run in there and just smash the place apart?" he suggested. "I could transform once we're inside and burn everything."

Miss Simone pursed her lips. "Our mission would certainly be accomplished in one fell swoop."

Abigail grew suddenly, returning to her full human size. She retracted her wings as she did so and leaned heavily against Hal in an effort to stay hidden in the recess. "There were at least five or six scrags in there," she said. "It would be hard to burn everything without burning them, too."

"I don't care," Hal said grimly.

She shook her head and smiled. "My brave Hal. Of course you care. Have you ever actually burned anyone before? I mean *really* burned them?"

"Well, no."

Miss Simone nipped across to the other side of the archway to give them and herself more room. From there, she whispered, "The last thing I want is death on your hands, Hal."

Hal instantly remembered the roc-riding scrags he'd caused to fall out of the sky. Those deaths were on his hands, but they didn't bother him too greatly. Why was that? And what was the difference between allowing people to drop from a great height and burning them with fire?

He shuddered. The difference was huge. With the rocs, he'd simply been trying to rescue Dr. Kessler. He'd meant to dislodge her only so he could catch her and fly to safety. Everything else—the frightened rocs bucking their riders loose and dropping calcified scrags—had been merely unfortunate in the ensuing chaos, outside his immediate control and therefore something he could live with.

But burning six scrags alive as he purposefully set alight a room? That was altogether more horrible.

"So what, then?" he asked, aware that Abigail was staring at him. She smiled, apparently relieved he'd chosen to avoid fiery murders.

"I have a few ideas," she whispered. "I could probably sneak in there and—"

What she planned to do was forgotten as a tremendous shout made all three of them jump. "It's her!"

Everything happened quickly. Without a word, Miss Simone leapt out from her hiding place into the corridor and dashed away, headed back toward the cobweb-smothered stairwell they'd come up earlier. A pair of booted feet thundered after her, a heavyset scrag who puffed and panted as he ran. Seconds later, doors flew open and a cacophony of yells filled the place.

Hal and Abigail cowered in their hiding place, squeezed together in their tight corner. The door right behind them remained shut, but it seemed the entire corridor was crowded with scrags now. Triumphant yells indicated they'd already caught Miss Simone.

"We have to move," Hal whispered to Abigail.

They slipped into the room behind them. It was empty. As Hal closed the door, he caught a glimpse of scrags marching Miss Simone past. She refused to look sideways, not giving the slightest indication that she'd come with friends, but already scrags were poking their heads around archways to check. Somebody would be in any second now.

Hal glanced around the room. Someone lived here. The top drawer of a massive, ornate chest was ajar, and women's clothing—dresses and ball gowns—hung on a rack by a wardrobe and gigantic mirror. A four-poster bed stood against the right-hand wall. Its spotlessly clean bedsheets and plush pillows had that crumpled look to suggest someone had lain here recently.

But whoever lived here was absent.

"Under the bed," Hal suggested, darting across the room.

As soon as they slid underneath, he wished he'd picked a better hiding place. The bedcovers didn't hang low enough for his liking, and he felt sure somebody would spot him immediately. Abigail was only halfway under when she paused and said, "Choose somewhere else. Hurry."

Abruptly she shrank and buzzed away, leaving him alone.

He scrambled across the floor and out the other side of the bed, then crawled to the corner behind the chest of drawers. This was no better. One quick look and he'd be found.

He scanned the room. Heavy drapes of purple velvet framed a wooden sink cabinet and metal basin. A giant intricate tapestry hung on the far wall behind a beautiful harp. An ornate table and four chairs stood in the center of the room. On the floor lay a trunk with leather straps. It *might* be big enough to hide in if empty, but already he heard footsteps outside the door . . .

He shrank into his corner, wishing he could transform into a faerie. He had no idea where Abigail had got to, but she would be very difficult to find at only six inches high.

The door flew open, crashing against a coat stand. Two scrags marched in, their boots first clacking on the stone floor then swishing on a plush rug. They paused then split up to search the room. Hal curled himself into a ball as one scrag ducked to look under the bed while the other pulled back the velvet drapes.

Any second now, Hal thought, steeling himself and willing a ball of fire to grow in his chest. He'd just have to fight his way out.

A scrag stomped around the bed toward his corner. At that moment, a high-pitched whine caught the man's attention, and he paused as Abigail zipped past his face. Both scrags turned to watch as she darted from one side of the room to the other.

"Get her!" one suddenly yelled as she headed for the door.

They tumbled over themselves in their hurry to catch her, but it was like trying to catch a dragonfly without a net. Hal watched her disappear into the corridor, knowing—hoping—she'd make herself scarce fairly easily. One of the scrags ran after her. The other paused in the doorway to watch.

In that briefest of moments, Hal slid out from his corner and scuttled under the bed. He was just dragging his feet under when the scrag swiveled and marched past the bed, heading to the corner Hal had just vacated. "Gotcha!" the man snarled as he pounced. He stared at the now empty space. "Oh."

The booted feet, which Hal watched with a thudding heart and bated breath, remained still for a second or two.

You already checked under the bed, you already checked under the bed, Hal thought over and over.

The boots swiveled, and the scrag stomped across the room to the trunk on the floor. Hal saw hands reach down, undo the leather straps, fling the lid open, and rummage through a lot of gaudy clothing.

Finding nothing, the scrag slammed the trunk shut and marched out of the room, leaving the door wide open behind him.

Only then did Hal roll onto his back and let out a long, shuddering breath.

He listened to the commotion out in the corridor. He could hear every word as though he were right there with the Swarm. Queen Bee was barking orders and generally getting ticked off with her drones. "How did Simone get down here? Did the guards fall asleep upstairs?"

"No, ma'am, they're all there, wide awake, all six of them, plus the ones in the courtyard. Nobody flew in, nobody snuck through the gates or over the walls or through the windows."

"And yet she's here!" Queen Bee snapped. After a pause, she said more calmly, "What about the back door?"

"It's impossible, my queen. They say people die trying to get in that way. There's a way, but only at low tide and even then it's dangerous, nothing but tunnels filled with seawater and—"

"She's a mermaid," Queen Bee interrupted. "If anyone can find their way through watery tunnels, it's a mermaid. Are you telling me you never posted guards at the other end of this corridor?"

"Uh, well, we did, but . . . well, I guess we never expected . . . uh . . ."

It seemed the entire corridor quieted at that point, every scrag in the place pausing to watch and listen.

"What you're saying," Queen Bee murmured, "is that you failed me."

"Ma'am," the scrag said shakily, "we caught the mermaid woman, and there's nobody else here. No harm done."

"Nobody else here?"

"Nobody, ma'am. Except for the faerie, but she—"

"The *what*?"

Now the silence was palpable. Hal couldn't see what was going on out in the corridor, but he could well imagine the scrag cringing before his petite mistress.

"The faerie. She was just—we chased her out of your room, my queen. We'll catch her soon, I promise."

Queen Bee let out a screech of rage. "You *idiot*! She was in my room and you let her go? If she's here, the dragon-boy is, too. Did you search it?"

"Yes, we searched, and he's not here. And if he is, he's someplace else. We'll find him. Everybody is looking."

Hal swallowed. Miss Simone was captured, Abigail had disappeared, and he was hiding under Queen Bee's bed with every scrag in the place looking for him. He concentrated on that ball of fire in his chest, cultivating it, getting ready to release it should someone come searching again.

As the chatter of scrags rose in the corridor and Queen Bee resumed her irritated barking of orders, Hal once more heard that mournful groan from the makeshift laboratory a few doors down. If it was indeed one of her shapeshifter experiments, there would likely be others, too.

He gritted his teeth. He would not be taken prisoner. Turning into a dragon was easy, and he could take on all the scrags with relative ease. The question was, how many of them would end up burned or killed in the process? How many innocent Brodon residents might get caught in the crossfire, used as human shields as the queen tried to escape?

And what kind of scrag shapeshifters would he have to deal with?

Chapter Seven
The Last Room on the Left

Hal lay under the bed feeling nervous, impatient, and a little ridiculous. The door to Queen Bee's private quarters stood ajar, and he could see scrags marching about outside, even the queen herself from time to time. All along the corridor, doors opened and slammed shut, voices rang out, and Brodon residents appeared briefly as they were hustled away.

"Listen up!" a scrag yelled. "All Brodon people get upstairs. We gotta search room by room down here."

"What's going on?" a haughty woman demanded. "I'm not used to being herded out of my quarters this way! The mayor will hear about this."

"We got intruders," the scrag replied. "Get upstairs or get yerself killed. Your choice, darlin'."

"Oh!"

Occasionally, Hal heard Miss Simone retorting loudly as she was badgered and probably roughed up by interrogators in a room nearby. "Who'd you come here with?" someone snarled, and she quite plainly denied everything. The rest of the noise in the corridor drowned her out for the most part. The place was in turmoil, and Queen Bee repeatedly demanded "full lockdown."

It was clear Hal was going nowhere anytime soon.

He waited. No useful ideas came to him. Escaping was one thing; he could transform and leave in a volley of roars and balls of fire, but even then he couldn't go far. A staircase waited at each end of the corridor, one leading up, the other down, neither fit for a dragon. Besides, the purpose of this mission was to destroy the blood and foil the queen's shapeshifting plans, not to run away.

Could he do that? Transform and rampage through the queen's makeshift laboratory? Perhaps—but he would still be stuck.

He had to stay hidden. Secrecy was his best chance of sabotage. Of course, if Queen Bee decided to move her operation upstairs to the castle . . .

Hal shook his head, frustration growing. He rolled onto his stomach and peered out from under the bed. Where could he hide? Not behind the velvet drapes, not in the corner behind the chest of drawers, not in the wardrobe—and certainly not under the bed! All those places were too obvious.

What about *in* a drawer? He stared at the chest, thinking it was a good size and probably large enough to hold him . . .

Then he mentally kicked himself. How exactly would he close the drawer on himself? He was being ridiculous.

The trunk, then. It was full of clothes, but he could scatter the garments, lay them out flat under the bedcovers and then climb into the trunk. He pondered on this idea for a moment, thinking it might work as long as they didn't decide to check the trunk a second time— which of course they would.

Clothes . . .

He held his breath as an idea formed. Could he disguise himself?

Without another second's hesitation, he crawled out from under the bed and darted across the room, shooting a glance toward the door. Scrags congregated in the corridor as Queen Bee barked orders. "Then check there as well! Why are you coming to me suggesting places he might be? See for yourselves!"

"But ma'am, we don't know for sure he's even here—"

"Simone is here, and that faerie girl is here somewhere. If they're here, the dragon-boy is here. Maybe the others as well. Bring me a prisoner in the next two minutes or someone will suffer."

While she was yelling all this, Hal was hunkering down behind the trunk, opening the lid and keeping an eye on the open doorway. He was safe enough from this angle. Someone would have to come all the way into the room to see him ferreting through the array of clothes.

He'd expected the garments to belong to Queen Bee herself, and he'd planned to dress as a scrag even if it meant donning some of the queen's own leather pants and jacket. But it looked like these were the possessions of a well-to-do resident of Castle Brodon. The problem was, they were all gaudy women's clothes—long dresses, skirts, and blouses of all colors.

Once more hearing Queen Bee in the corridor, Hal dragged out one of the less garish pieces, a dark-blue, knee-length frock. He also grabbed a hooded cloak even though it was bright orange and probably not intended to go with the dress. Or maybe it was. What did he know?

He closed the trunk and nipped behind the open door where he could peer through the crack and check for scrags. The corridor was full of Brodon locals, some of them dressed like hard-working laborers and others a little more regal, all being herded along like cattle.

Hal struggled into the dress, quickly realizing his pants showed below the knees. Rather than take them off, he rolled up the pant legs. Once he threw on the hideous orange cloak, pulled up the hood, and tied it around his throat, he figured he *might* pass for a Brodon resident if nobody looked too closely or questioned why he was hooded.

He waited. A scrag escort appeared alongside the slow, steady stream of residents. "Hurry up, move it along," he urged.

"But why do we have to go upstairs?" a teenage boy asked. He had his sleeves rolled up and looked like he'd been scrubbing floors.

"Safer for you," came the curt reply.

"We wouldn't want any of you getting hurt," Queen Bee said loudly. "We have intruders down here somewhere. My people can better protect you in the great hall upstairs." Her voice rose a few notches. "They'll surround you with weapons at the ready. Nobody will *dare* to attack us."

Hal knew this statement was meant for him, a thinly veiled threat.

"You don't need weapons," an unseen girl piped up. "You're shapeshifters!"

Not yet they're not, Hal thought grimly.

Again peering through the crack behind the door, he spotted Queen Bee standing in the middle of the corridor. She was suddenly beset by a group of youngsters as tall as she.

"You can turn into dragons and ogres and other monsters," the same girl persisted. "Show them!"

"Oh, we will if we have to," Queen Bee agreed, obviously forcing a smile. Obvious to Hal, anyway. These people were completely taken in by her.

Taking advantage of the brief crowd, Hal took a chance and slipped into the corridor with his head down, keeping his fingers crossed that nobody was looking his way at that precise moment, that short but vital two-second period as he exited the queen's room. He joined the shuffling group, staring furiously at the floor and noting that his feet and the sides of his smart shoes were filthy, very unbecoming of the young woman he was disguised as.

Unbelievably, nobody raised the alarm. Nobody yelled "There he is!" or "Who are *you*?" or anything remotely confrontational.

Raising his head slightly, he spotted the staircase ahead on his right. Four scrags stood there, waving everyone past.

Hal weaved through the line to the other side, his eye now on the final door on the left just yards away: the makeshift laboratory.

Keeping pace with the moving crowd, he suddenly ducked sideways and found himself in a gloomy room. Trembling with excitement, he paused only to find the best hiding place. He ignored the four unusually high tables in the center, which were too simple and exposed to hide under. The built-in closet at the back seemed too obvious, the first place they'd look. He veered instead toward three low wooden cabinets angled across a corner. Boxes, jars, bottles, and cloth-wrapped surgical instruments filled the tops. He clambered awkwardly over the cabinets and ducked down in the triangular-shaped gap behind. There he lay absolutely still, his heart pounding.

Any second now. Someone saw me. They're coming. They're probably already here, ready to pounce on me . . .

A man shouted, "Spread out! Search everywhere!"

Footsteps pounded on the stone floor in the corridor, accompanied by the familiar clack of poison-tipped spears. Doors opened and shut, scrapes and bangs filled the air, scrags called out to one another. Queen Bee repeatedly screeched, "He's here somewhere, I know it. Find him!"

Hal waited and waited.

As seconds and minutes ticked by, he began to think his silly disguise had actually worked. It seemed impossible. How had he slipped away?

Queen Bee's voice filtered through the doorway again. "Not now, Tadpole. Seems to me you lost your place in the line when you let that boy go."

"But, my queen—"

A resounding slap broke him off. "Don't you *dare* argue with me. Simone was right there outside my room! The faerie was *in* my room! That means the dragon-boy was, too. And you let him go."

"But I never even saw him—"

"Get out of my sight before I throw you off the castle wall."

Nothing more was said, but Hal heard more stomping feet and the murmurs of other scrags in the corridor.

Gradually, the search came to an end. Queen Bee demanded reports from every one of her Swarm, and she grew more agitated by the minute. "Did you check every room? Did you check the lab?"

Hal's heart skipped a beat, but several scrags said in unison that they had indeed checked the lab. It was just fortunate they'd checked *before* Hal had snuck in and hidden in the corner.

Afraid to break whatever spell of invisibility or luck he was protected by, he remained absolutely still, barely breathing. But after a while, a cramp developed in his left calf, and he carefully shifted so he could stretch out his leg.

Growing bolder, he raised his head to peep over the first cabinet. It was filled with jars, and he pushed a couple aside so he could look through the gap to the room beyond. Still no sign of anybody.

He took a closer look at the jars before him. They contained colored liquids and substances, some with creepy objects he couldn't make out. He shuddered. *Probably just as well. They might be brains or eyeballs or worse.*

The tops of the other two low cabinets were equally littered with random equipment and supplies. It all looked like it had been hurriedly assembled, brought in from elsewhere and thrown together. But for what?

Shapeshifting experiments, of course.

His situation had improved tremendously. He'd gone from being stuck under Queen Bee's bed to this, the heart of the Swarm's idea of a scientific environment. The blood vials had to be here somewhere!

He looked and saw cloth-bound packages, wooden boxes, metal devices with thumbscrews, fine cutting blades, saws, rolls of bandages . . .

The more Hal looked, the more he wished he hadn't. A shapeshifter lab was one thing, but this seemed more like a torture chamber.

He turned his attention to the four tables in the middle of the room. Each had a pillow at one end. The only thing missing were the patients. Lanterns hung from the walls, flickering softly.

Scrags continued to hurry back and forth out in the corridor. He listened to their exchanges for a second and chuckled. They were utterly confused as to his whereabouts. Queen Bee screamed incessantly at them, calling them imbeciles and nitwits, and Hal even saw her stride by the doorway from time to time, a tiny figure compared to most of the other scrags.

A mournful groan sounded from across the hall. There was nothing to see from where Hal hid, but he was glad to be away from whatever pitiful creature lurked there.

A couple of scrags entered the room a minute later. They paused, looked around, shrugged, and left again. "Try the animal house," one suggested.

"*You* try it," the other retorted.

Hal guessed they meant the room opposite. Did it contain only one patient or several? Were these patients suffering in some way, or was that awful moaning the mutterings of a sleepy monster?

The scrags disappeared from sight. Hal sank low in his private corner, finally believing he was safe. But where were Miss Simone and Abigail?

Outside in the corridor, a scrag yelled, "Looks like someone's been poking around in that trunk in your room, my queen. Could he have taken some clothes?"

A deathly silence fell.

Queen Bee finally spoke. "You think he just walked upstairs with the caretakers? Strolled right past the guards?"

"Um, maybe. I mean, it's possible. If he was even here."

"If that's true," she said so quietly that Hal could barely hear, "then he's probably long gone."

"Yes, ma'am."

Another silence. Then she spoke again. "Or he might be in the castle."

"Indeed, ma'am."

"Then perhaps you'd be good enough to resume the search upstairs?"

She spoke so softly now, so politely, that Hal imagined she was about to explode in rage.

"I'm on it, ma'am."

Seconds later, it seemed every scrag in the vicinity was tearing up the stairs two at a time, the steel of weapons clanking.

When the noise finally died down, Hal spent a minute removing the horrible hooded cloak and blue dress. Then he raised his head to inspect the tops of the cabinets again. He cringed at the awful things he saw there, clearly designed to cut people open, break or reset bones, inject them with drugs, and much more—but no vials of blood.

As far as he knew, Miss Simone hadn't needed to cut him open during his reboot as a new-and-improved adult dragon. Then again, Queen Bee hadn't known what equipment the Shapeshifter Program needed until recently. Maybe she'd set up this room weeks ago, bringing in everything she could think of that *might* be required when creating shapeshifters . . .

Someone entered the room, and Hal ducked and froze, listening hard. Another search party?

Multiple pairs of boots clomped across the floor. "Get it going again," the familiar voice of Queen Bee ordered.

"I don't recommend it, my queen," a deep voice replied. "We should wait and see what happens, take this in experimental stages. If anything should—"

"Don't you understand?" the queen snapped. "Simone's here! The faerie is flitting around like an annoying bug, probably spying on us right now. And the dragon-boy is somewhere in the castle upstairs. We don't have the luxury of time. We need to get this done."

"But, my queen—" the deep voice pleaded.

"Do as I say, Leech. And you, Croaker. I don't have time to wait for our test subjects to show us their powers before moving on to the next. If you carried out the procedure exactly as Dr. Kessler explained, then I'm sure we have our first three shapeshifters already."

"If she told the truth," Leech rumbled.

"And if we did it right," a nasally voice said. Hal assumed he was the one named Croaker. "Our lab is not exactly suitable."

Queen Bee lowered her voice, and Hal had to strain to hear. "You did it right. And I'm sure Dr. Kessler told the truth. She was too scared not to. Have you tried the glass ball on all three yet?"

"Yeah," Leech said. "No luck with the first two. Maybe we'll get lucky with the third."

As if on cue, the mournful groan sounded again from across the corridor.

"She sounds fed up," Leech commented. "I don't think she's seeing anything nice in that ball. How sad it must be to look back on your life and see nothing but heartache."

Queen Bee sighed. "Why is it not working for them? That glass ball helped other shapeshifters explore the full extent of their transformations."

Yeah, including me, Hal thought.

"Maybe they just need more time," Leech suggested. "Or a really good reason to change."

"Oh, they'll have a good reason to change before this day is out . . ."

Hal frowned. Leech's suggestion actually came close to the truth. A "really good reason to change" was what had caused Emily to finally switch to her naga form back on the island. It was either that or drown. As for Hal, even though he'd used the glass ball to figure out how to fly, he often wondered what would have happened if he'd fallen from a great height beforehand. Would he have crashed to the ground in a tangle of useless wings? Or would he have been saved by his built-in dragon instincts?

He raised his head and peered between large jars. He made out Queen Bee standing next to a table, staring down at it as though tending to an invisible patient. Two scrags stood by her side. One had a protrusion on his shoulder and neck, a hump that made him lean slightly to one side.

"Why did it work for Simone's lot but not for us?" the queen mused. "Why did the first drone only half-transform? Why has the second not transformed at all? Why is the third so *miserable?*" She let out a cry of frustration. "It's all so random! We need that faerie ball to work. We *have* to find that faerie."

Her humpbacked colleague scratched his nose. "We have that Simone woman. She must have answers."

"Oh, I know she does, Leech. But she's stubborn as a mule and won't talk. So let's get on with it. Bring in whoever's next on the list. Tell the next few to prepare as well. Let's crank out a dozen shifters tonight."

She stalked off without another word, leaving the other two to shake their heads in obvious worry. One muttered something, and the other exclaimed loudly that they'd better do as instructed.

Hal was no longer paying attention, though. He'd just spotted something that one of the scrags had brought in and placed on the table before him.

A shallow box containing vials of blood.

Chapter Eight
Blood Samples

The urge to jump out from his hiding place and throw the delicate vials of blood onto the floor was strong. Hal restrained himself for the moment.

"Go get the next on the list," the humpbacked scrag named Leech said. He had black, wavy hair, thick eyebrows, and ears that stuck out.

Croaker, small and thin with a cluster of dark pockmarks across the middle of his face as though somebody had spattered him with paint, wandered across the room and disappeared into the corridor.

Leech picked up the shallow box of blood vials and walked toward the cabinets. Hal sucked in a breath and ducked low.

He heard a clatter of equipment right above his head as the scrag pushed a bunch of stuff aside and set down the box of vials. The man was no more than two feet away. If he leaned forward, he would see Hal crouching there.

Instead, Leech collected a few things in his arms and turned away, his boots thudding on the stone floor. Hal risked a peek and saw him dump his armful of things on a table, mostly small surgical tools and cloths.

Hal's gaze fell on the shallow box that now lay within easy reach. *The blood*, he thought with glee. *It's right there!*

Since Leech still had his back turned, his hump sticking up, Hal shakily plucked a vial from the box. He glimpsed a label before the vial slipped from his hand and fell back into the box with a sharp *clink!* sound that caused the scrag to tense and look around the room with narrowed eyes. Hal ducked.

A long silence followed.

After a while, Leech resumed his task.

Hal sat still. He'd glimpsed the vial's label just now. Written in Miss Simone's neat handwriting was the word MINOTAUR. He vaguely remembered that creature from stories, a man with a bull's head chasing victims through a maze of corridors. It sounded dangerous.

But Hal knew he had the power to end Queen Bee's plans here and now. All he had to do was reach up, turn the box over, and smash the vials on the stone floor. Or better still, simply transform. The cabinets would go flying along with everything else, and he could blast the whole lot with fire, incinerating it all within a minute. Mission over. Then he'd just need to escape.

And rescue Miss Simone.

This gave him pause. The room was large enough for a dragon to maneuver, but the doorway was small and the walls made of stone. Could he smash his way through? Maybe . . . but he would definitely need to be human to navigate the winding staircase up to the castle. What if scrags blocked his way, as they undoubtedly would? Being a dragon shapeshifter was only useful if he had room to move.

He waited for the slower part of his brain to catch up. *So . . . I could burn the blood, but then it would be difficult to get away afterward. The element of surprise would be gone. I'd have to fight my way out of this place, somehow rescuing Miss Simone on the way.*

"Easy-peasy," he murmured to himself.

It might be better to dispose of the blood in secret. He twisted around and peeked over the cabinet again. Leech wasn't going anywhere for a while. The man seemed to be checking things for the sake of it, waiting for Croaker to return with the next hopeful shapeshifter.

Just as Hal thought this, Croaker returned. A grinning middle-aged man with the usual ugly scars followed him in and climbed onto the table without asking. "About time," he said, resting his head on the pillow and staring up at the ceiling. "My name was pulled from the hat ages ago. Let's get this done already."

"And you wanted to be what?" Leech asked.

"Dragon," the patient said. He lifted his head and smirked. "Think you can swing it, Humpty?"

Leech glared at him, clearly irritated by the nickname. It was Croaker who answered. "You know we can't. Duke's the man for that. Choose something else."

"Gah! Duke ain't even here. He's sucking up to the mayor." The man laid his head back down and sighed. "I guess a griffin, then."

Croaker nodded and started to head toward the bench Hal hid behind. Then he paused and looked back. "You do realize this may not even work? The first three are incomplete. We're not sure—"

"Yeah, yeah, c'mon, get it done."

"No, wait, you have to listen. You've heard the moaning from across the hall? It's Lola. She's got issues, like something's not working. These blood samples seem fresh, but that Simone woman had them stored on a wooden rack at room temperature! The blood should have gone bad long ago, but it seems *alive* somehow, so maybe it's okay, maybe it's not. If it were up to me and Leech, we'd hold off until we figured the whole thing out. This is dangerous business, and . . ."

While they were talking, Hal snaked his arm across the top of the cabinet and pulled out two vials at random, looking for the griffin blood. Unfortunately, these two read UNICORN and OGRE. He replaced them and pulled another. CHIMERA. This one rang a bell. Miss Simone had said it was a hard-to-find creature. The idea of smashing it on the floor and wasting valuable blood she'd gone to great lengths to obtain didn't sit well with him. He placed it carefully back into the box and grabbed another.

Being extra careful not to be seen, it took quite a few tries to happen across the vial marked GRIFFIN. He clutched it in his right hand, his heart beating hard. He had to hide it. Or destroy it. But either way, Croaker would rummage around for ages trying to find it, getting more and more agitated. Hal would likely be discovered shortly after as all three scrags started looking . . .

Maybe he could swap the label with another?

Excited by the idea, he tried peeling the label off, but it was stuck fast. Maybe swap the blood itself, then? He reached over the cabinet and had a quick hunt for one he'd picked up earlier. There it was: UNICORN.

Croaker hadn't finished talking. "You just gotta realize this is no simple matter. We don't know what might happen. What if you change and can't turn back? What if you only *half* change? Have you thought about this?"

The patient pushed up onto his elbows. "Listen, pal, if you don't turn me into a griffin right now, I'll reach down into your throat, grab your tongue, and yank it out of your cakehole. Quit stalling!"

With shaking hands, Hal pulled the stopper out of the vial marked GRIFFIN and tipped the blood onto the floor next to him. It was a horrible waste, but it had to be done. He stared at the spreading pool for a second. Something stirred within it, some kind of swirling light, a barely perceptible life force . . .

He shook his head, transferred the unicorn blood into the empty GRIFFIN vial, and replaced the stopper. Hal slipped the refilled vial into the box and ducked out of sight just as Croaker grumbled a last word on the subject and headed toward him.

Hal remained flat on the floor, listening to Croaker rummage in the box. The scrag was two feet away, grunting while he picked out vial after vial and read their labels.

"Got it," the man said at last. "Griffin blood. Looks like it's leaked a bit."

"Just bring it here," Leech complained.

The would-be griffin piped up, "Yeah, man, let's get this show on the road."

Hal risked a look again. He watched with intense fascination as the two scrags bent over their patient. "Gonna put you to sleep for a bit," Leech said quietly, brandishing a metal cup. "Drink this."

After the man took a few sips, he collapsed with eyes rolling and tongue sticking out.

Croaker used a syringe to suck about two thirds of the blood out of the vial. He handed the full syringe to Leech and kept the remaining third of the blood for himself, being careful to replace the vial's stopper.

Hal found that curious. If Leech was about to use two thirds of the blood on this patient, there wouldn't be enough left for another shapeshifter. It seemed to be one sample per shapeshifter—hence the patient list. All the scrags had drawn names in the hope of getting to choose first. In this case, the scrag who wanted to be a griffin would end up a unicorn.

"Okay, get me some DNA while I do this bit," Leech said.

Carrying his remaining sample of blood, Croaker strode to the door at the back of the room and disappeared inside.

Hal blinked. That was a *room*? He'd assumed it was a built-in closet. With the door ajar, it looked like a small space with tall wooden cabinets lining one wall and a bench along another. What was Croaker doing in there? All was quiet except for the soft noises of small objects being handled, the pouring of liquid, and tiny clinks of glass. How, exactly, did one extract DNA?

Meanwhile, Leech bent over his patient, whose shirt now lay open. Hal watched with morbid fascination as the scrag carefully plunged the syringe into the man's bare chest. Using his thumb, he injected about half the blood and stopped, then gently pulled the needle out.

At this point, Leech stared out from under his thick eyebrows as though waiting. It seemed that a scrag shapeshifter was in the making—except he would turn out to be something a little different than expected.

Hal agonized over his predicament. He may have prevented the creation of a potentially dangerous shapeshifter by switching the blood, but what about the rest of the vials? He couldn't wait for each and every patient to announce what they wanted to be and then fumble around trying to mix things up. He could, however, do some sabotage *now* . . .

Keeping one eye on the procedure, he reached for another vial. DRYAD. This one was perfectly safe. An army of dryad-scrags didn't pose a threat to the village of Carter, at least not a particularly dangerous one. Not unless they made the grass grow really fast overnight in an attempt to trip people up. He put the vial back in one side of the box and chose another.

SIMURGH.

What in the world was *that*? Hal puzzled over it and decided to leave it alone. He wished Abigail were here. She had studied so-called magical beasts of myth and legend and would probably know more about them. He picked another.

ELF.

This was safe. He guessed no self-respecting Swarm gang member would pick such an elegant, peace-loving creature, but it would be all right if they did. He placed it back in the box.

He paused. It might have been better to put the elf blood aside to use in place of something more dangerous. He grew more and more sure that his sabotage plan was the best way to thwart the queen's plans while giving himself a chance to escape alive. Destroying the blood outright or stealing it would cause a riot. Surreptitiously substituting the dangerous blood was far more subtle.

And it would give the scrags something to think about. Chuckling inwardly, he continued his painfully slow, silent work.

Leech was busy fussing over his patient. He regularly glanced at the man's chest, still apparently waiting for something to happen.

Hal found himself holding the vial marked OGRE. He'd picked that one up before, but now he stared at it, thinking that ogres would make a mean enemy. This sample had to go. Besides, Miss Simone could easily get more blood from plenty of real ogres with Robbie's help.

He pulled out the stopper and poured the blood away. Now he needed something to replace it with. Where had that elf blood gone? Or perhaps this one, FAUN, would do. He carefully transferred the harmless blood across and discarded the empty vial. He grinned as he slipped the refilled OGRE vial back into the box. Instead of griffins and ogres, there would be unicorns and fauns.

The silence in the room made it very difficult for Hal to do his job. He paused a moment, barely breathing, until Croaker reappeared in the doorway. "Just letting it stew for a minute."

Leech, running a hand through his oily-black hair, turned to him. "This is gonna take forever. Go get the next guinea pig. We can do a few at a time."

Croaker sighed and headed out to the corridor.

Careful to remain silent, Hal resumed his slow, silent search for blood vials. NAGA came next. A dryad, an ogre, now a naga . . . It was almost as though Miss Simone had taken blood samples from all his friends! But no, the blood had to be pure, from *real* creatures rather than shapeshifters. Miss Simone had simply been industrious, asking the shapeshifters for help the way her brother Felipe had brought along a genuine, pureblood dragon to her laboratory.

And speaking of which, somewhere in this box had to be dragon blood. Miss Simone had taken a very large sample and given Hal some of it, but there had to be a full vial here somewhere. That was definitely one to be poured out if he could find it. Perhaps he could replace it with will-o'-wisp blood or something equally ridiculous.

In the meantime, he spilled the naga blood onto the floor and looked for a suitable replacement. There! He held up the elf's blood. If anyone chose to be a naga, they'd end up a short, blue-skinned creature instead.

He continued his painfully slow work in absolute silence.

Croaker returned after a while. "Next one's on his way." He swept across the room and through the doorway at the back. He was gone awhile, during which time Hal started yawning. What time was it, anyway? It had to be late by now.

When Croaker finally reappeared, he held another tiny glass vial, this one partially filled with a colorless liquid and, presumably, DNA. "There you go," he said, handing it to Leech with a puzzled look on his face. "Got some nice strands again. Beats me how." He pointed to the patient. "And he looks like he's about ready for the next step."

Leech sucked in a breath. "So he is. All right, then . . ."

Hal couldn't see what was going on because Croaker stood in the way, so he went back to his own work, picking out vials from the box as the scrags muttered to each other. He came across the blood of a harpy and replaced it with brownie blood. He pondered over TRITON. Wasn't that a male mermaid? A merman? If so, it hardly posed a threat to the people of Carter or indeed any town. He ignored it and moved on.

CYCLOPS. All Hal knew of those creatures was that they had one eye. Were they big? Giants? If so, he should probably pour the blood away. It occurred to him that he needed to get rid of the minotaur, too. That was one he'd picked out earlier and put back before embarking on his plan of sabotage. He'd definitely need to find—

"Done," Leech said briskly, clapping his hands once. Hal jumped and hurriedly put the cyclops vial back in the box as the two scrags turned away from the table and stretched. "Just a few dozen more to do."

"There's gonna be a riot," Croaker said. "Extracting DNA isn't a problem, but we don't have much actual blood. We're gonna use up all the decent stuff and be left with leprechauns and what-have-you. Can't we use less?" He held up a vial, now empty except for a scarlet smear on the side. "Maybe we could get two monsters out of these instead of one."

Leech shook his head. "Best not to mess around. We have just about enough vials for everyone."

"Yeah, but the guy at the end of the list won't be happy being something pathetic like a pixie."

"Then he can wait until we have new samples."

Croaker approached the low cabinets in the corner. Hal ducked down again as the scrag lingered there, poking around in the box. "There's a leak somewhere. I keep finding a sticky mess."

Hal, once again holding his breath, closed his eyes and waited for the scrag to go away. He didn't, though. Croaker seemed intent on finding a particular vial. At last he let out a cry of triumph.

"Here it is!"

"Here's what?" Leech muttered.

"My future." Croaker's boots squeaked as he turned. Hal heard him stomp away across the floor. "When it's my turn, this is me."

A brief silence followed. Then Leech burst out laughing. "You want to be a *what*? What the heck is a hippocampus?"

Croaker snarled something in return.

Hal stole a sneaky glance. Trying to stifle his chortles, Leech took the lid off a tiny brown bottle and held it under their patient's nostrils. "Wakey-wakey," he said, still grinning.

The man lying on the gurney let out a strangled gargling sound and sat up clutching his throat. He frowned and checked himself over, taking a second to scratch at his bare chest. He looked from one scrag to the other. "Did it work?"

"Beats me," Croaker said. "Go walk around, get some air. And send the next patient in."

As the man staggered from the room, Leech began clattering around with his tools, straightening them up. "So what *is* a hippocampus, anyway?"

"An underwater horse," Croaker said sullenly. "With fins instead of hoofs. And a fishtail at the back. I imagine it's beautiful."

Leech collapsed into laughter again. "How are you supposed to gallop across the plains into battle with fins flopping about everywhere?"

"I don't plan on going into battle," Croaker said quietly.

This statement caused Leech's mirth to fizzle out.

"I didn't sign up for that," Croaker went on. "I just want to settle down, and being able to travel fast across the sea will open up my world."

"So will wings," Leech muttered.

"I don't like heights. I'll stick to water." Croaker paused, then tentatively asked, "What about you?"

Leech stared into space. "I'll be happy just to heal and be normal again."

"No more scars," Croaker agreed.

"And no more hump."

At that moment, another scrag walked in, a huge bearded man with bulging biceps thicker than Hal's waist. He wore only baggy pants held up with a rope. "My turn," he boomed, thumping his bare chest. "Gimme the ogre."

Hal swallowed. Luckily he'd poured the ogre blood away and replaced it with something else. This man was practically an ogre already!

Leech handed the metal cup to the giant and said, "Take a couple of swigs. Heck, drink it all."

The patient did so and thudded down flat on the table, already drooling as he stared sightlessly at the ceiling. Leech and Croaker began the procedure. First came the blood, two thirds of which Croaker sucked out into a syringe. "Think this is enough?" he mumbled.

"A minute ago, you wanted to use less and share it around more!"

"This one's different. Look at the size of the guy."

"Just stick it in there."

"That's *your* job, Leech. I'm a DNA specialist, not a surgeon."

"This isn't surgery, pal. Go ahead."

With a sigh, Croaker leaned over the giant. Hal strained to see from his hiding place. He couldn't be sure, but it looked like the scrag was injecting it directly into the man's heart. Certainly in that vicinity. But not *all* the blood; half was left in the syringe when Croaker straightened up again.

It was Leech's turn to lean closer. He stared hard at the giant's enormous barrel chest, his hand raised. "Whoa. It's started already. That was quick!"

"I must be better at this job than you," Croaker said with a chuckle.

"Or this guy is pumped up and ready for action."

Even from his poor vantage point, Hal spotted a faint glow appearing over the huge patient's chest, emanating from below his skin.

"Okay, *now*," Leech said.

Croaker plunged the needle back in, injecting the rest of the blood. The glow intensified, and they watched it with obvious fascination.

"I wish I knew why it glows like that," Croaker whispered.

"The human heart ... life force ... supernatural entities and divine spirits," Leech said with a shrug. "Who the heck knows? Gotta be some connection there somewhere. The wonders of the universe. Magic and all that."

"It just shows how little we know about anything. The creatures of this world are magic, and the blood itself must have magic in it. It's like—"

"Quit chin-wagging and go get the DNA before the magic wears off," Leech ordered.

As before, Croaker strode into the back room and started puttering about. Two more scrags walked in from the corridor.

Leech looked up at them. "Come in, lie down. Be with you in a minute." He turned his head and roared, "Croaker! Let's get busy!"

One of the newcomers exclaimed, "Hey, his chest is glowing. Looks like it's on fire! Is that normal?"

"There's nothing normal about this, my friend," Leech muttered.

With so many people in the room, Hal thought it best to lie low for a minute. He wished he'd managed to switch out a few more vials as there might have been some dangerous creatures he'd missed. But he'd get back to it shortly when the patients were asleep.

Unfortunately, even more scrags showed up. Queen Bee had apparently ordered them to be ready, and now a line of them had formed. Many commented on the patient's weird, glowing chest.

Hal lay in the corner worrying over the samples he'd missed. And what about the dragon blood? He'd not found that at all. It had to be around somewhere.

With scrags wandering around the room, some coming dangerously close to discovering Hal's hiding place and Croaker continually emerging from his room with DNA samples and then rummaging in the box of blood samples, it was all Hal could do to remain hidden. He lay on his back, stretched out alongside the backs of the cabinets, ready to transform if he needed to escape in a hurry.

But he hoped he wouldn't have to. He hoped to sneak out and rescue Miss Simone, to escape quietly, his sabotage undetected until far too late. If the scrags truly wanted to be shapeshifters, then shapeshifters they would be!

Chapter Nine
Scrag Shapeshifters

Hal lost track of time. He'd gotten so used to lying still that he'd actually grown sleepy. It didn't help that he found himself mesmerized by the small pools of blood on the floor next to him. Apparently, the blood of magical creatures had a special life of its own, a faint, swirling light deep within. There was something hypnotic about it, a little like gazing into Abigail's faerie ball, only this made him feel drowsy . . .

He jerked awake at the sound of yelling. He bolted upright, then remembered where he was and ducked back down. Astonished, he wondered how long he'd been lying there in a trance. Had he actually fallen asleep? He knew it was late, and the trek through the underwater tunnels had worn him out, but still—he'd *fallen asleep*?

The yelling came from the corridor. Several voices had joined in, some high-pitched and panicked, others laughing. Hal peeked over the low cabinets and tried to focus his bleary eyes and addled brain.

Four scrags lay on the tables in the room with him, three of them asleep, one beginning to stir. Thankfully the giant, bare-chested ogre wannabe was no longer here. That brute had already been and gone, possibly hours ago.

Hal groaned. How long had he been asleep?

There was no sign of the two scientists, Leech and Croaker. Scrags milled about in the corridor, clearly agitated by something.

The shallow box of blood vials just in front of Hal's face had been worked over, perhaps half the samples now missing. He kicked himself for falling asleep, but with the distraction in the corridor, now was probably a good time to do something about the rest.

With one eye on the waking patient, he thumbed through the vials looking for the dragon's blood. It wasn't there and probably never had been. Queen Bee most likely had it stashed somewhere safe, the ultimate blood sample saved for her most trusted drone—or perhaps for herself.

Even so, right here in the box were other creatures as dangerous as dragons. A basilisk, small and serpentine with a deadly death-gaze like a gorgon. That had to go. Hal replaced the blood with a gnome's.

The conscious scrag on the table was sitting up now, looking puzzled at the commotion in the corridor. He climbed down and staggered across the floor to see what was going on, leaving three scrags in deep sleep. This emboldened Hal, and he picked up the pace.

He came across a vial marked CERBERUS and switched it for something called a squonk. He was fairly sure a squonk was harmless. It *sounded* harmless, anyway. And he found a hippogriff. He searched the box for another small, friendly creature to substitute it with. There didn't seem to be any left, so he partially unstopped the lid and let the blood spill into the box. Croaker had noticed a leak earlier. Now he would understand where it was coming from.

"Take him upstairs," Queen Bee screeched above the noise. "Get him into the open air with plenty of room to move. Maybe that'll help."

Hal paused and watched as scrags surged along the corridor. In their midst, he caught sight of a very tall man. Something was wrong with him. He lurched all over the place as if trying to balance on stilts. His feet made a noisy clip-clopping sound like hoofs. Judging by the frightened expression on his face, he wasn't having a good day.

Hal suddenly realized this was a good time to escape. With just three sleeping patients between him and the door, he might not get a better chance. The noisy crowd in the corridor was thinning. Perhaps he could slip out behind them before Leech and Croaker returned.

He carefully climbed over the cabinets, one eye on the door, knowing that the last few scrags could look in at any moment. His fingers brushed against the box of blood samples, and he paused, wondering if he'd done enough sabotage. The problem was, the vials had been shuffled around so much as he'd slept that he was no longer sure which ones he'd handled. He had a very quick look-through again. How about a banshee? Was that something to be concerned about? What on earth was a sylph? And he imagined a hellhound was some kind of dog, but—

Another scrag began to stir. There would be trouble if Hal was caught red-handed with the box of blood, his sabotage exposed. Giving the vials one last glance, he hurried to the door, now eager to leave.

Had he done enough to prevent the scrags building a formidable army? He hoped so. He'd certainly rid them of some awful beasties such as a griffin, naga, harpy, basilisk, cerberus, ogre, and hippogriff. But he also had the nagging feeling he'd missed some. The minotaur, for instance. Now that he thought about it, he never had come across that one again. It was either still in the box or Croaker had already injected it into a scrag while Hal was asleep.

The dragon blood was missing, too. And what about those he'd been uncertain about and put back? What exactly was a simurgh? How terrible was a cyclops? Also, three scrags had been experimented on before Hal had even arrived! They were right across the corridor, Queen Bee's original guinea pigs. What kind of blood had *they* been injected with?

He loitered in the doorway. Most of the noisy crowd had disappeared up the stairs. The door across the hall stood ajar, and from there came that familiar mournful moan.

Hal edged out of the doorway and ducked into the recess behind the archway. Only Croaker remained in the corridor now. The scrag spun around and returned to his makeshift laboratory, coming within inches of Hal as he swept past.

And suddenly Hal was alone.

Where was Miss Simone? All he could do was check every room he came across, looking for a locked door with, hopefully, a key in the keyhole.

When the mournful moan came again, he knew he had to take a look. He tiptoed across the corridor to what a scrag had called 'the animal house' and peered in through the open door. As he understood it, there had been three scrag shapeshifters in this room. Now there were two.

One was a man wearing only pants. He lay on a bunk with great swaths of red fur across his face, shoulders, chest, and arms. Though scars riddled his skin, they seemed faint near where the fur started. His hands were unusually large and clumsy with much finer red fur and terrible black claws. His eyes shone blue when he looked up at Hal.

Mesmerized, Hal stared back. For some reason, all sense of secrecy fled him. "You're a manticore," he whispered, vaguely aware that something else lurked in the corner behind the door.

The scrag scowled, causing his flattened nose and broad forehead to wrinkle. "Not yet," he said in a thin, nasally voice. "But I will be."

Hal snatched a glance into the corner. There, a fully formed *thing* lay on its side, conscious but with its eyes closed, moaning from time to time. Though lionlike in shape, it had dull-grey reptilian scales all over, a perfectly human head, and a proportionally small, lithe body. Overall, the creature probably stood no taller than a large dog.

He gazed at it, fascinated—gazed at *her*, for it had a woman's face with silver hair and a strangely long, slender neck almost like there was a giant serpent mixed in with the feline body. Her curved claws unnerved him.

"Come on in," the manticore-scrag said with a half-smile, sitting up on the bunk. Though only partially changed, he still seemed fit enough to spring into action, ready to pounce. "I'm sure she'd love to meet you."

"What . . . what *is* she?" Hal said.

At the sound of his voice, the woman's head lifted and turned toward him. She stared with dark, soulful eyes. Then she jerked as if waking from a daydream. Baring her teeth and hissing, she leapt to her feet.

Staggering briefly, she took a moment to find her balance. Hal noticed her tail was definitely serpentine. She looked like a naga who had swallowed a large cat, and now her snake body was stretched ultrathin over the entire meal as it tried to run away . . . but of course that was ridiculous. She was simply a blend of cat and serpent—with a human head! Yet she was disturbingly beautiful and powerful, her muscles taut as she spun about and focused on him.

The manticore-scrag looked surprised at her sudden movement. "Well, look at that! She's on her feet at last. All it took was the sight of a young lad to feast on. Better run, kid. She's a lamia, and she's hungry for blood."

Hal didn't need to be told twice. He bolted, trying to pull the door shut behind him but failing because the lamia wedged her paws in and pushed through. Suddenly she was on Hal's back, throwing him down onto the corridor floor. She was surprisingly heavy, and he found himself pinned on his stomach, unable to move, her hot breath on his neck.

He twisted his head around just in time to see her stretching her jaws wide, reaching for his neck, her fangs long and gleaming.

"Stop!" he gasped. "What are you doing?"

She paused, her unblemished, oddly grey face screwing up into a frown. "What do you mean?"

Hal tried to wriggle out from beneath her and eventually gave up. "What are you going to do to me?"

"Well, I'm going to . . . to . . ." The lamia paused, blinking.

Though he had difficulty seeing her face, he knew she was disturbed by her own sudden desire to tear into his throat. "You're seriously going to drink my *blood?*" he said, laying it on thick. "That's gross!"

She relaxed her grip a little, and he turned partway onto his side. Now he could comfortably look up at her. She looked mystified as though she'd just woken and found she'd been sleepwalking.

"Do you know who I am?" he asked.

The lamia-scrag tilted her head. "Of course I do. You're one of them. One of Simone's little soldiers."

"I'm the dragon," he clarified. "And the second you stick your fangs in my neck, I'll transform and crush you against the ceiling. And if that doesn't kill you, I'll burn you."

Her expression turned to surprise, then to concern, and finally to what Hal took as misery. She let out a low, mournful moan that seemed to come from deep down inside. "I'm so hungry."

"Then eat a sandwich."

"I tried eating, but everything I put in my mouth comes right back up. My stomach can't hold anything. All I want is . . . is . . ."

"Blood?" Hal suggested.

"Not just any blood," she said slowly. "*Young* blood."

"Why?"

She screwed up her face as though trying to drag some deep-seated memories out from the back of her mind. "To . . . to purge myself. Only the blood of an innocent young person can wash away the burden and guilt of an adult."

"Well, it's not going to be mine," Hal said firmly. "Anyway, I'll be thirteen soon. I'm not as young as I look. Let me up or I'll burn you."

To prove his point, he willed a tiny ball of flame into his throat and belched it up. It flashed before his face and created a puff of smoke, not enough to burn the lamia but more than enough to show her he meant business. She backed off, releasing him.

He climbed to his feet and took stock. As he'd feared, his short clash with the lamia hadn't gone unnoticed. Naturally the half-formed manticore had emerged on two feet from the so-called animal house on the right, but also Croaker and one of his patients stood on the left outside the laboratory.

"Kill him, Lola!" the manticore-scrag suddenly yelled. "Tear his throat out!"

The lamia swung around and snarled, "He's a dragon!"

The red-furred scrag stepped closer, stooping into a crouch as if preparing to fight. "Right now he's just a kid. Get him, woman!"

He stooped lower, his body shape altering and becoming more lionlike. He opened his mouth wide, and now Hal saw three rows of needle-sharp fangs as his snout stretched wide. More red fur sprouted all over. His transformation was sporadic, but it wouldn't be long before he grew a segmented tail with a ball of poison-tipped quills and a deadly black stinger.

Hal backed off, separating himself from the uncertain lamia and those who stood beyond.

"Take him down!" the manticore-scrag yelled at her.

She crouched low, muscles tensing, but still she hesitated. "He's a *dragon*," she said again, this time in a mumble.

With a roar of irritation, the manticore ran toward Hal. As he did so, he tripped over his own pants, which had fallen to his ankles as his body continued to change. Sprawling on the floor, a long tail seemed to appear out of nowhere, its ball of quills bristling. As it swung around, those thin needles shot out in all directions, leaving the tail bare except for the black stinger.

Hal felt several quills pierce his shirt and stick into his skin. The lamia must have been hit, too, as well as Croaker and his patient, because all winced and cried out. Hal writhed on the floor, shocked at the intensity of the poison as it swept across his body. Moments later, everything around him started to swim.

His transformation was mostly instinctive. He was aware of his massive bulk filling the corridor, his wings pressing against the ceiling, his tail flicking around and smashing against doors behind him.

While everyone was dealing with the poison, the manticore—now a full-fledged monster—regained its footing and pounced, jabbing with its stinger. Gobs of yellow venom bounced off Hal's snout, and he felt a sharp, stabbing pain.

So much for these new shapeshifters lacking control, Hal thought as he conjured up a sheet of flame to ward off his red-furred attacker. *Both scrags are doing pretty well!*

He realized it was because of him. His presence had set both scrags off, whether through an urge to attack or a desire to feed. Breathing fire, he blackened the walls and heated up the corridor so much that everyone— manticore, lamia, and other scrags—leapt or crawled to safety through the nearest open door.

Alone once more, Hal gave a tremendous bellow before reverting to his human form. He staggered dizzily, his nose throbbing from the manticore venom. He felt like he'd been sucker-punched. Blinking rapidly, his eyes watering, he figured he had half a minute before anyone peeked into the corridor at him. Just about time to escape up the stairs.

Or should he look for Miss Simone down here?

Sighing with frustration, he stormed into the laboratory, aware that both the lamia and the manticore were already emerging from separate rooms and pursuing him. "Where's Miss Simone?" he demanded, yelling across the floor to Croaker, who cowered behind one of the four tables with his patient. Two other patients remained asleep on those tables, blissfully unaware of the ruckus.

Croaker raised his hands, his eyes wide. He looked woozy from at least three quills poking out of his left arm. "P-please, don't hurt me! The queen has her upstairs in the castle."

"Is she all right?"

"Leech drugged her earlier. She'll be sleeping like a baby by now."

"He *drugged* her? Why?"

"So she couldn't escape out the window. We know she's a mermaid."

A vision flashed into Hal's mind: her body straight and stiff, arms out wide, cloak billowing as she leapt from a great height into the sea just as she'd done back on the island.

He glanced across to the corner where equipment was piled on the cabinets. After all his work switching samples in secret, now it seemed logical to destroy it all and be done with it. The lamia and manticore alone proved that an army of scrag shapeshifters was something to avoid at all costs. There was only one way to prevent more shapeshifters, and that was to burn the blood.

Only it wasn't there.

He stared and stared. When he glanced back at Croaker, the man's eyes flickered to the tiny offshoot room at the back. "Is the blood back there?" Hal said. "Bring it out where I can see it, or I'll—"

Too late, he caught a flash of red fur as the manticore flew at him. Claws dug deep and teeth closed on his neck—but then Hal switched to dragon form again, and he heard a snap and yelp as the manticore's jaw, already hooked into his transforming flesh, stretched wide and broke.

He flung the creature off and clumsily spun around. Tables and patients flew across the room. The manticore scurried away, shaking its head, lower jaw hanging loosely. The lamia darted in the other direction.

Hal threw himself at the tiny doorway to the back room. The walls cracked and dust trickled down. He tried again, but nothing gave. He was big, but these walls were old and robust.

He could stick his head in, though. The wooden cabinets inside the room were shut, the bench cluttered with glass bottles and tubes and syringes. And there was the box of blood, hastily dumped in the middle of it all.

He set fire to everything. The wooden cabinets turned black and caught alight, and the shallow box began to smoke. He didn't know much about blood, but he was sure it would bubble and boil when heated enough, and the glass would melt, and everything would be mixed together in one nasty mess. It would be ruined, the shapeshifting experiments over.

Reverting to human form again, he gave Croaker a satisfied grin and dashed across the room to the corridor. Something bothered him about the way the scientist stared back. He didn't seem too upset with the inferno in his DNA-extraction room.

Hal tore up the narrow, winding steps two at a time. The last time he'd been here, scrags had chased him with poison-tipped spears, and he'd succumbed to the dizziness and fallen only to be picked up and rescued by Miss Simone and Abigail. This time he had a numb nose from the manticore's stinger, not to mention a few itches where the quills had stuck into him.

Gasping for breath, he wound up and up the dark stairs, terrified at how utterly vulnerable he was within this confined space. Torches flickered on the walls. Behind him came shouts and the snarl of the lamia, though she was snarling at her friends rather than him. "He's a *dragon!*" she kept protesting.

Hal finally reached the top and took a moment to catch his breath in a short hallway. Just ahead, bluish moonlight illuminated a doorway to one side.

Aware of distant voices, he emerged into a familiar hall. Great windows surrounded the place, though one had no glass in its frame from where he'd smashed his way in the other day. The fragments had been cleared up by the caretakers, but the main entrance doors still hung in pieces on their hinges. Hal doubted it was easy to find spare castle doors and huge windows.

The hall was heavily shadowed and completely empty. Everybody seemed to be outside in the moonlit courtyard.

He tiptoed across the floor. He stopped just inside the shattered wooden doors. He didn't have long because the two scrag shapeshifters were probably coming up the stairs after him.

But he paused long enough to take in a truly extraordinary sight.

Chapter Ten
Monsters in the Courtyard

Peering out through the enormous broken doors, Hal saw a large crowd of scrags cheering and laughing at a half-formed shapeshifter. Queen Bee headed up the audience, her voice carrying across the moonlit courtyard.

"Come on, Guppy, use your *mind*. You can do it. Just grow another couple of legs and be done with it."

The scrag named Guppy looked extremely unhappy at all the attention. He stood alone, a rather comical sight with the hindquarters of a horse tapering up to a thin-chested man. It was the weird proportions that everyone seemed to be laughing at—the long horse legs and large back end coupled with a puny upper torso. He stood taller than everyone else, yet he wobbled uncertainly as though on stilts, throwing out his arms for balance.

"I can't just grow front legs," he said plaintively. "Where are they supposed to grow from?"

"Get down on the ground," someone suggested. "Maybe your arms will turn into front legs if you crawl about like a baby."

"But centaurs have arms as well! I *need* these."

"You're thinking too hard about it," a scrag in the crowd suggested. "Come on, get on with it. You woke us all up with your yelling, dragged us out of bed—now show us something!"

Hal noticed the crowd wasn't entirely made up of scrags. He saw castle residents as well—men, women, even a few older children, most of them in pajamas where they'd hurried along to see what all the noise was about. They looked confused.

Guppy staggered and fought to right himself. His shirt and shoes were gone, his pants ripped to accommodate his horselike rear end. Hal saw blotchy, scarred skin on his upper body. Perhaps when he fully transformed into a centaur, those scars would begin to fade.

Queen Bee strode forward and took the man's hand. She looked tiny next to him. "Guppy, finish it off. You're embarrassing me."

"I don't know how!" Guppy exclaimed, his face darkening as another ripple of laughter spread through the crowd. "That stupid glass ball didn't help!"

Queen Bee frowned. "No, it didn't. Perhaps Simone will have a suggestion or two about this when she wakes from her beauty sleep tomorrow."

"I don't understand," a Brodon woman said. "I thought you people were already shapeshifters? Why is this man having so much trouble changing?"

The queen gave her a smile. "Guppy's new."

This simple explanation seemed to do the trick for many of the residents. Their puzzled frowns turned into grins as they joined forces with the scrags to celebrate the momentous occasion.

While Guppy was the center of attention, Hal recognized a few other scrags who had been experimented on earlier, notably the barrel-chested brute who'd wanted to be an ogre. Occasionally the man raised his hands and looked at them as though feeling the tingle of an upcoming transformation . . .

Hal heard a noise behind him, and he darted across to the corner of the hall where it was most heavily shadowed. There was nothing but a large, ornate plant pot to hide behind. He lay down flat and tried to conceal the pale skin of his hands and face with his dark smart clothes. He felt horribly exposed as scrags burst out of the narrow doorway from the stairwell.

Croaker was first, illuminated briefly by shafts of moonlight. Three other scrags followed, probably his patients. Then the dull-grey lamia emerged, looking wary. As the scrags crossed the floor to the broken doors, she hung back a little as though shy about her appearance. Behind her, the red-furred manticore lurked in the doorway, his jaw hanging at an odd angle and his tongue lolling.

"My queen!" Croaker called as he stepped outside.

From his shadowy corner, Hal clearly heard the queen's irritation. "What are you doing up here? Get back to work! I want an army by dawn, which gives you about two more hours."

"Queen, that boy—the dragon-boy—he was downstairs."

A silence followed. Even the chuckling crowd quieted. Then the queen hissed, "He's *still here?*"

"Yes, ma'am."

Another silence. Then: "Are the blood samples safe?"

"I hid them as soon as I heard noise in the corridor, but he came in and set fire to my DNA lab."

"Are they *safe?*" she barked again.

"No."

The queen sucked in a breath. "What?" she said hoarsely.

"Well, some are," Croaker said, his voice shaking. Hal heard a clinking of glass. "Look, I grabbed some good ones before the boy got there. The rest I left in the box for him to burn. They were mostly harmless things anyway, nothing we'd want in the Swarm. You still have the dragon's blood, right? And I saved the hellhound and—"

"But your lab is ruined," Queen Bee said.

"The small lab at the back, yes. We put the fire out. But I have plenty of spare chemicals and equipment. This is just a slight delay—"

"And where's the boy now?"

"H-he came up here. He's in the castle somewhere. Stick and Lola are guarding the stairs."

Hal heard the queen stomp across the courtyard floor and into the great hall. She stopped dead when she saw the lamia and manticore in the shadows.

"Come here, Lola," she said softly as scrags and Brodon residents shuffled into the hall behind her.

The lamia edged forward, and moonlight fell across her. Queen Bee reached forward and patted Lola's grey face. "Good to see you on your feet instead of lying around moaning. What happened?"

Lola tilted her head, and her silver hair hung across her face. "The boy. I saw him standing there and . . . and I just . . . I had an urge to drink his blood."

Queen Bee looked around the dark hall, her gaze settling on the numerous doors and archways deeper in, equally difficult to see in the blackness. "Why *his* blood in particular?"

"Because he's so young and innocent, and I'm so . . . so *burdened.*" In an instant, her soulful eyes filled with tears. "I just want to end my misery. I have so much guilt, so much pain. All the things I've witnessed since the virus broke out—it's weighing on me, rotting away inside. But if I drink the blood of someone young and innocent, someone free of the horrors of the world—"

"Yes, yes, I get it," the queen said. "Well, it's a good thing you stayed well away from young Seth, isn't it? I'd kill you if you hurt Seth."

The lamia's eyes widened.

Queen Bee looked around again, this time focusing on the enormous broken window. "But if you find that dragon-boy, you're very welcome to suck on his blood. In fact, I insist on it."

Though Lola licked her lips, she still seemed wholly uncertain about the idea of attacking a boy who could turn into a dragon.

As more and more scrags and townsfolk edged into the great hall and spread out, Hal wished himself smaller and smaller. How did he keep getting into these predicaments? This time he had nothing but a skinny plant and the shadows to hide him. On the plus side, he had plenty of room to transform if he needed to.

Queen Bee strode over to the destroyed window. There, a breeze tugged at her hair as she looked out across the bay, pale moonlight lighting up her face. "Well, if he wasn't gone before, he's gone now," she said at last. "Unless—" She spun around. "Somebody check on Simone!"

A scrag sprinted across the hall to a grand staircase at the far end and took the steps two at a time.

The queen paced back and forth. "Let's get some torches lit in here. Everybody on full alert." She approached the manticore lurking in the narrow doorway. "Stick? How are you doing?"

The manticore named Stick came forward, and everyone murmured with awe. He padded softly across the floor until he stood alongside the lamia. Much bigger and stronger, he was a formidable sight, especially when he arced his segmented tail over his head. It looked like it was already growing quills again.

"Well, look at *you*," Queen Bee said, standing with hands on hips. "Finally!" As if remembering she had company, she turned briefly to the nearest group of Brodon people. "He's shy. We hardly ever see him change." She looked again at Stick. "What, uh, helped you come out of your shell?"

The manticore said something, but his words were indecipherable.

Queen Bee frowned, then leaned forward and touched the manticore's slack jaw. "What happened here?"

Croaker answered for him. "He bit the boy just as the boy transformed."

When scrags starting chortling, she swung around in anger. "Enough! Not funny! Stick did good to attack. I want to see that kind of bravery from the rest of you when the time comes."

At that moment, footsteps sounded on the grand staircase at the far end of the castle. The scrag returned, breathless as he hurried across the polished floor toward Queen Bee. "Simone's still asleep in the tower. The guards swear nobody's been up there."

She nodded and turned to the manticore. "When you change back, your jaw will repair itself. Think about that." With one hand on his head, absently ruffling his fur as though he were a giant dog, she said to Croaker, "Get back downstairs and finish the procedures before Simone's friends come for her. Whatever blood you have in your pocket, use it!"

"And the dragon blood, my queen?"

Hal sucked in a breath as Queen Bee held up a tiny vial of her own. A silence fell. "This is for Seth," she said firmly.

Every scrag present stared at the vial as though it were the most precious jewel in the world. Mouths hung open, tongues licked at lips.

"Seth?" Croaker said, gently taking the dragon's blood from her. "I thought this was for Duke?"

"Duke's not here." The queen turned and pointed to a boy with mild scars on his face. Brown-haired and slim, he looked about Hal's age. "Seth will take the dragon blood. Is that understood?"

"But why *him*?" someone demanded. "He's a kid! Why should—"

"Quit stalling and get back to work," Queen Bee said shortly. She cupped her hands to her mouth. "Leech! Break's over! Get back downstairs!"

The scientist named Leech broke through the crowd, looking flustered even in the gloom. "Ma'am, I wasn't on break. You asked me to check on Guppy—"

"See, here's what I don't understand," a Brodon man said loudly, breaking into the conversation.

Everyone turned to him, and a silence fell. He was in his sixties, going bald, and it appeared his fellow residents greatly respected him judging by the way they nudged each other to listen up.

"You led us to believe you were all shapeshifters," he said in a gravelly voice. "You said you were here to protect us from others. The mayor told us the same thing. Yet it seems to me that only *some* of you are shapeshifters. You're talking about creating more! What's going on here?"

The queen sighed. "I don't have time to explain."

"Well, you'd better, young miss, because I'm the head caretaker in this castle, and I demand an explanation. I've lived and worked here forty-three years, and I don't appreciate the way you're—"

"Enough!" she screeched. "Everyone spread out. And get some torches lit! I want eyes on the windows. That dragon-boy might still be around. Maybe he's waiting for backup, or maybe he'll attack while it's still dark. Be prepared! And above all, guard those last few blood samples!"

"I'm not finished," the old caretaker said.

Queen Bee stuck her nose in the man's face. "Get in my way and you *will* be finished, you old coot. I suggest you and your people go back to bed. Things are about to get ugly around here."

The queen marched away. Some of the scrags surged after her, back outside to the moonlit courtyard. The manticore and lamia strutted out, too, apparently over their initial shyness. Other scrags ran deeper into the castle, some posting themselves at windows while the rest scampered up the grand staircase. One went around lighting torches. Three clustered together in the doorway to the narrow stairwell that led to the lower floor.

Leech and Croaker pushed past them and headed back downstairs to work. A few more scrags followed them, including Seth, next in line to be experimented on. Hal felt a pang of regret, knowing he should have stopped them while he had room to transform. But it was too late now.

The old caretaker stood quite still, many of his friends and colleagues clustered around him. After a long moment of deliberation, he said quietly, "I don't like this. I suggest we leave. Gather everyone up. Get the kids out of bed. Make sure everyone is accounted for."

As they all hurried away, Hal lay absolutely still, blanketed in darkness. He would be safe for a while longer if nobody lit any torches in this corner, but soon the rays of the rising sun would flood the place and chase the shadows away.

Where was Abigail? He'd been wondering about her for ages, but he hadn't been overly anxious because she was so small and hard to find. He had to assume she was still loitering about the place, probably up to mischief somewhere. But where? It was time she showed herself. He couldn't leave without her.

Scrags traipsed in and out. It was impossible to count them all, but there had to be a few dozen. How many had Leech and Croaker experimented on? Hal sighed with annoyance. He'd fallen asleep in the laboratory and had no idea. But if Queen Bee had her way, there would be more shapeshifters soon.

Through one of the east-facing windows, the sky was turning orange. Hal's hiding place behind the plant would soon be revealed. He almost relished the looks on the scrags' faces as they realized he'd been lying there in the corner all along! But it was a dilemma. He couldn't just wait around to be discovered, and he couldn't get up and walk away, either.

"It's starting!" a voice yelled from the shattered doorway.

Someone stumbled inside. The brightening dawn light outlined a large figure dropping to his knees and hunching over. Scrags came running. Once again, Hal had a perfect view—a little too perfect for his liking, with no more than thirty feet and a few remaining shadows separating him from inevitable discovery.

"Queen Bee!" somebody shouted. "We got another one!"

The crowd grew, and soon Queen Bee was pushing through followed by the anxious lamia and broken-jawed manticore.

"Are you making this happen, Ox?" the queen asked. "Is this your doing?"

"Naw," the one called Ox grunted. Hal suddenly realized he was the strong, bare-chested brute who wanted to be an ogre. "My fingertips have been itching for ages, and now my arms feel like they're somebody else's."

"Somebody else's?"

Ox nodded. "I feel . . . weak." Judging by the way he spoke that last word, clearly he was troubled. He lifted his arms and flexed them as though showing off his biceps. Even in the subdued light, Hal could see that he had thinned dramatically.

A murmur started through the crowd, and a few stepped back.

"This ain't right," Ox grumbled. "I'm supposed to be an ogre. I'm supposed to be getting bigger and stronger, not smaller and weaker. *Look* at me!"

His deep, rumbling voice had turned to a whine—and no wonder, for his bulky shoulders and arms were diminishing, his chest narrowing, and his lower legs beginning to stretch and contort. He sat heavily on his backside to watch the transformation along with everyone else. A hush fell.

Though he wore pants, these were now baggy. His shoes fell off to reveal the cloven feet of a goat and fine brown hair around his ankles. At the same time, horns sprouted from Ox's head and curled around and around while his ears stretched into points. When the transformation ended, the man was half his original size and weight, his pants hanging loosely.

Nobody said anything for a long while. Then Ox said, "Wh-what *am* I?"

A woman snickered. "You're either the smallest ogre in the world, or you're an adorable little faun."

Every scrag present burst into laughter. The noise echoed around the hall, and the only two not joining in were Ox and Queen Bee, both of whom looked angry.

"Shut up!" Queen Bee screeched.

The laughter trailed off.

She stood with her fists clenched, looking Ox up and down. "Are you sure you asked for ogre blood?"

The man exploded in rage. "What, you think I wanted *this*? Of course I asked for ogre blood! Those morons got it mixed up!"

He struggled up and tried balancing on his unfamiliar goat feet, then promptly fell flat on his face. The crowd laughed again, but Queen Bee spun around and lashed out. "If the ogre blood got mixed up with faun blood, some of the others might be wrong as well. Did you think about *that*?"

Silence descended. Now scrags looked at one another with concern, and it became blatantly obvious which ones had already undergone the experiment because they started checking themselves all over and holding their mouths like they'd just swallowed something nasty.

Queen Bee closed her eyes and pinched her nose. "How about we stop fretting about what you all *might* become and just get on with transforming?"

"How?" someone asked.

"Yeah, Ox—how'd you do it?"

"It just happened," the faun said miserably.

A heated discussion started up with scrags badgering the manticore and lamia about their transformations. The partially complete centaur joined in, too, the moment he staggered in through the doorway.

Rays of sunlight shone high on the walls, and Hal realized he was now mostly visible if anyone cared to glance his way. He had to move.

"Gruel," Queen Bee said, pointing at a lanky man with sunken eyes. He jumped at the sudden attention as everyone turned to him. "Blow on your conch shell and see if it helps you change."

He hefted the object in his hand, a large, twisted shell, yellowish in color. "I tried, ma'am. It doesn't work."

"Maybe you picked up the wrong kind? Or you're not blowing into it the right way?" She sighed with exasperation. "Come on, people, you're supposed to research your chosen forms and everything that goes with them."

Someone piped up, "The library's kind of lacking in the mythology section."

"This is the right kind of shell," Gruel said, "but it probably won't work until I change. Or maybe that whole conch shell thing is just a big fat lie."

Queen Bee shook her head. "Myths and legends come from stories passed down through the ages, and there has to be some truth to them." She pointed at the shell. "When you change, that thing will work. I'm sure of it."

"And how long before we change?" a scrag woman said.

"It takes as long as it takes," the lamia growled. "I changed straight away but couldn't find the will to get up. Stick only half-changed until that dragon-boy showed up. It's different for everyone. You just have to work at it."

"It's happening," another scrag said.

Everyone turned to him and fell quiet as he began a transformation of his own. Queen Bee approached, her eyes wide. "What are you supposed to be?"

"A griffin," the man said grimly as something slowly protruded from his forehead. He winced and gingerly touched the conical point that had appeared there. "Is this right? Does a griffin have this? I thought they were supposed to be giant eagle things mixed with lions?" The point grew longer and longer, extending straight outward. "Is . . . is this thing my *beak*?"

Hal couldn't help laughing to himself. The man's cross-eyed expression was too comical to ignore. The crowd gradually moved back, probably to give him room although it seemed they were afraid of catching some kind of disease.

The scrag abruptly transformed all the way, his clothes shredding and flinging in all directions. Where once was a scarred man now stood a fabulous white unicorn.

Much larger than the average horse, it danced around on the polished floor with a terrible racket, shaking its head about and swishing its full tail. The unicorn's horn, long with spiral indentations, came dangerously close to several scrags as they jumped clear.

The unicorn reared up and whinnied, then smashed its hoofs back down and caused the floor to crack. Snorting and huffing, the handsome beast turned and galloped out into the courtyard, disappearing from Hal's sight.

To his relief, the crowd surged after it—every man and woman along with Queen Bee, the lamia, and the manticore. And as soon as they were outside, somebody else exclaimed that he, too, was beginning to change.

Hal jumped up and tore across the hall to the grand staircase. He expected to run across guards higher up, but a blast of fire would hold them off.

Snatching glances over his shoulder, he glimpsed a menagerie of creatures staggering about among the crowd, creatures he didn't have time to study and identify. It seemed that the unicorn's dramatic transformation had sparked others; they were all at it now, like chickens hatching from eggs. However, the cacophony of unhappy shouts suggested very few satisfied customers.

Grinning, Hal ascended the sweeping steps and reached the castle's upper level. He found himself in a wide corridor with various grand doorways on both sides. But what interested him were the two highly alert guards standing at the entrance to another winding staircase, this one narrow and nowhere near as grand.

The tower! That was where he'd find Miss Simone.

The scrags stared at him as he skidded to a halt. One promptly charged him with his spear held high, and Hal—already prepared—let loose with a long-reaching arc of fire that sent the scrag scurrying to safety.

The other transformed.

Chapter Eleven
Sleeping Beauty

Hal had expected to deal with guards on his way up to the tower. For some reason it had never occurred to him that one would be a shapeshifter. Of course it made sense for the queen to utilize her new creations. It just surprised Hal that the scrag could shift so easily.

It seemed to surprise the scrag, too. As thick horns sprouted from the sides of his head, his shoulders and chest expanded and burst out of his dirty shirt. The man looked both shocked and pleased. "So that's what it takes to change?" he growled, his voice deepening with each word. "I just needed the wet-nosed dragon-boy to show up and threaten me?"

His brow bulged and broadened so that his eyes appeared to sink back into his head. Then they shifted sideways, becoming unusually wide-set, almost hidden around the sides of his face. This fluid, eerie repositioning seemed to push his lengthening ears up to the top of his head near his horns.

Meanwhile, coarse brown hair sprouted all over, extra thick and long around the top of his head but shorter on his face and down near his huge shoulders. Ugly scars vanished. Even where normal human skin showed through the man's ripped shirt, the scars had faded somewhat.

The transformation was complete within a couple of seconds, enough time for Hal to weigh up the monster that stood before him, something he recognized from descriptions as a minotaur. Though top-heavy, the beast crouched and moved with immense power. The man's torso and legs had probably toughened considerably as well, otherwise he would be staggering around with a huge weight on his shoulders.

Hal blasted the minotaur with fire. The minotaur let out a distinctly bullish howl of anger and leapt through the flames at him, thrusting his horns forward. One caught Hal's shoulder and ripped into it. Then the broad forehead slammed into him, knocking him ten feet through the air. Hal landed on his back, severely winded and in pain.

The minotaur-scrag, some of his hair blackened and smoking, came at him with his head down and horns angled forward.

What happened to stumbling around in their new bodies without built-in instincts? Hal thought as the pain in his shoulder flared up. *These first-timers sure are settling in fast.*

He didn't even have time to roll aside. The minotaur's heavy, booted foot thudded into Hal's chest and pinned him down.

"Don't make me angry," Hal said with a gasp. "You wouldn't like me when I'm angry."

"Lie still," the minotaur rasped in a voice that sounded like it rumbled up from underground. "If you start to change, I'll stick this horn in your eyeball so fast you'll end up skewered like a pig on a stick."

Hal knew he meant it. The horn's lethal point, backed by hundreds of pounds of coiled muscle, hung poised to strike.

But Hal meant it, too. He turned his head to one side and transformed.

During the swift change from human to dragon, the horn actually dug into him as promised, though his fluid metamorphosis and growth meant he actually got stuck in the neck rather than the eye. He expanded and thrashed, then rolled onto his belly and turned, and the minotaur ended up crashing to the floor and scrabbling aside.

Hal did a quick self-check. Whatever injuries the minotaur had inflicted had partially faded with the natural healing process. He was confident those wounds would be gone by the time he was human again.

The minotaur seemed to have suffered a severe injury, though. One of his horns had stuck into Hal, and Hal's sudden movement had caused it a nasty wrench, like a tree being half-uprooted. Blood poured down the scrag's head from the lopsided horn, and he howled with pain.

"Change back," Hal told him, though his voice came out as a roar. Seeing that the first scrag guard had disappeared, and knowing the tower's staircase was too narrow for a dragon, he reverted to his human form and stood before the minotaur as a simple, twelve-year-old boy. "Change back," he said again.

The minotaur peered up at him with one eye. The other was closed due to the scarlet mess that dribbled down his face. "What?"

Hal moved closer. A wounded, confused scrag was easier to deal with than one that was healthy and full of hatred. Still, maybe a bit of compassion would go a long way. Maybe Hal would gain an ally if he helped him.

"Change back and you'll heal up," he said. "It might take a few tries, but you'll heal a bit each time." He touched his own shoulder and neck, prodding for the wounds he'd suffered only moments earlier. "See? You stuck me twice, but I'm fine now. Mostly."

He felt a knot on his neck. Maybe another shift would take care of that. It didn't hurt, though. It was more like an old scar.

"I—I don't know how," the minotaur grumbled.

Hal could hear the distant shouts of scrags outside in the courtyard, their voices drifting inside and echoing off the walls. Though he probably had a bit of time to stand around chatting, he decided there were more pressing concerns. "You'll figure it out," he said. "Sorry, I've got to go."

Leaving the minotaur kneeling on the floor, he turned and dashed up the steps to the tower. Scrags would be after him in a moment, as well as numerous rookie shapeshifters. His brain hurt trying to remember which blood samples he'd either missed or left alone. The minotaur was one he'd picked up and put back before embarking on his blood-swapping sabotage. He'd dealt with the ogre, replacing it with a faun. He'd swapped the griffin for a unicorn. And the hippogriff—well, he couldn't remember.

He shook his head, annoyed. If only he'd been able to swap *all* of them. Then he might have faced a harmless dryad rather than a minotaur.

He was panting by the time he reached the top of the tower. He burst out of a doorway and stopped dead, realizing he'd gone too far. This was the roof of the tower, a circular space open to the daylight and surrounded by a thick, crenellated wall. A group of six lookout scrags swung around to face him.

Hal turned and headed back downstairs again, hearing the shouts of alarm and knowing they were following.

Straightaway he found a door he'd rushed past on the way up. It was clear enough to see, but it wasn't exactly grand, so small and modest that he'd mistaken it for a closet or something. The key was in the lock, so he twisted it, heard a clunk, tried the doorknob, and pushed the door open. Rushing inside, he grabbed the key out of the lock, slammed the door behind him, and locked it again. He was safe from the scrags for a few minutes.

The circular room took up most of the tower's diameter except for where the stairwell cut in. Ornate furnishings suggested this was, like other rooms in the castle, intended for wealthy tenants or lucky guests. Hal's attention wandered from the desk and chair under one window to the armchairs under the other, then fell on the huge four-poster bed with dark red drapes.

Miss Simone lay there, sound asleep.

Hal rushed to her side. "Miss Simone, wake up. Time to go."

He glanced at the two windows, seeing that one was open. They were small. To escape that way, he'd have to transform *after* diving off the windowsill. Either that or fight his way up the stairs to the roof . . .

"Miss Simone," he said again, giving her arm a shake.

She lay on her back on top of the covers, her silky green cloak spread out. No amount of shaking her arm and saying her name would rouse her. Leech really had drugged her. How long before she woke?

A high-pitched whining made him spin around. Before he could focus on the source of the noise, a figure appeared on his right, and he spun again. "I've already tried waking her," Abigail said as she retracted her wings.

"Where have you been?" Hal exclaimed, jumping up and running to her. He hugged her tight, and at first she tried to act nonchalant, but then she grinned and hugged him back even tighter.

"Where have *you* been?" she countered. "I've searched everywhere for you. I heard a story about a dragon-boy dressed as a girl who escaped upstairs to the castle, and everyone's been on the lookout for you since. I have, too."

"I never came upstairs," Hal said. "I hid in the lab."

"You hid in the—" Abigail stopped and blinked at him. "In the *lab*? Queen Bee's shapeshifter lab?"

"Now tell me where *you've* been all this time."

She shrugged. "Around. Scrags chased me a few times, but I just flew over their heads. They never came close. I searched the whole castle for you. I had no idea you were still downstairs. What were you doing in the lab?"

Somehow, Abigail had steered the conversation back to Hal. "I hid in the corner where the blood samples were. I switched some of them.

The scrags have started shifting, but they're not what they expected to be."

Abigail stared and stared, her eyes wide. Outside the door, Hal could hear the approach of multiple footfalls and hushed voices.

Finally, Abigail said, "Miss Simone told you to destroy all the blood—smash all the vials on the floor and burn it until it dries as one big, black scorch mark. I think Councilman Frobisher would have preferred that, too. Much safer."

Doubt crept through Hal's mind. "Well, I just thought it would be hard to sneak about and find Miss Simone if—"

"The thing is," Abigail interrupted, "if you'd done that—destroyed the blood, I mean—then Queen Bee would have gone and got more. It would have taken her a while, but she would have done it."

Someone wiggled the doorknob, then pounded on the door.

"As far as the scrags know," Abigail said, "they have just one shot at being a shapeshifter. By mixing up the blood, you've kind of ruined it for them. They're becoming shapeshifters but not what they wanted to be."

"Right," Hal said. "That, too. So . . . you're agreeing with me on this?"

She grinned. "Of course I am! If nothing else, think how much fun it will be to see their faces when they turn into the wrong monsters!"

Something heavy and powerful thumped against the door. "Again," a man's voice barked, and seconds later the door rattled in its frame.

Abigail rolled her eyes. "I guess we should leave."

"I guess so. If we can wake Miss Simone."

"One of the scrags drugged her," Abigail said with a sigh. She pointed to the open window. "Otherwise she might have jumped out and escaped. The sea's right below us."

"I know."

More thumping on the door caused them to glance over and watch. The door was thick and solid, but how long would it last against a minotaur or some other shapeshifter? And they might have a spare key somewhere.

"Well," Hal said, hurrying to the window, "we can either throw her out anyway, or we can try and carry her down."

"I thought of doing that myself, but I was afraid I'd drop her into the sea and she wouldn't wake up. I mean, she's a mermaid and all, but . . ."

Hal understood. What if Miss Simone didn't automatically shift as she sank to the seabed? What if she drowned?

Outside the window was a wraparound balcony. There were two, if he remembered correctly. This was the upper floor. Beyond that fencing was a sheer drop into the sea. The tower stood at the far end of the castle, and the castle on the edge of the cliff.

"Perfect," he said, nodding with approval. "The balcony's a bit flimsy and small, but there's plenty of time to shift on the way down."

They dragged Miss Simone off the bed and over to the window, struggling under her weight.

The door splintered, and something went *ping!* as a metal pin or bolt flew off. "Go," Hal told Abigail as he hoisted Miss Simone onto the windowsill. She was too heavy for him to handle properly, but all he needed was for her to tip sideways and fall.

Abigail leapt off the windowsill and sprouted her wings. She dropped a little, then buzzed back up again, coming to help. She took Miss Simone's hand and yanked while Hal picked up her feet and shoved.

At that moment, the door flew open with a terrible crunching noise and something spilled into the room. It wasn't the minotaur but something larger, so large that it had to bend double to fit through the doorway. The giant was maybe twice the height of a man and looked human except for one eye instead of two—a massive staring eyeball in the middle of his forehead. The giant was almost naked, wearing only a velvet drape wrapped around his middle, probably yanked from one of the windows downstairs.

A modest cyclops, Hal thought.

Miss Simone started to topple from the windowsill onto the balcony with Abigail still clinging to her hand. Hal threw himself after them, transforming as soon as he was clear of the frame. His heavy bulk filled the narrow balcony, and suddenly the fencing broke apart as he pressed against it, causing him to lose his balance and tip off the edge along with splintered railings.

He made a grab for Miss Simone with his clumsy reptilian paws, but he fumbled and missed, succeeding only in causing her and Abigail to spin through the air. The next two or three seconds were utter confusion as the three of them fell, twisting and turning.

Abigail pulled out of her spin first, buzzing away and then hurrying to catch up again. Hal tried in vain to right himself and make his wings work, but his simple plan to catch Miss Simone in midair and fly her to safety failed miserably. She dropped straight into the sea with a gut-wrenching smack and sank fast.

Hal followed with an even bigger splash. Underwater, he spun about to find her, at first seeing nothing but a stream of bubbles.

She woke at that moment and transformed, her fishtail appearing by magic and driving her back to the surface. By the time Hal righted himself and emerged above water, she was blinking in the morning sun and looking around.

"Sorry!" Hal told her.

His dragon growl made her jump. Then she relaxed. "What happened?"

Abigail buzzed closer and hovered over their heads. "Really, Hal? If dropping Miss Simone from a great height was your plan all along, I could have done the same thing *hours* ago."

Shouts came from above. The tower's upper balcony seemed impossibly high up, and Hal breathed a sigh of relief when scrags peered down and waved their fists at him. He caught a glimpse of the one-eyed cyclops, then the minotaur, and then Queen Bee herself, all spilling out of the window and clamoring to spot him far below. They gave the broken fencing a wide berth.

"I made a mistake," Miss Simone said, her face screwed up in pain. Hal could see she was clutching her stomach under the water. "I was sure newly created adult shapeshifters would find it difficult to transform. Unlike you and I, they weren't born and raised with the natural instincts of their alter forms. But it seems those instincts are just another part of the . . . the . . ."

"Magic?" Abigail said.

Hal instantly remembered the glowing chests of scrag patients.

Miss Simone shook her head. "I can't explain it any other way, so yes, part of the magic. I shouldn't be surprised," she added, sounding bitter now. "Shapeshifting itself is theoretically impossible. I suppose I felt a need to cling to some tiny semblance of scientific logic, so I tried to differentiate between the concept of physical transformation and the—"

"Look, we need to get away from here," Abigail interrupted as the shouts from above suddenly cut off. The silence was worse.

Miss Simone nodded and winced. "Ouch. I don't think I landed very well. I'll have to transform a few times as we go."

They began to swim, heading for the nearby beach. Something smacked the water near Hal, and he caught sight of a spear disappearing from view. Then another hit, this one a little closer.

Worse, something smaller and far more accurate zipped down and hit Miss Simone in the shoulder. An arrow. She cried out, clutching at it as blood leaked from the wound and soaked through her green silk.

"Dive!" Abigail shouted, zipping away.

Miss Simone and Hal didn't need reminding. They ducked under as another arrow *thwipped* through the air.

Deep down in the depths, the arrows lost their power and glided harmlessly past. Miss Simone swam easily, though she left a thin trail of blood in her wake, her face contorted with pain. *She'll be all right,* Hal thought, seeing the sloping sand that indicated the nearby beach. *We'll be out of range in just a moment, and then she can shift a few times and self-heal.*

The dull sound of a heavy splash caught his attention, too heavy to be an arrow or spear. He twisted around to look and spotted another fishtailed human figure. Another mermaid? Had she just jumped down from the tower?

He did a double take. The water was clear enough to see that this was a *male* mermaid. A merman. Hal paused a moment, almost amused at the idea of such a harmless creature coming after a dragon.

As the figure approached, he remembered one of the blood samples he'd spotted: the triton. He hadn't bothered pouring that sample away and replacing it because—well, it was a male mermaid! Hardly a threat.

The triton paused and faced him from thirty feet away. Meanwhile, Miss Simone continued on toward the beach, holding her leaking shoulder. Hal decided to hold off the triton until she was out of the water.

The scrag's scars were visible across his chest and arms, faint on his belly under a smattering of silver-colored scales, and nonexistent below the waist where a long fishtail took the place of his legs. This silvery-blue fishtail was split in two at the end like a forked tongue, with two separate tailfins.

Whereas Miss Simone in her mermaid form caused the hearts of men to flutter, the triton had no such power of enchantment. He had several long, trailing fins projecting from his forked fishtail as well as smaller ones from the backs of his forearms below the elbow. His gnarled, scowling face reminded Hal of a goblin. His teeth were long and pointed, his ears wide and flared.

Hal floated calmly, waiting to see what the triton would do. The scrag shapeshifter seemed uncertain and kept glancing around as if weighing his options.

Yeah, just as I figured, Hal thought. *No match for a dragon.*

Then the triton lifted something to his mouth. It was a large conch shell, something he must have brought with him when he'd dropped into the sea. Hal remembered seeing it earlier up at the castle. The scrag named Gruel seemed to be under the impression it would be useful once he'd transformed.

The triton gently blew into it, causing bubbles to erupt in a steady stream.

He's going to kill me with terrible music, Hal guessed.

Instead, the underwater current grew stronger. At first it didn't bother Hal too much, but after a few minutes he was unable to remain in one place and found himself being swept sideways and around in a powerful eddy. The triton continued blowing into his conch, oddly unaffected by the surge.

Hal clawed frantically as the current dragged him backward. *All right, that's enough*, he thought, grudgingly impressed by the triton's weird power. A harpy could generate storms in the air, and it seemed tritons could do the same in the sea. Still, if this was the extent of his attack . . .

At some point he tried to blow fire at the triton. It usually worked underwater if he was close enough to his target. Unfortunately he was not, and his flames bubbled and fizzled straight away.

Admitting defeat, Hal struck for the surface. It took all his effort to stick his snout out and catch a breath of fresh air, but then he was sucked under again, the current far stronger than his flailing paws and swishing tail.

When he managed to stick his head out of the water a second time, he noticed that the triton's storm was far worse above water. Though the morning sun shone in a clear sky, an enormous, fast-moving wave crashed up the beach and obliterated the promenade, then hammered the first line of houses. Many buildings simply collapsed under the pressure as though made of matchsticks.

The wall of water surged over and around the ruins, weaker now but still heading deeper into Brodon, taking with it small boats and masses of debris.

Miss Simone seemed to have vanished.

Chapter Twelve
Flood

The current sucked Hal under yet again. He glimpsed the triton's fuzzy shape in what was now cloudy water from all the sand and muck churned up from the seabed. The triton continued blowing into his conch shell. Clearly the scrag had read up about this. Did it say somewhere that tritons could create watery storms with music from a conch shell? It didn't seem fair that he and his scrag comrades had settled into their new forms so quickly.

Well, some of them, Hal corrected himself as he remembered the queen's three original shapeshifters. The centaur, manticore, and lamia had languished in the 'animal house' for hours, only coming fully alive when Hal had shown up—as if his very presence had spurred them on. The minotaur was proof of that. The bull-headed man had wasted no time fumbling around trying to get his balance. He'd launched straight at Hal with a skewering in mind.

Rather than try to swim against the raging tide, Hal changed course and went with it, following it around and gaining momentum before riding the waves to the surface. This time he exploded out of the sea. Finally free, he beat his wings and climbed into the air, letting out a triumphant burst of fire and bellowing.

On the outskirts of Brodon, the streets were awash with thigh-deep water and endless debris. Farther in, people emerged from doorways to find themselves up to their ankles.

As Hal flew around, checking out the damage with mounting awe and horror, he realized the bay had stopped crashing and rolling. The waves were calming now, the floodwater receding. He returned to the beach and watched the sand magically reappear as the water level slowly dropped, leaving saturated streets, endless pools, and a trail of destruction in every lane.

Where had Miss Simone gone? And Abigail! She was probably fine, buzzing above the rising tidal waves . . . but what about everybody else? The fisherman, Kinsey and her grandfather, her three-headed dog, numerous other people, even most of the small boats—all swept from the beach in an instant, probably dashed against the promenade and houses. They could all be dead.

Shocked at the power the triton had unleashed with so little effort, Hal flew around and around, searching for survivors and finding many wading and staggering to safety.

"What have you done?" he growled aloud, thinking of the triton blowing into the conch shell. And he couldn't help feeling partially responsible. If only he'd destroyed that blood sample when he'd had the chance!

He thudded down on the beach, causing a splash as he sank into the waterlogged sand. The sea pooled around him, several feet deep. Bits of wood swept past, then a shoe and a flowerpot and some books, all flipping under and back up again as the muddy water swirled and frothed.

He spotted a small girl, probably five or six years old, floundering and crying. He stamped closer to help, but a man came running down the beach, barefoot and soaked, yelling at him to stay away. Hal halted, and the man swept up his little girl and hugged her tight, then splashed away with occasional glances over his shoulder. The look of fury and hatred on his face left Hal feeling cold.

More shouts from where the promenade had once stood drew his attention. The houses there were wrecked, mere shells of twisted timber and piles of rubble. Residents wailed, some of them standing there among the ruins, others stumbling around outside. One bedraggled woman was kneeling, holding a motionless man and sobbing hysterically.

Stunned, Hal didn't care that his feet were deep in the sand by now, sucked down to his ankles with the seawater continuing to churn around him. How had it come to this? He shouldn't be surprised, though. After all, this kind of carnage was exactly the sort of thing Miss Simone had feared with the threat of irresponsible, uncaring scrags shifting willy-nilly into monstrous creatures with fearsome powers. But even so, the reality of it shocked Hal to the core.

"You're gonna pay for this!" someone screamed.

Hal squinted and found a small group of Brodon residents huddled on the beach where the water had receded. To his surprise, they were staring at *him*. They had the same look of fury and hatred the other guy had displayed.

Puzzled, he checked over his shoulder in case they were looking beyond him to the triton. The scrag was nowhere to be seen. When he glanced back, the Brodon residents pointed at him. "Get out of here!" a man shouted. "Go while you have the chance. Our protectors will be here any minute."

"Are you talking to *me*?" Hal said, and the crowd flinched at the snarl that emerged from his reptilian throat. He couldn't believe what he was hearing. These people thought *he'd* done all this damage?

The more he thought about it, the more it made sense from their point of view: the sudden eruption of tidal waves from the bay, the ensuing destruction, and then Hal bursting from the sea with a triumphant roar and blast of fire. The sea had calmed as he'd landed on the beach to 'gloat' at the damage—as far as the local people were concerned, anyway.

"No, no," he started to say, and again people flinched even though they stood well out of his reach.

The caretakers up at the castle would settle this misunderstanding. Hal was certain of it. *They* knew Queen Bee was full of lies, that she and her drones weren't really here to protect the people of Brodon. They must have left the castle by now. They were probably spreading the word already.

But would anyone bother listening to the caretakers after all this destruction? After what they'd seen with their own eyes?

More residents were showing up now, some of them dry except for their lower halves where they'd splashed along the streets to help. The majority were soaked through. Cries filled the air, some in terrible anguish but most, thankfully, in great relief as they found their loved ones alive. Still, even if one person was dead somewhere, that would be one too many. And everyone had gotten it into their heads that Hal was to blame!

He was so flabbergasted that he barely noticed when Abigail buzzed into view. He blinked and focused on her as she flew low over the water and hovered near his head. "What *was* that?" she demanded. "Wait, never mind. Tell me later. Nobody wants to hear you growling right now. Anyway, we need to find Miss Simone. I think she was pulled away with the tide. She's injured, and I'm worried she might be in trouble."

Hal's feet were still planted heavily, stuck fast in the sand. Even though he could pull himself free if he tried, somehow he lacked the inclination. The people of Brodon hated him. They thought *he'd* caused all this damage. The sense of injustice made him feel sick. And weary. He was tired of trying to do the right thing and getting it wrong. He was tired of being looked at with a mixture of fear and anger.

Maybe he *was* to blame for everything, at least in some indirect way. He'd blown up the Chamber of Ghosts, created smoking black holes everywhere, allowed droves of people including scrags to enter this world . . .

Rather than fly away with his tail between his legs, he abruptly reverted to his human form and floundered as the seawater crashed in around him. His feet came free briefly, but then the sand caved in over his toes, once more sucking him downward. The water splashed up to his chest as he stood there in full view of everyone, a tired and very wet shapeshifter.

"What are you doing?" Abigail said, her eyes widening. She buzzed closer, her toes dangling in the water. "Hal, we need to find Miss Simone. Get back into the water and look for her!"

He shook his head. "She's a mermaid. She'll be fine, unlike all *this*. I've done enough damage."

Abigail rolled her eyes and buzzed closer, leaning forward and reaching for his shoulder. "My dear, sweet Hal, you've done nothing wrong."

"Tell *them* that."

They looked toward the ever-growing crowd of townsfolk. Some were moving closer, edging down the sand and into the water as though debating whether or not to pounce on him.

Abigail retracted her wings and dropped into the water with a splash. She gasped briefly, then waded forward and gripped the front of his shirt. "Now, listen to me, buster. You didn't do this! You know it, I know it, and pretty soon everybody else will know it. So quit moping! Let's find Miss Simone."

"No."

"No?" Abigail withdrew slightly, frowning at him. "So you're just going to stand here chest-deep in water and sulk?"

"I'm not sulking," Hal said, though he knew he was. "I'm . . . I'm staying out of the way, that's all. Seems like whatever I do is wrong even when it wasn't me that did it."

"That's ridiculous."

"I'm not moving." As a wave slopped up into his face, he added, "Well, not far anyway. I'm just going to sit down and stay out of everyone's way."

With that, he sidestepped Abigail and waded out of the water until he was only ankle-deep. Then he set off away from the gathering crowd, heading back to where Kinsey's grandfather had been tending to his boat the day before.

The damage was just as bad there, too. The line of houses fronting the beach stood in shambles with owners picking through the saturated mess. There was no sign of the small boats that once stood leaning on the sand. It was like their existence had been wiped off the face of New Earth. Kinsey's grandfather was nowhere to be seen, nor Kinsey herself.

Hal became aware of Abigail buzzing along behind him. "All right, fine. Take a break. It's okay to sulk once in a while. When you're done, come and join in the search for Miss Simone." She moved closer and kissed him quickly on the cheek. "See you soon, mopey-boy."

He faltered and watched her zip away across the beach, zigzagging around and looking down at the water as she went. She'd never find Miss Simone that way, but at least she was *doing* something.

The sea glittered in the sunlight, now calm and peaceful under a clear blue sky. At the far end of the debris-strewn beach, the castle looked equally serene—except for distant shouts and hollers that carried on the breeze, and figures moving about in the courtyard outside the entrance doors. Hal could make out a number of large creatures, scrag shapeshifters of all types, though he couldn't identify what they were. Hopefully most were harmless. Some, though, would likely cause trouble before the morning was out.

A ferocious barking caught his attention. He swung around and spotted a three-headed dog crouching by the ruins of a house. Several people surrounded it, their hands extended, trying to calm the grey-furred cerberus as one brave man approached with a rope.

Hal held his breath. If Dog was here, maybe Kinsey was, too. Or . . . maybe she wasn't. Maybe that was why the neighbors were trying to catch her oversized pet before it attacked someone.

But then, as if by magic, Kinsey herself—barefoot and soggy—appeared out of nowhere, yelling at everybody to get back and leave Dog alone. They did, looking relieved as she darted through the crowd and threw her arms around her pet. The cerberus licked her face, its tail wagging wildly.

Well, at least she's all right, Hal thought.

"Hal!"

The voice sounded familiar, though it took Hal a moment to place it. He turned, scanning the beach, then searching the Brodon residents picking their way through debris. He didn't see anyone he recognized.

"Up here, idiot!"

He glanced up just in time to see a white-feathered bird-girl swooping down from the sky. "Lauren!" he yelled.

She thudded down on the sand, making a splash in the ankle-deep water. Her bright-white feathers gleamed in the sunlight as she stood with her wings outspread. Then she folded them and tilted her head, looking at Hal with yellow eyes. With her white-furred face, it was hard to read her expression. "What happened here? We just arrived. Looks like we're too late."

Hal gaped at her. In the chaos, he'd completely forgotten his friends had planned to come along this morning. "Where are the others?"

Lauren turned to the west and pointed. "See that dot in the sky?"

It took a moment for Hal to make it out. "Wait. Is that . . .?"

"The *CloudDrifter*, yes."

For some reason, the sight of Blacknail the goblin's rickety airship filled him with delight. After months of repairs, it was finally back in action—and it was like the cavalry arriving.

"About time you guys showed up," he said, grinning. "I think we might have a problem here."

Lauren surveyed the nearby damaged houses. "No kidding. We would have been here yesterday if Miss Simone had let us."

As quickly as possible, Hal explained how he, Abigail, and Miss Simone had snuck into the castle and gotten separated, how he had secretly switched many of the blood samples, and how the three of them had escaped just a short while ago. When he told her about the scrags emerging as fully functional shapeshifters, he gestured toward the carnage lining the beach. "That was a triton. He can do what *you* can do, Lauren—create a storm. Only he does it underwater."

Lauren was astounded. "A scrag shapeshifter did that?"

"Yeah, only most people think it was me because I'm the one they saw, not him. I flew about over the waves making some noise and breathing fire."

She raised an eyebrow at him. "Why'd you do that?"

"I was just happy to be out of the water!"

"Well, I'm going back to the *CloudDrifter* to let everybody know what's going on. They'll be here soon. Blacknail sent me ahead to make sure it was safe. We don't want to be attacked by rocs like the last time we traveled in that thing."

"I surprised Frobisher didn't send you with the helicopters," Hal said. "He must be pretty steamed after his meeting with the mayor?"

"Oh, he is! As soon as he got back home, he ordered Lieutenant Briskle and his troops to storm into Brodon and bomb the scrags *and* the castle. The lieutenant said no, that would be a slaughter. He said— what was it now?—he said this is a civil matter until his superiors tell him otherwise. Frobisher decided he needed us shapeshifters after all."

"So there are no soldiers coming?" Hal said.

"Not even to fly us out here, no. We're on our own." She looked around. "So where's Abi and Miss Simone?"

"Miss Simone's still missing. Abi's looking for her."

"And what are *you* doing?"

Hal felt his face heat up. "Um . . . well, nothing much."

Lauren batted him on the shoulder. "You're useless. Get to work, Hal. I'll be back with the others in . . ." She peered at the distant speck in the sky. "Maybe half an hour?"

She flew off, leaving Hal to digest what she'd told him. It was probably a good thing Briskle had refused to get involved. Helicopters thundering through the sky, bullets tearing through the castle, missiles blowing things up . . . It would be over in no time, but at what cost?

Hal shook himself and looked for Abigail. He found her way out over the bay, hovering slowly as she searched the water for signs of Miss Simone.

After transforming, he stomped down the beach and waded deeper and deeper until the waves lapped as high as his neck. Then he ducked under and swam this way and that, holding his breath and peering into the gloom. The sea had been clear until the triton's storm. Now it was cloudy and littered with all manner of things from destroyed homes.

Still, he could see well enough that his search was fast and wide-sweeping. Miss Simone wasn't here.

He worried that she'd been taken prisoner again. Maybe she'd been knocked senseless by the surge of water and snatched by the triton. Or maybe she'd drowned. *Could* mermaids drown? They breathed air like humans, but they could hold their breath underwater for a long time.

Glimpsing a shape flitting about above the water, he stuck his head out and sprayed a salty mist over Abigail, who squealed and shot upward.

"Eew!" she exclaimed.

Hal chuckled in a way most dragons were unaccustomed to. The light, humorous moment felt good for all of two seconds. Then they grew serious again.

"Where can she be?" Abigail said, hovering nearby. "She had an arrow stuck in her shoulder. I hope she didn't bleed out or anything."

Hal wanted to say there was no way she would have bled out with a simple arrow wound to the shoulder. He shook his head and huffed.

A roar echoed across the bay. Both Hal and Abigail glanced up at the castle on the cliff. They were too close, the angle too steep to see anything in the courtyard. Perhaps a giant was wandering about up there, a ferocious beast Hal had missed in his quest to render the blood samples harmless. He paused, trying to remember which ones he'd ignored . . .

Leaving the triton blood alone had obviously been a big mistake on his part. That thing had to be captured somehow. The cyclops? At twice the height of a man, the one-eyed giant had smashed down the door to the tower's bedroom. It wasn't to be trifled with. Nor was the minotaur.

The unicorn and faun were almost comical in terms of fearsome monsters, and the half-completed centaur was a joke. The manticore and lamia, impressive though they were, wouldn't stand in Hal's way for long.

Overall, then, only the triton so far promised to be a real nuisance. The rest were easy to deal with, at least while Hal was in dragon form.

But what else was up there?

A dragon.

The memory of Queen Bee handing the dragon's blood to Croaker gave him a chill. Was that the roar he'd heard?

With renewed urgency, Hal slipped under the water and resumed his hunt. He had to find Miss Simone while he had the chance. If she had an arrow stuck in her shoulder, perhaps she'd descended to the seabed to rest.

He scoured the sandy floor for ages, back and forth to the immense cliff and around its base, even checking the underwater entrance to the tunnels that led up to the castle. He found nothing. Even the triton had vanished.

When he popped back to the surface, gasping for breath, he guessed he'd been down twenty minutes or so. Everything had changed in his absence.

The *CloudDrifter* had arrived, a ponderous, elongated balloon the size of two houses. With its brown, leathery material stretched across a thin framework, Hal always thought it looked like the ribcage of a starving animal. Yet it also had a flimsy wicker cabin strapped underneath with long poles sticking out the sides, from which hung sails, so in some ways it resembled a giant, floating fish.

Nobody had come to greet the arriving shapeshifters. Instead, the townsfolk looked positively hostile toward them. A goblin, one Hal recognized as Flatfoot, had climbed down a peg-rope ladder and was, with Lauren's help, busy tying off the airship to a few remaining promenade struts. Many other faces peered out from the tiny openings in the wicker cabin—Fenton, Emily, Dewey, Thomas, Blair, and a few Hal couldn't quite make out. As for Darcy, he guessed she was sitting in a corner clinging to a support pole, suffering from 'height fright.'

His friends were here at last!

Hal suddenly found himself gripped by a monstrously strong current. It tugged him sharply downward, and he barely had time to take a breath and snatch a glance at something terrifying before the sea closed over his head.

What he'd glimpsed confirmed his earlier fear—a huge, fire-breathing dragon heading toward the beach.

Chapter Thirteen
Dragon Attack

Hal caught only a glimpse of the dragon that was headed toward the beach. Then he was once again sucked downward by a powerful underwater force. He thrashed and flailed in an attempt to break free, but the current continued to pull at him even when he was belly-down on the sloping seabed. He dug his claws in and watched in amazement as he left behind two deep trenches in the sand that slowly collapsed amid an ever-growing murky cloud.

He glanced over his shoulder, convinced some great monster had hold of his ankles. But no, it was just an extremely powerful undercurrent.

The triton appeared, blowing into his conch shell. This time he was not alone. He sat upon the back of a whalelike creature longer than Hal, something with long flippers at the front and a slender fishtail at the back. Its head struck him as odd, though—not a whale at all, but a giant horse.

A seahorse, he thought. *No, wait—a hippocampus.*

He remembered the conversation between the two scrag scientists up at the castle. The one named Croaker had said he'd wanted to be a hippocampus and had explained exactly what one was. Now he was right here, his wish granted.

As large as it was, the seahorse monster seemed like a gentle giant, obviously nervous judging by its flared nostrils and wide eyes. The triton rode its back like some kind of fearless warrior, gripping its mane with one hand and his conch with the other. His fishtail weaved behind, giving the impression he wasn't so much riding the hippocampus as hanging on for dear life. Still, somehow he spurred his anxious steed toward Hal until they were floating alongside.

Communication was impossible. The triton laughed and jeered, and Hal growled back, but that was the extent of it. Every time the triton stopped blowing into the conch shell, the undercurrent lessened slightly, and for just a second Hal felt it might be possible to break away. But then the moment was lost as the triton continued blowing with renewed vigor.

The towering cliff receded into the murky background and the sea deepened over Hal's head as he once more clawed at the soft sand. He tried breathing fire at the hippocampus, hoping to scare it and make it buck, but his flames barely crossed the gap before fizzling out in a ferocious column of bubbles. The triton laughed again.

Growing angrier by the second, all Hal could think about were his friends on the beach—or worse, still in the *CloudDrifter*, easy prey for a swooping dragon. But what could he do?

Well, if he couldn't break away from the powerful current, he could at least turn around and face front. He twisted and wriggled and finally managed it. The triton's grin faded a little, and Hal felt the surrounding water tighten its hold on him. He felt like he was inside an endless glass tube, its walls narrowing. Even facing front, he found he was unable to veer sharply away and escape.

And so, with growing frustration, Hal had no choice but to accompany the hippocampus and its rider farther out to sea. He jerked sideways often, testing the watery barrier. He thumped hard with his tail, finding his movements equally restricted. He tried to spread his wings and create more drag, but when he successfully managed to slow down, the triton just blew harder.

Hal did a double take. The triton's amusement had vanished. Now a frown plastered his face, and his conch-blowing developed longer and longer pauses. He was tiring! Maybe soon he would keel over and faint with exhaustion.

Yeah, right, Hal thought. But he watched the triton closely after that, waiting for an opportunity as he was dragged alongside the hippocampus. The seahorse glanced at him occasionally, then hurriedly looked away.

The triton paused again and hung his head, clearly taking a moment to rest. Hal felt the water pressure ease around him. He slowed just a little, and that was what caused the triton to resume his blowing.

A minute later, the triton paused again. Hal kept his eyes front. This time, when he felt the pressure ease, he flicked his tail gently to keep his speed going, matching the hippocampus's effortless pace. The triton's rest break lengthened, and for thirty seconds everything was peaceful and orderly. Out of the corner of his eye, Hal saw the triton glancing over. The scrag shapeshifter was probably surprised and pleased at how well his untested magic worked even when he wasn't blowing into the conch.

You keep thinking that, doofus, Hal thought.

Apart from the occasional blow, the triton seemed pretty relaxed now. The watery tunnel seemed to have evaporated for the most part, but Hal kept moving anyway, keeping up the pretense. He only had one shot at this.

When he acted, he acted fast. He veered toward the hippocampus and upward, extending his jaws. Shock flooded the triton's face as he hurriedly lifted the conch shell to his lips, but it was too late—Hal snatched him between his jaws and crunched down, forcing out a watery wail and causing the scrag to flail wildly. The shell tumbled away, sinking to the seabed.

Hal felt a moment of triumph. Ha! Now the triton had no power. He might go hunting for the shell again, though, so it would be best to take him away from this place, maybe dump him miles inland so that—

Something large and powerful slammed into his side, and he gasped, letting go of the triton. He twisted around to find the hippocampus already hurrying away again, its ears flattened, nostrils spurting columns of bubbles.

Hal swept his paws through the water, but the slippery, scaly triton was too fast, darting all over the place while trailing a cloud of blood. A second later, both the hippocampus and triton had disappeared into the murky distance.

"No!" Hal growled with frustration.

Well, maybe it would be all right. The triton was injured and might take a while to find his conch shell or another like it. And the hippocampus was no threat to anyone on land even if it came back.

Hal rocketed upward. When he burst out of the sea, he brought up his wings and began flapping to keep the momentum going. He soared higher, free of the ocean at last.

Land was miles away. He angled toward the distant cliff, shocked to see columns of black smoke lifting into the sky from the sprawling town below. There was no sign of the *CloudDrifter*, but everything was too distant to see clearly.

Where had the dragon gone? It had left a trail of destruction in its wake—numerous blackened rooftops and raging fires plus a haze of black smoke, all adding to Brodon's misery—but the dragon hadn't stuck around for long. Nor had the residents. The streets were deserted, as was the beach.

The *CloudDrifter* lay scattered in ruins on the sand. Hal thumped down nearby, terrified of finding his friends' charred corpses. But they, too, were missing. A morbid thought occurred to Hal. Had the dragon *eaten* them?

He couldn't believe that. Anyone else might assume such a thing had to be true, but being part dragon himself, he knew even the hungriest overweight adult couldn't eat more than a handful at one time.

As he stood there pondering, poking through the airship's splintered debris and sniffing at the sand as if it might yield some answers, he heard a tiny voice followed by a high-pitched whining buzz.

"Abigail?" he exclaimed, spinning around. His tail accidentally whacked the shattered wicker cabin, sending bits flying into the air.

He thought he heard a gasp and cry of fright.

"No, it's okay, it's *me*," he clarified. Of course he managed only the usual grunts and growls, so he reverted to his human form and stood there in his own dragon footprints in the sand, his arms outstretched. "See? It's just me."

Abigail came buzzing up in her tiny form. She grew as she approached, then landed lightly in front of him. "Please tell me that wasn't you just now."

Hal looked around at the deserted beach, the demolished seafront houses, the random fires and trails of smoke. "This? No way! What attacked you just now was a *scrag* dragon."

Abigail moved closer. "I thought so, but you and that other dragon look *exactly* alike."

"We would," Hal said grimly. "We came from the same blood sample. Miss Simone had a double-sized batch of it. That was a scrag just now." A name clicked into place. "Seth, I think. A boy my age."

"So where were *you*?"

"Underwater, held down by the triton." He frowned, looking around again. "Where is everybody?"

"I heard somebody yelling about hiding in basements. The dragon crashed right through the *CloudDrifter*, then came back to burn it. We all jumped clear and scattered in every direction."

As she said this, faces appeared up and down the beach. Fenton and Thomas emerged from part of a roof that had washed away down the sand. Emily, Darcy, and Molly crept out from under what remained of the promenade. Lauren came flying down from the sky, her white feathers flashing in the sunlight, and behind her came Blair with his scarlet, gold-tipped wings. Dewey, in centaur form, clip-clopped from an alleyway between crippled houses and stamped down onto the beach. It was only then that Hal spotted two goblins, Blacknail and Flatfoot, sitting morosely nearby, the airship's deflated balloon skin draped over them. As for Robbie, he popped out from behind a small upturned boat.

"Still no Miss Simone?" Hal asked Abigail.

She shook her head and opened her mouth to say something. Just then a voice rang out—a man's voice full of anger. "You! Stay where you are!"

Brodon residents had appeared, spilling out of the alleys and picking their way around debris. They were led by a very large, very familiar man with short, black hair. He puffed and panted his way down the sloping beach.

"You there!" Mayor Priggle shouted. "Stop this at once!"

Hal and Abigail exchanged a glance. "See?" Abigail whispered. "You're in big trouble."

When the big man finally arrived, temporarily out of breath, Hal used the opportunity to explain. "It wasn't me. It was another dragon. I was—"

He got no further. "I was right," the mayor shouted, making sure the nearest Brodon residents could hear him. They crowded behind almost like they were trying to stay in the mayor's shadow. "The shapeshifters of Carter are here to attack us. Arrest this boy! Arrest them all!"

"Now, hold on just a minute," Molly said, hurrying closer with her veil flapping wildly. Hal caught a glimpse of her eyes and was glad she had no magic at the moment. "Mayor Priggle, you've got it all wrong—"

Men shoved forward from the crowd and made a grab for her. She struggled but was no match for them. More townsfolk joined in the fray, intercepting the other shapeshifters as they ambled closer. Robbie hadn't gotten close enough yet, and he stopped dead when someone pounced on Fenton and nearly knocked him down. Another grabbed Thomas and held his arms tight. Darcy squirmed in the clutches of a fierce old woman. Lauren and Blair, who were still airborne, flapped away like startled birds. Dewey, in centaur form, stood quite still and challenged potential attackers with a surprisingly hard stare.

Somebody lunged at Abigail, but she zipped straight upward and smiled down at him, annoyingly playful even in this serious moment.

Nobody went for Hal, though. The mayor seemed to notice this and edged forward, his hands up and voice calm as though he were dealing with a cornered animal. "Easy, boy, easy. Just come with me for questioning, all right? You don't want to hurt anybody else. It's over."

Hal scowled at him. "I haven't hurt anybody. Don't you get it? It's the scrags! They're all shapeshifters now."

"And I suppose that was a 'scrag' just now, burning up our town and tearing through rooftops?" The mayor shook his head. "I don't know much about dragons, but we all saw it, and we saw you come back and land and change into the boy you are right now. And here you stand before us, lying to our faces."

"It wasn't me!"

The mayor grabbed Hal's shirt. "You caused that storm in the water earlier. We all saw you pop out of the sea right after and fly off. It was you—just like it was you that attacked our town a few minutes ago. Enough, now. You've caused enough damage, and someone is dead."

The news of that death hit Hal like a sledgehammer. He fought to keep from choking up. "I would never kill anyone. You have to believe me."

"You flooded the town!" the mayor shouted in his face, spittle flying loose. "What did you expect would happen? It's a miracle you didn't burn anyone to death just now!"

Abigail buzzed closer. "Now that you mention it, that dragon did seem kind of reluctant to hurt people. Did you notice how it smashed and burned things but deliberately avoided going after people when they ran to hide?"

The mayor glared at her, and she rose into the air, well out of his reach. "Perhaps your dragon friend developed a conscience in the last few minutes," he said sarcastically. "But he's still a murderer."

Molly found her voice again, though she spoke directly to the townsfolk rather than their mayor. "Don't listen to him. We're here only to help. The real enemy is up there at the castle. That gang of ruffians has figured out how to become shapeshifters, and now they're experimenting."

"They were already shapeshifters," someone shouted, "and they're here to protect us against *you*."

"No, no, they only said they were shapeshifters to gain your trust and earn a place to live. They knew they *would* be shapeshifters very soon, so they lied. Everyone is in grave danger."

"Ask the caretakers," Hal added. "They saw what was going on in the castle. They know Queen Bee is a liar. Ask them! They'll tell you—"

"Enough!" the mayor roared. "Take them away."

That was easier said than done. Thomas abruptly transformed and sent his captor scrambling backward in horror as a long, segmented tail with a stinger rose up and bristled with poison-tipped quills. The manticore swung around and let out a deep, throaty growl.

Next to him, Fenton shifted to his ten-foot lizard form, black and sinister, with red eyes and a long, pointed snout. His thin tail whipped and coiled about as his own captor backed off with his jaw hanging open.

Darcy turned invisible, but for an instant she showed her true dryad form complete with an oddly jagged head rather like a tree trunk that had been snapped in two. Then she was gone, and the woman that held her blinked and rather stupidly let go. If Darcy wasn't free before, she certainly was now.

Emily thrashed her way loose and, with a vicious baring of fangs, turned on the man that held her. All scaly coils, she slid away across the sand leaving a series of repeating scuff marks.

"You might want to rethink that idea," Abigail told the mayor. "We've all had just about enough of being locked up."

Though no prison can be as bad as the one outside Carter, Hal thought, *with its vine creature and endless days and nights.*

The mayor looked fit to explode. He jerked around in a circle, seeing that every shapeshifter was free and the townsfolk stood confused and scared. He swung back to Hal and glared, then turned again to Molly, who seemed to be the only one still in the grip of a captor, though even that looked like a halfhearted attempt now. "Where's Simone? Perhaps she'll see reason."

"We don't know," Molly said truthfully. She wriggled free and stepped away. "She was struck by an arrow. I saw her trying to pull it out right before the storm hit and swept her away."

Abigail dropped lightly to the sand and stilled her wings. "A scrag shot her."

"Why?" the mayor demanded.

"Because we escaped."

Priggle threw up his hands and turned to his people. "You see? Our protectors had these people in custody—and they escaped and wreaked havoc on our town."

"No, that's not what happened," Abigail said. "We were just—"

At that moment, a screech from the sky caused everyone to jump and twist around. Hal expected to see the dragon again, half-hoped it *was* the dragon if only to prove his innocence, but it was something else entirely, something enormous and birdlike with four feathered wings.

Four wings, Hal thought in amazement. *Four!*

As it descended from the direction of the castle, all the shapeshifters and townsfolk alike let out a gasp of awe. This thing was bigger than a roc, maybe twice the size of Hal's adult dragon form. Its copper-colored wings worked in perfect harmony, the front set beating downward while those at the rear came up, and so on, over and over, in constant motion to keep this monster in the air.

Its feet weren't quite birdlike. They looked more like the paws of a lion, though it only had three wide-spread toes. The tail was flared outward like a peacock's, perhaps to slow its descent. But though it was odd seeing a four-winged, lion-toed bird, nothing stood out more unusual than its head.

"Is that . . . is that a *dog*?" Hal said at last.

Copper-colored fur covered the blunt muzzle and pricked ears. Short whiskers twitched as the dog-faced creature snarled and barked once or twice.

"It's a simurgh," Molly murmured. "Uncommon in these parts, but not all that rare. Simone knew of one. I'm not surprised she snatched a blood sample from it. Isn't it fabulous?"

Hal would have chosen a more apt word like *terrifying*. It made rocs look scrawny and feeble in comparison. When it landed on the beach, its feet sank deep and caused the ground to tremble. It stretched its neck, lowering its dog-head so it could glare at them all with wide, baleful eyes.

To everybody's surprise, a figure was revealed sitting high up on its neck. Queen Bee looked down at them. "Trouble, Mayor?"

After working his mouth up and down a few times, the mayor finally sputtered his reply. "You betcha! Where *were* you? Have you seen what's been going on here this morning? The storm? The dragon attack?"

The queen nodded. "Simone and her team snuck into the castle last night and drugged our drinks. A few of us woke to find them escaping. Unfortunately, nobody was in a fit state to react until just now." She patted the simurgh's neck, and as tiny as she was in comparison, the monster tilted its head and shook itself all over, obviously pleased by her touch.

Hal and his friends shouted their protests at the same time.

"She's lying!"

"Nobody drugged them!"

"Liar!"

Queen Bee went on, addressing the mayor and his people. "We saw the dragon-boy's water storm. A terrible thing. And then he went around burning homes?" She shook her head and glared at Hal. "What is *wrong* with you?"

"It wasn't me!" Hal yelled, indignation flaring again as the Brodon residents turned to look at him with disgust. "It was a triton! I nearly caught him, but he got away."

"How convenient," Queen Bee sniped.

"Dragons can't even cause water storms!" Hal went on, facing the crowd. "Whoever heard of a dragon causing water storms?"

"A hydra can," an unseen woman called from somewhere. "You're obviously related to the hydra."

"A hydra has six heads," Hal exclaimed, his voice beginning to crack as it rose in pitch. "Do I look like I have six heads?"

"No, but you do have two faces," the mayor snapped, apparently seizing his moment to take back control. "The face of an innocent young boy—and the face of a deadly, murdering dragon!"

He delivered this line with a great deal of melodrama, and the crowd reacted by raising their fists and pointing accusingly at Hal.

Abigail dropped to his side and clung to him. "Go, Hal," she whispered. "Nobody's interested in our side of the story. And that simurgh thing could peck us up like chickenfeed. Get out of here."

"And go where?" Hal said as the crowd's volume rose.

At Queen Bee's command, the simurgh took a step forward, its jowls wobbling ponderously and saliva hanging in long, thick threads. Four gigantic wings spread outward, casting them all in shadow.

"Permission to execute this boy?" the queen called.

"Don't be ridiculous," Molly shouted desperately. "Civilized people don't perform public executions at the drop of a hat. There should be a trial first, and only then—"

"Trials are for people," Queen Bee retorted. "We're talking about a dragon here. Dragons are animals, and when tame animals turn wild, we put them down. This dragon-boy has gone wild and needs to be put down."

Some of the crowd yelled their agreement. Others looked troubled. Even with the recent attacks on the town, it was obvious most people didn't like the idea of answering violence with violence. The angriest, noisiest ones were at the front, though. It was them the mayor watched in silence, looking like he couldn't make up his mind.

The queen made it up for him. She raised her voice and announced, "I think that settles it. Kill the dragon-boy!"

Chapter Fourteen
Pursuit

The simurgh, twice the size of Hal's dragon, took a couple of giant steps toward him. Everybody scattered. Molly and the other shapeshifters shouted at Hal to get away.

Hal felt paralyzed as he watched the four-winged monster open its massive dog-jaws and lunge at him. He was aware of Abigail screaming in his ear and trying to push him aside. At the last instant, Hal transformed and hunkered down, knowing it was already too late to launch.

The jaws closed on him—but now he was much bigger than the simurgh had anticipated, too big to stretch its doglike mouth around. Hal shuffled around until he was facing the creature eye to eye. He snarled, and the simurgh snarled back. They stood like that a moment, and Queen Bee began screeching at her scrag shapeshifter. "What are you waiting for? Kill him!"

Hal breathed fire in its face as he backed off and spread his wings. He glimpsed Abigail buzzing around, once more in tiny form. Everyone else—shapeshifters and townsfolk—were running to a safe distance on the beach.

Once Hal had room, he sprang into the air and pumped his wings. Behind him, the simurgh snapped at his tail, missed, and launched after him. Hal was smaller and faster, but once the simurgh picked up momentum, it quickly caught up and came alongside with Queen Bee urging it on.

She was playing with him. He could tell by the huge grin on her face. "Fly, Hal!" she shouted. "You'll never outrun us!"

He was pretty sure she was right. He could dive into the sea where he doubted the simurgh could follow, but where would that get him? Once again he marveled at how quickly and easily a scrag shapeshifter had mastered his alter-form. It wasn't fair.

Still, Hal had a few tricks up his sleeve. He darted this way and that, testing his opponent's maneuverability. He blasted fire at it, and the monster shrugged off the flames as a minor irritation. He hammered it with his club-ended tail, and the simurgh refused to bat an eyelid. At one point he even flew close and raked his claws across the giant's flanks. He succeeded in pulling a few copper feathers loose and leaving faint scratches.

The queen laughed and laughed at his efforts as they all spun and circled over the town of Brodon. The beach lay far below, the residents no bigger than ants.

Hal had something in mind. It had worked with the triton and hippocampus, and it might work again now. He veered sideways and upward, climbing to avoid the flapping wings. When he was precisely centered overtop, with Queen Bee twisting to look up at him, he dropped and made a grab for her. She screamed and squirmed, and the simurgh suddenly took a dive so that Hal's claws never quite made contact with her. The trio ended up plummeting toward the beach, and Hal twisted and turned in unison with the simurgh all the way down.

No matter how much he tried to increase his speed, he just couldn't catch up. When he breathed fire, it just blew back in his face.

Then the simurgh did something unexpected. It angled so sharply downward that it fell vertically, then looped under and flew away upside down, twisting and turning as it went, Queen Bee hanging on for dear life. Hal might have been able to copy that maneuver if he'd had time to think about it, but instead he continued plummeting toward the beach.

For a moment it seemed there was a standoff in the sky. Then Queen Bee urged her scrag back to business, and the simurgh came after Hal with a vengeance. He guessed there would be no more teasing and messing about.

He headed for the castle. If he couldn't grab Queen Bee off the simurgh's back or outmaneuver it, he would just have to try something else. Maybe if he squeezed into a place too small for it to follow . . .

He smashed his way into the castle through another of those great windows in the great hall. Skidding across the floor, he came to a stop in the center of the room, panting hard. A few scrags yelled and ran for cover. A manticore sped past, and seconds later he spotted a lumbering one-eyed giant of a man who ducked and fled through a narrow doorway. Then Hal was alone.

Except for the simurgh, which hurtled through the same window, taking out part of the frame and wall in an explosion of dust and chunks of stone. The monster thudded into Hal, and they both slid across the floor until they hit the opposite wall. Another window cracked as they tumbled and fought. Queen Bee fell from her perch and scrambled away.

Hal snapped and breathed fire and roared with all his might, knowing he couldn't keep this dog-headed bird at bay for long. Its wings were huge, though, and they constantly brushed the high ceiling and got in the way. Hal, being half the size, had more room to thrash about. Still, he had no plans to stick around.

When an archway presented itself to him, he abruptly reverted to human form and rolled through it. He glimpsed a very surprised simurgh before darting off down a passage.

"Come get me!" he yelled over his shoulder.

The passage was short and turned sharply to the right. Around the corner, he came face to face with the minotaur and realized he'd put himself in a different kind of danger. He couldn't transform within these narrow corridors of stone, and he was no match for the minotaur even though it still sported a crooked horn and a mass of matted blood. Hal spun and sprinted back the way he'd come, and the bull-headed man snorted and thundered after him.

Dashing back out into the great hall, he found the simurgh still there, practically filling the entire place, facing the passage Hal emerged from. He ran past the monster before it had a chance to react and was already heading up the grand staircase as it started barking and twisting around to snap at him.

A small creature came down the stairs—a half-sized, goat-legged man with curled horns. It yelled at Hal as he ascended. *Great*, he thought, racing up to meet it. *A faun with attitude.*

He paused while the faun dipped its head and charged down the steps. Hal simply hopped sideways and gave it a shove, and the faun fell and tumbled the rest of the way down the flight to the bottom. The minotaur appeared then and gave a hearty bellow. Hal hurried on up.

Around the landing, he came across the lamia. He searched her expression. Was she afraid of him as she had been before? He wasn't sure.

She licked her lips. He saw hunger in her eyes, and he backed off. But he also saw fear. "I'll burn you," he warned.

"I know," she said. "But . . . I'm so hungry."

The minotaur howled on the staircase behind him.

"Let me past," Hal said, advancing toward the lamia.

Now it was her turn to back off. She glanced from side to side, flicking her grey, reptilian tail. Her shoulder muscles twitched. Behind her stretched a corridor with any number of doorways to hide behind and probably rooms with windows to escape out of.

Hearing the minotaur coming around the landing and up the final short flight of wide steps, Hal lunged toward the lamia with a sheet of flame. She flinched and cowered, and he marched past. Trembling, she said, "Please—I need to eat! It has to be healthy young blood. I'll die if I—"

"Can't help you," Hal retorted.

As the minotaur snorted again, Hal hurried along the corridor and rushed into the nearest room on the right, some kind of study with bookcases and a desk. He slammed the door behind him. There was no key, so he rushed to the window and pressed his face to the glass, seeing the ocean below.

Hadn't he been here before? Not this exact room, but certainly this situation. Was he really going to leap out again?

The door flew open behind him, and the minotaur snorted and roared. Like a bull, the scrag stamped and scraped at the floor, kicking back some imaginary dust while lowering his head and thrusting his horns forward.

Hal climbed up onto the windowsill and fumbled with the latch. There was no balcony outside this room, just a long, uninterrupted drop. It should be a little easier this time—if he could get the latch open! He jiggled and yanked on it, panic rising as the minotaur thundered across the room toward him.

At the last moment, Hal abandoned the window and jumped aside, rolling on the floor in his effort to get away. An explosion of glass and wood indicated the minotaur had crashed through it instead. Hal popped back up to find the bull-headed man leaning precariously over the sill, howling as he tried to pull his damaged horn free of the framework. Long shards stuck out of the wood.

Hal charged him—and bounced right off. He wasn't big and heavy enough to shift this mountain of a man. However, when the minotaur yanked his horn free, the scrag's hand slipped off the windowsill and caused him to lose his balance. He flailed, grunted, and finally toppled backward out of the window, taking some of the glass fragments with him.

A silence followed. Hal rushed forward and leaned out to see the minotaur crashing into the sea far below. Then he was gone.

Hal watched for half a minute until he heard noises outside the room.

"Where is he?" a woman's voice shouted from faraway. Queen Bee was on his trail. Muted voices replied to her, and she shouted, "Well, get after him!"

The lamia appeared then, blocking the doorway as she stared at Hal. "I'll hide you," she said quietly. "Get behind the desk."

"Not you again," he said as he turned to climb out of the window. There he paused, looking at the fragments of glass poking out of the frame. Some of them were bloody. He would need to be careful climbing out.

The lamia turned her back on him and faced the hallway, but she didn't yell out and bring scrags running. She just sat there. Hal wondered if perhaps she really did want to help him after all. And maybe she knew where the scrag dragon was. Besides, if she betrayed him, he could simply leap out of the window.

He ducked down behind the ornate desk and waited.

Footsteps stampeded the corridor. Queen Bee led the charge. A bizarre group of creatures and scrags hung close behind. "Where is he?" she demanded, looking straight at the lamia.

The grey, scaly-skinned cat shrugged. "Not sure. I heard someone pass by, but he was gone by the time I looked out."

"Gah!" the queen exclaimed, and carried on past. Trailing her, Hal spotted the cyclops, the manticore, a fully-transformed four-legged centaur, a tiny faun, a familiar blue-skinned elf, a thin creature the size of a small boy with large ears and long black hair that he thought was a brownie, plus a group of unchanged scrags. No doubt the unicorn had been told to stay outside rather than stampede about the castle waving its dangerous spiral horn about.

When they were gone, the lamia remained sitting by the door but turned to look over her shoulder. "Can you help me?"

Hal crept out. "How?"

"I need blood." She seemed pained by the idea. "I chose to be a lamia because I like cats. I was told I would be a giant cat. I didn't know I would keep the same face, the same human head. It's weird!" She grimaced. "And nobody told me I would crave human blood."

Hal found it hard to be sorry for her. "If you want blood, go chew on Queen Bee."

She scowled at him. "I don't *want* blood. I crave it. And I don't want to chew on anybody. I need to drink blood, not eat someone's flesh. That's repulsive."

Hal didn't know what to say to that.

"And it has to be young, innocent blood, not the tainted evil in adults. I don't know how I know this, but I do. If I try to drink nasty adult blood, I'll just reject it somehow. I need *young* blood."

"Yeah, so you keep saying." Hal was getting fed up with hearing it. "Look, you're not touching mine, all right? I'm sorry you crave blood, but that's what you get when you become a shapeshifter. You get weird urges. If you don't want that sort of thing, then be a scrag again. The craving should go away."

Queen Bee's voice echoed down the corridor again. "Check all the windows. Maybe he jumped out."

The lamia turned all the way around to face into the room. "How do I do that? How do I change back?"

Hal sighed. He didn't have time for this. He countered her question with one of his own. "Where's the dragon?"

She tilted her head, her silver hair hanging loose. "Seth, you mean? He's lying low. Queen Bee sent him to attack the town as soon as you were trapped underwater. You have to hand it to her—she came up with that plan on the fly. She sent Gruel and Croaker to trap you. We all stood up here watching to see if you'd go back into the water, and you did, and everyone cheered."

"Gruel is the triton, right?" Hal said. "Croaker is the hippocampus. And Seth is the kid?"

"About your age, yes. Queen Bee rescued him one day and made herself his guardian. He reminds her of the son she lost to the virus—"

As if on cue, the queen began screeching again. "Start over! He can't have shut and locked the window after himself if he flew out. There's either a window open somewhere, or he's still here. Get busy, people!"

The lamia edged into the room and pawed the door shut. It clicked softly, shutting out the stampeding feet on the corridor's stone floor. "Will you help me?" she asked.

Hal couldn't decide. "What's your name?"

"Lola."

Oh, yeah, I knew that already, Hal thought. "Why did Queen Bee make Seth into a dragon? I thought she would have kept that blood for herself."

"She dotes on Seth. The blood was supposed to be for Duke, but in the end she decided none of her Swarm was worth much of anything, so she gave it to her boy. He's a good kid and won't kill anyone, but she made him smash the town up to make it look deadly."

Footsteps outside in the corridor made Lola's eyes widen. "We're out of time. Help me. I don't want *this* anymore." She gestured at her sleek, reptilian body.

"Can you take me to Seth?" Hal asked.

"He's not here. If anyone in the town saw him return to the castle, it would be obvious he was one of us instead of you. Queen Bee wants everyone to think *you* caused all that damage."

"But why?"

"Because Gruel messed up."

"The triton?" Hal shook his head, confused. "I don't understand."

"Gruel got carried away. We saw everything from up here. He didn't realize his magic was so powerful. He caused the flood and someone got killed, so now the Brodon people are mad. Mad at us, the town's protectors! That's no good. But then *you* came out of the water and the people assumed *you* caused the flood. So Queen Bee went with the idea, and she thought she'd go ahead and make it worse for you, so she sent Gruel and Croaker after you, and they—"

"Dragged me underwater and made Seth burn things," Hal finished. "Where is he now? Can you take me to him?"

Lola nodded as footsteps sounded in the hall.

The door burst open. Queen Bee stood in the doorway, and for a moment she seemed confused as she glared at the lamia. "Why aren't you helping—?" Then she saw Hal. She jumped back and moved aside, shouting at the scrags and creatures behind her. "He's here! Get him!"

The giant cyclops doubled over to squeeze through the doorway, and though he was a formidable sight, he actually blocked the way for all the others and caused a delay. Hal darted toward the window and jumped up on the sill. "Coming?" he said to Lola.

The lamia seemed torn. But as the cyclops straightened up inside the doorway, she nodded and loped across the room.

Hal waited until she was perched on the windowsill with him, then said, "Grab hold."

It was a frenzied, awkward moment. He twisted to face the ocean while she gripped her front paws on his shoulders and leaned into him. They both tumbled forward, and Hal tried his best to remain belly down as he started to fall with her standing on his back as though he were some sort of magical surfboard.

When he transformed, she got a firmer grip on his much harder and broader back while he began flapping. In seconds he was soaring away from the castle.

"Where to?" he grunted.

Of course, Lola didn't answer. He was about to try again, perhaps formulate his dragon roars into something resembling human speech, when she let out a whimper. "It's Simmy."

Who the heck is Simmy?

He found out a second later when a volley of barks came from just behind him, and he twisted around to see the gigantic simurgh bearing down on him, snapping its jaws.

Simmy the simurgh? he thought. *Seriously?*

He ducked and swooped, trying to shake off his pursuer. Instead, the giant closed in on him, its four feathered wings pumping at crazy speeds. Hal had no choice but to dive for the sea.

Lola screamed. Any other time, Hal would have dropped in like a stone. Out of consideration for his passenger, he took a moment to slow his descent at the last second, skimming the surface before touching down and going under. The simurgh shot by overhead with another volley of barks.

Now underwater, Hal enjoyed the peace and solitude for all of half a minute before a shadow emerged from the gloom, swimming along at great speed with its curiously split fishtail. The triton was back. Meanwhile, Lola floundered nearby, her head above water.

Great, Hal thought. *All I want is to find Seth and take him to the mayor, to prove there's a second dragon and show it wasn't me who burned the town. How am I supposed to do that with Simmy the simurgh above the water and Gruel the triton below?*

Chapter Fifteen
Finding Seth

Seeing that Lola the lamia was floundering, Hal eased up underneath her and gave her a solid platform to stand on. She stood shaking and gasping as he trod water, a raft with huge leathery wings sticking up on either side like sails.

But the simurgh wouldn't let up in its quest to taunt and harass him. It swooped down again, dive-bombing him, and Hal sighed before ducking under and dropping his new friend in the sea again. Mindful that the triton was loitering somewhere, he waited until the simurgh's shadow passed overhead, then bobbed back to the surface where Lola splashed and panted. This time he offered her his tail, waving it in her face and making it obvious she should hang on.

She gripped hard, and he began paddling. He felt a little ridiculous, but he needed her. And right now she needed him.

When the simurgh came around, Hal ducked under and dragged her down with him. She let go immediately and went back to floundering. Growing impatient, Hal waited until the simurgh was gone, then reverted to his human form and swam to join her.

"You have to hang on," he gasped.

"I can't hold my breath like you can," she said, her teeth chattering.

He had to assume she was more scared than cold. "We can't stay out here all day," he told her. The beach was some way off, but the cliff loomed over them. No doubt Queen Bee was up there right now, looking down on him and ordering her drones to attack. What else did she have in store? "If you can hang on, I'll drag you away from here. Where should we head for? Where's Seth?"

"We'll never make it with Simmy flying around," she moaned. "And I'm so weak, I don't think I can stay above the water much longer."

"Sure you can," he said shortly. Unable to contain his curiosity, he said, "Hey, is Simmy really his name? Simmy the simurgh?"

She grimaced, looking annoyed. "He only chose that blood sample because he liked the word on the label. Turns out he chose well."

The simurgh was returning. Hal sighed. This routine was getting old.

At that moment, a hand gripped his ankle and yanked hard. The triton! He went under and nearly took in a mouthful of seawater as he flailed and kicked. He was about to transform when a face appeared in front of his—only it wasn't the triton's ugly mug. This face was beautiful and blue-eyed with long blond hair.

Miss Simone? he mouthed, astonished.

She smiled and pointed. He looked and did a double take.

Dozens of mermaids stared up at him from the depths of the sea. They floated silently, each very different but equally pretty. Blondes, redheads, brunettes, all draped with layers of thin, gauzy material that looked a little like sparkling seaweed. Miss Simone was the only one with a silky green dress and cloak, but even those had altered slightly to better suit her mermaid form and seemed to blend in perfectly with the mysterious underwater theme.

Three mermaids had a prisoner—the ugly triton, who struggled furiously to escape, a look of terror on his face. He had a bloody gash across his chest from when Hal had chewed on him earlier, but this seemed to be the last thing on the scrag's mind. He had to be completely out of his element in a situation like this. Despite mastering his new form and magical talent with relative ease, he had no experience with this underwater world and those who dwelled in it.

Miss Simone made a signal to follow her, but Hal shook his head and pointed to the lamia floating above. After a few more hand signals, he made it clear that she was on his side and they needed her help. After that, Miss Simone nodded and rose to the surface with Hal.

"Lola, we have help!" he gasped, popping out of the water.

Lola looked at Miss Simone with mounting concern. "*She* won't help me! Why would she?"

"Because Hal is vouching for you," Miss Simone told the lamia in a stern voice. She looked at Hal. "But she has a point. Why would I?"

The simurgh was approaching again. It flew low, dangling its three-toed lion-feet in the water and causing a spray.

"Can you make giant underwater air bubbles?" Hal asked Miss Simone. "So Lola can breathe?"

"We're mermaids, not miengu. Our powers are different. But wait here."

She ducked under, and the simurgh grew closer. Hal had to submerge again, and this time he was afraid the monster's feet would snatch him up if he didn't dive far enough. He felt the drag as the simurgh swept by, and when he returned to the surface, he found Lola weary and struggling to stay afloat.

"He snarled at me," she cried. "Simmy knows I'm helping you. I'm a traitor, and he's probably going to bite my head off next time he comes around."

"I'm surprised he hasn't already," Hal said.

"We go back a long way. He's angry that I've put him in this position. He doesn't want to hurt me, but if Queen Bee has ordered it . . ."

They floated together, bobbing around while the simurgh circled for yet another run at them. There was something different about it now. It moved slower, more deliberately, perhaps reluctant but determined to do its duty as a drone.

Four heads popped out of the water some distance away, smiling mermaids who looked up at the simurgh as they ran their hands through their hair. Water streamed down their faces, leaving behind dry locks that blew freely in the wind. The mermaids began to sing, each doing their own thing but in perfect harmony as if rehearsed many times before. Somehow their individual lyrics blended together and formed a whole, and the melody was both catchy and haunting, carrying easily across the sea.

Hal forgot all about the simurgh. He barely noticed the monster as he focused instead on the mermaids. Miss Simone and Lola faded from his periphery, too. Even the sound of the ocean dulled as the singing filled his head.

"Come on, Hal," a distant voice said. Dimly, he felt something tugging on his arm. "Wakey-wakey. Time to go."

"Huh?" he mumbled.

Miss Simone edged in front of him, blocking his view. The melodic voices seemed to fade a little, and he grew annoyed. "You're in the way!"

He tried to swim around her, but she slid smoothly through the water to intercept him. "Mermaid magic is powerful. Turn away and ignore it. They'll keep the simurgh busy while we go about our business."

It took all his effort to drag himself away from the singing. The giant simurgh had taken to hovering in place, something Hal didn't know it could do. All those fly-by attacks earlier . . . It must have enjoyed toying with them. Now it bobbed up and down twenty feet above the four mermaids, listening intently.

"Where are we going?" Miss Simone said in Hal's ear, shaking him from his trance. He almost swallowed water as he floundered, and Miss Simone grabbed him by the waist and held him in a hug, easily keeping him afloat. "What are we doing with this scrag?"

Lola was floundering, too, and with a click of her tongue, Miss Simone took a moment to duck under and call for assistance. Mermaids appeared all around, and soon both Hal and Lola were being carried along.

"Lola knows where Seth is," Hal said.

In the distance, the sound of the mermaid quartet drifted in and out on the wind, and when Hal glanced over his shoulder, he felt a pang of regret and longing. The simurgh was tiring, getting lower and lower, now only a few feet above the water.

"And who is Seth?" Miss Simone said in his ear.

Hal blinked and turned to face front again. "He's a scrag, about my age. He got the dragon blood." Miss Simone's eyes widened at this. "He attacked Brodon, but everyone thinks it was me because we look exactly the same, so now the whole town wants me dead. I figured if we found Seth, we could—"

"Prove your innocence?" Miss Simone finished. "Yes, well, Mayor Priggle may not want to know the truth. Or perhaps he *does* know the truth and doesn't care. In any case, we should still get that young scrag under control, so yes, finding Seth should be our priority. We can't have errant dragons." She glanced over her shoulder. "Or simurghs for that matter. Look."

With a splash, the monstrous bird with a dog's head touched down in the water and seemed to awaken, yelping in alarm and thrashing its four wings about, trying to lift off. This proved difficult, especially with four mermaids clinging to its feathery hide. The simurgh rose partway out of the sea, causing the mermaids to dangle their shimmering fishtails below, but the massive wings kept hitting the water and seemed unable to get coordinated. It eventually gave up and sank about halfway. The scrag named Simmy would probably have to paddle ashore and wade out before getting airborne again.

Hal eased back and enjoyed the ride. Miss Simone herself was propelling him through the water, her hands on his waist, and Lola the lamia had calmed down now that she was supported by other mermaids.

"Where did you go?" Hal asked Miss Simone. "We looked everywhere for you. We thought maybe that arrow had made you faint or something."

He caught a glimpse of her shoulder as she bobbed in the water next to him. The silky material was intact, though a little bloodstained. Once she'd pulled the arrow out, her smart clothes had repaired themselves nicely, along with the wound itself when she'd transformed.

"The arrow wasn't too much trouble," she said. "But a triton can be very bad news, as you saw with the water storm he generated. If a scrag shapeshifter can do that after transforming for the first time . . . well, there's no telling what else he can do."

Hal frowned. "What else *can* a triton do?"

"Apart from creating powerful currents? With the conch, he can call on virtually any weak-minded water-dwelling creature and lead them into battle."

An image of a passing whale and a few harmless dolphins sprang into Hal's mind. "And that's a problem?" he said doubtfully.

"Have you heard of a kraken? It's a general term applied to any giant of the seas. Some of the octopi in these parts are hundreds of feet long. Imagine one of those coming into the bay and pulverizing Brodon."

Now the picture in Hal's head changed to something far more destructive than a few leaping dolphins and a beached whale.

"Tritons are a scourge," Miss Simone said. "I knew I'd need assistance, so I went looking for mermaids."

Hal looked sideways at her and lowered his voice in case any were listening. The nearest were those carrying Lola, and they were submerged. "That must have been tough seeing as how you, uh . . . you know, don't like them much."

She nodded and whispered, "They've been helpful so far, but they're on the verge of being more trouble than they're worth. They have that look in their eyes."

Hal wasn't sure what 'that look' was exactly, but he imagined it to be a mischievous twinkle like Abigail often developed, only ten times worse.

Lola directed them around the cliff, leaving the simurgh behind. They all kept looking skyward, searching the castle windows for scrags, expecting to see Queen Bee leaning out. Hal took a moment to tell Miss Simone what the scrag shapeshifters had become. He proudly joked about the harmless faun, brownie, elf, even the unicorn and centaur, but sobered when he told of the minotaur, the cyclops, the manticore, the dragon, and of course the triton and simurgh.

"The minotaur fell from the window, so he's probably out of the picture for now," Hal said. "I don't think the hippocampus is going to be any trouble. He seemed pretty scared. He's probably gone for good. And Lola here seems to have switched sides."

"Yes, why *is* that?" Miss Simone asked.

The lamia flung her wet hair back and looked at them. "I just can't abide this hunger. Hal said he'd help me change back if I help him find Seth."

Miss Simone gave Hal a puzzled glance, and he shrugged.

The lamia wasn't finished. "I never asked for this. Leech lied to me. He said a lamia was a fabulous panther of legend. He never said anything about scaly skin or keeping the same face. And he definitely never mentioned feeding on *people*."

"What did you think you'd be feeding on?" Miss Simone said a little sarcastically. "What do all panthers feed on? Meat, that's what. You thought you'd be sitting down to dinner eating a nice salad while in panther form?"

"I didn't think about food at all," Lola protested. "Queen Bee made us write our names and put them in a hat, and she drew them out, and that decided the order of whoever got to choose next from the blood samples. Everyone wanted to be a dragon or a griffin. I didn't. I wanted to be something exotic and fierce but beautiful as well. Leech suggested a lamia and explained what it was. He said 'lamia' meant 'exotic panther,' but I think he lied."

Miss Simone snorted a laugh. "And these are the people you call friends?"

Lola was silent for a minute. The mermaids surged through the water carrying their passengers, and the castle fell far behind as they headed south along the rocky coastline to an unknown destination.

"Queen Bee's been good to me," Lola said at last. "She's a good leader. She has a quick temper, but she's fierce and loyal. It's just some of her drones I have issues with, like that Leech, who lied about—"

"There's a ship!" Hal exclaimed, spotting an old, wooden vessel leaning to one side just off the rocks in the distance. Clearly it was grounded, judging by the complete lack of motion.

"I remember hearing about this," Miss Simone murmured. "These mermaids do, too. They caused the wreck years ago. No wonder they're giggling so much."

"That's where Seth is," Lola said.

Hal looked for a dragon loitering on the deck but saw nothing.

Miss Simone was deep in thought. "I don't understand what Queen Bee *wants* from all this. She went to great lengths to take hostages, imprison us, and put on a charade here in Brodon while she worked on a plan for her Swarm to become shapeshifters. But *why*? What's her endgame?"

Lola shrugged. "Acceptance. A place to call home."

"I don't believe you."

The lamia shot her a glare. "I don't care if you believe me or not."

Hal jumped in before the two women could erupt into a full-blown argument. "It's just a bit hard to believe that all you want is a place to settle down."

"Why?" Lola demanded.

"Because all you people ever do is cause trouble and hurt people. It's like you enjoy it."

"When you live in an abandoned city with nothing but other gangs trying to survive, of course we have to put on a tough act. But don't you think we'd prefer to give up the violence and—"

"Become farmers?" Miss Simone finished with another of her derisive snorts. "Forgive me if I find that very difficult to swallow. Your queen continually does things that suggest you're all nothing but criminals."

"Such as?" Lola demanded, her voice rising. "Everything she does is for a good reason. She may come across as ruthless, and she is, but not because she's sick and twisted and enjoys it. She usually has a very good reason."

"Like destroying half a town and killing innocent people in a tidal wave?"

Miss Simone's voice had risen, too, and her question cut deep. Lola scowled and looked away.

"You see?" Miss Simone said to Hal. "She has no answer for that."

The lamia heaved a sigh. "Queen Bee was seriously irritated with Gruel for creating the water storm. She had to think fast, and she used Seth to—"

"Gruel is the triton," Hal interjected for Miss Simone's benefit.

Lola nodded. Her scowl lifted slightly. "Yeah. Queen Bee was furious with him. Destroying our new home and killing people wasn't part of her plan. It still isn't. Gruel went too far. He pretty much sabotaged the entire thing. The town isn't going to accept us if we destroy half of it first! Queen Bee spent ten minutes shouting obscenities down at him. Gruel was lucky he stayed in the sea or he would have been stung to death ten times over. In the end, Queen Bee came up with a new plan and threw Croaker over the wall." She grinned at this. "Did you hear him screaming on the way down? Probably not—it was around the far side of the castle. But he transformed before he hit the water just as Queen Bee expected. Then he and Gruel waited for you underwater, Hal. And while they kept you down there with them, she sent Seth to pretend he was you."

"To cause *more* damage?" Miss Simone said incredulously. "That's her solution? To right a wrong with another wrong?"

"To make it look like *you'd* done it," Lola murmured. "And it worked. The town is out for Hal's blood, and the Swarm is looking good right now."

Hal and Miss Simone exchanged a glance again. The scrags really did have a twisted way of ingratiating themselves into a society. "What's wrong with just showing up in town and asking to be accepted?" Miss Simone asked, more gently now, a hint of sadness in her voice.

"We tried that," Lola said bitterly. "We went to three different towns farther south. Nobody wanted us. They said we looked like trouble."

The mermaids were making good progress. Hal had been so focused on the conversation that he'd barely noticed the journey. The castle had receded into the distance behind them, and the ship loomed close ahead.

"Will Queen Bee come after us?" he worried aloud.

"Definitely," Lola said. "She's probably screaming at a few of her drones right now, telling them to get their act together and shapeshift. They'll be along soon, I promise."

"Who will?" Hal said. "Or *what* will?"

Before Lola could answer, Miss Simone exclaimed that she'd seen something moving near the grounded ship. It was a fairly big vessel with two masts, though the rigging was tangled and useless now, the sails nothing but ragged strips blowing in the wind. It reminded Hal of the galleons he'd seen in books, though smaller and probably a lot simpler. A gash down one side let the rolling waves flood in. Rocks poked up all around.

On those rocks behind the ship, something lurked—something Hal's size and shape, a large, dark-green reptilian creature with a knobby backbone and impressive leathery wings. Sticking out to the side was a long, thick tail with a triangular-shaped hunk of bone on the end. The ship was not quite big enough to successfully hide an adult dragon.

"There's Seth," Lola said.

"Thanks," Miss Simone muttered. "I don't think anybody would have guessed if you hadn't said that."

Lola shot her an even more heated glare than before. "I don't like you."

Miss Simone ignored her. She released Hal, and he found himself floundering again. "This is something you'll need to deal with, Hal," she said.

Several mermaids popped up around Lola, still holding onto her but looking on with interest as Hal paddled away from the group. As Miss Simone had suggested, they had a gleam in their eyes, clearly excited by the prospect of a confrontation between dragons.

Hal transformed. Looking around, he was surprised to find at least twenty more mermaids underwater with him, floating silently. They'd been following all this time? They, too, had a look of anticipation about them.

He turned his back on them and swam toward the shipwreck. There was no sand here, just mounds of jagged rock that clung to the vessel's wooden hull. Once in a while, Seth's tail would plop into the water. Hal headed for it, hoping to come up behind and surprise the boy.

As he motored smoothly through the water, he thought about his next move. Surprise Seth, and then what? It really depended on how Seth reacted.

A ridge of rocks surrounded the ship. He emerged from the rolling waves and stood up on hind legs, rising high. Seth noticed him immediately and jumped in alarm, swinging to face him, his feet half hanging off the narrow, rocky ledge he stood on. His tail whipped around and put a dent in the ship's rotting hull.

"I don't want to fight," Hal said. For once he expected his guttural dragon grunts to be fully understood.

To his surprise, Seth cocked his head to one side, clearly bewildered.

Hal tried again. "I have to take you to Brodon and prove that it wasn't me who attacked earlier. You have to tell everyone you're in Queen Bee's gang."

Again, Seth stared.

And then it dawned on Hal that the ability to speak a language couldn't be passed on with a simple infusion of blood and DNA. On this matter, the new Shapeshifter Program showed its limits. The scrags had done so well to master the complexities of their new forms and come up fighting, but it seemed they were destined to fall short when it came to a simple conversation.

However, though the boy couldn't understand what Hal was saying, apparently he had no trouble speaking. It made sense. He just opened his mouth, said what was on his mind, and grunts emerged. Grunts that Hal understood.

Bite me, Seth said.

"I will if you keep that up," Hal replied.

In truth, he was worried. What was Seth like, exactly? Was he a tough kid like Fenton, or a pushover like Dewey? Hal had never been much of a fighter and had never needed to be except where Fenton was concerned. Could he take on a boy his age in a fair fight?

Then he realized it made no difference how tough Seth was. The boy was a shapeshifter. He was a dragon. And not just *any* dragon, but the *exact same* dragon as Hal, a perfect copy, cloned from the same blood sample.

If a fight was imminent, he would literally be fighting himself.

Chapter Sixteen
Clones

Hal stood on a cluster of submerged rocks, up to his thighs in seawater. His opponent took a similar stance on taller rocks that projected out of the water alongside the rotting shipwreck.

"Have you ever messed with a dragon before?" Hal asked him.

Naturally, Seth didn't understand a word.

"I've been to the Labyrinth of Fire," Hal rumbled in his deepest, most menacing voice. "I've tangled with real dragons. I met the emperor. I might not look any different than you, but I have a lot more experience at this sort of thing."

Seth cocked his head again, and Hal recognized a puzzled look on the dragon's face.

He went on anyway. "Flying around smashing up a few houses is nothing. I'm warning you, Seth. Make me mad and I'll tear you to bits."

He let that threat hang for a second while Seth glared at him. The actual words might have been lost in translation, but Hal's tone was clear.

"Your side is losing," he said. He decided it might be a good idea to mention scrags by name. Maybe they would filter through somehow. "Simmy the simurgh is stuck in the water, Gruel the triton is being held prisoner by a bunch of mermaids, the minotaur guy is probably floating around dead after falling out of a castle window, and half your gang doesn't know what it's doing. Even Lola the lamia has switched sides. How do you think I found you?"

Seth remained silent.

"It's over," Hal finished. "So quit standing there trying to look tough and come with me. Look, all you did was a bit of damage. You didn't kill anyone. Nobody's going to come down too hard on you."

He had no idea if that was true or not. He also had no idea how the Brodon people would contain a dragon shapeshifter even if they wanted to. One of those iron collars would be useful but only if Seth could be persuaded to revert to his human form.

Are you done talking gibberish? Seth demanded.

Hal's heart sank. So they'd have to fight after all. The logistics of bringing down a dragon and transporting it over the cliffs to Brodon weighed on him. Well, one step at a time. First he had to—

Without warning, Seth blasted a fireball at him. Hal flinched, feeling the searing heat on his head. He had no choice but to duck sideways and launch into the water to cool off.

He turned the evasive maneuver into an attack by swimming hard underwater and circling around until he was barreling toward the ship. Then he exploded from the sea and spread his wings.

Momentum carried him straight toward Seth, and he let loose with fire of his own, a long, controlled stream that engulfed his opponent. Hal smacked into him with his claws ready, and the two of them toppled against the hull of the ship. Wood splintered. Seth roared with pain and anger. Smoke poured off his blackened scales as he tried to get back on his feet, but Hal rolled on top and pounded at him, clubbing him down and snapping at his neck, trying to get a good chokehold.

Every blow he administered made him feel bad, but sometimes the least damaging way to end a fight was to attack with such ferocity that the other submitted quickly. So he pummeled Seth without mercy, listening for the boy's pleas to stop.

They never came. Instead, Seth squirmed and roared and tried to blast fire every chance he got. He started using his tail, whacking aimlessly and sometimes connecting with the back of Hal's head. He got a hind leg in position and shoved hard, pushing Hal up and off, and then he started swinging his own paws, long claws fully extended.

Amid the thudding blows, Hal felt a sharp pain under his chin in a relatively weak part of his armored hide. Then another. Fire blazed in his face, and the searing heat burned his eyes, forcing him to clamp them shut and look away, which meant the side of his face and one ear started burning as well.

He rolled away, hitting the rocks as he fell into the sea. Smoke poured off his blistering face, and he panicked when he realized he couldn't open one eye. The pain was terrible. All he could think about now was escape, and so he submerged blindly, pushing away from the jagged rocks until he found deeper water.

He reverted to his human form somewhere near the rocky seabed. The pain eased somewhat, but his eye was still jammed closed. He dreaded to think what damage had been done. Had his face melted into a hot glob of flesh? He shifted again, intent only on fixing his injury. He switched back and forth several times, aware that he was creating a weird disturbance in the water whenever he shrank down small then expanded again.

Gradually, the pain subsided and he managed to open his eye. In dragon form once more, he blinked and scrunched up his face, flexing his jaw and widening his eyes. Everything felt better now.

Returning to the surface, he found Seth perched on one end of the shipwreck. The other end was a roaring inferno, flames licking high and black smoke pouring off. *Whoops*, Hal thought. He wasn't sure which of them had caused the fire, but it hardly mattered. He hoped the ancient wreck wasn't a tourist attraction, because it was toast now.

Come and get me, wimp, Seth taunted, apparently uncaring of the fire. His underbelly was blackened and still smoking. He had to be hurting, but he'd somehow turned his pain into anger. Maybe scrags had gotten used to doing that. Their painful scars had toughened them up over the past decade. Heck, Seth must have had scars his entire life, even as a baby. He had to be about the same age as the virus, born either just before or after the breakout. In that respect, he'd known nothing *but* pain. Pain and itching.

Flames reached up to one of the ship's masts above. It blackened and caught alight. Rigging and what was left of the old sails burned and came loose, falling in smoking lumps to the deck.

Hal was afraid to attack again. This scrag, as young and inexperienced as he was, had too much fight in him.

But what choice was there? He had to subdue his opponent somehow.

He glanced around. The nearby cliffs were barren, devoid of civilization. Brodon lay just the other side of the rocky ridge a little farther up the coast. For anyone to see the two dragons scrapping on the deck of the shipwreck, they'd have to be walking on top of the cliffs, perhaps on a hiking trail, and even then it would be a distant spectacle.

Anyone in Brodon could see the black smoke, though, if they were looking to the east. And if they saw that, they might see a couple of dragons flying around in the air . . . if Hal could bring the fight to the sky.

With a new plan in mind, he submerged, struck for deeper water, then spun and shot back to the surface. He exploded out and took to the air. As he circled the blazing ship, Seth turned to watch, hunkered down as if preparing to launch at a moment's notice.

Not too far away, Hal spotted Miss Simone floating in the sea alongside a few other mermaids and Lola the lamia. They were a little closer to the action than he would have liked.

With a bellow, Hal swooped toward the ship. He stretched out his claws and made his intention known—to rip into Seth for the second round of their battle.

As he'd expected, Seth sprang into the air and beat his wings hard, struggling to get airborne. Hal smiled inwardly. In this respect, he had far more experience and therefore the upper hand. Still, Seth flew to safety before Hal got there.

They shot low across the water, Hal right behind Seth and snapping at his tail the whole way. He suspected Seth was playing with him, and Hal was fine with that. Let him play as long as he forgot where he was and rose above the cliffs in sight of Brodon.

Can't catch me, Seth jeered, zigzagging left and right, up and down.

Hal said nothing, just continued snapping his jaws at the tail that whipped back and forth before his eyes. He dipped lower and put on a burst of speed, aiming for Seth's underbelly.

Seth jerked upward, and Hal went after him. Success! They were rising higher and higher above the sea. He moved to one side and snapped away, and Seth veered in the opposite direction. So now the two were rising *and* heading back toward Brodon. The rocky clifftop loomed closer.

I see what you're trying to do, Seth called back over his shoulder. *Think you're clever, huh?* And with that, he angled sharply to the right and down, heading back toward the burning ship and its column of black smoke. *You want to take me in? Then come and get me.*

Hal paused in midair, hovering as he collected his thoughts. Tackling the dragon directly seemed foolhardy. Tricking Seth into accidentally flying into sight of Brodon . . . well, it had seemed like a good idea at the time, but the boy clearly wasn't that stupid.

"Okay," he shouted, his roar carrying across the sea. "You want people to mistake me for someone else? That works two ways. I'm going to the castle. Let's see how close I can get to your queen before she realizes I'm not her beloved Seth. Close enough to chew her in half, I reckon."

It was almost a shame Seth had no way to understand that. Hal turned and flew off, leaving Seth to his thoughts and the mermaids and lamia far below. He had to hope Miss Simone would duck under if Seth came near.

Hal moved fast, his mind whirling as his new plan took form. He could actually turn his identical-dragon problem to his advantage. All he had to do was stoop to Queen Bee's level and use her own tactics against her, pretending he was Seth while he got close enough to grab her. And if Seth followed, Hal would simply treat him as the Swarm's enemy. Nobody would know the difference unless Seth managed to revert to his human form.

It didn't take long to arrive at the castle. He swooped lower, watching scrags scurrying for cover.

He thumped down as several creatures ran out onto the courtyard—the centaur, the cyclops, and something new, a massive black hound with blazing red eyes and flames licking up from its powerful shoulders.

Hal did a double take. Flames? The hound was on fire?

It trotted out to greet him, absolutely fearless. Everywhere it walked, it left smoldering footprints on the flagstones, small black smudges that trailed wispy black smoke and faded within seconds. It was a creepy sight.

Hal stood quite still, settling down and making himself comfortable as though he lived there. Scrags peered out from behind the busted entrance doors and several large wooden cages that still littered the place. The cyclops stomped closer, its single, staring eye unblinking. The giant still wore the velvet drape around its middle. The telltale scrag scars were faint across its chest and shoulders, even fainter on the face.

"What want?" the twelve-foot-tall giant slurred.

Hal offered a growl in response.

The hound—the *hellhound*, Hal suddenly realized as he remembered one of the labels on the blood vials—approached and sniffed at him. The heat it radiated was staggering, causing Hal to flinch even though he was in dragon form. Faint smoke rolled from its back as flames continued to flicker here and there. The creature was like a walking, smoldering ember.

"Is that you, Seth?" the centaur called from a safe distance. "Queen Bee told you to stay away. You're putting her plan in jeopardy."

Hal growled again, then shrugged.

The centaur trotted closer, eyeing the hellhound warily as he did so. "We can see smoke from the shipwreck. What happened? Was your hiding place compromised?"

After the briefest of pauses, Hal nodded.

"Was it Lola? Did she betray us?"

This time Hal shrugged.

"So what happened? We saw the other dragon-kid heading that way with Lola and some mermaids in the water. Did they find you? Did you kill them all?"

Hal shook his head.

The centaur scowled. "Did you at least kill the dragon-kid?"

Again, Hal shook his head. He might have said yes if Seth was likely to stay out of sight, but he half expected the boy to show up soon.

"You need to man up, Seth," the centaur snapped. "The queen favored you with that dragon blood, and you're squandering it." He spat on the ground, which Hal found unbecoming of a centaur. "Queen Bee should have picked a man for the job."

"Like you, Guppy?"

The queen spoke softly from the castle doorway. She stood there dressed in black as usual, calm and composed, with a spear in one hand.

The centaur jumped and clip-clopped around to face her. "No, not like *me*, ma'am. I just meant that Seth—I mean, he's the perfect guy to be a dragon, what with him being feisty and everything. It's just that . . . well, he might be a bit tender-hearted?"

"Instead of a killing machine like, say, Gruel?"

"Well, no. He went too far with that water storm. He never should have flooded the town."

The queen nodded. "Seth showed a lot more restraint, wouldn't you agree? He saw no need to kill, unlike Gruel, who was reckless."

The centaur looked doubtful now. "Right."

"Right. So perhaps my judgment of character is a little better than yours?"

"Right, my queen," Guppy said, bowing.

She slapped him hard on his side, and a couple of flies buzzed into the air. "Good. Having said all that, it's too late now for being nice. I should have held my tongue in front of the caretakers. Now they're gone, spreading the word." She looked at Hal again. "That's why we're changing things up, young Seth. I'm done with tiptoeing around. I think everyone else is, too."

Hal nodded and shuffled toward her. He couldn't believe his luck. He had her in his grasp. She was ten feet away. Eight. Six . . .

"Another dragon coming, Queen," a scrag shouted.

Queen Bee glanced to the south and narrowed her eyes. "What happened out there, Seth? Did you two boys fight? Did he get the better of you?"

Hal shook his head, taking another step closer to her.

Her eyes widened then. For some reason, she stared at his neck with a frown on her face, then took a step backward.

He lunged and grabbed her with one huge paw, encircling her tiny waist and clamping her arms to her side so that she was forced to drop her spear. He looked down, his snout close to her face. She gasped, a flicker of fear passing over her face. It was quickly replaced by anger. "Oh, I'm such a fool."

"Queen?" Guppy the centaur said, looking horribly confused.

The cyclops blinked a few times, a frown knitting his brow. Scrags stood all around, equally bewildered. The hellhound looked from Hal to the queen, flames dancing on the back of its head.

"It's him, you imbeciles," Queen Bee said, sounding tired now. "See the silky strap around his neck? This is the wrong dragon."

Ah, Hal thought, light dawning. *My smart clothes.*

After a moment's silence, pandemonium broke out. Hal watched with some amusement as the centaur galloped around shouting orders, and the scrags—men and women alike—started jabbing at Hal's tough hide with spears. The cyclops leapt in and started pounding with his fists, and the hellhound barked until it was hoarse, its coal-black coat glowing red as though freshly stoked.

Hal let them have their moment, taking the jabs and punches even though some of them actually hurt. He even waited as more creatures poured out of the busted castle doorway. Some were small and harmless like the faun and the brownie, others a little more impressive like the unicorn, which immediately leapt into the fray and began stabbing at him with its long, spiral horn. Those jabs were *really* painful, perhaps enhanced by magic, and Hal decided it was time to go.

He roared once, took a deep breath, and blew flames all around. Every man, woman, and creature ran screaming—except for the hellhound, which leapt into the fire with glee.

Queen Bee hung limply in his paw, submitting to whatever fate awaited her. She did, however, call sharply to Guppy the centaur, "It's on, do you hear? Gather everyone—"

Hal squeezed her so tight she gasped, cutting off her command. Seeing that Seth was bearing down on the castle at great speed, letting off fireballs as he went, Hal beat his wings, sprang onto the castle's stone fencing, and launched into the air with his prisoner.

Finally, the tables had turned. Hal grinned to himself. Not only had he the most important enemy in his grasp, Seth was making a big mistake in coming to rescue her. Hal could already see the townsfolk pausing in the streets to look up at not one but two dragons. Those on the beach looked especially surprised, so much so that they forgot to be frightened for a minute. Then they jerked into action, running in all directions to escape what they assumed was another onslaught.

Hal landed on the beach and held Queen Bee up for Seth to see. "Back off or she'll get hurt!"

Seth clearly understood the warning. He thumped down in the sand nearby, sending a wet clump into the air. *Let her go right now or you'll regret it.*

Not wanting to underestimate him, Hal lifted Queen Bee to his mouth and opened his jaws. It was hard to speak this way, but his meaning was obvious. Seth watched him warily, panting so hard that steam shot from his nostrils.

Okay, so now what? Seth grunted. *Everyone can see there's two of us. The game's up. So what? Doesn't change much.*

"It changes everything," Hal said, keeping Queen Bee's face near his jaws. In the background, he could see his friends approaching with caution. Abigail buzzed way ahead of them.

Why can't you speak my language? Seth snapped, stamping a foot. *We're the exact same dragon! How come I don't understand a word you're saying?*

Hal shook his head. He couldn't be bothered to explain.

"It's over, Queen Bee," Abigail shouted from a safe distance, darting from side to side as she glanced from one dragon to the other. She gestured up the beach to the crowds that were forming there. "Everyone can see this."

"It doesn't matter," Queen Bee said. She had a look about her that chilled Hal, tired and defeated on the surface yet with a cold, determined look in her eyes. She ignored Abigail, instead peering up at

Hal and talking directly to him. "Trying to ingratiate ourselves with these people was a waste of time. I should have known better than to try."

"So you're surrendering?" Abigail asked, buzzing closer.

The queen shook her head, still glaring at Hal. "Not a chance. We could have settled right in if you'd all just stayed away and left us alone. We could have been the town's protectors. They'd have felt safe and secure, and we'd have had a place to call home as well as a purpose in life. Everyone would have been happy. And I could have gone back to being a mother."

Seth gave a soft grunt and moved a step closer.

Queen Bee's jaw tightened. "But now look."

She nodded toward the Brodon residents. Dozens were amassed on the sand, confused and uncertain. The overweight mayor stood out in front, the scrag named Duke now by his side. Their guilty expressions suggested they'd been caught in a lie together.

"See?" the queen said. "It's all ruined. The castle's caretakers are mingling with the crowd saying ugly things about me. That means the mayor is finished, exposed as the power-hungry liar that he is." She laughed suddenly. "Did you know he wanted to be a dragon, Hal? That was the deal. He would be a dragon, and I would be queen of Brodon. Can you imagine it? Mayor Priggle, a *dragon*?"

The mayor heard this, and his face darkened even as people in the crowd looked at him with their mouths open.

"Everybody wants to be a dragon, Hal," the queen said, lowering her voice to a whisper. "See Duke over there? He knew the mayor was never going to be a dragon because I promised him *he'd* be one instead. In the end I realized there was only one person deserving of that precious blood. My young Seth here."

Where was she going with this? By now, all Hal's friends had arrived nearby. Molly waved Abigail back, clearly taking charge of negotiations. Hal had a feeling it was too late for that.

"I'm here to stay now," Queen Bee said. She raised her voice so everybody could hear. "My Swarm likes it here, and so do I. This is where we belong. I'm a queen, that's my castle, and I intend to stay!"

Hal remained still, coiled like a spring and ready to launch if she commanded Seth to attack.

Queen Bee smiled. "I don't need permission to live here, people. I especially don't need Mayor Priggle's blessing. I'm *taking* this town." She suddenly shouted, "Do it, Duke!"

Duke nodded and withdrew a knife. Before anyone around him had a chance to react, he turned and plunged the blade deep into the mayor's chest.

Brodon residents began screaming and yelling, pushing back from the stunned mayor as blood pooled on the front of his shirt. He looked down at the hilt of the knife. Then he staggered and dropped to his knees.

After a long, drawn-out hush, Mayor Seymour Priggle pitched forward and landed facedown into the sand.

At this point, Queen Bee shouted something at Hal. Trembling with horror and anger, he focused on her and realized she was gesturing toward the castle. "Here they come, dragon-boy. Are you ready for this? Are you sure you're fighting for the right team?"

Thundering down the long, sloping road from the castle came the Swarm's shapeshifter army, a mass of monsters large and small, most yelling and roaring, some of them screeching. A few soared overhead. Hal was sure many of these creatures were new, only recently transformed. A small stream of scrags brought up the rear, spears held high.

Meanwhile, just now clambering out of the sea, the angry simurgh shook itself off and reared up with a volley of barks.

Chapter Seventeen
Choosing Sides

Seth's attention seemed to be fixed on the body of Mayor Priggle. The man lay alone, facedown in the sand, while Brodon residents ran for their lives toward the nearby waterlogged streets. Duke, alone with his bloody knife, wiped it on his pants and stood waiting, licking his lips as he glanced up at the approaching horde of shapeshifting scrags.

You killed him, Seth growled to Queen Bee, and Hal thought he detected amazement, perhaps even shock.

Queen Bee wasn't paying attention to him, and she wouldn't have understood his grunts anyway. She was busy screaming at her army to attack.

But something else happened before the Swarm got anywhere close to the beach. Mermaids popped up out of the sea and started singing. Their melody carried across the bay, cutting through the hysteria and causing men and boys everywhere to pause and stare in wonder while droves of mothers, wives, and daughters urged them to quit standing around.

The simurgh had stomped out of the sea and shaken off its soggy wings. Now it froze. Hal had to remind himself that this was a man, too, a monster with the ordinary mind of a scrag. Though refusing to turn and look at the mermaids, Simmy seemed to be having trouble moving his feet as though stuck in mud.

The hollering horde of scrags continued pouring down the road from the castle. They were making too much noise of their own to hear the singing. Hal, though, heard every shout, roar, holler, and scream in the vicinity, and still the haunting melody prevailed. Mesmerized, he listened intently and tuned everything else out. He was vaguely aware that Seth, just yards away, was equally dumbstruck and motionless.

"Hal!" a voice barked in his ear.

He jumped and turned to find Abigail buzzing around his head at full human size. His friends were gathered there, too. All had transformed by now. Lauren the harpy, Emily the naga, and Darcy in a partially transparent state were attempting to distract the slack-jawed boys from the tuneful spell.

Robbie, in his ogre form, sat on the sand with a faint, toothy smile. Thomas the manticore lay on his belly, his arcing tail moving from side to side like a hypnotized cobra. Likewise, Fenton lay nearby, his black lizard body half-buried in the sand. Dewey stood quite still, his centaur hoofs planted deep.

Molly was there, too, slapping Bo's face. The man was just as mesmerized as the boys. Some distance away, two goblins stood with hands on hips, apparently perplexed by what they might call 'that awful mermaid racket' and quite obviously unaffected by it.

Shadows fell across the sand, and Hal looked up to find Blair the phoenix and Astrid the sphinx circling around high above. And a flying horse; Orson had come along, too. The whole team was here.

"Hal, *do* something," Abigail said. "Take care of the simurgh while it's in dreamland."

Shaking his head to clear the fog, Hal focused again on the simurgh. The monster's scrag mind had fully succumbed to the mermaids' charm. There were dozens of the beautiful water folk singing this time, their harmony far more complex than before, its magical potency greatly enhanced. The four-winged, dog-faced simurgh sat hunched on the sand, now twisting around to look at the mermaids, who were clustered waist-deep in the gentle waves.

Hal had no idea how to 'take care' of such a beast. It was twice his size, too big to lift, and too powerful to tackle on his own. A true dragon would burn it and tear into its throat, killing it within minutes despite its size. But Hal wasn't a true dragon. He was a twelve-year-old boy, soon to be thirteen. The idea of ripping into another creature with the intention of killing it was beyond him.

He had an idea, though. It would definitely involve some pain, but he was prepared to dish some of that out for the greater good. He gave Abigail a quick nod and tossed Queen Bee into Robbie's arms. If his friend wasn't already distracted from the mermaids' charm, he was now. He looked down in surprise to find the diminutive black-clad scrag leader squirming around, and he gripped her so tight she let out a squeal.

With Seth still slack-jawed, Hal launched straight over his head and headed for the simurgh. That oversized brute had to be first, Seth second. Then the rest of the Swarm.

Gritting his teeth, Hal cleared his mind and focused. He landed on the simurgh's back and gripped one of the four wings in his jaws. He clamped down and squeezed as hard as he could, twisting his head at the same time. A bone snapped, and Simmy jerked and yelped, then began thrashing and bucking.

Hal held on, digging his claws into feather-covered flesh. He'd already broken a rear wing on one side. Now he went for the front. Once he'd clamped on, it took only a few seconds to squeeze and twist with all his might until the bone splintered.

The simurgh barked and roared the whole time, trying to buck him off, sand flying up in all directions. Still holding on tight, pressing down on the monster while it turned in circles, Hal leaned forward and put his jaws near Simmy's head. For a second, he felt a strong temptation to dig in and rip a hole in his throat. Instead, Hal reverted to human form and scrambled to get hold of the tough fur right below one of the doglike ears.

"Hurts, doesn't it?" he yelled. "You can easily heal yourself, though. Just change back. The bones will mend."

He didn't bother clarifying that the wings would entirely disappear while in human form and completely regenerate during the next transformation.

Simmy tried to fly but ended up hopping around on the beach. Unfortunately for him, both his functioning wings were on one side. There was no way he'd get airborne like that.

"Go ahead and change," Hal shouted above Simmy's snarling.

Unlike his moment of genuine compassion when he'd hurt the minotaur, this time he had a good, logical reason to talk the simurgh into reverting to his scrag form. Remembering a trick Abigail had once employed, he put on his most mocking tone.

"Everybody's staring at you! You look like an idiot the way you're flapping about and not getting anywhere. I've never seen anything so stupid-looking in my life. How can you stand being like this? A four-winged bird with a dog's head? Really? And some stupid-looking feet, too! You're just a big—"

The simurgh barked savagely, twisting to grab at him, but Hal clung on and rode it out. As long as he kept a tight grip on the fur, he wasn't going anywhere.

He glimpsed Robbie running away with Queen Bee clamped in his arms, who flailed and screamed in fury.

Thomas sprang at Seth and jabbed him with his lethal stinger. At the same time, Fenton sprayed a long jet of water all over Seth's head, then leapt forward and tried to breathe on it from his low position in the sand. The vomited liquid would harden anyway; hot breath just sped up the process.

And Seth had plenty of hot breath as he woke from his mermaid-induced stupor. He began roaring with indignation, and though his jaws were smothered with a sticky, gluey film, his fire managed to break through and shoot out at a funny angle. He shook his head vigorously and bent to scratch at his snout.

Simmy the simurgh gave up trying to fly. He stood for a moment, panting hard, and Hal took the opportunity to speak to him again. "You have to learn how to change at will. You can't stay a monster all your life. I'm trying to help you." Inspiration struck. "Lola's on our side, now. We're teaching her to change back so she doesn't have to drink human blood to survive, and I'm pretty sure she'd like to see you again sometime. She's worried about you, Simmy."

The simurgh froze.

"That's right," Hal said, more softly now. "See, there's tons to learn about shapeshifting. You've done pretty good so far, but you can't just change into a simurgh and expect to survive. You have to learn about the simurgh's lifestyle." He was gabbling now, trying to hurry things along. "We can help with that. We have experts. See that flying horse up there? That's Orson. He's a teacher. He knows everything. He even knows where other simurghs hang out, in case you're interested . . ."

He trailed off. Simmy stood still, panting more softly now.

In the distance, the Swarm had reached the foot of the castle road. Now they stormed the submerged streets of Brodon, and Hal could hear screams of fright amid the bellows and roars of various creatures. Overhead, a trio of scrag shapeshifters skimmed the rooftops, but Hal had no time to study them because Seth had broken free of Fenton's gluey bonds and was hop-skipping along the beach in an effort to launch into the air.

The mermaids, realizing their singing now fell on deaf ears, ceased and sank below the surface. Hal wondered briefly where the triton was. He had to assume they still held him somewhere.

Abruptly, something happened to Simmy. Hal felt a shift in the monster's body mass. He clung tight as the simurgh shrank in tiny, jerky stages, a very bumpy ride that caused Hal's teeth to chatter. The wings melted away, becoming useless stalks that vanished into the simurgh's back. The dog-head shrank as fur faded. Feathers flattened and hardened, becoming a hard shell and then softening to pale skin as a knobby, human backbone appeared.

Hal leapt clear as the transformation came to an end. He'd planned on knocking Simmy unconscious—a hefty blow to the head would put him out of commission for a while—but the scrag, naked and curled into a ball in the sand, seemed to have lost the urge to fight. Hal paused, ready to strike if needed. "Are you going to cause any more trouble?" he asked.

The scrag looked at him and blinked. He sat up slowly and patted his bare chest, then his face. He seemed puzzled. Being naked seemed the least of his concerns at the moment. He was more focused on his skin.

"My scars," he said after a while.

Hal frowned. "What scars?"

"Exactly. They're gone."

The man's complexion was indeed free of scars. He was pale and clean, completely unblemished. "I don't itch," he said in wonder. "I don't hurt. I had scars all up my chest and arms, on my face . . . I've been scratching for years. I've forgotten what it's like *not* to scratch. But now there's . . . nothing."

Being free of itches seemed insignificant in the current circumstances. For a scrag, though, it was of monumental importance.

"I'm going to help my friends now," Hal said. "If you attack us again, we'll all work together to bring you down. You'll end up in jail for a long, long time. But if you help us, you can be part of our team. You can live in our village and be one of us. Like Lola," he added.

He had no idea if his promises would be honored by the likes of Councilman Frobisher, but that was a problem for another day.

"And shapeshifters on our team have special clothes like these," Hal added, plucking at his shiny shirt material. "They're smart clothes, made with magic. They stay with me even when I'm a dragon, and when I change back—"

His attention was drawn to the familiar noise of fire being expelled. Seth was coming in for an attack on Molly and the others, belching flames as he swooped.

Hal quickly stepped away from Simmy. "Gotta go." He transformed and took to the air, leaving the naked scrag behind.

Seth looked like he meant business. He descended from the sky and leveled off until he was hurtling along the beach a few feet above the sand. Hal's friends scattered in all directions. The dragon chose his target and ignored the rest. With his jaws open wide, he slowed at the very last second, tilted his head, and snatched at Emily as she tried to twist her serpentine coils away.

She screamed as Seth's jaws clamped around her thick, scaly body right about where her human waist would be. The dragon soared upward, yanking her into the sky. She dangled helplessly.

Hal tore after them, watching with growing horror as Seth flew higher and higher. Then he let go, and Emily began to tumble through the air, screaming.

Altering his course, Hal barreled after her. Everything else seemed to fade into the background. He'd plucked his friends from the air before—Dewey, Fenton, even Dr. Kessler—and he could do it again. But it seemed like he was too far away. Emily would hit the beach before he reached her.

Blair the phoenix came flying in, his spectacular scarlet and gold form an awe-inspiring sight. Orson the pegasus approached from another direction, equally fast, his black flanks shiny with sweat and his wings pumping hard. And Astrid the sphinx, with her oversized human head on her half-lion, half-eagle body, seemed intent on getting there first. She was slower but closer.

The three of them clashed in the air, a tangle of feathery wings. Somehow, somebody caught hold of Emily. It was all over a few seconds later, with Orson the victor, a winged stallion with a naga draped safely across his back.

Breathing a sigh of relief, Hal altered his course again, looking for Seth. The dragon was headed for Dewey, who galloped hard along the beach with sand and sea kicking up behind.

Obviously playing with him, Seth breathed fire in a long stream right behind the centaur, slowing so he didn't shoot past overhead. Hal pumped his wings until they ached, and seconds later collided in midair, ramming Seth so hard that the two of them hit the sand and skidded thirty feet before coming to a halt.

They began fighting immediately, Seth snapping and roaring while Hal clawed and stomped, both of them rolling around and digging craters in the sand.

I was just messing about! Seth panted, clubbing Hal on the snout. *I wouldn't have hurt him, you idiot!*

"Could have fooled me," Hal grunted, bringing his tail around and whacking Seth on the back of the head. "You dropped Emily! Was *that* just messing about?"

Seth twisted and shoved, causing Hal to topple backward. The two of them faced each other for a second or two, then clashed again, shoulder to shoulder, wrestling and biting. When Hal managed to pin his opponent down and put all his weight on him, Seth gasped, *I wasn't gonna hurt him! And I was gonna catch the snake-girl, I promise!*

"Liar!"

Hal pummeled Seth some more. He felt he was finally winning.

I never killed anyone in my life, Seth said, almost as though he'd understood Hal's last angry roar. *That's why Queen Bee chose me to be the dragon. I'm the only one she trusts.*

Pausing with his claws raised, Hal let out a barking laugh. "You're the only one she trusts? She made a big mistake."

Seth didn't react strongly, but again his reply seemed to fit. *I bet you and me are the same. We're definitely the same dragon. The only difference is that you grew up with a nice family in some nice home with some nice friends, everything all safe and cozy. I was raised by a group of crazy people.*

Dragons rarely spoke so many words at once. Hal lowered his claws, and the two of them took a moment to catch their breath, an unspoken truce.

The people I lived with were sorry losers, Seth went on, quietly now. His mouth barely moved, but a series of huffs and barks filled the air, which Hal translated internally without a second's thought. *They didn't care what they did to people as long as they got what they wanted. I hated them. That's why I left. I was always going off exploring, and one day I just walked away and never went back. I ran into the Swarm and thought I was dead meat, only Queen Bee took me in. She liked me, said I was just like her son.*

Reminded of the scrag leader, Hal looked for Robbie and found him still clutching her tightly. She was trying to wriggle free and failing.

Seth heaved a huge dragon sigh. *He got the virus on the very first day and died. It made her crazy-mad at just about everybody who escaped into bunkers and camps. A lot of them were rich and bought their way in. It wasn't fair.*

Hal stared at him. He didn't have time for this sudden outpouring, and yet he found this news about the queen oddly interesting.

She's killed a lot of people out of spite. Just like the mayor. She didn't need to do that, though. That was . . .

He trailed off.

"And you want her to be your new mom?" Hal said, barely able to contain his skepticism. Some role model she was!

Seth seemed to have given up the fight for now. *I wish I knew what you were saying. Do you even understand what I'm telling you?* He sighed again.

"I understand you just fine," Hal said.

An idea suddenly hit him, and he stepped back. He looked down at the beach, which was all churned up from their fight. A smoother patch lay just a few yards away, and he stomped over to it and scratched two words into the sand:

HELP US

Seth leaned forward and stared. It might have been a funny sight for anyone else to see twin dragons standing there looking at a message in the sand.

After a moment's thought, Seth began scratching a message of his own.

Anxious about his friends, Hal took a moment to check what was going on. The scrag shapeshifters had made it through town and were streaming out of alleys onto the beach, their intention to maim or kill made perfectly clear by their maniacal screeching and roaring. Any remaining Brodon residents on the beach ran for cover while Hal's friends gathered together. Even with Queen Bee gripped tightly in Robbie's arms, it was obvious they were all preparing for the onslaught. Hal wanted to be there with them.

LIT KWEEN BEE GO, Seth had written in the sand.

"Can't do that," Hal said, shaking his head firmly.

Seth growled in response.

Hal had no more time to dwell on the subject. He did, however, write one more message in the sand:

CHOOSE A SIDE

With that, he leapt into the air and took off, leaving Seth to mull that one over. He felt quite pleased with himself. His message was simple but thought-provoking. Of course Seth should choose a side, but he should choose wisely, because one side was about to lose.

He left the boy alone to search his heart—and, failing that, to at least weigh the odds and pick the side most likely to win.

A short distance away, Hal's friends had spread out to form a line stretching from the demolished promenade down to the water's edge. Robbie stood tall in the middle, Queen Bee held high above his head as though he planned to slam her to the ground if the scrags kept coming.

To both sides stood his friends—a centaur, a black lizard, a manticore, a naga, a blond-headed girl who might disappear at any moment, a buzzing human-sized faerie, and a gleaming white-winged harpy.

Also in the line stood Molly, with Bo and a couple of stout goblins next to her. A phoenix, a pegasus, and a sphinx circled overhead like vultures.

Hal wished *all* Miss Simone's classmates were here. Charlie the griffin, Canaan the elf, even Ellie the unicorn would complete the shapeshifter force. If Molly had her magic, she could turn everyone to stone and be done with it. If Bo could bring himself to transform into his unused sphinx form, he could join his sister in the air and be of some help.

But it was an impressive group nonetheless. And as he looked, Miss Simone emerged from the sea with Lola the lamia slinking along behind. When Lola spotted Simmy, she scampered to be with him.

Better find him something to wear, Hal thought, mildly embarrassed for the naked scrag. He hoped she would persuade Simmy to help, though. Then he could turn his colossal simurgh presence on the Swarm instead of sitting idly by the water contemplating his healed scars.

Or maybe Lola would switch sides again. Neither Hal nor Miss Simone had found time to help her yet. Maybe she'd lose heart, accept her new lamia form, and rejoin her scrag friends. If so, she'd urge Simmy to fight *with* the Swarm.

Everyone had better choose a side and get ready, he thought.

Chapter Eighteen
The Battle of Brodon

Hal landed on the beach a short distance from his friends and trotted closer, his feet sinking into the sand. Debris from the ruined, flooded houses littered his path. He stomped on a door, random clothing, and bits of furniture as he made his way to the shapeshifters that stood facing the castle ahead.

Abigail must have heard him coming because she swung around and buzzed over. "Hal?" she said tentatively. "I was worried about you. You *are* Hal, right?" She glanced at his throat, and her face cleared as she spotted the silky fabric of his reformed smart clothes. "Yes, you are." She flew up and landed on his shoulders. "You're just in time. The Swarm has a few new freaks."

Up until now, the scrags had been hollering and roaring as they ran down the castle road, trotted along the beach, and slowed to a steady march. Now a hush fell as they closed the gap. Three of them flew in circles overhead—a small dragon, a gaunt-faced woman who apparently had no need for wings, and a creepy greyish figure that trailed smoke. They stayed close to the group, swooping around.

The cyclops led the Swarm. At twice the height of a man, he lumbered along with his arms swinging. The velvet drape wrapped around his middle was now secured with a rope.

The manticore loped alongside, his broken jaw still hanging open but his tail arced and ready to sting.

The centaur trotted along with a small figure on his back, the tiny faun that had once been a large, muscle-bound brute. Hal thought that was funny. The man would be better off in his human form! But this proved none of the scrags had figured out how to change back.

Except for the simurgh, Hal corrected himself as he glanced back over his shoulder. Simmy was still sitting on the sand, half in the water, with Lola sitting nearby in her grey, reptilian lamia form. They seemed to have no interest in anything but their own private conversation.

The scrag unicorn dwarfed a number of other small creatures. Abigail confirmed his guess that the small, thin person with big ears and long black hair was a brownie. Molly muttered that the squat, ugly woman was a gnome. She waddled along, scowling and clutching her oversized head in her hands.

"Give it up!" the centaur shouted, trotting out to the front of the group. "Release our queen and maybe we'll go easy on you."

"In your dreams!" Fenton shouted.

Molly reached sideways to give him a jab. "Leave the negotiations to grown-ups, my boy."

Among the scrags' ranks, a curious figure caused Hal to blink and stare—a man made of sticks and mud, eight feet tall. "It's a golem," Emily said with a gasp of wonder. "Isn't it, Molly? I've heard about those. They're like magically animated clay people."

"Exactly like that," Molly agreed.

"How did Miss Simone get a blood sample from a clay person?" Fenton demanded loudly.

Again, Molly jabbed him. "Voice down, Fenton. And I don't know how. Golems are made of whatever materials come to hand, but once animated, they are technically alive and can't be killed unless the spell is lifted. So I hear, anyway." Molly stroked her chin. "Not sure how the rules apply to a shapeshifter, though."

"I'll tell you another time," Miss Simone said quietly, and everyone turned to look as she strode closer. She spotted Robbie's prisoner, Queen Bee, clasped in his arms and nodded with satisfaction.

"Our army is bigger," the centaur warned. "Stand down."

Hal glanced around, confused. A bigger army? He doubted that. The scrags had three things flying around in the air and a couple of dangerous-looking monsters on the ground. The rest were harmless. And inexperienced. There was no way they had a 'bigger army' than Miss Simone's team.

"What is *that*?" Abigail whispered from her perch behind his head.

It snuck out from behind the golem and cyclops as if they'd been waiting to unveil their secret weapon. At first, Hal assumed it was a scrag shapeshifter gone wrong. It had the head and body of a lion—but also the head and shoulders of a goat sprouting from its back as though two animals had become fused.

"Chimera," Molly said. "Look at its tail."

The tail was actually a long, thick snake. It twisted around to face them, making the bizarre creature a three-headed horror.

"Watch out for that one," Molly added. "The chimera breathes fireballs."

Reminded of fire, Hal also noticed the sinister hellhound nearby. The charred-black, superheated canine hung close to the chimera, perhaps because it was attracted by the prospect of fire being breathed in its direction.

"Last chance," Guppy the centaur called. "Hey, you—centaur-boy! Talk some sense into your mob."

Dewey scowled and said nothing.

"They have another dragon," Darcy said, and everyone looked up to study the reptilian creature as it circled around. It was about the size of a man, small and slender, with only two legs and no arms. "Molly, does it breathe fire?"

"No, that's a wyvern. No fire, but a vicious bite and nasty tail."

The wyvern's snout was long and pointed, full of fangs. The tail had a curved barb on the end.

Molly glanced toward Miss Simone, who was edging closer to Robbie and giving Queen Bee a steely stare. The two seemed preoccupied for the moment, so Molly took a few steps forward and spoke to the centaur herself. "Nothing good will come of a fight. People will get hurt, and in the end you'll lose."

"Are you sure about that?" the centaur said, grinning.

Again, Hal looked around. He still thought Miss Simone's side had the upper hand, especially if Seth the dragon and Simmy the simurgh made the right choice. Maybe the centaur scrag thought he could rely on their help instead.

"We have your triton," Molly said, pointing out to sea.

A few mermaids bobbed about there, and they held in their grasp the silver-scaled, gnarly-faced triton.

"So?" the centaur said, shrugging.

Molly moved forward a little more, raising her hands in a placating gesture. "What's your name, young man?"

After a pause, the centaur folded his arms and sighed. "Guppy. Why? You wanna get to know me?"

"I want to reason with you. This whole business has gone far enough. Look at you all! You're meddling with forces you don't fully comprehend. But if you join us, you—"

"*Join* you?" Guppy threw back his head and laughed. "You want to be our friends now that we're an army of shapeshifters? Queen Bee was right. We tried to fit in, but our scars just frightened people off. Nobody wanted us. So we'll take what we want instead."

"What scars?" Molly asked simply.

"What, are you blind?" Guppy pointed at his chest.

"I can barely see them."

Though still visible, the scars were probably far less severe than they had been. Guppy peered down at his chest and frowned.

"See that?" Molly said, speaking loudly even though she now stood right in front of him. "Being a shapeshifter means you can self-heal. Each time you transform, you heal a little more. If you switch back to human form, I'll bet the scars will be gone."

"She's right!" a woman's voice shouted.

Everyone turned in surprise. All the flying creatures on both sides seemed to stutter in midflight, and those standing on the beach swung to face Lola the lamia as she strolled up the beach.

She gestured back toward her friend Simmy, who remained in the water. "Simmy's completely healed. No scars at all. We don't need to fight. We're not scrags anymore. We're just ordinary people."

"Don't listen to her!" Queen Bee shrieked from Robbie's grasp. "I'm still in charge even while this oaf has hold of me." She glared up at the ogre's toothy grin, then faced the centaur again. "Quit standing around and *attack*. And be sure to give Lola the stinging she deserves."

"You heard her, people—get 'em!" Guppy yelled over his shoulder.

A cheer went up as the Swarm hurtled toward Hal and his friends.

Molly went down under the weight of the cyclops, her veil flying off but her stare having no effect.

The hellhound came flying out of the crowd to pounce on Fenton, flames leaping off its head and shoulders. The big boy transformed just in time, his scaly body sizzling the moment the hellhound touched him. He let out a howl and thrashed around, trying to smother the burning with cold wet sand.

The unicorn galloped forward with its horn lowered, aiming for Emily. She barely had time to twist her snake-body aside to avoid being stabbed, but the side of the unicorn's head slammed into her and knocked her flying.

The golem lumbered up on long legs, quickly covering the short distance and making a grab for Bo. Being a non-shapeshifter, he could do little to protect himself and ended up dangling high off the ground, hands of wood and mud squeezing him tight. Astrid came flying in to help him out, screaming, "Leave my brother alone!"

Hal was frozen into inaction. Everything was happening at once, and he caught it all in several snapshot moments that seared into his brain—the cyclops flinging Molly aside and stamping over to grab Thomas by the scruff of the neck—the bizarre chimera roaring with its lion-head, hissing with its snake-head, and shooting a fireball with its goat-head—and the wyvern swooping in and whipping its tail around, catching Robbie's shoulder and causing him to grunt with pain.

The gaunt-faced flying woman darted close to Hal's head, screaming a terrible noise as it went, so piercing that it hurt his ears and made him want to bury his head in the sand. *A banshee*, he realized suddenly. They wailed when someone was about to die—and right now he believed it.

The other flying figure, the grey phantom trailing smoke, shot toward and *through* Dewey. The boy tensed and grew wide-eyed, then sagged and turned as grey as the creature itself. The phantom soared away a shade lighter.

"The sylph got Dewey!" Abigail yelled.

What the heck is a sylph? Hal wanted to ask. But he had no time. After a few seconds of standing around dumbly watching everything unfold, he finally got a grip and sprang into action.

He lashed out at the cyclops, breathed fire toward the chimera, clubbed the golem with his tail, and clawed at the hellhound as the pandemonium continued. Screeches and yells filled the air along with the smell of fire and smoke. He quickly lost track of his friends amid the chaos, all his attention on whatever scrag was in front of him at any given moment.

Amid the confusion, Queen Bee got loose. While she sprinted away with a huge grin on her face, Robbie stood wiggling his fat ogre fingers as though she'd vanished into a puff of smoke. She weaved in and out of the combatants, urging them on, even giving the chimera a hefty boot up the rear when it dithered too long. The snake-tail hissed at her, but she was already past, racing away across the sand. Miss Simone yelled something and went after her, clearly angry.

Hal saw all this as he was facing off with the hellhound. The creature kept lunging toward him, and each time he felt heat rolling off its charred body. When he breathed fire at it, it just leapt deeper into the flames the way most dogs would dance about in a fountain. He would have picked the creature up and dropped it in the sea if it wasn't too hot to touch.

He couldn't find Abigail and hoped she'd had the sense to get clear the way Bo had. After being saved by his sister, the man had bravely gone to attack a few ordinary scrags, but they'd charged toward him with spears and overly joyful expressions, and he'd stumbled away.

Darcy sprang to mind, too. Being invisible was great for secret missions but no good for full-on battle. Then again . . .

He blinked as her footprints appeared in the sand behind the hellhound. Distracted, he watched as they hurried past and headed toward a scrag. The black-haired man had a hump on his shoulder. It was Leech, one of the scientists from the lab. Out here in the midst of battle, he looked as dangerous as the rest of them, ready to slice someone's throat with the vicious ten-inch knife he wielded.

The hellhound leapt again, and Hal clubbed it with his fist. It was like punching a red-hot ember, and he knew the back of his paw was going to smart in a moment or two. But the hound toppled over and lay there in the wet sand shaking its head, steam sizzling out from underneath.

Hal returned his attention to the humpbacked scrag. The man looked confused now, turning quickly as if looking for someone, his knife held high while clumps of wet sand mysteriously flew up and smacked his face and chest. Darcy couldn't put him out of commission like this, but she could distract him.

Dewey staggered about, his face ashen. He looked somehow drawn, the life sucked out of him.

Was that what the sylph did? Hal spotted it flitting about in the air. As he watched, it descended toward Fenton and tried to ghost through him, but Fenton was too low to the ground for that to work, so the sylph moved on to Thomas instead. Thomas leapt sideways and shouted a warning, and the sylph continued on toward Emily.

Emily was wrapped tightly around the golem, probably trying to squeeze the life out of the bizarre giant. The ghostly sylph hesitated and backed off, smoke curling up around her feet.

The golem had planted its feet in the sand and was trying to get a good grip on Emily's thick coils to rip her off. She held tight and repeatedly bit the giant's neck. Hal couldn't remember if she was venomous or not, but the golem seemed more irritated than anything and kept batting at her face.

The hellhound leapt back up and, apparently deciding Hal was too big and indestructible, darted toward Molly instead. She screamed as the hound pounced—but just before it hit her, something slammed into its side and knocked it flying. Astrid had again arrived out of nowhere. Now she flapped away, howling with pain as her front paws and underbelly sizzled and smoked.

Fenton came rushing in. He sprayed stomach-stored water all over the hellhound as it was climbing onto its feet. The water evaporated instantly on its heated body, hissing and creating a thick cloud of steam. The hound didn't like it, though, and tried ducking sideways, but Fenton easily kept his endless jet of water trained on it, and in the end the hound had to retreat. When it scurried out from the backend of the steam cloud, it was bedraggled and shivering, its black fur like a coat of oil.

But Fenton wasn't done. He slithered after it on four short legs, now blowing with all his might, trying to catch up to the much faster hound.

Hal thudded after them both, flapping his wings as he went and getting airborne just in time to sail over Fenton's head. Instead of breathing fire, he blew hot air instead. The hellhound toppled over, its legs seizing up as Fenton's glue hardened. Whimpering noisily, the hound's blazing eyes widened as its entire body became encased in a tough, translucent shell that slowly turned grey.

Hal would have stopped to give Fenton a high-five. Instead, they shared a glance and nod, then returned to the battle.

One at a time, Hal thought. *Deal with one at a time.*

Above his head, Lauren swooped by and slammed into the banshee, cutting off the hideous wailing and causing the scrag woman to gasp. Both came crashing down onto the sand, and Lauren was clearly much tougher with her fierce talons. The banshee seemed more suited to nighttime fright tactics than battle. Though her screeching was like nails being driven through the brain, it was still nothing but noise and mostly harmless.

"Enough!" Lauren yelled at her, stomping on the banshee's shoulder and pinning her down. "Make one more sound and I'll *really* give you something to scream about!"

The chimera came at Hal, lion-jaws snapping and snarling. The goat-head kept bleating, which Hal found almost funny. *Almost* funny, because that same goat-head suddenly shot out a fireball the size of a human head. The fiery cannonball whacked Hal in the chest, knocking him back a step. It *hurt*. And when he looked down, he realized it had seared its way through his scales to raw flesh.

"Ow!" Hal yelled as pain exploded across his chest. The goat-head started bleating again, and now Hal recognized that it was working on a new fireball the way Lauren's cat, Biscuit, might cough up a furball.

Though he wanted to flee and transform a few times, Hal knew he had to take out this chimera creature. Even while it wasn't shooting fire, the snake-head at its rear kept whipping about and jabbing at anybody nearby, whether friend or foe. It didn't seem particularly smart. *Because the brain's in the front*, Hal thought as he leapt high into the air and came down hard on the three-headed monster.

The goat kept on bleating, and there was an intensity to it now as though a fireball was imminent. Hal grabbed the beast tightly in his claws and launched into the air, dragging it up with him. The lion-head roared.

Another fireball erupted. This one, spat from an awkward angle, zipped past Hal's snout and arced high. The goat-head bleated loudly, the lion continued roaring, and the snake-tail whipped around and jabbed at Hal's underbelly.

The fireball eventually began to fall. Hal watched, fascinated, as the flames died. The whole thing dimmed and began to look like an actual cannonball, hard and round, a dense ball that glowed red and slowly turned black. It fell into the sea with a splash.

Hal decided the sea was a good place for the chimera, too. He let go, and all three heads exclaimed in unison, snarling, bleating, and hissing all the way down. It made a splash far greater than the fireball had, and it was ten seconds before the bizarre creature returned to the surface in a frenzy of kicking limbs.

Not wanting to stick around, Hal flew back toward the beach. From afar, the battle looked like a crowd of random bugs, the screeches and roars oddly muffled. It was a surreal, oddly serene moment. But reality kicked back in once he was in the thick of it—the frantic cries, the heavy smell of sweat and blood, the faces of his best friends as they fought for their lives . . .

The cyclops was attacking Robbie. The ogre should have been the clear winner being taller and much heavier, but the one-eyed giant seemed to be made of much sterner stuff than Hal could have imagined. The scrag threw his shoulder into Robbie's stomach and lifted. The ogre's feet came off the sand, and for a moment it looked like he would roll all the way over the cyclops' shoulder and fall flat on his back. But the ogre was simply too heavy, and the cyclops buckled under the weight. They went down together, scrapping and rolling.

Hal knew Robbie was probably enjoying himself right now.

The sylph was at it again, now darting toward Molly. Hal roared a warning far too late. The sylph ghosted on through, and Molly stiffened. The veiled lady remained like that as the sylph shot upward, now another shade lighter.

Whatever the sylph was doing, Hal had no way to help. Both Dewey and Molly seemed to be in a daze now, and it was a miracle none of the scrags cut them down while they had the chance. Or maybe they just knew the two were done for, their souls or magic stolen.

Emily finally succeeded in getting the better of the golem—by twisting the thing's head off! She threw it away, and it bounced and rolled in the sand before coming to a stop. The golem's body paused, then felt for its head. Emily jumped clear and slithered away as the headless creature turned in a slow circle.

So not dead, then, Hal thought. *But headless. I bet that'll hurt when the golem turns back into a scrag.*

He shuddered at the thought of it. Was there hope for the scrag if he reattached his head before reverting back?

The rest of the Swarm stayed clear of the fight, content to stand around cheering and jeering. They were a motley bunch of men and women, maybe eight in all, wielding spears and knives. Hal came down hard directly in front of them, and they yelped and scattered, some of them tripping and dropping their weapons in their haste. Hal snorted at their cowardly retreat.

The wyvern screeched closer and whacked him on the face with its barbed tail. It stung, and he glared at the wily, fast-moving, flying reptile. It had been buzzing him and others throughout the battle but was way too quick for anyone to grab hold of. It seemed a little uncertain with its flight, though, sometimes swooping a bit too close to the beach and almost crash-landing.

Hal made a point to keep an eye on it and make a grab next time it passed.

"I've been stung!" a familiar voice cried.

Swinging around, Hal spotted Lauren kneeling in the sand, her wings spread but hanging low. She was gripping one of her knees. Just a few feet away, a manticore loomed over her, its scorpion-tail held high.

The scrag-manticore named Stick said something, but his jaw was still hanging at an awkward angle. The gleam in his eye said it all, though. He was waiting for her to die at his feet.

Hal stomped closer and gave the manticore an almighty backhanded swat. Stick flew sideways and collapsed, unconscious. If his jaw wasn't broken before, it certainly was now.

Lauren swayed, her eyes rolling up. The wound on her knee stood out clearly, an angry red swelling. Muscles in her thigh twitched violently as the manticore's poison took hold. She fell backward, suddenly as unconscious as the creature that had stung her.

Unable to pick her up and talk to her, Hal looked for Robbie. The ogre was still fighting with the cyclops, and it was hard to tell who had the upper hand. All in all, the shapeshifter battle seemed fairly even.

Hal reverted to his human form and knelt by Lauren as monsters clashed all around. "Lauren, wake up," he shouted in her ear. "You need to change!"

He gently slapped her face a few times, and she stirred and complained about it. He did it some more, trying to wake her. He knew she'd be fine if she switched back and forth. But what if she slipped into a deep state of unconsciousness and never woke?

"Lauren, you need to—"

"Oh, NO!" someone yelled.

It was Emily. Still in full naga form, she stood tall as she stared south.

Guppy the centaur heard her. He shielded his eyes against the sun and began to laugh. "Yeah, girl, that's what I'm talking about. I *told* you we had a bigger army."

Hal groaned. The odds had suddenly shifted with the appearance of a dozen or more gigantic rocs. Even from a distance, he could make out the shape of a long-haired man astride one bird out in front. The rest followed his lead, all heading toward the beach.

Chapter Nineteen
The Birdman

Cheers filled the beach as rocs flew in from the south, led by the mysterious long-haired New Earther known simply as the birdman. The battle continued unabated, yet eyes turned to the sky.

"It's over now, kids!" Guppy the centaur shouted. "Give it up while you're still breathing."

The headless golem stumbled around in circles, lashing out with arms of sticks and mud. Robbie and the cyclops were beginning to tire, both panting as they clobbered each other over and over. Fenton remained standing over the hellhound, repeatedly squirting his gluey spit to keep the creature from getting free. Thomas got into a scrap with several non-shifter scrags, and it was hard to say who was taunting who as he ran around between them, avoiding their spears. It was impossible to tell where Darcy was. Hal suspected she was darting about causing whatever mischief she could.

Molly and Dewey had by now wandered dreamily out of the battle zone. The centaur was heading along the beach toward the castle, and Molly into the water, her robes drenched.

Over their heads, Blair and Astrid did their best to keep the wyvern at bay. Neither were equipped to capture and subdue a small dragon, but they collided with it over and over, knocking it off course as it tried to dive-bomb the battle on the beach.

The sylph took another soul, only this time it was a scrag's. A straggly-haired woman had stepped in front of Thomas at the wrong moment and frozen when the sylph ghosted through her. After that, she stood perfectly still while the other scrags continued their runaround.

The banshee resumed its irritating wailing but otherwise did little to help nor hinder the battle. Nor did a few other scrag shifters. In this respect, Hal had been successful with his blood-swapping.

He watched, bemused, as the large-headed gnome-woman repeatedly head-butted the goblins, Blacknail and Flatfoot. The goblins deliberately took the punishment as, bit by bit, they led the scrag away from the battle.

The pointy-eared brownie with long black hair scampered away, yelling that this was not what he had signed up for. He didn't go far, just darted among some of the larger debris from the flooded houses to find a place to hide.

The petite, blue-skinned elf tore away, too, zigzagging up the beach and vanishing. Hal wasn't surprised. Tiny creatures like that had no business wrangling with monsters that could breathe fire, shoot poison quills, squirt glue, or crush skulls with bare fists.

That didn't stop the tiny faun, though. He had the ferocity of a tornado but the strength of a mild breeze. He tried to cause some damage but could barely lift a sword, lacked the height to throw a spear, and was so light on his feet that the slightest nudge from a careless elbow sent him flying. The faun was a giant of a man locked inside a puny body.

When Hal tore his eyes from the chaos, he was horrified to see Lauren was still unconscious. "Lauren! Wake up! You need to change!"

She didn't respond. Hal knew there was a serious threat of a shapeshifter dying if they fell unconscious instead of transforming one way or another. He shook her roughly, slapped at her face, then looked around for help. Where was Miss Simone? He'd seen her earlier, but she'd vanished around the time Queen Bee had escaped.

And where was Abigail? Hal hoped she was hiding under a rock somewhere. This was *not* the place for a faerie.

He scooped his arms under Lauren and tried to lift her. She was too heavy for him. One day he might be a big, strong man like his dad. Right now he was short and feeble. Grunting with disgust, he dragged her across the sand away from the battle, keeping his eyes open for attacking scrags and monsters.

The manticore that had stung her lay still, tongue hanging out. The chimera was still some way out to sea, splashing frantically as it headed toward shore. Once in a while, a fireball shot into the sky.

As for Simmy and Lola . . . The two were still at the water's edge, talking in earnest as the battle raged on. "Thanks for your help," Hal muttered as he put Lauren down again. The poison was a huge concern. Was it a fatal dose? Maybe Thomas would know since he was a manticore himself.

"Be right back," Hal told Lauren before heading off.

It was then, purely by chance, that he spotted Miss Simone. She was far along the beach, rolling on the sand with a small, black-clad woman. So she'd gone after Queen Bee after all—and now they were mere yards from Seth, who hunkered in the sand watching them with a cocked head.

As worried as he was for Miss Simone, Hal couldn't do everything at once. He tore through the crowd of battling shapeshifters and right into the middle of the cat-and-mouse game that Thomas and a gang of six or seven scrags were involved in. Leech was one of them. Duke was another; he'd joined the battle on the beach after murdering Mayor Priggle in front of everybody. Another scrag—the woman who'd been 'sylphed'—was now sitting idly on the sand, staring into space.

"Thomas!" Hal shouted.

The manticore swung around. The scrags paused, clearly surprised at the interruption.

Hal spoke loudly. "If you sting these people, is it fatal?"

Thomas grinned, baring three rows of long, pointed teeth. "If I want it to be. Or I can divvy it out between *all* these scrags. I should probably stop messing with them and get on with—"

"Lauren got stung," Hal said shortly. He pointed, and Thomas looked. "Can you do something?"

"Uh . . ." Thomas said, his eyes going wide.

At that moment, the scrags charged with spears held high. Their own poison-tipped stingers glistened in the sunlight, and Hal had no desire to be their victim again. He transformed and reared up high. The scrags backpedaled, a couple dropping their spears, as Hal leapt forward with snapping jaws.

He ensnared one straight away, but even as he bit deep, the idea of chewing on a human being—or a wild animal for that matter—filled him with disgust and horror. He spat the man out and grimaced as the other scrags yelled in anger.

Thomas took off, loping around the battleground and heading for Lauren where she lay some distance away.

Hal returned his attention to the scrags and belched up some fire. Even then he couldn't bring himself to burn them, so he allowed two men to pick up their fallen comrade and hurry away. The trail of blood horrified Hal. What use was he as a dragon if all he could do was *pretend* to be dangerous?

Someone let out a shriek. Hal looked that way, seeing nobody. Then he noticed footprints in the sand, appearing by magic before his eyes as though someone invisible were running at full speed. Darcy!

Coming after her, flapping its leathery wings and zipping from side to side, the wyvern snapped its jaws and swung its barbed tail, trying to zero in on whatever it could smell right in front of its snout. Hal could see its nostrils flaring, its small, beady eyes scanning the ground.

Before he could react, a huge, three-headed dog tore into view and pounced. One pair of jaws crunched down on the wyvern's left wing. The weight of the grey-furred cerberus slammed the dragon into the ground, and Hal heard the *snap!* of a wing bone followed by a terrible roar of pain.

Darcy ran on, zigzagging up the beach to safety, as the cerberus gnawed on the wyvern's wing. Seconds later, the barbed tail whipped around and caught the dog in the side. Three heads yelped in unison, and the cerberus took off with its tail between its legs.

Wimp, Hal thought. But he was grateful to Kinsey, who had to be watching from somewhere as her pet cerberus, Dog, ran away.

Familiar screeches told him the rocs had arrived. He'd successfully blocked them out of his mind until now, but when a large shadow passed over him, he looked up to find three monstrous birds descending with wings and claws outstretched, seeking to snatch up victims.

Hal leapt high, breathing fire and sweeping it around in an arc. All three rocs veered off course, one squawking in panic as thc flames caught its tail feathers. The birds split up and rose higher, apparently done with the battle already.

"Hey, get it together!"

The birdman was astride one of these rocs, yelling at them. Scrawny and barefoot, his clothes were dirty and raggedy. Hal spotted him holding aloft the wooden instrument he used to control these gigantic birds, some sort of flute but rounded and held sideways in his palms. *He's like a triton of the sky*, Hal thought grimly, *blowing into his conch shell.*

Sure enough, the man brought the instrument to his lips and started blowing, and the effect was instantaneous—a jerking of heads as the two flanking rocs angled toward him.

More rocs flew in, five of them and nearly a dozen more close behind. Panicked, Hal knew he'd never win this fight. He'd already scrapped with this flock outside Miss Simone's laboratory and nearly gotten himself pecked to pieces. But he also knew they weren't all that interested in fighting; they were simply obeying the instructions of the strange birdman. They lacked *commitment*. It should be relatively easy to dissuade them from joining in the fight.

But first he had to take out the birdman.

He launched skyward and set off after the leading roc. The birdman's hair streamed in the wind as he made fluty, melodic noises with his wooden instrument and led the rocs around in a gentle arc. They would soon be back in the battle, and Hal was sure they'd each grab a victim. Whether they'd distinguish between friends and foes was unclear.

With a feeling of *déjà vu*, Hal soared high above the birdman and dropped fast, his own claws outstretched. He'd tried this same maneuver with Queen Bee astride the simurgh, and it hadn't worked very well.

Rocs squawked in warning, and the birdman glanced backward— but too late. Hal collided hard right behind where the man sat, making the giant bird flap wildly at the sudden extra weight of a dragon. Hal grabbed the birdman in one paw and flew away, reaching for the sky with his prize and leaving the roc behind.

As expected, the entire flock seemed startled and confused, their formation breaking as the birdman's melody cut off.

But not for long. The birdman hurriedly resumed blowing into his curious flute. It wasn't so much a tune as a warbling sound, actually quite soothing. When Hal glanced back, he saw the rocs responding and beginning to follow.

You want to lead them away from battle? Hal thought with a surge of hope. *That actually suits me just fine.*

Ordinarily, he would have laughed with glee at the way his plan had unfolded so neatly. The threat of rocs had ended as quickly as it had begun, at least for those still in the throes of battle on the beach.

For Hal, though, it was a problem.

The bare-footed birdman reminded him so much of the triton. Both used a device to create sound, and somehow that sound had a controlling magic. But the birdman was much older, easily in his sixties, wrinkled but surprisingly spry. With his long, dark-grey hair, raggedy pants and shirt, and a face as gnarled as the triton's, maybe the two would get along well together—in the ocean!

Hal nearly dropped him right then and there, but it occurred to him the birdman would simply swim to the surface and continue blowing his flute. Before long, a roc would snatch him out of the sea and the attack on the beach would resume. The best solution was to separate him from his wooden flute the way the triton had been separated from his conch shell. Without that, he was worthless. The trouble was, Hal's claws were too big and clumsy for the delicate task of plucking a small object from a man's hand.

Kill him, then, a voice in the back of Hal's head said. *Squeeze the life out of him. Or just drop him from such a height he can't possibly survive.*

If he had to do such a thing as kill a man in cold blood, the second choice sounded less horrible. He climbed into the sky, higher and higher, and prepared to release the birdman from his grasp. The wiry man continued playing. He probably had no idea what was in store for him.

Hal's claws seemed to have locked up. He found he couldn't unclasp his meaty digits and release the man. The problem was all in his head, of course. It should be a simple matter to let this man drop. He would scream on his way down, and then it would be over with a dull smack as he hit the water far below. From this height, the sea would feel like solid ground. After that, the rocs would probably fly around for a bit and then disperse.

Just do it, he told himself. *Go on, I dare you.*

The birdman had stopped playing. The silence was worse. It was as though the man had suddenly realized what Hal planned—only Hal couldn't do it.

"Please," the man said, his voice shaky and high-pitched. "If you're planning to drop me, don't! The birds will never reach me in time. I'll hit the water too hard. It'll kill me."

"I know," Hal growled, trying to sound menacing.

"I had no choice," the birdman gabbled. "Queen Bee threatened my son. She said he'd be safe if I helped her a couple of times. She said nobody would get hurt. I was just supposed to transport the hostages and then help win the battle, that's all. I didn't know the casket had an actual dead man inside. I thought that was a bluff. Please let me go. She'll kill my son if I let her down!"

A likely story, Hal thought angrily. The memory of the birdman and his roc delivering that casket to Carter was hard to shake.

He'd risen so high now that his wings were beginning to feel tired, his body heavy. The air was thinner up here. The rocs, far below, had begun to flock around in circles. If Hal dropped the man now, *maybe* one would catch him on the way down. And maybe not.

It would be so much easier if he could just pluck the wooden instrument from the birdman's grasp and toss it away.

"I'm not a bad person," the birdman pleaded. "I'm not one of *them*. I'm harmless, I promise. I'm just a simple man who sells ocarinas for an honest living. Everyone likes the sound of them, even rocs."

He waved his wooden instrument around at this point, but Hal missed his chance to snatch it.

"The birds follow me whenever I make music," the birdman said, sweat glistening on his forehead. "I've been playing to this flock for twenty years now, training them to understand simple commands, riding on their backs. That's why Queen Bee came to me—because nobody knows rocs like I do." He barked a nervous laugh. "I'm living proof that you don't have to be a shapeshifter to communicate with animals."

Hal was torn. Should he drop the man? Would his pet rocs catch him? If only it were possible to form a few simple human words with his dragon mouth, he could demand the birdman toss the instrument— the *ocarina*—and that would be the end of it.

"I *know* you people," the birdman said. "Well, not you kids, but the older ones—Simone and Blair, and that *Molly*." He spat out her name with obvious distaste, causing Hal to blink at him with surprise. This curious man knew them? "It wasn't her fault," the birdman went on, wiping his perspiring forehead. "She was young. They were *all* so young."

"What are you talking about?" Hal grunted under his breath. He couldn't hang around here. He tried batting at the man's arm, but it didn't help. The birdman absently gripped the ocarina tighter and tucked his arm behind his back, now talking even faster.

"Look, I'm just an old fool who's spent too long living alone. Let me go, and I'll help you fight the Swarm—but only if *you* promise to help *me*. My son, you see, is on a journey, traveling alone, and Queen Bee's gang is following him, and she keeps threatening to kill him if I don't help her, and that's why I . . ."

Hal tuned him out because, back on the beach in the distance, he saw a short flash of fire. Seth the dragon was up to something. Maybe

Queen Bee had just ordered him to burn Miss Simone! Meanwhile, not far away from that flash of fire, the shapeshifter battle seemed to be easing off. What kind of conclusion had been drawn?

". . . seen him in a long, long time, and I didn't even know he was alive until recently, and when I found out, I wanted to go see Simone straightaway, but Queen Bee threatened me . . ."

Hal brought the man up to his snout.

". . . a-and sh-she'll vouch for me, I promise! She knows me! Put me back on a roc and I'll come with you to—"

"Shut up!" Hal roared. The birdman squeezed his eyes shut and raised his hands, one of them still clutching the ocarina.

It was like time stopped. Hal stared at the instrument. Elliptical, smooth and round, a series of holes and a single jutting mouthpiece, the ocarina had been lovingly crafted and maintained with a soft polish. In the right circumstances, he'd be interested in learning how it worked.

Hal snapped it up in his jaws—along with the birdman's hand. Something made a sickening crunch, and the man's eyes bulged.

When Hal released him, the ocarina fell to pieces and scattered to the wind. The birdman hardly noticed because he was busy sobbing at the sight of his bleeding hand. It wasn't so bad, though—a little mangled but otherwise intact.

Hal plummeted with his prisoner toward the flock of circling rocs. When he was close enough, he headed for one of the birds. It saw him coming and flapped away in a panic, but Hal was too fast. He threw the birdman onto the roc's back and sped away, heading back to the beach.

Enough time had been wasted on that curious man, but at least the threat of rocs was no more, not without their tune-playing guide leading them into battle. Something nagged at him, though. Given more time and a less stressful situation, he might have stopped to listen to the old man's ramblings. Did he really know Miss Simone and the others?

By the time he arrived over the beach, the battle had wound down. The hellhound was still incapacitated. The manticore obviously felt sorry for itself as it nursed a broken jaw and sore face. The golem still searched blindly for its head. The cyclops had a black eye. And the wyvern suffered from a bent and drooping wing so that all it could do was flap about uselessly on the ground, whipping its long tail around and screeching.

The unicorn, elf, and brownie had disappeared. The banshee still wailed but hoarsely now. The sylph seemed another shade lighter than it had been before, though its most recent victim was hard to spot among the crowd. The large-headed gnome sprawled facedown on the sand with two goblins astride her back. The chimera still hadn't made it back to shore.

The remaining Swarm force—an angry faun, Guppy the centaur, and several spear-wielding scrags—seemed reluctant to give in. They stood shoulder to shoulder as Emily, Astrid, Orson, Blair, Darcy, and Bo closed in.

Somewhere out in the bay, a group of mermaids held a triton prisoner, a minotaur floated dead or alive, and a hippocampus kept to itself.

The battle was just about won.

Hal looked for Robbie. The ogre shouldn't be hard to spot, and yet . . .

There! He had reverted to his human form and gone running to Lauren. Shoving Thomas aside, he knelt to hold her. Thomas watched for a second or two, then took off back to the battlefield where he joined the others in surrounding the remaining scrags. At that point they seemed to sag in surrender.

Lola trotted across the sand to be with Robbie and Lauren. She hunkered down and pawed at Lauren while Robbie glared suspiciously at the grey-skinned reptilian cat. Was she trustworthy? There was no way of knowing.

Simmy stayed where he was in the water, watching silently.

With a jolt of fear, Hal spotted Seth in the distance standing tall over Miss Simone. Perched on the dragon's back, Queen Bee shouted something, maybe trying to egg him on.

As Hal turned toward them and put on speed, he happened to glance back in time to see the lamia lunging at Lauren. Yelling, Robbie tried to push her off, but Lola already had her head down, tearing into Lauren's leg.

Despite everything, the lamia had succumbed to her bloodlust.

And in the opposite direction, much farther along the beach past endless debris, Miss Simone let out a piercing shriek.

Chapter Twenty
Death on the Beach

Torn with indecision, Hal very nearly turned around and headed straight back to help Lauren. He was much closer to her than Miss Simone, and it would take mere seconds to swoop down and knock the lamia flying.

On the other hand, Miss Simone probably needed him more. Lauren had Robbie the ogre right there by her side and a whole team of others nearby. Miss Simone had nobody to protect her from Queen Bee and a dragon.

Hal hurtled onward.

Miss Simone's piercing shriek had sounded unnatural, the kind of noise she made when angry. He could see her standing there on the beach staring up at Seth—only Seth was now turning away and flapping his wings, already lifting off. As Hal approached, Miss Simone ran after Seth and shouted to him, but the dragon gave a snort and flew up into the air.

She's angry, Hal realized. *Not hurt or in fear of her life, just angry.* Now he wished he'd gone to help Lauren instead.

Seth came soaring past just fifty yards away, Queen Bee on his back. She looked pretty angry herself, and she shot Hal a glare as they passed. He twisted his head to watch them. They were headed back to the battle.

Confused, Hal thudded down in the sand a few yards from Miss Simone and stamped closer.

She ran to him and began climbing aboard. "She won't admit it's all over. Hurry—she's going to rally her team again."

Hal took off back along the beach. He thought it funny that two identical dragons were currently flying low over the sand, each carrying the leader of a small army. Seth had already made it back and was dive-bombing the weary shapeshifters, not seeming to care who he aimed for. Hal saw Emily slithering fast alongside a scrag, both ducking as Seth's clawed feet made a grab for them.

"Lauren!" Hal rumbled, and headed her way.

Long before he got there, he glimpsed the lamia and Robbie leaning over the white-winged girl. Everything looked peaceful enough, though. Robbie hadn't switched to his ogre form, and she was still in one piece.

"Queen Bee's furious," Miss Simone shouted above the wind that rushed through her hair. "Your swapping the blood samples made her look a fool. And some of her scrags have let her down. Her army isn't quite what she expected."

"So what's she doing now?" Hal asked, one eye still on Lola in case she leapt at Robbie's throat.

His question was answered soon enough. Shouts filled the air as Hal's friends and some of the scrags ran around in a panic. Thirty feet above, Queen Bee yelled at Seth, and he veered toward a small figure with pointed ears and long, black hair—the odd little brownie creature that had run away earlier. He hadn't run far enough, though. He was ducking beneath a demolished, upside-down cart, but Seth tore into it with his jaws and ripped it apart, exposing the little fellow. The brownie's eyes opened wide right before the dragon snatched him up.

Hal swept in over the battlefield and circled around. Seth flew closer with the brownie hanging from his front paws. Queen Bee shrieked at the top of her lungs, "This is what I do with deserters!" Abruptly, Seth angled upward and shot high into the air as she barked orders into his ear.

The beach fell oddly silent. Enemies stopped running around and attacking one another. Everyone paused exactly where they were, their quarrel temporarily forgotten as they stared up at the sky.

Seth rose higher and higher, the brownie wriggling in his grip.

Then, after a long pause, Seth dropped him.

There were gasps and cries as the tiny, screaming figure began to plummet. Seth continued onward through the air, glancing over his shoulder as he went. It was hard to see what Queen Bee was doing. Patting the dragon's shoulder? Whispering "Good boy" in his ear?

Either way, the brownie fell toward the rooftops of Brodon. Not only would he die, someone else in town might get hurt as well.

For a fleeting moment, Hal felt sorry for Seth. The boy had made a point of explaining he didn't like to kill people, and yet Queen Bee—his self-appointed guardian—had just talked him into it. Some mother she was!

Springing into action, Hal put on some speed and headed toward Brodon with the hope of intercepting the falling brownie. Blair, Orson, and Astrid did the exact same thing. Blair was easily the fastest, and he snagged the brownie long before the others would have got there. He made it look so easy, too. In a matter of seconds, the phoenix was turning and heading back to the beach.

He deposited the brownie on the sand near the battleground and flew off. The small figure, shaking like a leaf, promptly fainted.

Something changed in the stunned silence that followed. Everybody looked at each other—humans and monsters, scarred or otherwise—sharing a moment of disbelief at what had just happened. At what Queen Bee had done to one of her own and how gallant Blair had been to save the enemy.

The moment only lasted a few seconds, though. The scrag named Duke piped up, "He deserved that for running off. He was lucky he didn't get a stinging."

"He still might," the tiny faun shouted. "The queen's coming back."

Seth came hurtling down from the sky, Queen Bee screaming something nobody could make out. "She's not amused," Miss Simone said from behind Hal's head. "Take me closer to our people, Hal."

He flew in, unsure of her intentions. As he passed over the crowd, she shouted, "Retreat! Move away!"

And, just like that, everybody Hal knew hurried away from the scrags, leaving them standing. In less than five seconds, the two sides were separated with a huge space between.

As Seth came tearing in, Hal wondered if he should try to ward him off. Miss Simone might get hurt in the process, though. *He* might get hurt. Anything could happen if two identical dragons clashed in the air. One of the passengers could easily topple off.

As it happened, he didn't need to do a thing because a frantic barking started up behind him, down by the water's edge. He spun about in time to see the simurgh—the gigantic dog-headed bird—heading up the slope of the beach. Simmy was back. He flapped all four wings and lifted off from the sand.

Told you, Hal thought. *I knew your wing bones would heal up if you shifted back and forth.*

He looked over his shoulder to see Seth breathing fire on his final approach. Still seventy or eighty feet up, it was unclear whether he was angling toward the Swarm or Hal's friends. Perhaps both. Either way, shifters and scrags scattered in all directions.

Then Simmy was there, flying up toward him, his massive bulk casting a huge shadow and causing Seth to jerk in surprise. Too late, though. The simurgh thudded into him. Both were knocked off course. The simurgh righted itself quickly, but Seth tumbled through the air with flailing limbs, wings, and tail.

"Yes!" Hal hissed with delight. Simmy had finally made up his mind which side he was on, and his massive bulk made a tremendous impact—literally.

Queen Bee came loose and fell to the beach from a great height, dropping toward the empty space somewhere between the two small armies. She landed hard on her back and lay there wide-eyed, her mouth opening and shutting as she tried to catch a breath.

"Grab her!" Miss Simone shouted.

Everyone surged toward Queen Bee, one side hoping to save their helpless queen, the other to capture her.

Hal would have leapt into the fray except he wanted to make sure Seth was out of the picture first. The dragon had not landed quite so heavily as Queen Bee. Instead, he'd skidded and bounced before coming to a rest.

The simurgh, still flapping around and causing a strong downdraft, moved closer and descended, thumping down on the sand near Seth. Standing over him, he growled and planted a large, three-toed foot on the dragon's neck.

Several scrags exclaimed their disappointment at Simmy and threw down their spears with disgust. They stood there with slumped shoulders. The cyclops groaned and sat down to rest, and Emily, who had been constantly jabbing at him with her fangs, slithered around in front. Though twice her size, he had a swollen, puffy eye and looked thoroughly worn down.

The battle, which had resumed with vigor moments ago, had quickly ended again. Now that the simurgh had defected, and the cyclops had given up, the rest of the scrags followed suit. Some of the most fearsome—the manticore, the hellhound, the wyvern, and the golem—were all injured or incapacitated in some way. The golem still couldn't find its head. And the chimera languished out to sea, no doubt exhausted.

When Hal looked around and thought about it, he decided that the most damaging scrag shapeshifter had turned out to be the ghostly sylph. She had rendered two of Hal's friends utterly useless. Molly and Dewey were still wandering around in a dream state.

But the sylph seemed flighty and hadn't darted into battle as much as she might have. Or maybe ghosting through people and taking their souls wasn't as easy as it looked. Maybe she had simply had her fill for now. Even the biggest, deadliest carnivores became too stuffed to move after a hearty meal. Maybe the sylph was full up with souls or whatever it was she stole from her victims.

Hal spotted the weird phantom woman floating around over the water, trailing wispy smoke. She was definitely a few shades lighter than when he'd first seen her. She might be ready to eat again soon, though.

He landed and reverted to his human form the moment Miss Simone had climbed off. Lauren was still lying on the sand, Robbie and Lola hunched over her. The first thing he noticed was the tiny faerie buzzing around their heads.

"Abi!" he shouted, running to her.

She saw him and expanded in size, then retracted her wings—just in time for Hal to throw his arms around her.

"I was worried about you," he said. It was only then he realized how much that was true.

"I was more worried about *you*," she said. "Nobody could catch me, but you were in the thick of it as always." She pointed down the beach to where Dewey had come to a halt. "I've been taking care of those two—Dewey and Molly—whispering in their ears and guiding them away from the battle. They'll sorta-kinda do as they're told, but they're pretty much out of it."

Hal spotted Molly somewhere entirely different, stumbling across some bits of wood that littered the sand. "What's happened to them? Can they be . . . ?"

"Fixed?" Abigail said. "Not sure. Let's ask."

She went to pluck at Miss Simone's sleeve, but the blond-haired woman ignored her for the moment. She was too busy leaning over Robbie's shoulder to look at Lauren.

Hal almost didn't want to see how bad the harpy girl was hurt. She was still lying on her back, her wings spread out beneath her like a fine quilt. He imagined the poison had spread throughout her body, causing painful swelling and fever. If she'd only been conscious enough to transform back and forth . . . Yet he knew she was all right even though the lamia had lunged at her earlier. Robbie was too calm for her to be anything other than safe.

What he saw freaked him out a little. Lola had her front paws on Lauren's injured knee. Blood smeared the lamia's chin. Her scaly body and human face had been a pale grey color before. Now she'd turned a richer, more golden color.

"You didn't," Hal said with narrowed eyes.

"She did," Robbie answered for her. He grinned. "She saved Lauren's life."

Lauren pushed herself up on her elbows. "Hey, Miss Simone," she said with a weak smile, "now I know how you felt when Thomas stung you."

Miss Simone shook her head. "Why didn't you change? You could have self-healed. You *still* haven't changed. There's no reason for this person to be sucking blood out of your knee."

"I fainted," Lauren said. "Lola saved me."

Robbie nodded. "Lola needed young, innocent blood to drink, and Lauren needed the poison sucked out of hers, so we're making sure it's all gone."

"Making sure the blood's all gone?" Hal repeated, horrified.

"The poison, idiot. It should be gone by now. She sucked it out and spat it over there." He pointed to a nasty splash of red and bright yellow in the sand nearby. "Now Lola's drinking good, clean blood. Just a little bit. Once she's had enough, she can stop and Lauren can change and heal up, and that'll be that. We're killing two birds with one stone."

Lauren batted at him. "That's a terrible thing to say."

Robbie looked confused for a second—but then he glanced at her wings and laughed. "Sorry. Yeah, bad choice of words."

As Lola dipped her head to Lauren's knee, Hal's mouth dropped open. He stared, morbidly fascinated and grossed out at the same time.

Miss Simone stood and began striding back up the beach. "Let's take care of Queen Bee before she slips away again."

Leaving the macabre trio behind, Hal and Abigail stayed close to Miss Simone. Hal couldn't help feeling excited. Finally, things seemed to be going their way. Then he checked himself. Nothing was over until it was over.

The small scrag queen lay on her back staring up at the sky. Nearby, Seth looked like he was wondering whether he could jump up and escape, but the simurgh's heavy foot on his neck persuaded him to lie still.

"It's over," Miss Simone told Queen Bee without preamble as she stood over the motionless woman. "Your people are done in. It's time to call it a day."

Queen Bee slowly turned her head and lifted her arm to shield her eyes against the sun. "You've ruined *everything*," she snarled as a hush fell. "I hope you feel good about yourself, Simone. All I ever wanted was for my people to be accepted, but nobody would take us because of the way we look."

"That's not true—" Miss Simone started to protest.

"No?" She barked a hoarse laugh. "You have *no idea* what it's like to be us. What we've been through. You live in your cozy house in your cozy village, safe from the virus, enjoying the countryside and the good, clean air . . ."

She had such a look of contempt on her face that Miss Simone turned away. Queen Bee didn't stop there, though.

"The rest of us have had to scavenge on the streets for food. It wasn't so bad at first, plenty of houses and stores to raid after everyone had dropped dead, but you'd be surprised how quickly *that* gets old, especially with corpses stinking things up. The army cleared away the dead eventually—and took most of the canned food as well, anything with a good shelf life. The rest of us? Scrounging and stealing, fighting to stay alive while dealing with the pain of our scars and what we'd lost."

She shook her head and closed her eyes, wincing as her chest rose and fell.

"I had a child once," she said, gritting her teeth. "A boy. I haven't spoken his name aloud in years, and I won't start now, not in front of you people."

Hal had a feeling 'you people' referred to *everyone* present, scrags and all. Her Swarm didn't seem put out by her sweeping contempt, though. They hung onto every word.

"He was thirteen when the virus took him. I lost my home to invaders in the months after. I lost everything I had."

She chewed her lip as everyone in the vicinity shuffled closer. Pretty soon, a large circle had formed around her. Still she lay flat on her back.

"I killed to stay alive," she said quietly, almost to herself. "I got so good at it that others wanted to follow me around. I formed a gang. The Swarm became feared across the city. I was the queen of the scrags. Other gangs joined me or got out of my way. I spent years trying to forget how much I'd lost, and I did it by building a new family—a family of scarred people like me, people who had lost as much as I had." She lifted her head and looked around, clearly straining with the effort. "It was better than nothing, right?"

The crowd murmured their agreement.

Resting her head on the sand again, she sighed with what sounded like irritation. "We picked up a young man who was immune to the virus. A weasel named Ryan. He set fire to my home and ran away."

Because you filled his sock with virus spores and scarred him for life, Hal thought.

"So I went after him," Queen Bee said, "and he led us to you, Simone."

She looked up at Miss Simone with such an intense glare of hatred that Hal would rather have faced Molly's death-gaze in that moment.

"A whole new world," Queen Bee snarled, trying to raise herself up again. "People walking around in clean air. Villages full of happy families. Amazing creatures that are only supposed to exist in the imagination. Plenty of room for my people to settle. Only nobody would accept us. Nobody!"

She spat that last word out. She collapsed then, pale and trembling, breathing hard and obviously in pain. Some of the Swarm edged forward, but others held them back, shaking their heads.

"And then Seth came along."

Queen Bee turned her head to look for him. Scrags moved aside, forming a narrow gap through which she could gaze at the dragon beyond.

"He needs me. He's like my son was—impulsive, curious, too ready to go off exploring, liable to get himself in trouble. He needs parenting. He needs *me*." She swallowed and winced. "And now you people have gotten me killed."

Hal frowned. He glanced sideways and found Miss Simone narrowing her eyes and inching forward.

All around, scrags stared in silence.

Queen Bee opened her eyes again. This time, when she spoke, her voice was decidedly hoarse. "I think I ruptured something."

Miss Simone moved closer. "There's a doctor in Brodon."

The queen tried to laugh at that but instead winced and screwed her face up. "You really think people here would help me? I don't."

She squinted, now too weak to shield her eyes. Miss Simone moved into a position that blocked the sunlight.

"I should have had Leech and Croaker fix me up as a shapeshifter," Queen Bee said. "I could have transformed and self-healed. Right, Simone?"

Miss Simone shrugged and nodded.

"Well, at least some of my Swarm can get rid of their scars. Maybe things will be better for them if they look like everybody else instead of monsters." She winced again, struggling not to laugh. "The irony, Simone. I had to make them into monsters so nobody would perceive them as such."

The circle of scrags had closed tightly around her again. Behind them, the gigantic simurgh made a startled noise, and a few heads turned to look. Hal saw nothing wrong until he realized Seth had vanished.

He gaped. How had a full-sized dragon managed to slip away undetected?

More heads turned, and a few exclamations told Hal what had happened. The crowd parted again, and Seth—in human form, wrapped in a shirt a scrag had just passed to him—crept forward. He looked ordinary enough, a twelve-year-old with dark-brown hair that needed cutting. He had no scars whatsoever.

He knelt by Queen Bee and stroked her hand. "Bee?"

She woke, having apparently slipped away for the last minute. Blinking, she smiled. "Well, look at you. You clean up nice."

Miss Simone knelt also. She ducked low and lifted Queen Bee's arm, trying to see underneath her. "I don't see any blood," she muttered. "Tell me if this hurts—"

"Get away from me, woman!" the queen snapped with every last ounce of energy. A spittle of blood appeared at the corner of her mouth, and she licked it and frowned. After that, she sighed and closed her eyes, clinging tightly to Seth's hand as he leaned over her. "I think it's time," she whispered.

One of the scrags started up with a long, drawn-out hum. Others immediately joined in, and pretty soon the air was filled with the noise. When one or two broke off to draw breath, others filled in for them, and so on, their voices overlapping so they produced a continuous, unbroken drone. The effect was creepy, and Hal had no doubt the sound carried all the way up the beach to Brodon.

Queen Bee's lips curled into a smile, and she stayed like that while Seth rested his head on her shoulder and the entire Swarm closed in tighter and tighter, a curious bunch of humans along with a cyclops towering over them, a few smaller creatures, Lola the lamia, a manticore, a broken-winged wyvern, and others. Even Simmy joined in, though his was more of a howl than a hum.

Overhead, the banshee floated silently.

Chapter Twenty-One
The Nature of the Sylph

The scrags had lost the urge to fight. "Now what?" the tiny faun said, sounding like he was prepared to launch back into battle at the slightest provocation.

"Now you face a fair trial," Miss Simone told them all in a stern voice. She sounded like she were talking to a class full of children, and some of the scrags took umbrage at her tone and gave her hateful looks.

They were all sitting on the sand, shoulder to shoulder. Simmy, back in human form, had taken a leaf from Seth's book and borrowed a scrag's shirt to wear around his middle. He strutted around showing off his scar-free skin. Non-shapeshifter scrags stared at him with a degree of jealousy while the rest, a menagerie of monsters, looked hopeful as Simmy tried to explain how to revert back to human form.

"You just do it," he said, spreading his hands. "You have to want it so badly that it just comes naturally without thinking about it. If you think about it too hard, it won't work. Just . . . just *do* it."

His pep talk didn't seem to be working very well, though. Not a single scrag managed to morph back into their human form. The manticore was groaning by now, his jaw hurting badly, and the wyvern kept trying to flap its damaged wings to no avail.

"They'll get it eventually," Hal said to Abigail.

He was standing guard over the scrags along with Fenton, Thomas, and Emily. Robbie and Lauren still sat apart with Lola. Astrid had flown off to fetch some of the dead mayor's guards. Perhaps they would be able to rustle up a large force to take the scrags into custody—but not before the new shapeshifters among them reverted to their ordinary size and shape, and that might take a while.

Miss Simone touched Abigail on the shoulder. "I need your help."

"With what?"

"Dewey and Molly."

"About time!" Emily exclaimed, overhearing from her position fifteen or twenty feet away.

"Yeah," Fenton added. "Who am I supposed to trip up and make fun of without Dewey around? He's no good to me at the moment."

None of them had liked seeing the two wander so aimlessly, but Miss Simone had assured everyone their situation was in no danger of worsening. She'd added that in fact it couldn't *get* any worse, but that hadn't stopped her dealing with the more immediate problem first— explaining to the Swarm that the battle was over and that their esteemed leader, Queen Bee, had died from internal hemorrhaging and shock, maybe even a few broken bones that had punctured an organ or two. Though the queen looked unscathed, almost peaceful, there was no way she would be walking away from this.

"The sylph is an elemental," Miss Simone told Abigail. "They're notorious for stealing the life force from people. Their essence, if you like."

"Their soul?" Hal suggested.

Miss Simone scrunched up her nose. "I'm not sure I'd use that word, but I suppose it works as well as any other."

They all looked up at the strange phantom creature. She was floating around above the group and leaving a trail of thin smoke.

"Why would you want a blood sample from something like *that*?" Abigail exclaimed. "Who wants soul-snatching ghosts floating around the village?"

"Nobody," Miss Simone said grimly. "That's exactly the point. There's a place to the west that's overrun by sylphs. They're infested with them. I thought it would be useful to have a shapeshifter sylph so we could find out more about them, talk to them, perhaps discover an alternative substitute for souls. It's what the Shapeshifter Program is for, after all."

Hal and Abigail said nothing for a moment.

"So *how* did you get a blood sample?" Abigail asked. "How do you take blood from a ghost?"

"They can take solid form and walk around on the ground, mingle with people and so on, but they can only do that if they weigh themselves down first. That's why they steal souls. The more they steal, the heavier and more substantial they become. That place I mentioned? Sylph hunters pounced on one as soon as she was vulnerable. I took a sample before they . . . disposed of her."

"This one's had three souls that I know of," Hal said. "Molly, Dewey, and a scrag woman. The sylph got lighter the more she took."

"Lighter in color, maybe," Miss Simone said, "but more substantial, too. I'd say she has a way to go before she's solid enough for us to grab hold of—which presents a problem. We can't grab her unless she's solid, and becoming solid means stealing more souls, which obviously we can't allow."

"Can . . . can souls be returned?" Abigail said with a tremble in her voice.

Miss Simone scratched her nose, frowned, and finally gave a nod. "Yes—but it's very rare simply because they don't want to. While they have souls, they're solid enough to be with ordinary people. As time passes, the souls diminish and the sylph slowly turns back into a phantom. Why would they willingly give up souls and return to a ghostly state?"

Many of Hal's friends were listening to this, and it seemed some of the closest scrags were, too.

"So how do we persuade her?" Hal asked. A thought occurred to him. "What if she just switches to human form? She won't need souls then. Will they return to their bodies?"

"I don't know, Hal. This is why I wanted a sylph shapeshifter—to learn exactly this kind of thing. What if she reverts to human form and *doesn't* release the souls? They might be lost forever. Or they might linger until she transforms into a sylph the next time. I just don't know. Solid sylphs have been put down in the past, but nobody has known souls to return."

Lauren walked into the circle at that moment. She was back in her own human form, her green, silky dress smothered in wet sand. She seemed fine.

Robbie held her hand, grinning as if everything was all right with the world. He looked around with raised eyebrows. "What are we talking about?"

"Molly and Dewey," a voice next to him said.

Robbie swung around, squinting. "Whoa! Darcy?"

The blond-haired girl materialized out of nowhere, and several scrags let out cries of surprise. "Sorry. I've been here the whole time. I forgot I was invisible."

"I want to be what you are!" a scrag woman called out. "If we get to be shapeshifters like the rest of the Swarm, I want to be invisible and—"

"Forget it," Miss Simone said sharply. "You people have done enough damage. You're not responsible enough to be shapeshifters."

"And these kids are?" another demanded. This was Leech, the humpbacked scientist. "Listen, lady, you don't have the right to stop us. Look at Simmy! All his scars are gone! He turned into that giant dog-bird thing, and now he's completely normal, all healed up. I want to heal, too. We *all* do."

The non-shifting scrags shouted their agreement.

Miss Simone opened her mouth to retort, but Hal tugged on her sleeve and whispered, "They might be less trouble if you tell them maybe."

She frowned, looked from one expectant face to another, and sighed. "Maybe." As a babble of excitement started up, she raised her hands and shouted over them. "But not anytime soon—not without a fair trial for all the things you've done, the trouble you've caused, and of course the people you killed."

"We only killed a few," someone blurted. As heads swiveled, the scrag named Duke shrugged. "Only three by my reckoning."

Orson the pegasus whinnied loudly, stamped his hoofs, and fluttered his shiny, black wings. Astrid the sphinx was the one who spoke. "Only three?" she shouted, her voice rising in pitch. "*Only* three?"

An argument broke out then. As Miss Simone, Astrid, and Bo pointed fingers, scrags tried to defend their position, quickly turning on Queen Bee who lay dead on the sand not too far away. Seth, still by her side, scowled at the sudden wave of blame, and Hal saw his fists balling.

Abigail must have seen that, too, because she sprouted her wings and rose into the air above the squabbling crowd. "Enough!" she screamed.

Voices trailed off. People frowned up at her.

"Can we *please* stop arguing and get my friends' souls back?"

At this, mutters and murmurs filled the air, and the tension eased. The sylph, who had paused midair, spun about as everyone looked up at her. She suddenly looked worried, and she opened her mouth to speak. Though her lips moved, nothing came out but a whisper that nobody could hear.

Miss Simone spoke quietly. "This is why I need your help, Abigail. Go talk to her. But be careful."

Looking doubtful, Abigail buzzed up into the air above the crowd and toward the sylph. The phantom woman backed up a little, but she seemed curious about what the faerie might have to say.

Hal strained to hear. The two were drifting higher and farther away, and Abigail's voice came in bits and pieces. ". . . Let them go and . . . maybe another way to . . . can't live without their souls . . ."

She placed her hands together, obviously pleading now, but the sylph wore a confused, standoffish scowl. She kept shaking her head and backing up even more. By this time, the two of them were several hundred feet away.

The sylph's scowl deepened. Suddenly, she shot forward and through Abigail, emerging easily from the other side and leaving the faerie gasping.

"No!" Hal yelled along with a crowd of others.

He jumped up and started running as the sylph drifted away, another shade lighter. She was grinning now, descending slowly as though she'd gained weight.

Abigail remained frozen in midair, her wings buzzing sporadically. They stuttered, and she began to fall, but then she buzzed again and hovered before stuttering again. By the time Hal got to her, she was only just out of reach. He jumped for her, grabbed her foot, and pulled her downward. Her wings stopped, and she fell into his arms.

"Abi!" he yelled in her face.

She gave him a dreamy, glassy-eyed stare.

A commotion had started up again, but Miss Simone yelled at the scrags to sit back down. Only then did she come running.

"What's your name?" she shouted up to the floating woman.

The sylph stared down at her.

"Your name," Miss Simone repeated, slowing as she approached. Craning her neck to peer up at the sylph, she spoke more softly now. "Tell me your name."

"Her name's Stretch!" a scrag shouted.

Miss Simone raised an eyebrow. "That's not a name," she said quietly to the sylph. "Tell me your *real* name."

But the sylph said nothing.

"All right, Stretch it is, then." Miss Simone took a deep breath. "Listen, Stretch, you can't do this. I know you have an urge to do what comes naturally—to take people's life force—but you're a *person*. You're one of us. If you want to better yourself and be accepted into a village somewhere in this world . . . well, you need to step up and do what's right. You need to let those souls go."

The sylph shook her head. Her mouth moved, and this time Hal thought he heard her say, "I'd rather die."

Could sylphs be killed while intangible like this? Hal couldn't imagine how. Certainly not by physical means. He hugged Abigail tighter, wishing she'd just snap to it, wake up and blink rapidly, give even the slightest indication that she was *there*.

"It doesn't have to be this way," Miss Simone said. "Nothing good will come of taking all these souls. If you want to be solid and walk on the ground, you just have to become human again. You're a *shapeshifter* now. Come down here."

To Hal's surprise, the sylph descended until she was maybe fifteen feet above their heads, tilted forward with that odd, wispy smoke trailing from the raggedy dress she wore.

"That's good," Miss Simone said, nodding. "Just a little more, and then we can talk—"

The sylph shot forward and ghosted through her.

A roar of indignation filled the air. Even the scrags were upset. Miss Simone staggered, then stood quite still, a blank look on her face.

The sylph smiled as she floated just above the ground, once more a shade lighter and looking almost human. The smoke petered out, and when she clapped her hands together, Hal heard a soft, dull thud, somehow distant. "I'm growing solid," she said in a faraway voice.

"And as soon as you're solid enough," Hal growled, "you're gonna wish you weren't."

He could barely contain his fury. The heat in his chest was growing, and he knew he was about to transform and lunge at her whether she was solid enough or not. The woman had lost her mind. Even her fellow scrags thought so.

The sylph turned to him with a tilted head and a smug look. "You can't stop me. None of you can. I can take all your souls. I'm getting the hang of it now. It was overwhelming before, almost smothering. It took my breath away each time. Now it's different."

Hal carefully pressed down on Abigail's shoulders and forced her to sit so she wouldn't go wandering off. He straightened up and turned to the sylph—

And she came at him.

Before Hal had a chance to react, she was already passing through him. He gasped, and everything turned to a haze.

* * *

"Oh, no," Hal muttered.

He was in that place again. That void of nothing, a world of darkness against which nearly-black clouds rolled all around as he floated there. Tiny orange glows moved about in random directions like a star-studded night sky that had decided to rearrange itself.

He'd spent maybe an hour here when Molly had transfixed him with her death-gaze and turned him to stone. The only difference this time was that he *knew* where he was and how to get around.

And people he knew were here with him.

"Miss Simone!" he called to the mysterious, human-shaped, smoky figures that floated nearby. "Abi!"

At the sound of his voice, both figures jerked. He waved his arms and moved closer, letting his imagination flesh out what he saw before him. In an instant, one featureless figure became Abigail, the other Miss Simone.

"What—?" Miss Simone said.

Abigail swung around, her eyes wide. "Hal!"

Hal moved toward her. "It's okay. I've been here before. Just try to relax. You're seeing me as a shadow at the moment, but that's because souls don't have faces. Just picture me as you know me, and your mind will do the rest."

Both of them stared at him wide-eyed. He edged closer so the three of them formed a triangle, facing each other.

"Oh!" Miss Simone said. "I see you!" She reached for him, and though clumsy, she managed to cross the small space and fling her arms around his neck.

Startled, Hal froze as she clung tight. Her arms sank into his shoulders, and something about that repulsed him—and not because Miss Simone was acting strangely clingy.

"Where *are* we?" she said, her mouth by his ear.

"Uh . . ."

"And where are Molly and Dewey?" Abigail said, turning away. "I've never known anything like this. I have to say I'm stumped. Is this the place you talked about, Hal? The place you visited when Molly turned you to stone?"

"Uh, yeah," Hal said as Miss Simone continued to cling to his neck. He suddenly realized what was wrong. "Hey, Miss Simone?"

"Mm?" Abigail said.

Hal mentally kicked himself. He blinked and re-imagined the two souls so they had the correct faces and voices. Suddenly it was Abigail clinging to his neck and Miss Simone looking around in wonder. He sighed with relief and hugged Abigail tight, ignoring the odd feeling as his fingers sank into her waist.

"We need to find the others," he said, finally disengaging from her grip. "They can't be far. Time moves slowly in here—or fast outside, depending on how you look at it. The three of us practically arrived together, but Molly and Dewey got here a few seconds earlier."

"A few—" Miss Simone turned and looked at him, her mind clearly working overtime. She shook her head. "This is difficult to fathom."

"Chase figured it out. He said every six minutes in here is a day outside. So we need to find the others fast. They've been gone—what, an hour at most? That means they've only been in this place for . . ."

He paused, trying to get his head around the complicated math problem. In the end he gave up.

"There!" he said instead, squinting into the darkness. "I think I see someone."

Grabbing Abigail's hand, he started to move through the void. He reached for Miss Simone's hand as he passed, and she took it without pause, then recoiled at his touch. He waited, and she tentatively took it again. The hand-holding was bearable after that. It just took getting used to.

The three of them drifted toward a shadowy figure floating upside down not too far away.

"Who's there?" Hal shouted.

The shadow glanced his way. Or at least the head rotated. It was hard to tell where the face was because it was completely black.

"Who *is* that?" Hal asked again, approaching fast.

"M-Molly. I—where am I? Is that *you*, Hal?"

Grinning broadly, he brought his passengers to a halt in front of Molly as she slowly rotated. She was already fleshing out in his mind, and within a second she was complete, her robes billowing in a non-existent wind, a veil hanging across her face, and her familiar wide-brimmed hat tipped forward.

"Now we need to find Dewey," he said, looking around.

"I don't understand," Molly moaned. "I can't see. You're all smoky and dark. Are you wearing masks and black clothes? Where's the ground? Why—?"

This is where you send people when you turn them to stone, Hal thought. How ironic that she was here now.

"I don't understand, either," Miss Simone said. "But Hal's been to this place before. We just need to keep it together and do as he says."

"Picture us as you know us," Hal said helpfully. "We can look exactly how you want us to look. All you need to do is imagine it."

"Didn't work for me," Miss Simone muttered. "Maybe I don't have any imagination."

More black figures were popping up. Hal frowned, confused and concerned. Something wasn't right. "Dewey!" he yelled.

"Here!" a distant voice cried. "Who said that?"

"It's me! Hal!"

It took about thirty precious seconds or more to gather the five of them together. In the process, someone else called out. "Hal? Where are you?"

Hal felt a horrible, sinking feeling. "Emily?" And then another voice he recognized. "Fenton?"

This was a nightmare. His mind raced as he finally caught up with the math problem. According to the time difference Chase had figured out, one whole day outside equaled only six minutes in the void. So Molly and Dewey had arrived ten or fifteen seconds earlier than him. Now other friends were popping up. Overall, perhaps five minutes had passed just getting to grips with their predicament.

Nearly a whole day had gone by outside already.

"She got me," Emily moaned. "We had the sylph woman calmed down, and the people of Brodon had started clearing up some of the mess from the flood, and it got dark on us, and we were all wondering what we were supposed to do next. Two of the scrags—the manticore and the wyvern—changed back into people, and they were pretty happy about it, too. In the end, Brodon guards came along to take the scrags away to jail. Nobody liked that idea, so Astrid said we should shift and help out. Some of us did—but that sylph went crazy and attacked us, just ghosted through us one after another."

"Is anyone *not* here?" Hal demanded.

He realized that was a silly question. Nobody could see anybody's faces, and voices were nondescript until fleshed out with an identity. Aware that time was pressing, Hal quickly gathered the group together and asked them to say their names out loud. Listening to that roll call was like being told of all the people who had died in a horrible accident—and the truth was, they *were* dead unless the sylph let them go.

Meanwhile, time moved on. That was the worst thing, Hal realized—the fact that every passing minute in the void was about four hours outside!

And what was happening to their bodies in the meantime? They wandered aimlessly on the beach, utterly vulnerable if the scrags wanted to cut them down.

"Shut up!" he yelled as the clamor of frightened voices grew.

When everyone fell silent, he stared around the group. Some faces he'd filled in. All his friends were there, each and every one of them. The sylph had spared no one. There were three scrags, too. When they spoke, he recognized Lola and Simmy straight away. The third identified herself as Delores, who'd been snatched earlier in the battle during Thomas's cat-and-mouse game. He couldn't remember her face, so he left it blank.

Hal fought to control his terror. He couldn't let everyone know how hopeless the situation was. If the sylph didn't let them go, then they were done for. After everything they'd been through, to be taken in such an effortless way seemed grossly unfair. But what could anybody do to stop a phantom?

"How solid was the sylph toward the end?" he asked, his mind elsewhere. He needed to keep the others calm. Any outbreaks of panic would just cause more delays if and when he managed to work up a plan.

"She was talking to us," Bo offered. "Right before the Brodon people showed up to arrest the scrags, we were *reasoning* with her, trying to persuade her to let you go, and the scrags were helping. I think everyone was scared of her. She kind of hopped around like there was hardly any gravity, like she was on the moon, and everybody kept moving away from her."

"So how solid was she?" Hal asked again.

"She grabbed Thomas, then Fenton, and then me," Emily said. "She was still a phantom—and she had to be to ghost through us, right?"

"She *bumped* into me," Simmy pointed out. "I was one of the last, I think. She called me a traitor. Lola, too. She didn't ghost *through* me, but she bumped into me and I kind of got *pulled* into her."

"So she's solid now?" Hal said. "She could be stopped? Someone could jab her with a spear or cut her throat or—"

He broke off. Panic had driven him to talk this way. But somebody killing her might be the only chance Hal and his friends had of returning to life.

Then again, Miss Simone had said souls did *not* return to their bodies when sylphs were put down. Was a shapeshifter sylph any different? Somehow, Hal doubted it.

But he had another idea.

Chapter Twenty-Two
Lost Souls

Hal led the way across the void. Short of something happening in the real world that would miraculously change the sylph's mind and spit out the souls, all he could think about was going to see the Gatekeeper—and quickly.

"Where are we going?" Miss Simone asked as the crowd, with linked hands, sped through the endless, cloudy void. None of them liked the feeling of touching like this. Souls tended to overlap.

"It's hard to explain," Hal said. "We're going to see, uh . . . Well, think of her as . . . Well, I call her the Gatekeeper. She, uh . . ."

He broke off. Even here, in this impossible place of magic and supernatural entities and glowing balls of energy, he found it difficult to say out loud what the Gatekeeper was even though he'd already told Miss Simone months ago after his last visit. She had *tried* to believe him back then. Perhaps she really had.

"You'll see," he said in the end. "Make up your own mind about her."

The scene ahead brought about a collective gasp. More black, shadowy figures, but thousands of them, perhaps millions, so densely packed together they formed a solid impenetrable mass spreading into the distance where they surrounded a dazzling bright white light.

"Is that where we're headed?" Abigail whispered, clinging to one of his hands. Miss Simone clung to the other. The entire group was linked in this way, with Hal at the center and the rest spread out to the sides and trailing a little behind. Together, they formed an arrow shape, and Hal imagined he was like the leading bird in a flock.

"Look, there's the Gatekeeper," he said, swallowing hard as he looked ahead to the tall figure that manifested within the bright light.

He didn't fear her. He knew she wasn't some kind of monster that would roar and chew him up and swallow him. What he *did* fear was the answer "no" when he asked if she could see her way clear to freeing them.

Did she even have such a power?

They flew over the heads of droves of shadow people, rows upon rows that stood shoulder to shoulder, pressing toward the light. Hal wondered—not for the first time—why the vast majority of them stuck to a two-dimensional plane as though they were standing on ground. They weren't. They were floating around in a nothingness, and they could easily skim over heads or dart underneath. There was a strange order to the ceremony as though to cut in line and approach the light in any other way would be grounds for rejection.

Hal *wanted* to be rejected. Last time he'd been here, the Gatekeeper had pushed him away because he'd been in suspended animation rather than dead. It occurred to him now that he and his friends might actually qualify as dead this time. He needed to step carefully.

He slowed his approach, only mildly embarrassed for cutting in line. The masses below barely gave him a glance, just continued pressing forward—but without touching one another.

Some of Hal's group began to whimper and whine, and a commotion started at one end where most of the scrags were. "It's hideous!" one cried. "It's the Devil Himself!" another gibbered.

Dewey began crying out, too. "I'll do better! I'm trying, I really am. Hal, I can't do this yet. I don't want to be sent down there."

"Quit your jabbering, horse-face," Fenton snapped. "He looks pretty friendly to me, like an old granddad."

"He?" Darcy squawked. "You think she's a *he*?"

They squabbled like that while Hal concentrated on what he saw for himself within the blinding glare—a tall, slender woman with an elongated face and large, black eyes so shiny they reflected his own image back at him. She hovered effortlessly above a pit of light, and it was into this pit that shadowy figures surged, dropping out of sight.

Aware that his friends were still arguing over what they thought they were looking at—a hideous demon, a motherly figure, an old man, even a gnarled, hulking monster—and just as aware of the ticking clock, Hal spoke loudly to the Gatekeeper. "I need to ask a favor."

Her head turned toward him. In that moment, the babble of voices around him ceased, and he felt like he'd been ushered into a private chamber with the powerful creature of light.

An image filled his mind: the beach near Brodon, upon which he wandered aimlessly. The sun was rising in the east behind the castle. He looked down on himself from a height of twenty feet.

His friends were spread out everywhere, equally blank and dreamy as they sat or stood or shuffled. Dewey was still in centaur form. Hal spotted Thomas the manticore snoozing, Fenton staring into space with his red eyes, and Emily swaying as she slithered along. Robbie and Lauren were in human form, holding hands. Darcy stood knee-deep in seawater staring out across the horizon. Miss Simone, Molly, Bo, Orson, Astrid, Blair . . .

They were all there, each an empty shell, all except Blacknail and Flatfoot, who had apparently been elsewhere at the time and avoided the sylph's curse. This was a good thing, because they were now busy herding the group together, their short legs pumping as they ran around like sheep dogs.

Seth the dragon was there, too. He'd avoided being taken by the sylph probably because he'd stayed well away from the group. Even now, in this vision, he hunkered some distance away amid a pile of debris, watching silently as though trying to decide if he wanted to take revenge for the death of Queen Bee.

The rest of the scrags were long gone.

The bizarre, unnerving vision suddenly flickered and jumped like a cobbled-together dream sequence, fast-forwarding to what Hal knew was *right now*. It had to be two mornings later. The beach was certainly a lot cleaner, and Brodon residents were out in force. Even Seth was gone now.

"Yes, that's us," Hal said, excited that the strange woman instantly knew his predicament. She probably knew everything there was to know about everything. "I need to know if you can put us back? The sylph took us, and now she's gone along with everyone else, and—well, we're not dead yet, are we? Are you able to send us back to our bodies?"

He held his breath, awaiting the reply. The woman tilted her head and stared at him in silence.

Another image flashed into his mind: the Chamber of Ghosts exploding with a deafening boom and shaking the countryside for miles around. Geo-rocks everywhere went bang, and smoky holes appeared. The scene fast-forwarded to people stepping through from the old world to the new—soldiers, civilians, and scrags. The montage of scenes flickered past too quickly, but he got the gist.

"Yes, people came through," he said, impatience brewing. "I did as you asked and united the two worlds. Nobody believed in me, and people still hate me for it, but I did it." He paused. Then he added, for good measure, "I did it for *you*, so you owe me a favor."

He knew that wasn't quite true, though. He'd blown up the mines and united the worlds not because she'd told him to but because of the images she'd fed into his brain, which he had no doubt were factual. She'd made a good presentation. Those images had made him a believer.

"Time's marching on," he said with a nervous laugh. "Can't hang around. Every minute I'm here, hours pass by outside."

He reeled as another jerky film played out in his head. This one confused and revolted him: a massive wall, slick and white, shuddering from time to time, obviously a living thing. He didn't want to know what it was. He tried to shut his eyes, but the image was plugged directly into his head. Gritting his teeth, he forced himself to watch the awful thing without screaming in horror.

The living wall—which looked to him like some kind of giant brain—pulled away from him. Or rather he floated backward so he could see it better. He knew the thing was big, gigantic, but he had no real sense of scale until he picked out the rocky, textured walls of a cavern surrounding the creature.

Then he knew this thing had to be miles wide.

He blinked and shook his head. Nothing that huge could survive in an underground cavern. It had to eat, surely? No morsel in the world could ever be big enough to feed such a colossal beast. Did it even have a mouth?

His view of the monster changed. Somehow, he followed the glistening wall of the creature—the brain—through miles of cavernous tunnels. The thing wasn't just a big round lump. It had no real shape at all. It just oozed into gaps deep below the ground. Throughout its length and breadth, thousands of delicate tendrils stuck up on top rather like hair. They vanished into numerous fissures in the rocky ceiling, each taking their own path to the surface.

Except they're not tiny, he realized, trying to get his head around the sheer size of this monstrous underground brain. If the thing was as big as he thought it was, then each hairlike tendril had to be thicker than a two-hundred-year-old oak tree. Not delicate but sturdy and incredibly powerful, more like the tentacles of some kind of gigantic octopus . . .

He gasped at a sudden idea. Eager to learn more, he allowed his impossible journey to continue, following one of the many enormous tentacles upward through thousands of feet of solid rock, through endless fissures on a long, roundabout route to the surface where, at last, it emerged and split into dozens of thinner tentacles.

These slender appendages could have spread out across the ground and snaked through the bushes. Instead, they stayed together and bent sharply toward a manmade wall of stone. They shoved their way in through an opening and disappeared inside—into a building Hal recognized as a prison.

He sighed. The concept of such a beast was mind-boggling and spectacular and awesome, but its purpose eluded him. So the huge brain under the ground was tapping into the prison's cellmates and absorbing . . . what? Nutrients?

Information, a voice whispered.

With that single word, Hal understood: a nerve center, a hub, a network of connections to the outside world. His own body and nervous system made use of his five senses—touch, sight, hearing, smell, and taste—but the giant underground brain had no such luxury. Instead, it absorbed information by listening in on people, scanning their knowledge, hearing their memories, feeling their emotions. Secondhand knowledge. Perhaps not as rich as the real thing, but far more attainable. What it lacked in quality it made up for in sheer quantity.

"Yeah, but *why?*" he asked. He had a feeling he'd asked that same question the last time he had visited.

The woman appeared again. Hal's private time ended with a slow fade back to the void. Souls continued to throw themselves into the blinding pit as she hovered above with her white robes hanging in space. His friends were still arguing, though Abigail and Miss Simone at his left and right were gazing at him.

"Hal?" Abigail whispered. "She's looking at you."

"Yeah, I know that," he muttered. He spoke again to the Gatekeeper. "What *are* you? Where did you come from? Why are you here?"

She stared intently at him but said nothing. Maybe she didn't know how to answer that in a way he could understand. How would *he* answer such questions? Then again, he wasn't a know-it-all alien-demon messing with life on Earth. He wasn't the one who'd created New Earth just as an experiment to see what would happen if magical creatures co-existed with humans.

He tried again. "At least tell me if you come from outer space."

She tilted her head sideways, her expression blank. Then she fuzzed into a variety of different personas: a horned demon with deep-red skin, then a glowing, white-feathered angel, then an elderly man with a long, white beard, and so on through a collection of what Hal guessed were fairly common perceptions of godlike, divine beings. They just confused him further.

"So you're *not* from outer space?"

Abigail prodded him and whispered in his ear, "Hey, I don't like to interrupt, but if time is moving fast the way you said . . ."

"Yeah," Hal said to the Gatekeeper, "why *is* that? Why does time pass so quickly outside? Can you slow it down?"

This time he received a brief but powerful suggestion in his head. A tree standing in a field, nothing more than a sapling. He stared at it for ages, but nothing happened. It just stood there, peaceful and alone.

Then the sky darkened and it was night. The moon shot across the sky, and the sun rose in the east and began tracking south, heading for the western horizon. Still nothing happened with the tree.

This wasn't real time. This was just a vision.

Another night passed. Another day. Another night. The sky brightened and darkened so quickly now that it seemed to flicker. The days looked like flashes of lightning in a storm, and during those blink-of-an-eye moments, Hal saw the leaves turning brown, then vanishing as winter set in, and then budding again for the spring, and throughout all this, the tree slowly grew.

"Oh," he said. "I think I get it."

"Get what?" Miss Simone asked.

He realized his friends had gone quiet. They all hung together, floating in the air, and it seemed his one-sided conversation with the silent Gatekeeper had gotten them worried. Meanwhile, the shadow people teemed just below, pushing forward and dropping into the pit of light.

"I guess if you're going to do experiments on the world and mix tons of magical monsters with humans," he said slowly, "it would be helpful if you didn't have to wait hundreds of years to see how things turned out. It would be great to speed things up, right?" He nodded, pleased with his assessment. Then he reconsidered. "Or . . . maybe slow things down here in the void?"

The Gatekeeper gave a nod.

"So we're all moving really, really slow right now?" Hal said with awe. "We just *think* we're moving at normal speed in this place. What about the tentacles back at the prison? Are they moving slow, too?"

He couldn't get his head around that one. He felt he was on the edge of understanding how everything tied together, but the logic seemed off, somehow reversed. But after a moment's thought, and perhaps a nudge from the Gatekeeper, he figured it out.

He turned to Miss Simone. "The tentacles leak magic. When we were in the prison, the magic started to get to us. Everything seemed to drag by, but that's just because we weren't used to the feeling. If we'd been there a bit longer, our brains would have adapted to the magic, and then our days and nights in the cells would have started to seem normal to us again—but everything outside would have started speeding up, faster and faster." He blinked, amazed at how obvious it all seemed now. "It's magic versus our biological clocks," he said slowly as the information filtered into his head. "Our brains have to adapt so that we—"

"This is fascinating, Hal," Miss Simone whispered, "but we should go."

"Oh. Yeah."

He turned to the Gatekeeper. "What do you want me to do?" he asked, knowing she had a reason for all the visions of a giant underground brain.

She dipped her head and closed her enormous black eyes a moment.

Feed me.

When she reopened her eyes, she was looking elsewhere as though she had no further interest in him. He was dismissed.

And with a sudden yanking motion that made him gasp, Hal blinked awake in the moonlight, sure that he'd just woken from a dream.

* * *

He was standing on the beach at nighttime, his feet cold and wet from the waves that lapped over his toes. All was quiet except for the familiar, annoyed shout of a goblin in the distance. Glancing around, Hal started picking out his friends in the gloom: a centaur, a sphinx, a blond-haired girl . . .

Amazingly, he'd somehow negotiated his way out of the void. His soul had been wrenched from the sylph and returned to his body.

But what about his friends?

"Abi!" he yelled at the top of his voice.

He began running, squinting in the darkness. If he was the only one the Gatekeeper had saved, then he was going straight back in there to argue about it. There was no way he planned to be the only survivor. If she wanted him to make it his life's mission to feed the giant brain somehow, then she'd better come through for him now. The panic he felt at that moment threatened to overwhelm him as he dashed toward the nearest of the moonlit figures.

Dewey stood there with his back to him, his horse tail flicking back and forth. Hal ran around to his front end and peered up at him, searching for a flicker of something on the boy's face, just some sign he was here and not lost in the void.

"Dewey? Are you okay?"

A frown creased the boy's forehead. Dewey blinked and looked at him. "What happened?"

Intense relief flooded through Hal then. He laughed out loud, then turned and raced off across the beach. "Astrid! Are you all right? Darcy!"

One by one, his friends came to life and spoke to him. They were spread out across the beach down by the water's edge, most of them still in their varying alternate forms, barely visible except in silhouette. He ran panting from one to the other, barely able to contain his happiness.

"Miss Simone!" he yelled as she turned to face him.

"Hal?"

Behind her, Robbie and Lauren were staring in wonder at the night sky. Robbie was in human form, but Lauren had spread her white-feathered wings, moving them gently as though testing them. Thomas busily licked at his red-furred paws. Fenton lay in the sand nearby, long and sleek, his red eyes glowing.

The two goblins, Blacknail and Flatfoot, appeared out of the gloom and came waddling. Then Emily slithered into view, and after her Molly, pulling her veil into place and straightening her hat.

Orson, in his shiny pegasus form, trotted around snorting and tossing his head about. Blair, for once in human form and wearing smart clothes, kept looking upward like he wanted to fly off without a word.

Hal spotted Abigail. She sat on the sand with the water lapping around her legs. He ran to her and practically yanked her onto her feet, where she staggered and grimaced. "What are you sitting around for?" he said with a grin.

She looked bewildered. "Why is it nighttime? It was the middle of the day just now. I don't remember anything in between except—" Her eyes grew big and round. "The sylph! She got me!"

"Yeah, but you're okay now." Hal put his arm around her. She was shivering. "So . . . you don't remember anything else?"

"It's just one big blank."

Hal sighed. Once again he was alone in his recollection of the void and the mission he'd been assigned with. But at least everyone was alive.

They came together: six adult shapeshifters, nine younger ones, two goblins, and three scrags. Fenton stood up straight as he approached, returning to his human form as his smart clothes arranged themselves around him. The shirt Simmy had tied around his middle wasn't enough to keep away the night chills, and he shivered badly in the cool night air. The straggly-haired scrag named Delores refused to give him one of her layers. Lola remained in her lamia form, apparently quite comfortable with the nighttime drop in temperature.

The large group slowly gathered, all talking at once, trying to figure out what had happened to them. One of the last to arrive was the sphinx, who walked unsteadily, stumbling at times.

"You okay, Astrid?" Molly called out.

"I'm right here," Astrid said quietly from behind her.

Molly jumped and spun around. Though her veil covered her face, her surprise was obvious. "Huh?" She turned again, and everyone sucked in a collective breath as a *second* sphinx hobbled toward them.

"A scrag?" Robbie suggested.

"No, not a scrag," Astrid said breathlessly. "That's my brother."

Bo—in full sphinx form—had a look of horror on his oversized face. "How did *this* happen?"

Even in the darkness he looked every bit as strange and impressive as Astrid, with the body of a lion, wings of an eagle, and enlarged human head. But he walked like his shoes were too tight.

"I remember that sylph coming after me," he moaned. "I don't know what happened next. I just—"

"Transformed?" Miss Simone said, smiling. "Join the club, Bo."

"And not a moment too soon," Fenton said rather sarcastically.

This comment earned him a punch on the arm from Darcy.

"All right, so what exactly happened to us?" Molly said. "Where did the day go? How did we wake after being taken by the sylph? What time is it?"

"Flatfoot was just starting the nightshift," Blacknail complained. "'Bout time you all woke. We've been rounding you up the whole time. You keep wandering off. Dunno what's gotten into you all."

"You didn't see us get taken by the sylph?" Darcy said incredulously.

"Pah!" Blacknail said. "That floating hag didn't come anywhere near me."

"Nor me," Flatfoot agreed. "She knew better."

"She probably didn't like how you smelled," Molly chimed in, and everyone chortled and giggled.

The goblins shared a glance. "You can talk," Flatfoot muttered.

Though very dark on the beach, their pale faces shrouded in shadow, Hal could tell by the light tone that everyone was all right. He was mortified, though, about the damp patch down the middle of his pants.

"Uh, how long have we been gone?" he asked, trying to sound casual about it and grateful it was so dark.

Blacknail huffed and shook his head. "A day would have been bearable. You were gone for three."

This news was shocking. Everyone stared in astonishment—except Hal, who grudgingly accepted that sounded about right. Three days outside was nearly twenty minutes in the void.

"That's . . . that's not possible," Bo said finally.

Blacknail shrugged. "'Tis. That other dragon hung around long after the other scrags left. Then he flew off on his own."

The news that Seth—and the rest of the scrags—had escaped barely seemed to register. "We can't have been just wandering about the beach for that long," Miss Simone protested. "I feel hungry, but not *that* hungry. And a person can't survive more than a few days without water."

The annoyed goblins shared another glance. "You think we don't know that?" Blacknail said shortly. "What do you think we've been doing here all this time? Force-feeding you, that's what. Tipping water down yer throats."

"Tipping . . ." Molly repeated slowly. "So we've been unconscious?"

"No," Abigail answered, "we've been wandering around in a daze. You were the first to go, Molly, so you wouldn't have known."

"Wandering about like fools," Blacknail grumped. "Opening your mouths like babies when we came to tip water down your gullet. We shoved food in at the same time."

"You *shoved* food in?" Darcy said. "What kind of food?"

"Meat pies, mostly."

Hal automatically touched his lips, feeling a dry, crusty patch stuck on one side. Even soulless sylph victims couldn't resist Brodon's finest pies.

"We've been running around after you," Flatfoot added, "putting up fences to stop you wandering too far. Bunch of mindless sheep, the lot of you!"

Blacknail nodded and pointed into the darkness. Now that he mentioned it, Hal could just about make out flimsy structures all around: posts made from whatever splintered lengths of wood had come to hand and linked together with rope. It wasn't much, but it seemed the mere suggestion of a perimeter had been enough to deter the dreamy sylph victims.

"Everyone in Brodon," Blacknail went on, "has been busy picking up debris and clearing away rubble while you've all been standing around drooling."

Astrid opened and closed her mouth like a fish. "But—but this is awful! How—I mean, surely we've needed to—Is there some kind of portable toilet somewhere that we've—?"

Flatfoot snorted. He pointed out to sea. "Right there. That's why we kept you on the beach. Think we're nurse maids or something?"

Hal dipped his head and stared at his feet. He was sure the embarrassment was felt by all. Many of them had been lucky to be in their alternate forms the whole time. Others, himself included, had been in human form and wearing clothes. He liked to think that, even in his dream state, he'd at least pulled his pants down in the water while doing his business!

Miss Simone cleared her throat after a while and, rather shakily, thanked the disgruntled goblins for everything they'd done. As grumpy as they were, Hal recognized that they'd been true friends in sticking around and keeping them safe. He was glad it was *them*, a couple of ugly, foul-tempered goblins instead of, say, one of his friends. Especially the girls.

"Now," Miss Simone said, rubbing her hands in the gloom, "let's get busy. We have scrags to catch."

"I can help with that," a man said, approaching out of the darkness.

Hal tensed. The voice was familiar, someone he'd spoken to recently. Everyone craned their necks and squinted as the figure came into view. He wore threadbare clothes and had long, dark-grey hair.

"The birdman," Hal muttered to Abigail. "What's *he* doing here?"

Chapter Twenty-Three
Escapees

Hal's surprise at seeing the birdman here on the beach was nothing compared to Miss Simone's reaction. She gasped and reeled, then leapt forward like she was going to attack the man. Instead, she grabbed the front of his shirt and stared hard at his face. "It's *you*," she whispered.

The birdman shrugged. "Sorry."

"You're *sorry*?"

"Sorry that woman dragged me into it." The man sighed and looked down at his bare feet, then squinted up at her. "Queen Bee said Chase is alive. Is it true?"

Miss Simone nodded. "Blair broke the spell. Chase is as young as he was when Molly turned him to stone twenty-something years ago. He's out looking for you right now, Richard. Looking for his father."

Several gasps filled the air. Hal could hardly believe his ears. The birdman was *Chase's dad*? He was certainly old enough—in his sixties—but Hal had always imagined a clean businessman, not this wrinkled, weathered long-haired hermit. Words failed him.

"I know he's looking for me," the birdman said, nodding. "Queen Bee told me. And she said she'd ensure his untimely death on the side of a trail if I didn't help her. I'm sorry, Simone—I just didn't know what else—"

"We'll talk later," Miss Simone said shortly. "Right now we have to find the rest of the Swarm. You said you could help with that?"

"Yes—and then you can tell me Chase's route so I can find him?"

Miss Simone nodded. "Of course. But the Swarm first."

The birdman bowed his head. "Queen Bee had an emergency rendezvous location in case things went south. She told me because my rocs were part of the escape plan. They're not far from here. Let me fetch my birds."

"Get the cages, too," Hal blurted. "Uh, you know, the ones outside the castle? It'll be good to see the scrags locked up in those like the hostages were."

The birdman was already nodding vigorously, his long hair falling in front of his face. "I'll be back shortly. Look, my ride is just over there."

Hal and his friends could barely see the birdman's 'ride' in the darkness until they came within a hundred feet of it. Then they could make out the giant bird's white plumage and hear its occasional deep-throated chattering as it arranged huge chunks of debris into a pile as if building a nest.

The birdman climbed aboard and brought out his ocarina— obviously a replacement for the one Hal had crushed earlier that day.

More like three days ago, he remembered. *The birdman's probably been home most of that time.*

There was nothing to do but wait while the roc flapped away into the night, heading toward the castle on the cliff. Tiny pinpricks of orange light indicated that the caretakers had returned to their duties. Hal guessed they'd be very happy to see those wooden cages gone from the courtyard at last.

"Richard Stockwell," Molly said, breaking the silence.

Blacknail gave a grunt. "He's been hanging around here the last couple of days. Never cared for the man."

The adults came together to discuss their old acquaintance while Hal and his friends worked on correcting their mental image of the standoffish father Chase had described in his stories. Gone was the clean-shaven, slightly awkward businessman. In his place was a wiry old hermit sitting astride a giant bird!

"You owe me a ride," a girl's voice said behind him.

Hal turned to find a familiar face staring back at him. "Kinsey!"

She scowled as everybody crowded around. "Hey, back off. I didn't come to chat and make friends. I just want what's due."

Next to her, the huge, three-headed cerberus growled in warning. Instead of flinching away like everybody else, Darcy hurried forward to pat the beast on the head. Dog stiffened, apparently unused to such affection from strangers.

"Thanks for your help the other day," Darcy said, stroking Dog's fur while looking at Kinsey. "You two saved me from that wyvern."

Kinsey looked indifferent. "Wasn't me. It was Dog."

Darcy smiled. "But you sent him to help."

"No, he ran away," Kinsey retorted. She shrugged. "But yeah, whatever."

Abigail patted Hal's arm. "The dragon-boy will be happy to give you a ride, Kinsey. Won't you, Hal?"

"Sure," he agreed. "Now's a good time while we're waiting for the rocs." He glanced down at the cerberus, who glared back with three pairs of eyes. "Dog will have to stay here, though."

"Well, *obviously*," Kinsey said, rolling her eyes.

Her grumpy manner was soon replaced by breathless excitement as Hal took her up into the night sky. Once above the clouds, she gasped at the clear moon. He plummeted through the clouds and back up again, then tore over Brodon where she could look down on the rooftops. Everything was hard to see in the darkness, though, so he took her to the castle and flew past the glowing windows.

Out in the courtyard, the birdman was just leaving. His roc, along with four others, ascended with a noisy flapping of wings. Each bird carried a wooden cage about six feet square, a horizontal bar mounted on top that the rocs could grip in their enormous talons.

Hal followed the birdman back to the beach and landed. Kinsey's ride was over. Now it was time to round up those scrags.

Once Kinsey had dismounted, a few of his flightless friends—Miss Simone, Molly, and Darcy—came to take her place on his back. "Hope you enjoyed the ride, Kinsey!" Abigail called, buzzing alongside them.

"I couldn't see anything," Kinsey grumbled. "It'd be better in the daytime."

"Well, maybe Hal will come see you again soon."

"He'd better," she said.

Hal thought it was a shame Seth had disappeared. If he'd only stuck around and gotten to know this Brodon girl, maybe they could have been friends. Then again, it was hard to imagine the grumbling Kinsey being friends with anyone.

"Here's our first prisoner," Robbie said, growing rapidly and sprouting shaggy hair on his thickening arms. He grabbed the straggly-haired scrag named Delores and shoved her into a cage, then slammed the door shut, ignoring her sudden torrent of abuse. He then turned to Simmy and Lola.

"We can help catch the others," Lola said quickly.

"They won't get past me," Simmy added.

Miss Simone pointed at them. "You are by no means excused from your crimes. You associated with the wrong crowd, and you need to be accountable in part for what happened."

"We get it," Simmy retorted. He took Lola's hand. "We're not going anywhere. We'll help you find the others, then turn ourselves in. We're tired of running. Tired of *surviving*. A jail sentence sounds good right now."

It was an impressive fleet of monsters that finally left Brodon behind: the four-winged simurgh, five rocs, a dragon, a pegasus, a harpy, a phoenix, not one but *two* sphinxes, and several passengers spread between them all. Hal chuckled, thrilled and proud at being part of such a large force. And flying *with* the rocs was far better than going against them.

He still couldn't believe the birdman was Mr. Stockwell, Chase's father. How had Queen Bee found him? Someone else asked this same question out loud, and the birdman twisted around and shouted from his perch.

"She followed the same route Chase had laid out, the route you devised, Simone. Her drones jumped ahead and found me before he did. I think they were going to use me as some kind of bargaining chip, maybe even take me hostage, but when Queen Bee found out I could control rocs . . . well, she switched gears and, uh, *persuaded* me to join her."

His hair streamed backward in the wind as the rocs pushed onward, their great wings beating slowly. Hal kept up easily, but he suspected the two sphinxes were struggling. They fell farther and farther behind, and eventually Astrid shouted that she and Bo were going to rest. Of course, Bo was new to flying. He'd looked wobbly from the start and seemed no better now.

"See you at home!" Astrid shouted as she and her brother dropped out of sight. "We might be some time!"

The rest cruised along. Hal had Abigail on his back along with Darcy, Molly, and Simone. Fenton and Thomas had each grabbed a roc, and so had Blacknail and Flatfoot. Emily and Dewey shared another. Lola, still in her lamia form, clung to Simmy's back, and Delores yelled from her cage dangling below.

They came across the Swarm twenty minutes later, a long way on foot but only a short flight. The scrags were indeed at their rendezvous point, a narrow ravine with a river running through the center. Hal put on some extra speed and surged ahead of the rocs, believing his fiery breath should be the very first thing the scrags saw when they looked up into the night sky. He descended fast, looking for the chimera and expecting a fireball to shoot into the air at him.

To his surprise, the scrags barely reacted. He thumped down in front of the three-headed monstrosity and tensed, waiting for the goat-head to start bleating. It didn't. Instead, the chimera paused a moment, then turned and shuffled off.

Tents and shelters stood all around, and there were several burnt-out campfires. But the place was in disarray as though something had wandered aimlessly through the shelters and pulled them apart. One tent was a charred mess, still smoking.

The hellhound lay on its belly, panting while flames licked up from its back. The golem stood perfectly still, its head tucked under its arm. The cyclops and centaur seemed to be lost, turning about as if trying to decide which way to go. Some of the others were there, too—the long-haired brownie, the tiny faun, the large-headed gnome, and of course a group of ordinary scrags. The banshee floated around above, listless and silent.

The manticore was missing. So, too, was the wyvern. And the sylph.

The group had spread itself lengthways along the ravine, hemmed in by the high walls to either side. Hal thought it would be fairly easy to herd them together if they didn't decided to hunker down and fight.

But they had no fight left in them. As Hal's flying friends came alongside him, he stared in wonder at the chimera, then the cyclops and the centaur. All gazed into space, unaware or uncaring that their days of freedom were over.

The rocs dumped the cages on the ground and landed nearby. When Fenton jumped down to open one up, Hal stepped closer to the chimera and nudged it with his snout. The creature's lion-head merely glanced at him and looked away again. The goat bleated once, feebly.

"The sylph got them!" Fenton shouted.

Hal let out a sigh. Fenton was right. It made sense now that he thought about it. Their escape from the world of darkness had left the sylph empty again. She'd immediately sought out the nearest replacement souls—those of the Swarm.

As Hal and his friends worked together to herd the scrags into the cages, it became obvious that the manticore and wyvern were here after all. They were simply in human form. That explained the two scar-free scrags wandering about. As for the sylph herself . . .

"Over here!" Emily yelled, changing into her naga form and taking up a defensive posture.

Everyone hurried over. Hal stomped carefully, ready to breathe fire again. He was *not* going back to the world of darkness.

The sylph had hidden away behind some boulders the moment she'd seen the shapeshifters and giant birds approaching. When Hal's blast of fire illuminated her, she screamed, "Get away from me! I'll take all your souls! Stay back!"

Miss Simone and Molly shouted for everyone to do as they were told. The sylph lady, Stretch, was about as solid as anybody else, heavy with stolen souls, but that didn't mean she couldn't take more if she tried. When Hal lit up again, he saw that her dirty face was streaked with tears.

"What do we do?" Darcy said.

"She needs to be in a cage on her own," Lauren said.

Molly shook her head. "That won't help. If she releases those souls, she'll simply escape again. I *wish* I had my powers back. Or maybe if Blair was charged enough, he could perform a rebirth for her benefit alone . . ."

The sylph, crouched as though ready to pounce on anybody who came too close, looked at Molly with wide eyes. "How do I do that? How do I release souls? I didn't want to take my friends'—it was an accident—I couldn't control myself. Tell me how to release them so I . . ."

She trailed off, and Fenton sneered, "So you can take ours again? No way. Get her, Thomas!"

Before anyone had a chance to say another word, Thomas leapt forward, red-furred and powerful as he pounced onto the rocks behind the sylph and stood over her. She flinched away, and he swung his tail around. Poison quills shot out, and she screeched and swore, holding up her arms as dozens of them struck.

She went down in a woozy, moaning heap, unconscious seconds later.

"*Now* try and take our souls, doofus," Fenton said to the motionless sylph. He grinned around at the astonished group as Thomas jumped down to join him. "You can thank us anytime."

* * *

The rocs landed just outside Carter, as close to the woods as they could get. The prison was only ten minutes' walk from here. Miss Simone issued orders and got everything organized, and soon Molly was dashing off to Dr. Kessler's house while Orson and Blair flew around to gather some goblins.

"The rest of you can go to bed," Miss Simone announced, walking between the cages and peering in at the menagerie of monsters and scrags. "I think we can handle this quickly without you. My trusty goblin friends and I will transport the prisoners to the prison and lock them up. Dr. Kessler will administer a sleeping drug for the sylph to make sure she stays asleep until we figure out what to do with her. So go home, get washed up, and go to bed."

And that was that. Hal and his friends trudged into the village and began going their separate ways, mumbling goodnight as they went. Robbie headed off to see Lauren home, and Hal walked with Abigail.

All was quiet. It had to be well after midnight judging by the darkened windows. Only the street lanterns lit their way, and they were few and far between at this hour.

"It's a shame Seth escaped," Abigail said with a sigh. "Queen Bee's dead, and we have most of the scrags locked up, but Seth is missing."

This bothered Hal, too, but it could have been worse. At least most of them would be locked up in the prison soon, feeding the tentacle-monster with whatever thoughts soulless people had.

They were all the way through the village to Abigail's house before Hal slowed to a stop. "What's wrong?" she asked.

"I, uh . . . There's something I want to do before I go to bed."

"Like?"

"Go back to the prison."

"What? *Now*? It's the middle of the night! I stink. *You* stink. Why can't this wait until morning?"

"I'm not tired," Hal said. "Go to bed if you like. I'll see you in the morning."

He turned to go, but she grabbed his arm. "Seriously? You think I'm going to let you have a midnight adventure on your own?"

Shaking her head with annoyance, she slipped her arm through his. Smiling inwardly, Hal led the way back through the village to the other side, then out onto the trail leading to the prison. They passed the five, empty wooden cages at the edge of the woods. The rocs were gone now.

They walked through the dark woods with huge nighttime bugs chirping all around. Abigail again complained about his need to see the prisoners.

"I just want to make sure everybody's locked up," he fibbed.

"You don't trust the goblins to do that? You don't think Miss Simone and Molly and the others are capable of locking the cage doors?" She threw up her hands. "Dr. Kessler would have given the sylph some kind of sleeping potion, too. What more is there to do?"

The truth was, Hal wanted to visit the tentacle-monster behind the prison. The Gatekeeper's words, *Feed me*, kept rattling around his head. The prison was full now, but were soulless sylph victims the right kind of food? How would the tentacle-monster's magic affect them?

"What are you thinking about?" Abigail said, holding his hand. "Are the woods creeping you out?"

"No, it's just . . . prison stuff."

She gave him a look, and he sighed. He didn't want to go into the details, but he had to give her something to chew on.

"Those tentacles at the prison," he said. "It was pretty bad, time dragging so slowly when we were locked up. But maybe it was because we were so stressed. You know, worried about everything that was going on."

After a moment's thought, Abigail said, "You mean it might be different if you're *not* stressed? If you *want* time to drag?"

"Right."

She looked down at her feet as they walked. "Okay, let's suppose you upset me really badly by kissing Darcy."

"What? Why would I do that? I'd never—"

"Calm down, I'm just giving an example."

"Oh."

She squeezed his hand. "If you kissed her, I might fly into a jealous rage and attack you both. I might beat you up and do other things I'd regret later."

Hal stopped in amazement. "You'd fly into a jealous rage?"

"No, silly. But someone not so well-adjusted might. But, see, what if I were so mad that I wanted to cool off? Maybe it would take days, maybe a week. The thing is, I wouldn't want to show my jealousy and look like a crazy, clingy person. I'd want to cool off in private. But you'd notice if it took me a week to warm up to you again. You'd see I was giving you the cold shoulder and acting weird."

"So?" Hal said. All this talk of cooling off and cold shoulders reminded him that the night was chilly.

"So I might want to go to the prison and stay there awhile. Maybe I could voluntarily admit myself for an attitude adjustment. I could stay there a few hours, which would feel like a few days. In that time, I'd calm down, get myself under control, forgive you and Darcy, and leave with a much happier, brighter outlook on life. Everything would be fine in no time."

"Sounds a bit dramatic over a simple kiss."

She punched his arm. "As I said, it's just an example."

Hal mulled it over. "So not a prison but a sort of . . . hospital?"

"More like a time-out clinic. An attitude adjustment center."

"Are you serious?"

She laughed and batted his arm. "I'm always serious. Except when I'm not."

"You're so annoying."

They came to a campsite in a clearing. Here, three goblins sat in a circle around the fearsome scrag hellhound. It blinked occasionally but otherwise stared into space as it lay smoldering on its belly, flames crackling behind its head. The goblins rubbed their hands together over the hellhound's superheated back. One even held a metal pan full of roasting chestnuts over the flames. The ground beneath the creature was scorched black, but the monstrous canine shapeshifter couldn't go far wearing heavy chains and manacles.

Besides, it was docile now. All the scrags were.

"If you're looking for Simone, she just left," a goblin said grumpily. "And here *we* are, out in the cold."

"Aw, come on, you *love* a nighttime nut roast," Abigail said cheerily as she and Hal walked past. Once out of earshot, she lowered her voice. "Wow, they didn't waste any time taking advantage of that monster! Saves them lighting a fire, I suppose."

Hal shrugged. "It's not like you can put a hellhound in a nice, wooden kennel with straw on the floor."

The woods crowded the prison ahead, and he shuddered with anticipation. With a new, long-term mission taking shape in Hal's mind, he first needed to experience the time-lagging effects for himself—voluntarily this time, without the fear of being locked up. And

Abigail would be there to snap him out of it. *Baby steps*, he thought as they approached the old building. *She can interrupt after two minutes tonight, maybe five minutes another time, then ten . . .*

They slipped in through the double-door entrance and tiptoed across the dark lobby. The place smelled as musty as ever, but that didn't seem to bother the two goblins who sat there at the desk in the small office, puzzling over a game of chess in the light of two lanterns. They barely glanced at the visitors.

Hal and Abigail passed through the lobby to the main corridor, which was lit by a dozen more lanterns. A statue stood there—a calcified scrag named Dungbeetle. Rather than move him and risk breaking something off, he currently served as an ugly reminder of what happened when people messed with Molly the gorgon. Now that Blair was home again, maybe he'd wake the scrag with a regeneration. Hal doubted he'd be in any great hurry about it, though.

Heavy bars formed the fronts of five large cells on the left, a solid wall between each. Robbie had previously bent most of these bars out of shape. Now it looked like somebody—either goblins or Robbie himself—had set them right again in anticipation of scrag prisoners.

The cells were simple, square, and quite large, their ceilings smothered with vines and thin, milky-white tentacles. Though designed for two cellmates each, with two simple bunks and a single toilet, currently the prison was full thanks to the late-night delivery of scrag prisoners.

The first barred room contained seven ordinary, disheveled men, either standing or sitting but all with dreamy looks on their faces, staring into space.

The second cell was filled with some of the Swarm's male shapeshifters—a tiny faun, a long-haired brownie, an enormous golem with its head under one arm, and a cyclops curled up on the floor nearby.

Three ordinary female scrags sat on bunks in the third cell. One was Delores, who seemed to have given up her indignant screeching. All were looking up at a not-so-ordinary woman floating horizontally above their heads. Thankfully, the banshee was too drowsy to wail. The gnome shapeshifter was there, too, standing in the corner and gently banging her large head on the wall.

Hand in hand, Hal and Abigail wandered past, not daring to speak in case they disturbed the peace and caused a sudden ruckus.

The fourth cell held the chimera monster. Judging by a few scorch marks on the wall opposite, the three-headed creature had, perhaps inadvertently, let off a few fireballs from time to time. No wonder it had a cell to itself!

In the fifth and final cell lay the scrag named Scarecrow. He'd been there since the hostage situation, and now his mind was so deeply entrenched in the tentacle-monster's magic that he had even more of a slack-jawed expression than his soulless neighbors. He wasn't alone now, though. Guppy the centaur shared the cell with him. His arms hung loose, his head bowed as he stood perfectly still in what Hal guessed was centaur slumber. Two other men, both in human form, stood motionless—the manticore and the wyvern.

"That's everyone but the sylph," Abigail said quietly.

"And the triton," Hal said. "I guess he's still with the mermaids."

Abigail smiled. "Miss Simone mentioned that he'd prefer to be here than with those giggling underwater pests. I think she plans to go rescue him soon."

"Croaker got away, too. But that's okay, I guess. I think he wanted a quiet life anyway." He frowned. "There was also a unicorn and an elf. They're both missing. They ran away before the battle on the beach got started. Oh, and a minotaur. I guess he drowned."

"And Seth." She sighed. "Okay, let's go home now. I'm tired."

"Well," he said slowly, "actually, I kind of want to sit by the monster out back for a couple of minutes."

She swung around. "What? Why?" She clicked her tongue. "Is this why we're really here?"

"Just for two minutes. You can interrupt, okay?"

She grumbled about it as they grabbed a lantern and walked around the corner toward solitary confinement. Then they both fell silent, not wanting to wake the sylph within. The ceiling here was extra thick with foliage and tentacles. The door strained at the chains as though the vines and slippery appendages were trying to burst it open.

"Walk on past," Abigail whispered, tugging at his hand.

They hurried on to the end of the dark corridor. The back door stood wide open, hanging on its hinges where Hal had whacked it with his tail. How long ago that seemed now! Or was that the tentacle magic at work on him already?

It was pitch-black out back. The lantern barely penetrated the darkness. Here they found the source of the tentacles—a strange, white trunk sprouting from the ground like an albino tree. It split into dozens of tentacles, but rather than spread outward like the branches of a tree, the entire cluster bent sharply toward the building, disappearing through a rotting, crumbling crack above the door.

"I'm going back inside to the front office," Abigail said quietly. "How long did you want again?"

"Two minutes."

"All right. I'll start counting, and I'll be right back."

She hurried inside.

Holding the lantern high, Hal sat down with his back against the weird creature that sprouted from the earth. It was hard to believe this thick trunk was the very tip of a horrendously long tentacle that had worked its way through miles of rock from deep below.

The magic was strongest here. When he'd last come into contact with the tentacle-monster, he'd only been 'gone' a few seconds before Robbie had woken him. Those few seconds had dragged terribly from his point of view, but he'd been anxious at the time, worried the scrags were escaping. As Abigail had said, perhaps one's emotional state would make a vital difference.

Technically speaking, he was now feeding the creature. But the thoughts of a solitary thirteen-year-old boy were nowhere near enough to satiate the monster, and he suspected a bunch of soulless prisoners weren't much to gnaw on, either. He needed to work on a plan to bring more active-minded people to the prison—not necessarily as prisoners, but as voluntary knowledge-givers, or even as patients who recognized they needed time-outs and attitude adjustments.

Or maybe those who wanted to mourn the loss of a loved one without impacting others around them. Or to get away from a busy lifestyle and spend a day letting the mind rest and recuperate. Or for those who simply wanted to *think*. Hal was sure someone like Fleck the centaur would find it wonderful to sit and work through complex equations for months in his head while staying on schedule in the real world.

This prison couldn't be the only place tentacles emerged from the ground. Hal guessed there were plenty of similar sites—perhaps a mountain cave where white tentacles spread across its roof, a swamp with tentacles along its banks, that sort of thing, probably all as creepy as the next. He needed to come up with some way to demystify the sites, make them less creepy and frightening and turn them into something more *enticing*, something wonderful where people traveled miles for an incredibly relaxing experience that would seem like hours of bliss but in reality was only ten minutes . . .

These tentacle sites were spread far and wide. A task like this was going to take years of traveling.

But he was only thirteen. He had plenty of time ahead of him.

Chapter Twenty-Four
Birthday Boy

Hal slept heavily and refused to budge until the afternoon sunlight streamed through the window of his bedroom.

Even then, he stayed where he was as long as possible. They'd all arrived home in the small hours of the morning, he and Abigail later than the others. His parents hadn't cared what time it was, though. His mom had made him a sandwich and run a hot bath for him, and he'd finally collapsed in bed and fallen sound asleep. Clean and happy, he'd dreamed of a hero's welcome the next day, of parading in the streets with cheering onlookers, his stigma finally lifted . . .

Yeah, right, he thought as he rubbed his eyes and stared up at the ceiling. Did anyone in Carter have a clue what had happened in Brodon? When word got back that a portion of the seaside town had flooded and burned, a poor man drowned, and their greedy mayor knifed in the chest, would the residents of Carter see the shapeshifters as heroes in all this? No matter whose side the children were on, from an outsider's point of view it probably looked like a shapeshifter squabble gone wrong, with innocent people caught in the crossfire.

Councilman Frobisher was going to have a field day dishing out the blame. Miss Simone would no doubt take the brunt of it.

Hal dragged himself out of bed and got dressed in fresh smart clothes. It felt good to be clean and rested. And fed. Blacknail had done well to stuff food down the throats of all the sylph victims to keep them going, but of course it hadn't been enough, and they'd all been ravenous and thirsty.

"Good morning," his mom said with a smile as he wandered into the kitchen.

"Hey, Mom," he said, sliding into a chair. "Is it too late for breakfast?"

She came around and kissed him on the cheek. "You can have lunch, sleepyhead. And afterward, we'll go out to the fields and see your dad."

He frowned. "Why?"

"We have something for you, Birthday Boy."

That took a moment to sink in. "Is it *today?*" he exclaimed, rising out of his seat. "Yeah, I guess it is. Wow! Getting stuck in limbo for a few days really messed with my head."

He couldn't believe he was finally thirteen. A *teenager*. The first of his friends. For a short period only, he would be the only teenager of the group, and he intended to make the most of it.

After lunch, he went with his mom out to the fields. It was a bit of a trek on foot, but the trail was well worn and the weather nice, so he enjoyed the walk. He suspected his mom did, too, judging by the way she kept reaching out to hug him. Or maybe she was just grateful he was still alive.

His dad and four other men were busy plowing one of the fields. Hal stood watching the horses struggle with the huge wood-and-iron contraption until his dad came wandering over. "Hey, kiddo! Who's thirteen today, eh? Come on, we've got something for you."

The three of them headed to a rundown barn at the edge of the field. Inside, Hal's dad opened a small door and ducked into a dark storeroom. He was gone just a few seconds.

"We thought you could do with a slice of normal life," Hal's mom said, putting a hand on his shoulder. "You don't have to be a dragon all the time."

When his dad emerged wheeling a shiny bicycle, Hal couldn't help grinning. "My bike! You went back to the island for it?"

"Well," his dad said, "I know you could have done that anytime, no big deal for a dragon and all that, only you never did."

Hal took hold of the handlebars. "It'll be great to go riding again," he admitted. "I wish Robbie had his, though, so we could ride together."

His parents exchanged a glance. "That's why we got his, too," his dad said. "And everybody else's. They're all in there." He jerked his thumb toward the storeroom.

When Hal wheeled his bicycle closer and peered in, he saw them lined up within, all shiny and clean, like new. "This is *really* cool. Thanks!"

His mom looked almost sheepish. "It's not much. We had gifts put aside while you were growing up on the island, things you might grow into. You kids were grateful for anything new. But now you have the world at your fingertips. What do we give a boy who can turn into a dragon and fly everywhere?"

"This is perfect," Hal said. He meant it. Birthday gifts hadn't even crossed his mind. He'd just been looking forward to being thirteen. As it happened, there wasn't a single thing he needed or wanted more than the return of something precious he already owned from his days growing up on the island.

He carefully laid the bicycle down and went to give his parents one of his tightest hugs.

* * *

He rode his bike to Robbie's house first. When he pounded on the door, it was a minute before his friend answered. He looked bleary-eyed, but his eyebrows shot up at the sight of Hal's bike. "How'd you get *that* back?"

"Birthday present," Hal said, grinning.

Robbie's mouth fell open. "Oh! That's today? Wait, yeah, it's today!" He suddenly looked mortified. "I didn't get a gift or anything."

"You did," Hal told him. "All you need to do is agree to going on a bike ride with me, like we used to on the island. Just us. We'll keep going until we get completely lost, and then we'll fly home."

"That sounds cool but sadly impossible with only one bike."

"Yours is at the barn in the field. My mom and dad brought all of them across from the island."

It took a moment for Robbie to take that in. Then he beamed. "Cool! Okay, give me a minute to get ready."

Of course, Hal realized he couldn't just go off without telling Abigail first. Robbie, for once, agreed. "Lauren needs to know where I am," he said. "I guess that's the price of having a girlfriend, right? We have to tell 'em everything."

"Like you mind," Hal murmured.

Robbie couldn't contain his smile. They set off to Abigail's first, since she was closest, but she wasn't there. Nor was Dr. Porter. So they went to Lauren's, who also wasn't in.

Her mom, Mrs. Hunter, said, "She's in the village. There's a public hearing going on, and Miss Simone's in the limelight." Her gaze traveled to Hal's bicycle, and she smiled. "Happy birthday, Hal. How do you like having that back?"

"It's great," he said. "I can fly and everything, but I've missed just riding along. We're going for a ride in a minute. We just wanted to let the girls know."

"And they're going with you?"

Hal glanced away. "Uh, yeah. Sure."

Luckily, Mrs. Hunter seemed to miss his less-than-enthusiastic response. The truth was, he and Robbie wanted to ride like they used to, tearing around, daring to jump across streams, slip-sliding down hills and not caring if they went flying. Abigail and Lauren *might* be up for that, but . . .

"Anyway, I guess we'll head out," Robbie said. "We'll go into the village first and see if we can find them."

Robbie had no intention of doing any such thing, but Hal couldn't help being curious about the public hearing Mrs. Hunter had mentioned. He persuaded Robbie to come with him and see what was going on.

"Oh, *man*," Robbie grumbled.

The two-story building where the council members held their meetings had a very large crowd outside. A long table had been set up, behind which sat the council, almost like they were using the table to protect themselves from any angry mobs that might rear up. Everything seemed fairly calm, though, as Hal pushed his bicycle through the crowd with Robbie in tow.

There were eleven council members. Councilman Frobisher, old and wrinkled with thin-framed glasses on the end of his pointed nose, sat in the middle, squinting in the sunlight. An unfamiliar man stood before them, and he'd just finished mumbling some kind of statement.

Frobisher dismissed him with a wave of his hand. "Thank you, Bennett." He raised his voice. "So we've heard testimony from a messenger who, in the official capacity as an investigator on behalf of this council, visited Brodon and spoke personally with Mayor Seymour Priggle several days ago. Let the record show that the mayor was not forthcoming with regards to the presence of scrags at his castle. Indeed, he claimed he knew nothing of such a group of people—and yet, unbeknownst to Bennett, the mayor had previously announced to the people of Brodon that the scrags were there as so-called 'protectors' or 'defenders' of the town. Why, then, did he fail to mention any such thing to Bennett?"

He pounded the table, and several men and women to his sides jumped.

"The reason is because Mayor Priggle *knew* these scrags were trouble. He knew they had taken hostages and that we would come after them had we known they were there. He deliberately held back from informing our investigator, thus hampering our efforts and prolonging the dreadful hostage situation . . ."

"This is boring," Robbie whispered to Hal. "Let's just go."

"Okay."

As Hal wheeled his bicycle back through the crowd, Darcy stepped in front of them. "And where have you boys been? We've been waiting to see the birthday boy all morning."

Robbie muttered something under his breath, but Hal shrugged and answered for them both. "Couldn't be bothered to get up. Hey, how do you like the bike?"

She frowned and pointed. "That's . . . that's *yours*! From the island!"

"Yep. My mom and dad brought it back as a birthday present. Yours, too. They're all in the barn outside the village, up in the fields."

Darcy looked at him and broke into a grin. "So we *all* got a piece of your birthday present?"

"Well, it wouldn't be much of a present if I was the only one with a bike."

She stepped closer and put her hands on his shoulders. "Hal, I want you to know this is nothing personal. It's your birthday, and I'm obliged to give you a really big kiss. So close your eyes and—"

"Hands off, Darcy," Abigail said in a stern voice.

Hal spun around to spot her standing there with all their other friends. She had one eyebrow raised high.

Darcy sighed and dropped her hands. "Aw."

Hal couldn't decide if he was relieved, disappointed, or a bit of both. He felt his face heating up as Fenton laughed and nudged Thomas.

"Happy birthday, Hal," Abigail said.

Shouldering Darcy aside, she stepped closer to Hal and leaned in to kiss him. Everyone immediately complained out loud, and Fenton made noises like he was vomiting. Darcy rolled her eyes and stuck her tongue out.

"What did I tell you about kissing Darcy?" Abigail whispered in Hal's ear. "Do you *want* me to go ballistic and beat you up?"

He grinned at her as she stepped back with a gleam in her eye.

"Going somewhere?" she asked, looking down at the bicycle.

Before Hal could answer, Robbie jumped in a little too enthusiastically. "Yeah, Hal has his bike back, and we were coming to get you and Lauren so we could go on a bike ride together. Just the four of us. Or all of you if you want, I guess. But definitely the four of us at least. All our bikes are in the barn up at the fields."

"Yeah," Hal agreed. "My mom and dad brought them from the island. They're squeaky clean and shiny. Can't wait to go riding!"

"Sounds boring," Fenton said. "Count me out."

"All right," Robbie said, nodding vigorously.

Emily had moved closer. She patted the handlebars and grinned. "I'll come. Can we have a picnic, too? I'll organize baskets and food if maybe some of you others can bring blankets to sit on. In fact, maybe I should write up a list of things we need so we don't forget anything."

"I have to be back after supper," Darcy said. "Miss Simone wants me at the lab this evening. I'm working with the dryads today, trying to figure out how they concoct their herbal medicine for gout. It works so well, and Miss Simone would love it if we could make it ourselves—in other words, if I can make it using my special dryad powers."

"I'm supposed to take some Old Earthers to the centaur shelter," Dewey said. "A bunch of teachers, I think. They want to study the centaurs, and the centaurs have agreed as long as I lead them in and introduce them."

"Oh, I have to do that, too!" Emily exclaimed. "Only with the naga."

Dewey nodded. "Well, I need to take them in a minute, but I should be back in a couple of hours."

"A couple of hours?" Thomas complained. "So if we can't leave just yet, and Darcy has to be back for supper, that means we'll have two or three hours at most."

"Can we take Ryan, if he'll go?" Lauren suggested. "He doesn't have a bike, but we could maybe share. If he rides one and someone runs for a bit, then we could switch and—"

"He can have mine," Fenton interrupted. "I told you, I'm not going. Sounds boring."

"Good. Let's swing by the river and fetch him. He's fishing there somewhere. He shouldn't be too hard to find."

"We should plan our route so we don't get lost," Emily said thoughtfully. "Who do we know with a good map of the place? Blacknail?"

Hal and Robbie were already sharing a look by this point. *This* was why they preferred to go off on their own. Add even one person into the mix and suddenly there were complications and delays. Their simple, unplanned bike ride had turned into a massive, organized headache.

Thankfully, Miss Simone wove into view at that point. "Happy birthday, Hal. A quick word, please?"

"Rapid," he quipped. "Speedy. Fast."

She gripped his arm and pulled him aside, then bent close to his face. She didn't appear to be annoyed at him, just businesslike. "Frobisher wants me to detail everything that happened on the beach. I'll summarize as much as I can, but he'll probably press for details."

Hal's friends moved closer around them, listening in.

"Okay," Hal said, puzzled.

Miss Simone pursed her lips before speaking. "I can detail everything except what happened with the sylph. I've drawn a blank there. She took us, and then we woke on the beach three days later."

"Right."

She looked expectantly at him. "So? Any ideas?"

He glanced around at his friends. They looked like they were waiting for an answer, too. "You probably know as much as I do," he said carefully.

"You don't have any recollection of those three days?" Standing up straight, Miss Simone put her hands on her hips and frowned. "It's extremely rare for a sylph to willingly release its stolen life force, its collection of *souls*. Do you know something we don't?"

Again, everyone stared at Hal. He felt uncomfortable with all eyes on him like this. "Look," he said at last, "even if I remember what happened, there's no point telling Councilman Frobisher. He'd never believe you. I don't think you'll even believe *me*."

She narrowed her eyes and said nothing.

An idea struck him. "You could tell the council that the scrags persuaded the sylph to let us go. She's a shapeshifter, remember? She's not like other sylphs. And even scrags can change their minds, right? Look at Simmy and Lola. They're not so bad."

"There's hope for them," Miss Simone admitted.

When pressed, she went on to explain how Simmy and Lola were safely locked up in Carter's small jailhouse, the back of which had been boarded up. Obviously smitten with Lola, Simmy seemed quiet and thoughtful, occasionally fingering his iron collar—something goblin guards had been told *not* to remove under any circumstances. Nobody had forgotten his crucial, last-minute help during the battle, but Miss Simone feared he might change his mind again and try to escape if given the chance.

Meanwhile, Lola lounged in her lamia form, unable to change back. She'd figure it out eventually, especially with Simmy encouraging her from the next cell. Her desire to drink young blood seemed to have faded. In fact, since drinking some of Lauren's, she claimed that her burdens had been lifted, her guilt eased, and now she seemed determined to serve time in jail without fuss. She hoped, one day, to emerge a free woman and work as a resident shapeshifter.

"I'd certainly like to work with her," Miss Simone said, her eyes shining. "If anything good has come from this, it's that we have a couple of new shapeshifters among us. Once they've served their time, that is." She nodded and turned to go, then paused a moment. "Oh, and Hal? I'm not finished with you yet. I want to know *everything* about what really happened. We'll talk later, all right?"

As she headed back into the crowd, Hal couldn't help being glad she was so keen to hear his wild tale of a giant brain under the ground. His mission would be far easier with her support.

* * *

Darcy announced her bright idea for the bike ride. "Let's all go home and change into ordinary clothes. No smart clothes, okay?"

"Why?" had been the obvious question.

"Because it's way too easy for us to transform at the slightest sign of inconvenience. If we get lost, someone will fly up into the sky. Or Robbie will uproot bushes so we can get through the woods. Or Hal will start a fire so we can warm up our soup."

"I can do that without transforming," Hal muttered. Abigail giggled.

"Let's change into ordinary clothes so we're not tempted to be shapeshifters," Darcy went on. "Just for this afternoon, let's be *ordinary* again."

"Why not wear iron collars while we're at it?" Fenton demanded.

Darcy put her hands on her hips and glared at him. "Because that would be stupid. If we run into actual danger, we need to be able to protect ourselves. I'm just saying we should try to be ourselves for a while."

Everyone agreed to humor her. And secretly, Hal got a thrill out of the idea of experiencing their afternoon bike ride without any shapeshifting.

They finally headed out. Loaded up with baskets of food and supplies, and dressed in ordinary clothes that would rip apart if they tried to transform, they tore away from the village on their shiny bicycles. Hal felt strange wearing his old socks and sneakers. He hadn't worn them since the winter months.

The group followed a path over the grassy slopes on the north side of the village, then veered east around a stand of trees. The map Emily had brought turned out to be almost worthless, and they quickly abandoned it, deciding instead to just cycle at random until they were ready to eat. Then they'd see if they could find their way back via a more direct route, following the direction of the sun. It would be a challenge, and they'd be worn out by the time they made it home that evening.

"We can split into two teams," Lauren shouted as they rattled and bounced down a bumpy hill. "Maybe girls versus boys? We'll see who's the smartest."

"The boys will cheat, though," Darcy replied, her blond hair streaming as she passed Dewey. "Hal will fly them home or something."

"I would not!" Hal protested.

It was late afternoon by the time they stopped to eat, and they had all developed what Robbie called *wobbly legs*. They stretched out on the grass on top of a rise and stared up at the sky, munching on sandwiches and guzzling water. Hal felt something crawling over his hand and jerked away to find a six-inch beetle struggling through the grass. He nudged Robbie, who promptly forgot about his sandwich and spent the next five minutes studying the bug.

"I thought you wanted to bring Ryan along with us, Lauren," Fenton said in a sleepy voice.

"I thought *you* weren't interested in coming," she retorted. "But even if you'd stayed home, I started thinking about how he rode your bike once before, and how it was too small for him. I couldn't see him coming along without a bike his size. Besides, he could be anywhere. He doesn't hang around the village much."

"No, he doesn't," Abigail said, flicking bits of grass at Dewey. "He's happy, though. He practically lives in the woods, as he's always done, only now without the fear of scrags coming after him."

"Now he just has to worry about manticores stinging him to death," Fenton said with a laugh.

A lazy silence fell, and they lay there listening to the buzzing of huge bees and dragonflies.

"Dewey, stop chewing with your mouth open," Emily murmured.

"I will if you stop snoring," he said.

"I am not!"

"Not now you're awake," Dewey said. "But you were a second ago."

"Well, if I was snoring, your chewing woke me up."

Dewey paused, then fumbled in his pocket. "I might write a poem about that. 'While kids are snoring and chewing, cows are boring and mooing.'"

Lauren giggled, but Darcy sighed and shook her head. "Absolutely awful, Dewey. Your worst yet."

When some of them fell asleep, Abigail climbed to her feet and brushed herself down. "I'm going for a walk," she told Hal, nudging his foot. "Coming?"

He groaned and got up. "Yeah, okay. Bugs keep crawling over me anyway."

They left the others behind, strolling down the slope.

"I can't wait for Chase to come home," Hal said. "I reckon his dad will find him and bring him back on a roc."

"If they come back at all. The birdman isn't exactly in Miss Simone's good books at the moment."

"She'll get over it. He didn't do any harm. He was just the driver."

Hal was about to say that Councilman Frobisher might have something a little stronger to say about that when they heard a brief roar. They stopped and looked up, frowning.

"That sounded familiar," Abigail said, clutching Hal's hand.

"Did it?"

"Yes. It sounded like *you.*"

When they ran back to the top of the hill, all their friends were sitting up and staring over the trees. Darcy spun around and glared at Hal for a moment, then looked puzzled. "Oh."

"What?" Hal said.

"We all thought that dragon was you. It *looked* like you, anyway. We were just thinking you'd cheated and gone home, and we were wondering why you'd left your bike behind. It must have been another dragon that—"

She stopped, her eyes widening.

"Seth!" everyone said in unison.

They all stared at the line of trees, waiting for Seth to reappear. But he didn't. Hal was sorely tempted to go after him, to find out what the boy was doing, where he was planning to live, but he didn't want to ruin his clothes. By the time he found a bush to hide behind so he could strip down, Seth would be long gone.

He sighed. "Well, I guess he's around somewhere."

Wide awake now, they all picked themselves up and started packing away their things. Fenton and Thomas headed off first, followed by Emily, then Robbie and Lauren. Dewey and Darcy finally got loaded and set off next, though Darcy looked back over her shoulder as she wobbled away. "Are you coming?"

Abigail smiled. "Sure. We'll beat you home!"

"Not unless you cheat," Darcy retorted, putting on a burst of speed. A few seconds later, she was all the way down the hill and disappearing into the trees.

"So *are* we going to cheat?" Abigail asked, turning to Hal. "Do you want to carry us home, bikes and all?"

"No!" He looked down and fingered his clothes. "Anyway, I'd have to take these off first."

"I won't look."

"It's not happening," Hal said. He frowned at her. "You don't really want to cheat, do you?"

She looked thoughtful. "Don't think of it as cheating. Think of it as getting home before all the others without any effort at all."

He sighed. "Sometimes, I just don't understand you."

"Which is why you love me so much."

He shrugged, trying to feign indifference. But he couldn't keep up the pretense for long, not with her gazing at him with her big, brown eyes. "Yeah," he admitted, and leaned forward to kiss her.

She neatly sidestepped him, putting up a hand to block him. "No way. I'm still mad at you and Darcy."

"*What?*"

She grinned. "Come on, Birthday Boy. If the others beat us home, it'll be all your fault for standing around trying to talk me into flying. Honestly, what am I going to do with you?"

Author's Note

The last nine books in this series has chronicled Hal's transition from an ordinary twelve-year-old boy living on a foggy island to an experienced thirteen-year-old shapeshifter in a bright new magical world.

His adventures took place over five months between October and March. That's a lot of story for a short period of time! He's pretty exhausted now, so we'll take a break and leave him alone for a bit while he recuperates and plans his ongoing mission for the future—to feed the monstrous underground brain. We'll check back in on the shapeshifters in Book 10, *Forest of Souls*, which picks up a few months later.

In the meantime, look for the ISLAND OF FOG CHRONICLES, a series of short stories and novellas which delve a little deeper into Hal's world before, during, and after his adventures.

And take a peek into the future with the ISLAND OF FOG LEGACIES, a series of full-length novels featuring Hal and Abigail's twelve-year-old son, Travis, who yearns to be a shapeshifter just like his parents. Set twenty years from now, you'll get to see all the old friends as well as new characters and monsters. Turn the page to sample the opening chapters of the first book, *Unicorn Hunters* . . .

UNICORN HUNTERS

Special Preview

Chapter 1
Poachers from Old Earth

Travis moved through the trees, whistling tunelessly, hands in pockets, his eyes on the narrow trail because it had a habit of tripping him the moment he looked elsewhere. He normally headed straight home across the fields, but today he wanted inspiration. This longer, far more scenic route always managed to surprise him with its hidden wonders.

Birds chirped high above. A dragonfly the length of his forearm buzzed past his face, causing him to jerk backward and look left. As it happened, he then spotted two glowing will-o'-the-wisps circling a tree trunk. The tiny creatures were smaller than faeries and with fuzzy blue fur.

When he moved on, an ugly squonk shuffled off the trail ahead and into the bushes, its folds of fat wobbling. About the size of a dog and with four spindly legs, the pitiful creature sobbed mournfully as it went, leaving a watery trail. It was said that a squonk could dissolve into a pool of tears if too many people stared at it at once.

Travis smiled. He'd been right to come this way. The forest was teeming with fascinating wildlife, magical or otherwise.

Fleeting movement distracted him. He glanced off to the right, squinting through the vegetation. There he saw a tree-colored, man-shaped figure, possibly a dryad—

He tripped on a root and went sprawling.

When he picked himself back up, the dryad was gone. Or if not gone, then absolutely still as it blended into the background and studied him. Wishing he could be the first of his classmates to meet one face to face, he scanned the trees with a keen eye, looking for even the slightest movement, the tiniest blur that would give away the dryad's location.

Nothing.

Sighing, Travis continued on his way. "A dryad," he muttered. "That could work. Not as cool as a wyvern, though."

A wyvern remained at the top of his shortlist. He'd seen one a week ago, and its slender orange-and-blue reptilian body and blood-red wings had awed him. Though not much bigger than a man, they had razor-sharp teeth and barbed tails. To be able to transform into one . . .

He heard the cracking of a twig to his left and paused. A bush quivered, and he tensed, waiting to see what would emerge. To his relief, a tiny childlike female moved into view—tan-colored skin, large mischievous eyes, oversized pointed ears, long black hair, dark-brown tunic and pants, and fine leather boots. She stood no taller than his waist.

"Oh, it's *you*," Travis said. "Can't believe you followed me out here, Nitwit."

"What did you expect?" she said in her squeaky voice. "I'm an imp. It's my job to annoy you."

"And *only* me," he murmured. "Nobody else."

Nitwit grinned. "Is school over already?"

"Yep." He felt a renewed surge of excitement. "And guess what? I got approved."

The imp frowned as she joined him on the trail. "For what?"

"To be a shapeshifter!" Travis said, unable to contain his joy. "Dad filed the paperwork with Lady Simone, and she presented it to the committee, and they approved. No big surprise, really. Both my parents are shapeshifters, so it's in the blood." He paused. "Well, not *literally* in the blood, otherwise I'd be half dragon and half faerie. How would that work? But shapeshifting kind of runs in the family, so the committee didn't have to think too hard about it."

"Because you're a *natural*," Nitwit said, rolling her big brown eyes. "Everyone else has to be nominated by at least two dozen non-family adults before the paperwork can even be filed to the committee. You skipped all that."

"Well," Travis said, continuing on the winding trail, "I can't help it if my parents have friends in high places."

"I suppose not."

"They're old heroes, you know, and my dad—"

"Yes, we all know about your dad," the imp mocked.

"What's *that* supposed to mean?"

She avoided the question. "What do you want to be?"

"I'm not sure yet. Maybe a wyvern."

"Why a wyvern?"

"Because they're cool."

She squinted up at him. "You know wyverns can't breathe fire, right? If you want to be a dragon like your dad, why not just—"

"I'm not allowed to be a dragon," Travis grumbled. "There's a whole bunch of things I'm not allowed to be. These days, shapeshifters have to be something safe and nonthreatening."

"In case you turn bad and go on a rampage," Nitwit said, nodding.

Like twenty years ago when scrags stole the top secret formula for creating shapeshifters, Travis thought. *A gang of villains turning into deadly monsters like the chimera, hellhound, dragon, and the massive simurgh. Not good.*

"Yeah, but also we have to be something *useful*, something that can contribute to society. Like a dryad. My dad knows a dryad shapeshifter, and she makes medicines. And his friend Robbie's an ogre who builds houses."

Nitwit frowned. "So what use is a wyvern? They're vicious things! They don't breathe fire, but they have a nasty, poisonous barbed tail."

"But they're cool."

"And how is being cool useful to society?"

"I don't know."

"Are they even allowed? They seem pretty dangerous to me."

"Sometimes the committee will make exceptions if—"

The roar of an engine sounded from outside the forest ahead. The sound was so unexpected that it took a moment for Travis to register what it might be.

He picked up speed, muttering as he went. "Sounds like Old Earthers. They shouldn't be driving around in these parts. Come on, let's see what's going on. Probably joyriders again."

He didn't care much for Old Earthers in general, though he had to admit some were okay. There were a few in his class. Twice a week they stepped off the yellow bus, one of the few vehicles allowed to rumble into Carter on a regular basis. Those kids couldn't get enough of New Earth; they stared wide-eyed at literally *everything*, even the mundane stuff, always expecting something magical to happen. They couldn't wait for the Friday field trips.

Travis had tried Alter-Education a while back. He'd gone to an Old Earth school once a week until he'd had his fill of it. The other world was impressive with its massive cities, impossibly tall buildings, flying machines, and super-fast road vehicles. But machines literally left a nasty taste in his mouth, and he'd dropped out.

The forest ended, and the trail opened out into a lush meadow. Normally it was peaceful here, nothing but the buzz of bees. Today, however, four mud-splashed off-road vehicles shattered the serenity as they spun about and left deep wheel marks in the grass surrounding a small thicket.

Travis felt a surge of anger at the Old Earthers. Did they have nothing better to do than tear up his beautiful countryside? Why couldn't they stay in their own world instead of fouling this one?

Then he froze as a flash of white bolted from the thicket. A unicorn!

The vehicles roared after the creature, one of them hot on its heels. Unicorns were larger than horses and much faster, but the open-topped Jeeps were built for scrambling on rough terrain, and they quickly matched the frightened equine's speed. With unerring precision, the four vehicles pressed in tight on both sides as well as in front and behind. The one bringing up the rear looked like it might clip the unicorn's hooves at any second.

The leading driver jammed on his brakes, and the startled unicorn leapt into the air, clearing the entire length of the vehicle in one bound. It came down hard just ahead, then bucked and caved in the front of the Jeep with a savage backward kick.

The unicorn galloped away with three Jeeps in pursuit, leaving the fourth to halt with steam pouring from its radiator grille. But the other hunters seemed more determined than ever now, and they quickly closed in despite the frenetic pace. Travis watched in amazement as the unicorn danced about and frequently changed directions, trying to shake off the drivers. They spun and tore up the grass, leaving a crisscrossing mess of tire tracks and a haze of noxious exhaust fumes.

Travis wrung his hands and hopped from foot to foot. "They can't *do* this! It's illegal to hunt unicorns! It's illegal to hunt *anything* without a license! They're not even supposed to be *driving* in New Earth!"

He realized after a moment that Nitwit had disappeared, and he clicked his tongue with annoyance. She had a habit of showing up when not wanted and disappearing when he needed her. Not that an imp could help in this situation.

"I wish my dad was here," he growled. "He'd chase them off."

The unicorn grew desperate and began ramming the moving Jeeps. It lunged and stuck its horn deep into a side door, briefly tilting the Jeep to one side before wrenching loose. The driver of that vehicle yelled and then started laughing at his lucky escape. Meanwhile, the unicorn shook its head and bucked wildly as the hunters once more closed in and began driving circles around it.

A flock of rocs flew over. Travis imagined them glancing down at the ruckus and most likely not caring one bit. If he were a roc shapeshifter, he'd use his massive talons to pick up the Jeeps one by one and take them off into the sky, then drop them from a great height. At the very least, he could easily slam down and break up the hunt in short order.

What other kind of shapeshifter would help? A wyvern could lash out with its barbed tail and inflict a few well-aimed bites. An ogre or troll could stomp on the Jeeps and tip them over. A manticore's poison-tipped quills could easily find their mark and take the drivers out.

But Travis was no shapeshifter, at least not yet, and he watched helplessly as the unicorn grew weary, its eyes wide and nostrils flaring. As big and fast as the creatures were, they weren't much for fighting and were easily shocked. The Jeeps maneuvered into formation around the poor equine and herded it down the grassy slope. It tried to veer off once or twice but lacked the energy to leap away.

Where were the hunters taking it? Travis scanned the way ahead, looking for—

Ah! There it was on the fringe of the sprawling forest opposite: an inky-black dome of smoke twenty feet across, protruding from the ground and pulsing rhythmically, growing larger one second and sucking inward the next, breathing in and out. His old-fashioned parents still called them holes, but Travis and everyone else of his generation knew them as portals. This one was pretty big, and it definitely hadn't been there last time he'd come this way. The hunters must have created it recently.

"That's illegal, too," he growled, clenching his fists. "If my dad were here . . ."

The three Jeeps disappeared through the smoky portal and vanished, taking the unicorn with them. Just like that, they were gone, their noise cut off.

Travis started running down the slope after them, then changed his mind and headed for the fourth Jeep. It remained motionless, the hood up, steam drifting from its radiator. The driver rummaged in a compartment at the rear, produced a large can, and unscrewed the lid as he hoisted it around to the front. When he poured water into the radiator, more plumes of steam erupted. Even from a distance, Travis could see the water running straight out the bottom of the radiator, but it probably helped cool things down a little.

Panting, he hurried closer, fearing the man would turn and see him at any moment. Travis's luck held, and he darted to the back end of the Jeep while the driver slammed the hood down. Then it was a case of keeping the vehicle between them, hiding behind it while the man threw his half-empty can onto the passenger seat and climbed in. When the engine roared into life and the twisted radiator fan screeched in protest, Travis clambered into the back seat and ducked low, still amazed he hadn't been spotted.

"Come on, baby," the driver grunted as he swung the steering wheel around and made the Jeep spin. "Just down the hill, okay? Don't overheat on me yet."

No more steam erupted from the radiator, probably because its contents had already poured out into the grass. It was running dry now. But the smoky portal was just down the hill, a short ride in a speeding, bouncing Jeep.

Travis remained low on the back seat, looking up at the wispy clouds. When blackness filled his vision for a second, he knew the Jeep had just passed through the portal. The sky returned immediately, now deeply overcast, the air ten degrees cooler and somehow thinner. He felt sprinkles of rain on his face.

He'd crossed into Old Earth.

Fear gripped him. *What am I doing?*

Chapter 2
Unicorn Rescue

The Jeep skidded to a halt almost straight away, and the engine died. The screeching fan cut off, too. "We hoofed it outta there," the driver shouted with a laugh. "My ride's a wreck."

"Bagged us a cool fifty, though," another replied. "Ran straight up onto the truck."

Travis identified three or four more voices as he lay there squeezed into the smallest form possible. After half a minute, he twisted around to peer between the front seats and through the windshield. He saw the other three Jeeps parked alongside a gigantic, dark-blue semi-trailer truck. Its rear doors were open and a ramp down, but just inside the trailer was a sturdy metal gate, through which Travis could see the unicorn.

It stood panting, sides heaving and tail swishing. It started to turn around but stopped when the ivory-colored, spiral-indented horn caught on the wall. The unicorn stamped and whinnied, then let out a deep-throated growl before resuming its frantic panting.

The hunters—a group of six men in all—stood on the very end of the ramp, looking up at their prize. "So are we going back for another or not?" one asked.

"I'm game."

"We only have three Jeeps now, though."

"I still think it would be safer to tranq the unicorns. Safer for us, safer for them."

"Yeah, and then what? We drag their sleepy butts out of New Earth and onto the truck?"

Trying to calm his nerves, Travis took in his surroundings. The terrain was vaguely familiar, with open hills all around, only this version of the world had a smooth road stretching to the horizon. The truck had pulled over onto the hard shoulder, its rear end facing the smoky-black portal. There was no way this gateway between Earths had been there already. It was brand new, created by poachers for their dastardly expedition.

"This portal might be closed by tomorrow," one of the men said, "And Portal Patrol will be watching for us. Right now we have the advantage of surprise. I say we go in again now, while we can, and nab a couple more."

"Another hundred thousand?" another said, and let out a low whistle. "I'm in."

"We got lucky with this one. The herd is spooked now, so it won't be as easy next time. Maybe we should take a foal."

They kept arguing, and Travis grew angrier by the second. He looked over his shoulder. The portal, a dome of black smoke, stood fifty yards away on the roadside. He'd seen dozens in his lifetime and would never get used to them. Some floated above the ground, others high in the air or even deep underwater. All were carefully monitored these days, but there was a time when such a task had been impossible. Thousands of portals had exploded into being twenty years ago, pockmarking the landscape and bridging the two worlds, unifying them. Travis's own dad had been responsible for that event. It had been a time of awestruck wonder as people from a virus-stricken Old Earth had wandered across into a magical land filled with creatures they'd always believed to be the stuff of myth and legend.

The novelty had never worn off. Naturally, everyone wanted to see unicorns and dragons and other so-called exotic creatures, and some rich Old Earthers paid handsomely for private zoos filled with the most exciting beasts, dangerous or otherwise.

The poachers came to an agreement. Five of the men climbed into the three vehicles while the sixth sauntered back to the truck's cab, which seemed far away. As engines roared into life, Travis laid low and waited, thankful that his driver had left his crippled Jeep alone and gone off with the others.

He glimpsed the vehicles tearing past as they headed back to the portal. Craning his neck, he watched as, one by one, they vanished into the blackness—and as they went, the noise of their engines cut off until an abrupt silence fell.

The truck driver climbed up into his cab and slammed the door shut.

Travis leapt out from his hiding place and hurried to the back end of the trailer. The unicorn turned its head and banged its horn on the metal wall. There just wasn't room for it to spin around. It was, however, able to watch him out of one eye.

"It's okay," Travis whispered. "I'll get you out of here."

Up close to a unicorn like this, he couldn't help feeling intimidated. Horses had always made him nervous, and this was no ordinary horse, standing at least a foot taller than most and packed with twitching muscles across its flanks. He'd never seen such pure white hair. Even its mane, long and flowing, gleamed like it had been thoroughly shampooed. The unicorn's horn had to be over three feet long.

He unlatched the gate and paused, wondering how this was going to work out. "Now, when I open this," he said, trying not to sound so nervous, "I need you to run back through the portal and hide. Okay? Do you understand me?"

The unicorn merely stared back at him, unmoving.

"Don't get yourself caught again," he added. "Go find your herd and stay with them. Warn them."

As far as he knew, unicorns were no smarter than horses, which meant his words were futile. This was where being a shapeshifter came in handy. If he were a unicorn shapeshifter like one of his dad's friends, it would be a simple matter to transform and help this poor, dumb creature understand. He sighed and pulled the gate all the way open, keeping his fingers crossed that all would go well.

"Shoo!" he urged, stepping off the ramp and around to the side of the trailer out of the way.

The unicorn backed up in a hurry and swung its head around—too early. Again it banged its horn on the side. But it was halfway down the ramp the second time it tried to turn, and it cleared the end of the trailer and spun about in obvious excitement. Then it was off, galloping away as fast as its legs could take it.

In the wrong direction.

Travis's jaw fell open at the sight of the unicorn tearing across the field toward the trees, completely ignoring the smoky portal. Or perhaps willfully avoiding it.

"Whoops," he muttered. But at least the unicorn was free.

"Hey!" a voice yelled.

The driver had witnessed the escape in the side mirror and jumped down from the cab.

Travis turned and ran, heading for the portal, aware that his only chance was to outrun the middle-aged man until he could lose himself in the forest. What if the Jeep drivers abandoned the unicorn chase and came after him instead? Could he make it home? Not with those Jeeps tearing after him! But if he was going to run and hide, he'd rather it was in New Earth than this unfamiliar place.

He made it to the portal without breaking a sweat and had time to glance back and see the hunter's angry face—and then Travis was plunging through blackness and out the other side. The temperature rose, and everything brightened considerably. Even the air smelled sweeter.

The noise of Jeeps filled the air. In the distance, the three of them had spread out around a herd of a dozen unicorns, some of them foals. Travis kept running, glad they were so far away but upset they were closing in on one of the younger creatures. One Jeep tore ahead, and the foal reared and darted sideways—exactly as the hunters had intended. Now cut off from the herd, the foal found itself galloping alone with noisy, frightening vehicles pursuing it.

As the rest of the herd stampeded away, one of the adult unicorns paused and looked back, then let out a screeching whinny and went after her foal.

Travis kept running, panting as he climbed the grassy hill. Glancing back, he saw the truck driver emerge from the portal and pause to look around. Travis concentrated on his own two feet, knowing he had a good lead and could probably keep his distance as long as he didn't trip and sprain his ankle. The truck driver already looked ready to give up the chase.

The next time Travis looked back, the three Jeeps had herded the foal almost all the way down the hill to the portal. But the drivers hadn't noticed the much larger unicorn bearing down on them from behind. It moved with purpose, head low and horn jutting forward, and Travis stopped to watch with a sense of dread as the furious equine closed the gap.

This couldn't end well. He imagined the horn ramming into the rear end of the Jeep, snagging on the metal, and the unicorn tumbling and twisting, being dragged along and severely injuring itself in an effort to save its foal . . .

But at the last second, the Jeep at the rear suddenly veered away from the danger. The unicorn swung its head in vain but missed, saving itself from serious injury in the process.

Flanking the foal on either side, the men aboard the two remaining Jeeps either didn't notice the charging unicorn or didn't care. But they shouted in alarm when it inserted itself between the fast-moving vehicles and swung its head viciously to one side. The horn pierced a windshield, and fragments of glass flew everywhere. Then the horn swung the other way and nearly took out a driver. Both vehicles split off and peeled away, their tires spinning and sending up clods of dirt.

The unicorn and her foal ran on side by side, now free.

"Yes!" Travis yelled.

Then he, too, hurried on his way. Maybe the poachers would give up the hunt now. They seemed pretty shaken and fed up judging by the way they slowed their Jeeps to a halt and threw up their hands in disgust. Maybe the news of the escaped unicorn would dash their resolve once and for all.

Or infuriate them further.

He made it to the brow of the hill and slowed, out of breath. Looking down into the valley ahead, he could see his home nestled in a stand of trees. He'd lived there all his life, and he loved it despite it being so far outside Carter. His parents had moved here long ago when the village had expanded well beyond its perimeter and become a town. In fact, most of the shapeshifters had left around the same time, preferring the solitude. Travis knew their reclusive nature had something to do with a sheltered upbringing, a life on a lonely, foggy island.

Whatever the reason, he enjoyed being well away from the busy, bustling town.

He started down the hill—and at that moment heard the sudden roar of an engine as one of the Jeeps rumbled up the slope toward him.

Sagging at the knees, he knew he'd never make it home. The hunters would be on his tail in less than ten seconds. Still, he broke into a sprint and yelled until he was hoarse.

"Mom! Dad! HELP!"

The Jeep hurtled over the hill, bumping and sliding as it circled around in front and skidded to a halt. Two men leapt out, their faces screwed up in anger. One hunter held a rifle.

"You just cost us a fortune, kid!" the driver snapped.

"Hunting unicorns is illegal," Travis said shakily, looking past the men toward his home. It seemed so close yet so far away. If only his mom or dad would look out the window.

One of the men laughed and spoke sideways to the driver. "You hear that? Hunting unicorns is *illegal*. Man, I feel so bad right now."

"They're just horses with spikes on their heads," the other snarled. "Never saw the fascination. What's so great about them? They're bigger and faster, but so what? Are they magic? I didn't see any fireballs or rainbows. What's the big deal?"

"They're sensitive," Travis said, trying to remember everything his dad had told him. The one and only unicorn shapeshifter, an elusive lady named Ellie, had learned a lot about them over the past two decades. "They can make poisoned water drinkable. They can heal sickness. They're just really gentle and harmless, and they scare easily—"

"Yeah, they do," the second man said, laughing again. "We were just getting the hang of it, herding them straight through the portal into the back of the truck. We shoulda left the foal alone, though." He glared at his colleague. "I *told* you."

"Lesson learned," the driver admitted.

Travis remained still and quiet, hoping they would grow bored and leave *him* alone, too. What could they do to him anyway? Being paid to hunt unicorns was one thing. The murder of a twelve-year-old human boy was something else entirely.

Unfortunately, they had other plans. The driver waved him closer. "Come on. Get in."

"Wh-what?" Travis stammered. "Why?"

"Because you know stuff. Unicorns can heal? My boss is gonna want to know everything about that. So come on, get in."

Travis backed away. "No way!"

"Get in, kid." The man raised his rifle. "I won't ask nicely again."

Both men watched Travis with narrowed eyes, and he looked from them to the rifle, his heart thudding. Whether they would actually shoot him or not didn't matter. Even if he turned and ran, they could easily climb into their Jeep and catch up to him, then reach out and grab him. He had no chance.

But he smiled, a wave of relief flooding through him. "I'm not going anywhere. But you'd better run before it's too late."

"Huh?"

Travis pointed behind them. Both men swung around—and gasped.

Soaring toward them from the direction of his home, with massive leathery wings beating hard and steady, came a giant adult dragon with a hard, knobby spine and club-ended tail. With claws flexing and casual bursts of fire shooting from its jaws, the monster was a terrifying sight for those who didn't know him.

"You messed with the wrong kid," Travis said with a grin. "That's my dad."

Chapter 3
A Very Famous Shapeshifter

The dragon's rapid approach spurred the hunters into action. They yelled and clambered into their Jeep, and moments later the vehicle roared away, tearing up the grass and showering Travis with clods of earth.

Down the hill, the truck driver and the other two Jeep crews must have seen the approaching dragon, because they wasted no time in skedaddling. The whole lot of them vanished through the portal before the third team had made it halfway there.

Travis watched with mounting excitement as his dad—a very famous shapeshifter—flew almost lazily over the hill to catch up with the last remaining hunters. His massive shadow fell across the field, twice the speed of the vehicle and closing fast.

"Go, Dad!" Travis yelled.

While the driver hunched over the steering wheel, the passenger twisted around in his seat and pointed his rifle into the air. A *crack!* rang out, then another, and the dragon veered off. But then a huge sheet of fire leapt from his fearsome jaws toward the Jeep below, and both hunters yelled as flames licked over their heads.

Travis's dad swept by, turned, and thumped down in front of the smoky portal, thwarting any attempts at escape. The driver had no choice but to skid to a halt less than twenty paces away—just a couple of short hops where the dragon was concerned. As the rifle came up once more, a blast of fire engulfed the front of the Jeep and blackened the windshield. Both men cowered behind the glass, screaming with terror.

Their hands shot into the air in surrender when the stream of fire cut off. The dragon thumped closer and leaned over the vehicle, giving another bellow just to make it absolutely clear the chase was over.

Laughing inwardly, Travis raced down the hill, eager to hear the stern lecture his dad was about to unleash on behalf of Portal Patrol. The dragon abruptly shrank down and took the form of a man dressed in silky clothing of varying greys and greens—a knee-length coat, a loose-fitting shirt, comfortable-looking pants, and a pair of finely tailored boots made from the same silky material only much thicker and sturdier.

Smart clothes, the magical garments that adapted to fit a shapeshifter's form. With Travis's dad, they became a strap around the dragon's throat, rather like reins. When he reverted to his human form, they instantly reshaped around him.

Travis almost lost his footing in his haste to catch up to the Jeep. His dad had already started into his lecture as the two men stared in amazement, one loosely grasping his rifle as though he'd forgotten it was there. Both their mouths hung open. In a moment, they'd get over their shock and probably rise up in anger, but for the moment they listened like meek schoolboys.

". . . Creating a new portal," the shapeshifter scolded, counting off on his fingers, "entering New Earth without a permit, hunting without a permit, bringing a vehicle through without a permit, tearing up the countryside, harassing the wildlife, *capturing* the wildlife, firing a weapon at a dragon—" He broke off and frowned. "So stupid. Wounding a dragon will always result in a deadly attack on the assailant and probably wider retaliation on a nearby settlement."

"You're not a *real* dragon, though," the driver argued. He rose out of his seat and leaned over the windshield. "You're a shapeshifter."

Travis's dad raised an eyebrow at him. "And that's better how? Do you think I won't roast your hides in a heartbeat?" He waited a half-second, then added, "In fact, firing on a shapeshifter is an even worse crime. Last time I checked, killing a human is murder."

"Yeah, well, whatever," the driver grumbled. He scowled. "So what now? You gonna arrest us?"

The other hunter hung out of the passenger seat with his rifle still hanging loosely. Travis sidled alongside the Jeep and reached for the weapon. "I'll take that," he said nervously. As he clamped his hand around the barrel, the man jerked in surprise and yanked it away.

"Hand the rifle to my son," Travis's dad warned from up front. "Don't make things worse than they already are."

To make his point, he let out a quick belch of fire.

The driver gasped. "H-how did you do that?"

Travis reached for the rifle again, and this time the passenger released it.

"Now, both of you out of the vehicle, face down on the ground, hands behind your back."

The hunters moved slowly, their eyes darting about, obviously looking for a way out. Travis watched nervously, holding the rifle but doubtful he could shoot anyone with it even if he knew how. His dad was unarmed but amazingly calm.

"Son, take the keys out of the Jeep."

Travis hurried to the driver's side and removed the keys. He tossed them to his dad, who caught them deftly.

At that moment, one of the men jumped up and shouted, "Now!"

Both sprinted off in exact opposite directions, not looking back.

Travis's dad sighed. "They always run. Go on home, Travis. I'll have to take these men straight off to jail instead of waiting for backup."

"But there's a unicorn, Dad. They took one earlier, and I followed it through that portal into the back of a huge truck. I let it escape, and it ran off—but it's stuck in Old Earth!"

His dad looked at him with raised eyebrows. Then he smiled. "I'll have to call Ellie, then. She'll track the unicorn down, don't worry." He hurried over to the portal and disappeared into it, then reappeared after a few seconds. "The truck's gone. I'll go look for it in a minute. First, let me catch those two men and drop them at the jail. Back soon."

Once more, he transformed and took to the sky, his massive wings beating hard and his tail swinging around. Travis watched with glee, wishing he could be a dragon just like his dad. Of course, even if he were allowed, he wouldn't be *that* big. Not yet, anyway. But it wouldn't take long. As a human youth on the cusp of adulthood, he might only gain another ten or twelve inches in height, but his dragon form would grow three or four yards in length and probably put on a few thousand pounds of weight.

As his dad flew off after one of the hunters, Travis wondered for the umpteenth time how a human could transform into such a monstrous animal. Where did all the extra mass come from? Lady Simone had always dismissed this mysterious aspect of shapeshifting as "too difficult to explain," probably because she had no clue herself.

In fact, the reverse was true of his mom. She could grow faerie wings and remain at five and a half feet, but she could also shrink down to faerie size, about six inches tall. Where did the surplus mass go?

He watched as his dad descended and snatched the frantic hunter off the ground. Soaring high again, he swept around in an arc and headed back to fetch the other. By now, that hunter was nearly at the line of trees . . . but the dragon got there first, casually grabbing the man by the scruff of the neck and yanking him into the air.

With a hunter dangling from each of his front paws, Travis's dad headed off to the town.

Travis turned to look at the portal, anxiety growing. The others would get away if his dad didn't hurry back. Right now they had to be still in sight. Maybe his dad just hadn't seen them on the horizon. Still holding the rifle, he edged past the silent Jeep and toward the pulsing cloud of black smoke.

Steeling himself, he plunged through, walking fast. The ground under his feet felt the same all the way through, nothing but long grass, but the air temperature changed again, and everything looked dingy. He raised the rifle, half expecting to face a crowd of hunters.

But nobody came at him. The massive semi-trailer truck had gone, and the three Jeeps had disappeared with it, including the one with the smashed-in front. Maybe they'd towed it away.

He looked all around, puzzled. He could see for miles. Surely he should be able to see the tail end of the slow truck in the distance? How could it have driven over the horizon so quickly?

He shook his head. Maybe it had taken longer than he realized dealing with those other two escapees, and the rest of the crew had wasted no time making themselves scarce. It was a shame they'd gotten away. Though two men down, they would probably be back some other time.

He returned to New Earth and started up the hill toward home. If his dad hadn't gone off with the keys, Travis might have been tempted to try and drive the Jeep home, too!

* * *

"All taken care of," his dad said when he returned home a little later and walked into the living room. "Those two hunters will be in the town jail today and then moved to the Prison of Despair for a week. The council is contacting Portal Patrol to get that hole secured and shut down, but it might take a while. Apparently, there's been a spate of poaching in the area—seven new holes to deal with!"

Travis's mom jerked upright on the sofa. "Seven? Wow! What's happening around here?" She pushed her dark-brown hair away from her face and frowned. "I don't like it. We've had poachers before, but this is different."

"Yeah, more organized. Abi, these people are serious. Well funded and professional. Someone is paying big money to nab our wildlife." He turned to Travis. "So those men are in jail, and the goblins came and took their Jeep away. There's no sign of the others anywhere, not even that truck you mentioned."

Travis shook his head. "I can't believe they got away so fast."

"I flew up high and looked, but I didn't see anyone for miles. I would have spotted a convoy like that from the air. They must have hidden somewhere."

Travis smiled. "If only I had wings of my own . . ."

"Oh, there he goes again," his mom said, throwing up her hands. "Hal, your son wants to be a dragon just like you. So he can work for Portal Patrol and deal with illegal visitors."

Travis had always liked the sound of Portal Patrol, and not just because "Portal" was an anagram of "Patrol," something he found amusing. To be a shapeshifter assigned to policing the gateways between Old and New Earth? It was his dream job. Of course, he had to finish school first, but he could be an apprentice until then. And who better to train with than his dad?

"Well, it'll be your turn soon, son," his dad said, coming over to squeeze his shoulder. "Now, is that dinner I smell?"

Travis's mom looked stern. "Yes, but you have to earn your keep if you want to eat, Hal Franklin. All you've done today is sit around in caves with nasty white-tentacled monsters."

"Just one cave, Abi, and one nasty white-tentacled monster. And someone has to do it."

She rolled her eyes. "Feeding the brain? Sitting there daydreaming under the pretense that you're providing information to a giant being under the ground?"

"It likes its regular updates."

"It gets plenty of fresh news from everyone else who visits the hundreds of sites you've unearthed across the land—"

"*Eighteen* sites."

"—And now it's going to drain the brains of two hunters in the Prison of Despair."

"It doesn't drain their brains, it just reads their minds and makes time slow to a crawl."

Travis had heard this routine many times. He smiled, almost tuning them out. Many people already thought his dad was crazy without him going on about the weird white tentacles and what they were supposedly attached to. Most scientists believed they were simply plants of some kind, growing wild like ivy, completely smothering a cave or ceiling but always originating at a thick, treelike trunk in the ground. His dad insisted those trunks were merely the tips of massive arms reaching out of the Earth from deep within, part of a colossal underground brain, and he had a huge following of devoted believers offering their services as daydreamers.

Yes, his dad was crazy—but in a good, lovable way.

End of Special Preview

Like it? There's plenty more! *Unicorn Hunters* is the first book in the growing ISLAND OF FOG LEGACIES series.

The ISLAND OF FOG series

If you enjoyed this book, the author would greatly appreciate your review. Thank you!

The popular Island of Fog series follows the adventures of Hal and his friends as they harness their shapeshifting abilities and settle into a world vastly different from their own. If you want more, there are also short stories known as the Island of Fog Chronicles (ebooks only) as well as the Island of Fog Legacies, a spin-off series that takes place twenty years in the future with a new generation of shapeshifters.

Please visit the author's website for more information and to keep up to date with the latest releases.

http://www.unearthlytales.com

10556168R00155

Made in the USA
San Bernardino, CA
29 November 2018